Honoured Enemy

by

RAYMOND E. FEIST
&
WILLIAM R. FORSTCHEN

Voyager

Raymond E Feist

&

William R Forstchen

Honoured Enemy

HarperCollins*Publishers*

Voyager
An Imprint of HarperCollins*Publishers*
77–85 Fulham Palace Road,
Hammersmith, London W6 8JB

www.voyager-books.com

Published by *Voyager* 2002
9

First published in Great Britain by *Voyager* 2001

A catalogue record for this book
is available from the British Library

ISBN 0 00 648388 7

Set in Minion

Printed and bound in Great Britain by
Clays Ltd, St Ives plc

ACKNOWLEDGEMENTS

As always, I am indebted to many people. They include:

The original mothers and fathers of Midkemia, and those who contributed after to the world's development. Without them, the landscape would be far less colourful.

I would also like to thank Rich, Andy, Jim, Rick, and the other regular diners at Flemming's every Friday who made many weeks more tolerable during the last year through their humour, sensitivity, and grace. And to Mira, for being such good company and keeping my mind off my troubles from time to time.

Jonathan Matson, as always.

And my children, Jessica and James, for just being the most marvellous things in my existence.

Raymond E Feist

Many thanks of course to my mentor, Dr Gunther Rothenberg, yet another example of honour and courage, Dr Dennis Showalter, a grand advisor on so many fronts, and Brian Thomsen, Bill Fawcett, and Eleanor Wood.

Finally, a special thanks to Bruce, Gus, John, and my friends from Nomads and the University of UlanBaator. We trekked together across the steppes of Mongolia discovering a fascinating world of adventure, beauty, lost history waiting to be rediscovered, and the culinary delights of fermented horse milk and roasted marmots.

William R Forstchen

DEDICATION

This one's for Janny Wurts, who showed me that
two heads often were far better than one.

Raymond E Feist

When I think of Honour, Colonel Donald V
Bennett, Fox-Green, Omaha Beach, and Sergeant
Andy Andrew, Easy Red, Omaha Beach stand before
me. When duty called, they served unflinchingly. I
am honoured to call them my friends.

William R Forstchen

Contents

NORTHLANDS

The Great Northern Mountains

Stone Mountain

The Lake of the Sky

Elvandar

Tyr-Sog

Yabon

Crydee

LaMut

Loriél

THE GREEN HEART

The Grey Towers

Zūn

Hawk's Hollow

THE KINGDO

THE FAR COAST

Walinor

Hūsh

Natal

Ylith

Queeg's View

Carse

Jonril

Bordon

Calastius Mountains

dim

Tulan

Port Natal

Sethanon

THE FREE CITIES

Margrave's Port

Queg

Sarth

THE GREAT

THE ENDLESS SEA

THE STRAITS OF DARKNESS

Lan

Palanque

THE KINGDOM OF QUEG

SORCERER'S ISLE

Darkmo

Krondor

Dors

LiMeth

Land's End

Landreth

THE BITTER SEA

SEA OF DREA

Elarial

Durbin

Shamata

VALE OF DREAMS (DISPUTED BORDER)

The

Ranom

JAL-PUR DESERT

Caralyan

Trollhome Mountains

The Pillars of the Stars

THE EM

MIDKEMIA

PROLOGUE

Intelligence

The rain had stopped.

Lord Brucal, Knight-Marshal of the Armies of the West, entered the command pavilion, snorting like a warhorse and swearing under his breath. 'Damn weather,' he finally said. The elderly general, still broad-shouldered and fit, ran a gloved hand back from his forehead, getting the damp hair out of his eyes.

Borric, Duke of Crydee, and his second-in-command looked at his old friend with a wry smile. Brucal was a steadfast warrior and a reliable ally in the politics of the Kingdom of the Isles, as well as an able field general. But he had a tendency towards vanity, though. Borric knew he was getting irritated by the regal mane of hair now being plastered to his skull.

'Still sick?' Borric was a striking man of middle years, with more black in his hair and beard than grey. He had on his usual garments of black – the only colour he had donned since the death of his wife many years before – and over this he wore the brown tabard of Crydee, emblazoned with a golden gull above which perched a small golden crown, signifying Borric's royal blood. His eyes were dark and piercing, and currently showed a slight amusement at his old friend's bluster.

As Borric expected, the old grey-bearded duke swore an oath. 'I'm not sick, damn it! Just a bit of a sniffle.'

Borric remembered Brucal when he was a young man, visiting Borric's father at Crydee, his laughter, with his robust joy and a glint in his eye. Even when his reddish-brown hair and beard had turned grey, Brucal had been a man who lived each day to the fullest. Today was the first time Borric recognized that Brucal was now an old man.

On the other hand, it had to be said that Brucal was an old man who could quickly draw a sword and do considerable harm. And he refused to admit he was ill.

Brucal pulled off his heavy gauntlets and handed them to an aide. He allowed another to remove the heavy fur-lined weather-cloak he had worn from his own tent. He was dressed in simple blue trousers and a grey tunic, his tabard left behind in his tent. 'And this bloody rain doesn't help.'

'Another week of this and the snows will be falling in earnest.'

'According to our scouts, it's already snowing heavily up north, around the Lake of the Sky,' replied Brucal. 'We should consider sending the reserves back to LaMut and Yabon for the winter.'

Borric nodded. 'We might get one more week of clement weather before the winter storms come, though. Just enough time for the Tsurani to start something. I think we'll keep half of the reserves close by; I'll order the other half back to LaMut.'

Brucal looked at the campaign map on the large table before Borric. He said, 'They haven't been doing much, lately, have they?'

'The same as last year,' said Borric, pointing at the map. 'A sortie here, a raid there, but there's little evidence they seek to expand much any more.'

Borric studied the map: the invading Tsurani had taken a large chunk of the Grey Tower Mountains and the Free Cities of Natal, but had seemed satisfied to hold a stable front for the last five years of the war. The dukes had managed one successful raid through the valley in the mountains the Tsurani had used as their beachhead, and since then intelligence about what was occurring behind enemy lines was non-existent.

Brucal blew his nose in a rag used to oil weapons, and then threw it into a brazier nearby. His large nose now looked red and shiny. The nine-year campaign had taken its toll on him, Borric noticed.

Borric thought back a moment to when the first sightings of the Tsurani invaders had been reported, by two boys at his own keep

2

who had found a wrecked Tsurani ship on the headlands near his castle at Crydee. Later, word had been brought by the Elven Queen of aliens in the forests that lay between her own Elvandar and the Duchy of Crydee.

The world had changed: the fact of an alien invasion from another world via a magic gate was no longer a source of wonder. Borric had a war to fight and win. He had added some marks with brush and ink to the campaign map.

'What's this?' asked Brucal, pointing to a notation Borric had added earlier in the morning.

'Another migration of Dark Brothers. It looks as if a fairly large contingent of them are moving down the southern foothills of the Great Northern Mountains. They're treading a narrow path near the elven forests. I can't understand why they'd come over the mountains at this time of year.'

'Those blackhearts don't have to have a reason,' observed Brucal.

Borric nodded. 'My son Arutha reported a large force tangled with the Tsurani while they were besieging my castle five years ago. But those were Dark Brothers driven from the Grey Towers by the Tsurani; they were striking north to join their kin in the Northlands. They've been quiet since then.'

'There's one possibility.'

Borric shrugged. 'I'm listening, old friend.'

'That's a bloody long trek for nothing,' observed Brucal, as he wiped his nose with the back of his hand. 'They're not fools.'

'The Dark Brotherhood is many things, but never stupid,' agreed Borric. 'If they're moving in force, it's for a reason.'

'Where are they now?'

Borric said, 'Last reports from the scouts near the Elven Forest. They're avoiding the dwarves at Stone Mountain and the elven patrols, heading east.'

'Lake of the Sky is the only destination,' said Brucal, 'unless they're going to turn south and attack the elves or the Tsurani.'

'Why Lake of the Sky?'

'It makes sense if they're trying to get up to the eastern side of the Northlands. There's a spur of mountains that runs north-east out of the Teeth of the World, hundreds of miles long and impassable. Over the Great Northerns, past the Lake of the Sky, and up a trail back north over the Teeth of the World is a short-cut, actually.' The old duke stroked his still-wet beard. 'It's one of the reasons we have so much trouble with the bastards up in Yabon.'

Borric nodded. 'They tend to leave us alone in Crydee, compared to the encounters your garrisons have with them.'

'I just wish I knew why they were out in force, heading east, this close to winter,' muttered Brucal.

'Something's up,' said Borric.

Brucal nodded. 'I've been fighting Clan Raven since I was a boy.' He fell silent for a moment. 'Their paramount chieftain is a murderous dog named Murad. If this bunch from the Northlands is looking to join with him . . .'

'What?'

'I don't know, but it'll be bad.' Looking over the rest of the map, Brucal asked, 'Do we have anyone in that area now?'

'Just the garrison forts along the Tsurani front, and a few last patrols before winter,' Borric replied.

Brucal leaned close to inspect each of the small ink marks on the map, then made a sound half-way between a snort and a laugh. 'Hartraft.'

'Who?' asked Borric.

'Son of one of my squires. Dennis Hartraft. Runs a company of thugs and cut-throats called the Marauders for Baron Moyet. He's up there.'

'What's he doing?' asked Borric. 'The name is familiar, but I don't recall any reports from him.'

'Dennis is not one for paperwork,' said Brucal. 'What he's doing is unleashing bloody murder on the Tsurani. It's personal with him.'

'Can we get word to him about this Dark Brothers migration?'

'He's an independent. He'll come back to Moyet's camp for the winter in the next week or two. I'll send word to the Baron to get whatever information from Dennis he can.' Then Brucal laughed. 'Though it would be fitting for him and Clan Raven to tangle if it comes to that.'

'Why?'

Brucal said, 'Too long a story to tell now. Just say there's even

4

more history between his family and Murad's blood-drinkers than there is between him and the Tsurani.'

'So what happens if this Hartraft and the Dark Brothers meet up?'

Brucal sighed, and wiped his nose. 'A lot of people are going to get dead.'

Borric took a step away from the map table and looked out of the pavilion's door. A light mix of rain and snow was starting to fall. After a moment, he said, 'Maybe they'll miss each other and Hartraft will get back to Moyet's camp.'

'Maybe,' said Brucal. 'But if that bunch from the north gets between Dennis and Moyet's camp, or some bunch from Clan Raven moves to meet with them . . .'

Brucal let the thought go unfinished. Borric knew what he thought. If that many Brothers got between Hartraft and his base, the chances for the Kingdom soldiers returning home alive were nearly non-existent. Borric let his mind wander for a moment, considering the cold hills of the north and the icy winter almost upon them, then he brushed away the thoughts. There were other fronts and other conflicts to worry about, and he couldn't help Hartraft and his men, even if he knew where they were. Too many men had already died in this war for him to lose sleep about another high-risk unit out behind enemy lines. Besides, maybe they'd get lucky.

ONE

Grieving

The ground was frozen.

Captain Dennis Hartraft, commander of the Marauders, was silent, staring at the shallow grave hacked into the frozen earth. The winter had arrived fast and hard, and earlier than usual; and after six days of light snow and freezing temperatures, the ground was now yielding only with a grudge.

So damned cold, he thought. It was bad enough you couldn't give the men a proper funeral pyre here, lest the smoke betray their position to the Tsurani, but being stuck behind enemy lines meant the dead couldn't even be taken back to the garrison for cremation. Just a hole in the ground to keep the wolves from eating them. *Is this all there really is in the end, just the darkness and the icy embrace of the grave?* With his left hand – his sword hand – he absently rubbed his right shoulder. The old wound always seemed to ache the most when snow lay on the ground.

A priest of Sung, mumbling a prayer, walked around the perimeter of the grave, making a sign of blessing. Dennis stood rigid, watching as some of the men also made signs to a different god – mostly to Tith-Onaka, God of War – while others remained motionless. A few looked towards him, saw his eyes, then turned away.

The men could sense his swallowed rage . . . and his emptiness.

The priest fell silent, head lowered, hands moving furtively, placing a ward upon the grave. The Goddess of Purity would protect the dead from defilement. Dennis shifted uncomfortably, looking up at the darkening clouds which formed an impenetrable wall of grey to the west. Over in the east, the sky darkened.

Night was coming on, and with it the promise of more snow, the first big storm of the year. Having lived in the region for years, Dennis knew that a long, hard winter was fast upon them, and his mission had to be to get his men safely back to their base at Baron Moyet's camp. And if enough snow fell in the next few days, that could prove problematic.

The priest stepped back from the grave, raised his hands to the dark heavens and started to chant again.

'The service is ended,' Dennis said. He didn't raise his voice, but his anger cut through the frigid air like a knife.

The priest looked up, startled. Dennis ignored him, and turned to face the men gathered behind him. 'You've got one minute to say farewell.'

Someone came up to Dennis's side and cleared his throat. Without even looking, Dennis knew it was Gregory of Natal. And he understood his lack of civility to the Priest of Sung was ill-advised.

'We're still behind enemy lines, Father. We move out as soon as the scout comes back,' Dennis heard Gregory say to the priest. 'Winter comes fast and we'd best be safely at Brendan's Stockade should a blizzard strike.'

Dennis looked over his shoulder at Gregory, the towering, dark-skinned Natalese Ranger attached to his command.

Gregory returned his gaze, the flicker of a smile in his eyes. As always, it annoyed Dennis that the Ranger unfailingly seemed to know what he was thinking and feeling. He turned away and, pointing at the squad of a dozen men who had dug the shallow grave shouted: 'Don't just stand there gawking, fill it in!'

The men set to work as Dennis stalked off to the edge of the clearing which had once been a small farmstead on the edge of the frontier, long since abandoned in this the ninth year of the Riftwar.

His gaze lingered for a second on the caved-in ruins of the cabin, the decaying logs, the collapsed and blackened beams of the roof. Saplings, already head-high, sprouted out of the wreckage. It triggered a memory of other ruins, but they were fifty miles from this place and he forced them out of his mind. That was a memory he had learned long ago to avoid

He scanned the forest ahead, acting as if he was waiting for the return of their scouts. Normally, Gregory would lead any scouting patrols, but Dennis wanted him close by, in case they had to beat a swift retreat. Years of operating successfully behind Tsurani lines had taught him when to listen to his gut. Besides, the scout who was out there was the only one in the company able to surpass Gregory's stealth in the forest.

Resisting the urge to sigh, Dennis quietly let his breath out slowly and leaned against the trunk of a towering fir. The air was crisp with the smell of winter, the brisk aroma of pine, the clean scent of snow, but he didn't notice any of that; it was as if the world around him was truly dead, and he was one of the dead as well. All his attention was focused, instead, on the sound of the frozen earth being shovelled back into the grave behind him.

The priest, startled by the irreverent display, had watched Dennis leave the group and then stepped up to Gregory's side and glanced up at the towering Natalese, but Gregory simply shook his head and looked around at the company. All were silent, save for the sound of a few desultory shovels striking the icy soil; all of them were gazing at their leader as he walked away and passed into the edge of the surrounding forest.

Gregory cleared his throat again, this time loudly and having caught the men's attention he motioned for them to get on with the work at hand.

'He hates me,' Father Corwin said, a touch of sadness in his voice.

'No, Father. He just hates all of this.' Gregory nodded at the wreckage of battle that littered the small clearing: the trampled-down snow – much of it stained a slushy pink – broken weapons, arrows, and the fifty-two Tsurani corpses that lay where they fell, including the wounded who had been finished off with a knife across the throat.

His gaze was fixed on the priest. 'The fact that you accidentally caused this fight, that wasn't your fault.'

The priest wearily shook his head. 'I'm sorry. I was lost out here and didn't know the Tsurani were so close behind me.'

Gregory stared straight into the pale-blue eyes of the old priest but the priest looked straight back at him, not flinching, not lowering his gaze even for an instant. Mendicant priests of any order, even those of the Goddess of Purity, had to be tough enough to live off the land and whatever bounty providence offered. Gregory had no doubt that the mace at the priest's belt was not unblooded and that Father Corwin had faced his share of dangers over the years. Besides, Gregory was an experienced judge of men, and while this priest seemed meek at the moment, there was obvious hardness beneath the apparently mild exterior.

'I wish I'd never left my monastery to come here and help out,' the priest sighed, finally dropping his gaze. 'We got lost, brothers Valdin, Sigfried and I. We were making for the camp of Baron Moyet, took a wrong turn on the trail and found ourselves behind the Tsurani lines.'

'Only Rangers and elves travel these paths without risk of getting lost, Father,' Gregory offered. 'These woods are treacherous. It is said that at times the forest itself will hide trails and make new ones to lead the unwary astray.'

'Brothers Valdin and Sigfried were captured,' the priest continued, spilling out his story. 'I escaped. I was off the trail, relieving myself, when the Tsurani patrol took them. I ran in the opposite direction after my brothers were dragged away. I was a coward.'

The Natalese Ranger shrugged. 'Some might call it prudence, rather than cowardice. You denied the Tsurani a third prisoner.'

The priest still appeared unconvinced.

'There was nothing you could have done for them,' Gregory added with certainty, 'except join them as a captive.'

Corwin seemed slightly more reassured. 'It was foolish of me to have run, you'll agree. Had I been more stealthy I'd not have led them to you. When I saw one of your men hiding off the side of the trail, I just naturally went straight to him.'

Gregory's eyes narrowed. 'Well, if he'd been doing a better job of hiding, you wouldn't have seen him, then, would you?'

'I didn't know they –' he pointed towards the Tsurani corpses littering the field '– were right behind me.'

Gregory nodded.

What should have been a clean, quick ambush incurring minimal loss had turned into a bloodbath. Eighteen men from the Marauders – nearly a quarter of Dennis's command – were dead, and six more were seriously wounded. As it was, the engagement had been a Kingdom victory, but at far greater cost than was necessary.

The priest rambled on, starting his tale yet again. Gregory continued to study him. It was obvious the man was badly shaken. He was poorly dressed, wearing sandals rather than boots. A couple of toes were already showing signs of frostbite. His hands shook slightly, and his voice was near to breaking.

The priest fell silent, and took a long moment to compose himself. At last, he let out a long sigh, then looked over to Dennis who stood alone, at the edge of the clearing. 'What is wrong with your commander?' he asked.

'His oldest friend is in that grave,' Gregory said quietly, nodding down at the eighteen bodies lying side by side in the narrow trench hacked out of the freezing ground. 'Jurgen served Dennis's grandfather before he served the grandson. The land the Tsurani now occupy, part of it once belonged to Dennis's family. His father was Squire of Valinar, a servant of Lord Brucal. They lost everything early on in the war. Word of the invasion hadn't even reached Valinar before the Tsurani. The old Squire and his men didn't even know who they were fighting when they died. Dennis and Jurgen were among a handful of survivors of the initial assault; Jurgen was his last link to that past.' Gregory paused, transferring his gaze to Father Corwin. 'And now that link is gone.'

'I'm sorry,' the priest replied softly, 'I wish none of this had ever happened.'

'Well, Father, it happened,' Gregory said evenly.

The priest looked up at him, and there was moisture in his eyes. 'I'm sorry,' he said one more time.

Gregory nodded. 'As my grandmother said, "Sorry won't unbreak the eggs." Just clean up the mess and move on. Let's find you some boots or you'll lose all your toes before tomorrow.'

'Where?'

'Off the dead of course.' Gregory indicated boots, weapons, and cloaks that had been stripped off the dead before they were buried.

'They don't need them any more, and the living do,' he added matter-of-factly. 'We honour their memory, but it's no use burying perfectly good weapons and boots with them.' He motioned with his chin. 'That pair over there looks about your size.'

Father Corwin shuddered but went over and picked up the boots, the Natalese had indicated

As the priest untied his sandals, Alwin Barry, the newly-appointed sergeant for the company, approached the edge of the grave, picked up a clump of frozen earth and tossed it in.

'Save a seat for me in Tith's Hall,' he muttered, invoking the old belief among soldiers that the valiant were hosted for one night of feasting and drinking by the God of War before being sent to Lims-Kragma for judgment. Barry bowed his head for a moment in respect, then turned away, heading over to the trail that went through the middle of the clearing, and called for the men to form up in marching order.

Others hurriedly approached the grave, picking up handfuls of dirt and tossing them in. Some made signs of blessing; one uncorked a drinking flask, raised it, took a drink then emptied the rest of the brandy into the grave and threw the flask in.

Burial was not the preferred disposition of the dead in the Kingdom, but more than one soldier rested under the soil over the centuries and soldiers had their own rituals for saying farewell to the dead, rituals that had nothing to do with priests and gods. This wasn't about sending comrades off to the Halls of Lims-Kragma, for they were already on their way. This was about saying goodbye to men who had shed their blood alongside them just hours before. This was about saying farewell to brothers.

Richard Kevinsson, the company's newest recruit, was one of the last to approach. A young squire from Landonare, who had escaped from there when the Tsurani had overrun his family's estates, he had joined full of blood and fire, vowing vengeance. Now there were tears in his eyes, his features were pale, and a trickle of blood coursed down his cheek from a slashing blow that had laid open his scalp just below the edge of his dented helmet. 'I'm sorry,' he gasped quietly. He knelt down and picked up a clump of earth, his gaze fixed on the old sergeant-at-arms lying in the centre of the grave, surrounded by his

11

dead comrades. The grave-diggers were hard at work, but no earth had yet to fall on Jurgen. The man could have been asleep; except for his blood-soaked tunic he almost looked as if he would sit up and smile, revealing his crooked teeth. The young man had often dreamed of his first battle, and the heroic deeds he would accomplish. Instead he had been on the ground, looking up at his enemy like a frozen rabbit, fumbling for his dropped sword and screaming in terror ... and then Jurgen had stormed in, cutting the Tsurani down with a single blow.

In saving Richard, however, Jurgen had left himself open to an enemy spearman who had charged straight in. Jurgen had been looking into Richard's eyes when the spear struck; there had been a brief instant, almost a flicker of a smile, as if he was a kindly old man helping a child out of a minor scrape, just before the Tsurani spear struck him from behind. Then the shock of the blow distorted his face and the spear exploded out of his chest.

Richard had watched the life fade out of the old man's eyes. It was only a moment, yet it seemed an eternity, the light fading, Richard knowing that the old man had made the sacrifice of his own life without hesitation.

He looked down at Jurgen now. The corpse's eyes were closed, but in his mind, and in the nightmares that would come for the rest of his life, the eyes would be open, gazing back at him.

'It should have been me instead of you,' Richard whispered, barely able to speak for his grief.

He bent almost double, sobs wracking his body. He knew the others were watching, judging him. Why didn't they cry? he wondered, and he felt ashamed for all his failures this day.

He let the earth fall from his hand, recoiling as the clump hit Jurgen's face. Embarrassed, he drew back and turned away, shoulders hunched, shaking as he struggled unsuccessfully to hide his tears.

The few who followed Richard, most of them silent, tossed the ritual handful of earth into the grave then turned away, eyes empty of emotion.

The company formed up for the march, Alwin detailing men off to bear the litters of the wounded.

The grave-diggers were nearly finished. In spite of the cold their faces were streaked with sweat and their hot breath made clouds of steam in the air, as they hurriedly worked to complete their task.

At the edge of the clearing Dennis continued to stare with unfocused eyes at the forest. Something, a sensing, refocused his attention. A lone bird darted through the branches overhead. The angry chatter of a squirrel echoed.

His left hand drifted down to the hilt of his sword. He looked back over his shoulder. Gregory had been kneeling beside a Tsurani, studying the face of the enemy soldier as if he might learn something about the alien invaders from this man's still features. He had sensed what Dennis had sensed, that someone was approaching. His gaze flickered to the men lining the trail. Several of the old hands were already reacting. Others, noticing this, started to react as well.

Dennis watched Alwin and was disappointed, for the new sergeant-at-arms was several seconds behind Gregory and himself, but finally he raised his left hand, palm outward, at the same time drawing his right hand across his throat, the signal for everyone to fall silent and freeze. Dennis turned to look back at the forest, not yet giving a command.

Gregory listened for a moment, then relaxed. He looked at Dennis and nodded once, then smiled.

A flicker of a shadow moved in the darkness of the forest on the trail ahead and Dennis relaxed, too.

The shadow stepped out from behind a tree, raised a hand and Dennis motioned for him to come in. The scout sprinted forward. He was clad in a white tunic streaked with cross-hatching lines of grey and black, the uniform designed by Dennis for the Marauders to wear during winter campaigning in the deep forest. He ran lightly, in the way only an elf could run, so softly that even in snow it was said they at times they would leave no prints.

As he approached Dennis, he nodded, and with a hand signal motioned for him to follow.

It was a bit of protocol that at times bothered Dennis. The scout was Gregory's companion, not officially part of Dennis's command, and as such he would report first to his friend. This, as much as anything else, was the reason Dennis preferred having Gregory lead any scouting mission; when the Natalese Ranger returned from a mission, he reported to Dennis. Dennis, for not the first time, considered it a petty irritation, yet he couldn't rid himself of it.

'Tinuva,' several of the men sighed, as the elf came into the clearing. They were obviously relieved. Weapons were resheathed.

The elf nodded a greeting. He looked over at the burial detail, busy filling in the grave and paused for a moment, head lowered, offering his thoughts for the fallen. At last, he looked back at Gregory. 'You were right, two of them did escape.' he announced.

'And?' Gregory asked.

'Good fighters, tough, a long chase,' Tinuva said, matter-of-factly.

'So you got all them?' Dennis asked.

The elf shook his head. He was obviously winded after the long chase.

Dennis pulled a flask out from under his tunic and handed it over. After nodding his thanks, the elf drank then handed the flask back.

'Not sure,' Tinuva replied. 'Their commander might have sent a runner back before the fight even started. There were too many tracks on the trail to tell. If I had more time to follow the way they came, I would know for certain, but you stressed getting back here quickly.'

Dennis cursed silently.

'Then we must assume someone did get out,' Gregory announced.

'I always assume that,' Dennis said coolly.

Gregory did not reply.

'I sense something else here as well,' the elf said.

'The Dark Brothers?' Gregory asked and the elf nodded.

'Did you see signs?' Dennis interjected.

The elf reached into a pouch dangling from his belt and drew out the broken shaft of an arrow. 'It's their make – Clan Raven. Not more than a league from here. I came across tracks as I was returning here after finding the two Tsurani. There was blood on the snow. Someone killed a stag, quartered it and then headed back north. Four of them, early this morning, an hour after the snow started to fall today.'

'Only four?' Dennis asked.

The elf shook his head. 'No, there are more. What I found was just a hunting party foraging for food. The forest whispers of them.

They're out here: something is stirring.' The elf nodded towards the mountains to the north, barely visible in a gathering darkness, to the north.

'How many?'

Tinuva closed his eyes for a moment, as if to aid his thinking. 'Hard to tell,' he whispered. 'We eledhel have history with the moredhel.'

Gregory gave a quick shake of his head to Dennis, warning him not to ask anything more.

'They are as difficult to track as we are, unless they are close by or out in large numbers.' He looked northward again. 'Up there, distant, but in large numbers, I would judge.'

'Why?' asked Father Corwin, who was standing at the edge of the group.

Several of the men turned to look at the priest. Suddenly embarrassed, Father Corwin lowered his eyes.

No one answered. Finally the elf stirred.

'Holy one,' Tinuva said, softly. 'Something is beginning to stir amongst those you call the Brotherhood of the Dark Path. This war with the Tsurani diverts us away from the threat of the dark ones to the north. Perhaps they see an advantage to be gained from humans slaughtering each other. Perhaps they seek to return south to the Green Heart and the Grey Towers – it isn't hard to imagine they've worn out their welcome with the clans of the Northlands after nine winters.'

Gregory said, 'Are they moving south?'

Tinuva shrugged. 'The hunters whose signs I saw may have been foraging ahead of a larger company, or on the flank. It's difficult to know if they're heading south or in this direction.'

'All the more reason for us to get the hell out of here now,' Dennis interjected sharply. 'We've been behind the lines too damn long as it is; the men deserve to spend the rest of the winter in Tyr-Sog getting drunk and spending their pay on whores.'

He looked back at the burial party. They were nearly finished; a couple of men were dragging out deadfall and branches to throw over the grave. Several of the men were already returning to the ranks, hooking the short-handled shovels onto their backpacks. A trained eye could easily pick out the burial site today but if it continued to snow, by tomorrow the grave and the nearby Tsurani dead would have disappeared. By springtime, when the snows melted and grass fed by the richness beneath sprang up, it would have disappeared back into the forest.

'Alwin, move the men out.'

'Sir, you said you wanted to speak to the boy first,' Alwin replied softly.

Dennis nodded, scanning the line of troops. His gaze fell on Richard Kevinsson. 'Boy, over here now,' he snapped.

Nervously Richard looked up.

'The rest of you start moving,' Dennis rapped out 'we want to make Brendan's Stockade and our own lines by morning.'

Two men acting as trailbreakers sprinted forward, darting off to either side of the trail, lightly jumping over deadfalls and around tree trunks. Within seconds they had disappeared into the forest. Half a dozen men, the advanced squad, set out next, moving down the trail at a slow trot.

Richard Kevinsson approached, obviously ill-at-ease. 'Captain?' he asked, his voice shaking.

Dennis looked at Gregory, Tinuva, and the priest, his eyes commanding a dismissal. Tinuva stepped away, bowed in respect to the grave, then joined the column, but Gregory and the priest lingered.

'Father, go join the wounded,' Dennis said sharply.

'I thank you for rescuing me, Captain,' Father Corwin replied, 'but I feel responsible for the trouble this lad is in and I wish to stay with him.'

Dennis was about to bark an angry command, but a look in Gregory's eyes stilled him. He turned his attention back to Richard. 'When we return to Baron Moyet's camp I will have you dropped from the rolls of the company.'

'Sir?' Richard's voice started to break.

'I enrolled you in the company because I felt sorry for your loss, boy. It reminded me of my own, I guess. But doing so was a mistake. In the last fortnight you have barely managed to keep up with our march. I heard a rumour that you fell asleep while on watch two nights ago.'

He hesitated for an instant. It was Jurgen who had reported that, and then defended the boy, reminding Dennis that *he* had done so as well when out on his first campaign long years ago.

'It was you that the priest saw from the trail wasn't it?'

The boy hesitated.

'It's not his fault,' Father Corwin said, impassioned. 'I stopped because I was exhausted from running. I was staring straight at him, I couldn't help but see him.'

'That doesn't matter,' Dennis snapped, and the look in his eyes made it clear that he would not tolerate another word from the black-robed priest. 'Well?'

'Yes, sir,' Richard replied weakly. 'It was me.'

'Why?'

'I thought I was well concealed.'

'If that old man could spot you, be certain a Tsurani trailbreaker would have seen you. You are a danger to yourself and to my command. I'm sending you back. You can tell your friends what you want. I suggest you find a position with a nice comfortable mounted unit down in Krondor. No brains needed there, just ride, point your lance, and charge. Then you can be a hero, like in the songs and ballads.'

'I wanted to serve with you, sir,' the boy whispered.

'Well you did, and that's now finished.' He hesitated, but then his anger spilled out. 'Go take a final look at that grave over there before we leave,' he said with barely-contained fury, his soft voice more punishing than any screamed insult. 'Now get out of my sight.'

The boy stiffened, face as pale as the first heavy flakes of snow that began to swirl down around them. The he nodded and turned about, shoulders sagging. As he rejoined the column the men around him looked away.

The priest took a step forward.

Dennis's hand snapped out, and a finger pointed into the old man's face. 'I don't like you,' Dennis announced. 'You were a bumbling fool wandering around out here where you had no business. Damn you, don't you know there's a war being fought out here? It's not a war like the ones that fat monks and troubadours gossip about around the fireplace. I hope you got a good belly full of it today.'

'Two of my "fat friends", as you call them, are prisoners of the

Tsurani this day,' Father Corwin replied, and there was checked anger in his voice. 'I volunteered to serve with the army as a healer. I just pray I don't have to work on you some day. Stitching together flesh that has no soul is bitter work.'

The priest turned and stalked away. The middle part of the column, made up of the stretcher-bearers was starting off and Corwin joined them.

Gregory chuckled softly.

'What the hell is so funny?' Dennis snapped.

'I think he got you on that one. You did go a bit too hard on the boy.'

'I don't think so. He almost got us all killed.'

'He made no mistakes, I was but ten feet from him. I made sure he was well concealed.' As if thinking of something, Gregory added, 'That priest has unusually sharp eyes.'

'Nevertheless, the boy goes back.'

'Is that what Jurgen would have done?'

Dennis turned, eyes filled with bitterness. 'Don't talk to me about Jurgen.'

'Someone has to. There's not a man in your company that doesn't share your pain. Not just over losing a man they respected, but because they bear a love for you as well, and now carry your burden of sorrow.'

'Sorrow? How do you know what I feel?'

'I know,' Gregory announced softly. 'I saw what happened too. Jurgen made his choice, he left himself open in order to save the boy. I would have done it, so would you.'

'I don't think so.'

'You and your Marauders have become hard men over the years, Dennis, but not soulless ones. You would have tried to save him, even at the cost of your own life, as Jurgen did. The lad has promise. You might not have noticed, and I'm not even sure he remembers it, but he did kill the first Tsurani that closed on him. The one that almost got him came up from behind.'

'Nevertheless, the boy goes.'

'It'll kill him. We both know the type. Next battle he'll do something stupid to regain his honour and die doing it.'

'That's his problem, not mine.'

'And what if he gets a half-dozen others killed as well? What would Jurgen say of that?'

'Jurgen is dead, damn you,' Dennis hissed. 'Never speak to me of him again.'

Gregory stepped back, raised his hands, then shook his head sadly, and walked over to the grave. Looking down at the rich brown earth being covered by the falling snow, he whispered, 'Until we stand together again in the light.'

Then he went to join the company. Tinuva fell in by his side and the two of them headed up the trail in the opposite direction, double-checking to make sure that nothing was following the unit.

Dennis was left alone as the last of his men abandoned the clearing.

The heavy flakes swirled down, striking his face, melting into icy rivulets that dripped off a golden beard which was beginning to show the first greys of middle age.

When all were gone, and he knew no one was watching he walked up to the grave, reached down and picked up a clump of frozen earth.

'Damn you,' he sighed, 'why did you leave me like this, Jurgen?'

Now there was no one left. Nothing but a flood of memories.

The holdings of the Hartrafts were not much to boast about; forest lands lying between Tyr-Sog and Yabon. A scattering of frontier villages on the border marches, a rural squire's estates that the high-blood earls, barons, and dukes of the south and of the east would have scoffed at, or tossed aside as a trifle in a game of dice. But it had been his home, the home of his father and his father's father.

Jurgen had been a young soldier for Dennis's grandfather, old Angus Hartraft, called 'Forkbeard', who had first been granted the lands on the border for his stalwart service against the dark things that lived to the north. Jurgen had also been his father's closest friend. And when his father died on the first day of the Riftwar, when the Tsurani flooded into their lands, it was Jurgen who had saved his life the night their keep was taken.

Dennis stared at the grave.

Better I had died that night, he thought, and there was a flash of resentment for old Jurgen.

Malena, his bride of barely six hours, died that night. His father had ordered him to take her through the secret passage out of the burning chaos of the estate's central keep. He had fought his own desire to stay with his father and had taken Malena through the tunnel. Then outside the escape tunnel, just as freedom had been in reach, a crossbow bolt had stilled her heart forever. He had briefly glimpsed the assassin in the flickering light from the burning keep, and the image of the man as he turned and fled burned in Dennis's memory. Jurgen had found him kneeling in the mud, clutching her lifeless body. He had fought to stay with her, until Jurgen knocked him out with the flat of his sword, then carried him down the river to safety.

Fifteen men from the garrison, including Jurgen and Dennis, survived that night. Carlin, the next to last had died just a month earlier from a wasting of the lungs. Now, of those fifteen men, only Dennis was left.

So now you're dead old man. Died because of a damn stupid boy and a fat old priest. It would be like you to die for that, he thought, a sad smile creasing his features.

The 'Luck of the Hartrafts', it was called. No glory, no money, no fame. Just a retainer of a family with a minor title and nothing else. And then, in the end, you get a spear in your back because of a clumsy boy.

Yet, he knew that Jurgen, old smiling, laughing Jurgen, would not have wanted it any other way, that he had been more likely to die for the sake of a stupid squire than for any king. In fact, if it had been the mad king in far Rillanon, he most likely would have leaned on his sword and done nothing, figuring that such high and mighty types should take care of themselves.

A breeze stirred, the wind moaning softly through the rustling tree branches. The snow was coming down hard now, hissing, forcing him to lower his head.

Opening his hand, he let the clump of earth fall onto the grave. There was nothing left now of the past except a half-forgotten name and a sword strapped to his side. His father, Jurgen, Malena; all of them were in their graves, and the graves were all returning to the uncaring forest.

'Dennis?'

He looked up. It was Gregory.

'Nothing behind us, but we'd better move.'

Darkness was closing in. Tinuva was barely visible but a dozen paces away, waiting where the trail plunged back into the forest.

He looked around the clearing for a final time. Eventually the forest would reclaim all of this. The wind gusted around him and he shivered from the cold.

'You still have the Marauders,' Gregory whispered.

Dennis nodded and looked down at the Tsurani bodies scattered about the clearing. *All that they have taken from me,* he thought. He glanced up the trail where the men waited and while none of them was from Valinar, he saw faces that had become as familiar to him as those from his home. The Marauders still lived, and he had a responsibility to them.

He nodded. 'And the war,' he replied coldly, 'I still have the war.'

Without a backward glance Captain Dennis Hartraft turned from the grave and left the clearing, disappearing into the darkness.

Gregory watched him and sadly shook his head, then followed him on to the path to Brendan's Stockade.

It was cold.

Force Leader Asayaga threw a handful of charcoal on the warming brazier, pulled off his gloves and rubbed his hands over the fire.

'Damnable country,' he sighed.

He picked up the orders addressed to him and studied the attached map.

Madness. The first heavy snow of the season was falling from the skies and yet he was expected to start out at once with his command to reinforce a column which would strike a Kingdom outpost at dawn.

Why now? A day march would have been easy, but now darkness was closing in. Outside his tent the wind was stirring, the frozen canvas cracking and rattling, and he could hear the heavy snow falling from branches in the woods surrounding the camp.

The Game, always it was the Great Game, he realized with a detached fatalism. He knew with certainty he was being sent on a futile mission so that shame might be attached to one of his clan cousins. His House, the Kodeko, was not significant enough to warrant attention on its own, but it was related to those who were in the Kanazawai Clan. He put down the orders and sat back in his small canvas chair, wishing not for the first time that it had some sort of back support. Even more, he wished the frozen ground was covered in the soft lounging cushions that provided such comfort in his home. He ran his hand over his face, shaking his head. He was growing too suspicious. This was not necessarily part of another Minwanabi ploy to embarrass a political enemy back home; it could simply be a well-intentioned, badly-planned attack. Either way, his duty was clear.

Asayaga called for Sugama, his newly-appointed second-in-command.

'Order the men to form. Full marching gear, five days' rations. Make sure they have on those new furs and footwraps. We march before sunset.'

'Where, Captain?'

He handed over the map and Sugama studied it intently.

Asayaga said nothing. Sugama, without a doubt, didn't know a damned thing about what he was looking at on the parchment, but nevertheless he was staring at it determinedly, acting as if he were a scholar thinking profound thoughts.

'Kingdom outpost. We were to take it today but the commander, in his brilliance, decided he needed more men first, and thus we are volunteered.'

'It is an honour then that our commander selected us.'

Asayaga snorted.

'Yes, an honour. In the Kingdom's tongue our destination is called "Brendan's Stockade".'

Asayaga stumbled over the last two words, dropping the 's'.

'Then it shall be a name of glory for the Empire.'

'But of course,' Asayaga said, features frozen in a mask that revealed nothing. 'Another act of glory in a glorious war.'

22

TWO

Discovery

Icy rain lashed down.

Carefully, silently, Dennis Hartraft slipped through the column of weary troops. In the early morning down-pours, his men crouched motionless, many with arrows nocked to their bows. In their dirty grey cloaks they were one with the forest. Even so, he could sense their tension; something was wrong. Their eyes followed him as he darted from tree to tree, staying low. During the night the snow had changing to a mix of sleet and icy rain. It had made the night march a misery, but some inner sense had compelled Dennis to push on, a decision that Gregory and Tinuva had fully endorsed. Swinging east of Mad Wayne's Fort, which had fallen to the Tsurani the previous spring, they followed a path little more than a game trail back to Brendan's Stockade, approaching from the north-east.

They were less than a quarter of a mile from Brendan's when Alwin Barry, leading the advance squad, ordered a halt. A keen anticipation of downing pints of hot buttered mead and cold ale in a cosy tavern at the fort, instantly gave way to a grim foreboding.

Raised in these woods, Hartraft knew them intuitively. More than once that intuition had kept him alive, where sound logic would have got him killed.

Jurgen had taught him long ago truly to listen to the rhythm of the ancient woods, to be completely still, so quiet that eventually you became one with the forest and could sense the beating of its heart. That sense told him to be ready for the worst.

Jurgen . . . He pushed the thought away as he passed the head of the column and cautiously followed the tracks of the advance squad. Looking over his shoulder he saw Gregory stealthily moving opposite him on the trail to his right.

The two pressed forward as the rain began to let up.

Dennis heard the chatter of a squirrel, looked up and caught a glimpse of Alwin, crouched behind a fallen tree just back from the top of a low rise. He made for him, crawling the last fifty feet to stay concealed from whatever might be on the other side of the ridge.

Alwin didn't talk, he simply pointed to Dennis, then pointed with two fingers to his own eyes and gestured towards the top of the rise, the hand signal for Dennis to go forward and see for himself.

Dennis nodded, crawling under the fallen tree and followed Alwin's track on the slushy ground, trying to ignore the icy dampness seeping through his clothing.

As he moved slowly, he suddenly became aware of the scent of smoke hanging heavy in the air. It had been masked by the rain. On a clear day, he would have smelled it a half-mile farther back. There was more than wood scent to it, something else – cooking meat, perhaps?

He reached the crest, picking a spot between two boulders, crawled up between them, then cautiously raised his head.

Smoke concealed most of the clearing. The smoke was thick, clinging to the ground, and there was far too much of it to have come only from morning cooking fires. He knew what it meant even before an errant breeze blew the smoke away for a moment. The entire clearing, several hundred yards across, was revealed. In the centre, on top of a low ridge, Brendan's Stockade was nothing but a flame-scorched, still-smouldering ruin. With a cold chill he realized that the scent of cooking meat was the stench of burned bodies.

What had happened?

His eyes darted back and forth, trying to soak up information, to evaluate if there was an immediate threat to his men, to see if they had just walked into a trap.

Nothing moved on the far ridge.

The wooden stockade had been breached at the gate with a battering ram mounted on rough wooden wheels. Scaling ladders leaned drunkenly against the wall to either side of the gate.

The moat had never been much, really nothing more than a ditch full of water that stank in the summer and froze over in the winter. He could see where the ice had been broken and had yet to refreeze. The fort must have been attacked late yesterday evening or during the night.

The open slopes around the fort were carpeted with Tsurani dead, perhaps a hundred or more. He stared at them for a moment. Curiously, many were lying facing downslope, as if killed while running away – and Dennis knew the Tsurani never ran away; a knot of them were clustered in the south-west corner of the clearing, piled on top of each other. Obviously they had made a last stand there, but against whom? Had the garrison been strong enough to sally forth and attack the Tsurani downhill, the walls and gates would still be standing and Hartraft's Marauders would be inside at this very moment eating a warm meal.

If Brendan's Stockade had fallen, where were the Tsurani? Dennis had been fighting them for the entire war, and they never left their dead to rot unless killed to the last man. Either way, the winners should now be putting out the fires and repairing the gate, for either side would hold this stockade once taken.

Nothing moved. It was a stockade of the dead.

'There's nothing right in this.'

Gregory had slipped up so silently that his whispered voice gave Dennis a start. Damn him, he enjoyed doing that, sneaking up and thus showing his skill, but Dennis didn't let his flash of anger show.

'Brendan and his lads are finished,' Gregory whispered, 'but so are the Tsurani.'

Dennis said nothing. In spite of the snow vultures were already circling in. A mile or more back he had noticed an absence of crows and ravens in the forest – inactive at night, they were usually noisy and busy first thing in the morning – now he knew where they were . . . enjoying a feast. A vulture dropped down inside the smoking ruins of the fort and did not come back out, yet another indicator that no one was left alive inside.

Could it be that the Tsurani had retreated at his approach?

No. If there were enough of them to take Brendan, they would stay and make a fight of it. The fall of this stockade, along with the Tsurani holding Mad Wayne's to the north-west, made a hole twenty miles wide in the picket chain that covered the northern front. Why take this crucial point only to abandon it?

Ambush?

He looked back over his shoulder. Gregory was carefully looking about as well, and Dennis realized that the Natalese scout had been scanning the woods to either side, looking for any indicators that a trap was closing in.

Nothing. The crows and ravens were all down in the clearing, feasting, so there was none of their noisy cackling in the forest. The other sounds were normal: the ice-covered trees creaking in the breeze, the tinkling sound of now-light rain, the calls of other birds, and nothing else.

There was no ambush: it would already have been sprung.

Their eyes met and both had reached the same conclusion.

'Dark Brothers,' Dennis whispered.

Gregory nodded an agreement. 'Unless the last Tsurani and the last Kingdom soldier conspired to kill one another at the same moment, that's my guess.'

What he saw started to fit together. A Tsurani force had besieged the fort. Ringing the edge of the clearing he could see where the snow had been trampled down, and the torn remains of a dozen of their tents littered the ground, bits of canvas sticking out of the icy slush. Their besieging camp was at the edge of the forest less than a hundred yards away. Cooking pots still hung over cold fire-pits, and a battle pennant leaned against a half-collapsed tent covered with ice. He could even make out the spot where they had forged together their rough-hewn battering ram, for the stump of the freshly-cut tree was coated with melting ice.

Perhaps the Tsurani had just taken the fort, or were venturing an attack when the Dark Brothers had hit them, pressing right through to finish off Brendan's defenders as well. The pattern of bodies indicated that the Tsurani had tried to break out, heading towards the south-west corner of the clearing and the trail that ran straight back to territory they held. The piled-up knot of dead were stopped a good hundred yards short of the main trail which headed into the heart of Tsurani-held territory.

He stared at the trail for a moment, feeling a knot in his stomach. He had walked it often enough as a boy; it was the trail back to his family's estates . . . He forced his attention away from bitter memory and back to the present.

With fifty men in Brendan's garrison the Tsurani would not have ventured an attack with less than two hundred. If the Dark Brothers had come into the fray it meant there were at least three hundred of them, maybe more. They didn't risk a fight like this unless the odds were on their side. He had to know. With only sixty-five of his men left, four of the wounded having survived the night march and still needing to be carried, it was a deadly situation if the moredhel were still in the area.

He caught the scent of Tinuva. It was strange, there was something vaguely different about the scent of elves, not a perfume, but it seemed to carry a warmth, a vitality of life with it, like the first morning of spring. He felt the elf's breath.

'They're here. Moredhel,' Tinuva whispered, his voice drifting so gently it could not have been heard more than half a dozen feet away.

Dennis nodded. 'How many?'

Tinuva weighed the question for what seemed to Dennis a long time. The elves' sense of time was far more stately than humans'. After a long while, he said, 'At least two hundred, maybe more.'

'Are you certain?' asked Dennis.

'No,' replied the elf. 'But do you see any moredhel bodies out there?'

'No,' conceded Dennis.

'Any dead or wounded they carried off. They would have had to come in numbers so overwhelming that the garrison and the Tsurani were quickly overrun, else we would see more sign of them. Look.'

Dennis looked to where the elf pointed and not understanding, finally asked, 'What am I looking for?'

'There are no broken moredhel arrows. They have cleared this area of their passing. They don't want us to know they've been here.'

Gregory nodded. Pointing to the smoking char that had been the stockade, he said, 'That's sort of difficult to ignore, my friend.'

Tinuva said, 'But if you found it in the spring, might you not think the Tsurani had overrun the fort and left behind this memento?'

Dennis didn't hesitate. 'No, the Tsurani would have claimed this position. To the north is the abandoned mine road that leads into the mountains. To the east are the marshlands and mountains. With the Tsurani controlling Mad Wayne's and most of the land west of here ... From here they could raid south behind our lines until we drove them out.' Suddenly Dennis felt a stab of alarm. 'The Dark Brothers are still close by!' he hissed quietly.

'They're probably tending their wounded and waiting for the snow to stop before they return to dispose of the Tsurani dead,' Gregory said in a hoarse whisper. 'I don't think they know we are here though,' He glanced skyward as the snow slackened.

'Don't risk your life on that thought, my friend,' Tinuva said, again his voice was a drifting shimmer barely heard.

'Circle,' Dennis whispered.

Dennis slid back down from boulders. Spying Alwin, he gestured for him to remain in position, indicating that the three of them would circle around the fort and that moredhel were in the area. After nine years in the field, the Marauders had a sophisticated system of hand signals to cover most situations. Alwin signed that he understood and would comply.

Having approached the fort from the west, Dennis started north, following the direction of the low ridge. The realm of the moredhel was to the north, though it didn't necessarily mean that was the direction they had attacked from. Besides, the next major trail, the one that connected Brendan's Stockade and Mad Wayne's Fort, entered at the north-west corner of the clearing. Perhaps there would be signs there that could help unravel the mystery.

As he drifted along the ridge, staying low, he kept the remains of Brendan's Stockade in view. *Yet another link to the past lost within the last day*, he thought.

The stockade was one of a dozen such along the Yabon frontier, garrisoned out of Tyr-Sog. Unlike the mountains to the east, which were dominated by major passes guarded by the border barons –

Ironpass, Northwarden, and High Castle – the western mountains were shot through with trails and little passes. Smuggling in the west was common, but none of the passes was sufficient for any large-scale invasion southward. So the stockades had been constructed over the years.

Each was owned by a trader or innkeeper, who kept it repaired out of profits, while the Baron of Tyr-Sog and the Earl of LaMut paid for the garrison ensconced within; they were much-utilized stops for traders and caravans heading down into the heart of the Kingdom and as such very profitable before the war.

Brendan's had been one of the more successful stops on the trade routes; from here one could turn south to the Kingdom proper, west toward Ylith or LaMut, or north for a shortcut route that would eventually lead to Yabon. Now Brendan and his family were certain to lie dead within.

Dennis kept his eyes busy as he circled, but he felt regret. Brendan had been a good sort, open-handed to those he liked, always ready to offer a pint and a joint of meat to someone down on their luck. As a boy Dennis had stopped there often enough with his father and Jurgen when they went hunting together. Brendan was that type that never seemed to age, perpetually frozen at a stocky middle-age, gravel-voiced, with an expansive girth that cascaded over a thick leather belt, a first-class brawler; and a damned good friend to all who lived a precarious existence along the frontier.

He was, as well, a notorious cheat when it came to gambling, a fact Dennis had witnessed when Jurgen had caught him at it. The fight that resulted had become something of a legend, with Jurgen's nose permanent mashed over to one side and Brendan missing part of an ear.

The two had been good friends after that, both appreciating the mettle of the other, but never again did they venture into a game of dice or the new craze of cards with numbers and pictures painted on them. During the night march Dennis had thought about Brendan, and had pondered how he would react to the news that Jurgen was dead. No need to worry about that now and he wondered which had greeted the other at the entrance of Lims-Kragma's Hall. Perhaps now they could gamble together again, if such games were allowed over there, while they waited to be judged by the Goddess of the Dead.

After covering two hundred yards the rise of ground dropped down towards a narrow forest stream, partly frozen over. The trail to Mad Wayne's Fort, a position now in Tsurani hands, followed the stream and he paused, looking down on it from above.

There were tracks ... and lying by the stream on the far side of the trail was a body, a Tsurani, his throat cut, the ground around him an icy pink.

The three waited for several minutes, carefully scanning the trail, stream, and surrounding woods. Dennis finally looked at Tinuva, who nodded. The elf pulled a bow out from under his cloak, nocked an arrow, and drew it half back.

Dennis took a deep breath and slipped down the trail, pouncing catlike, wincing slightly at the sound of the icy slush crunching beneath his feet. He looked first to the north-west in the direction of Mad Wayne's and away from the smoking ruins of Brendan's Stockade. The trail disappeared into the early morning mist.

Nothing.

Gregory landed beside him, swung out his bow and drew it, pointing it up the trail, tensed and ready.

Still nothing.

Dennis looked down at the ground and his heart stopped. It was churned into a muddy slop which was quickly icing over. He moved slowly, scanning for details. A large number had passed down the trail, heading towards the stockade; he could see frozen imprints that must have been made during the night.

The prints weren't made by the heavy sandals and footcloths of the Tsurani, but by the booted feet of moredhel, men, and the deeper hoofprints of horses and mountain trolls.

What was chilling, though, was that there were prints heading back up the trail and they were fresh, so fresh that droplets of moisture were still oozing into them as ice formed. But not as many as had come in. It was hard to tell – perhaps fifty at most, and no horses.

Battle losses? No, he had not seen any moredhel corpses around the fort. There should have at least been some wounded, drops of blood, a dragging footstep, but these moredhel had been running. Why the haste?

He looked up. Tinuva was still above him, watchful. Dennis pointed to the trail then to the north-west and made the gesture for moredhel, then held his finger tips to his throat, indicating that it was only minutes, a matter of heart beats since their passing.

Tinuva nodded and moved out. Dennis looked at Gregory who set off as well, crossing to the other side of the trail and moving into the stream where he could travel without leaving tracks.

Dennis slipped down to the Tsurani body and touched its leg. The body was just stiffening, dead several hours at the most; had he died earlier in the night rigor would have set in. Looking at the ground, he could figure it out easily enough. The man was a sentry, guarding the trail while the attack on the fort went in, or had in fact already taken the position. It had been a clean kill, stealthy, throat cut from ear to ear and no sign of struggle other than the final spasmodic thrashing of a dying man.

Dennis looked back to the north-west and caught a glimpse of Gregory who was looking back. Dennis pointed to himself and then towards the stockade. Gregory nodded and disappeared into the mist-shrouded forest.

Choosing speed over caution Dennis got back up on to the trail and started off at a slow trot.

The task now was to find out which direction the rest of the moredhel had taken. If the band had split up, scattering after the attack to throw off any pursuit, he'd swing his own men in behind the group heading towards Mad Wayne's Fort, finish them, then reoccupy Brendan's. He'd send Gregory and Tinuva back to Lord Brucal's base camp to ask for reinforcements while Dennis and his company repaired the stockade. But, if the moredhel were indeed returning in force to clean up the Tsurani dead, as Tinuva speculated, Dennis wanted to be well clear of the area before they got back. Defending a rebuilt stockade was one thing; fighting among the ashes on an exposed hillock while being hit from all sides was quite another.

He slowed as he reached the edge of the forest, slipping in behind a towering pine. Closer now to the stockade, he could pick out more details though the smoke was still thick. There were only a couple of Tsurani dead around the northern approach, for the bulk of them were by the gate and the road that headed south-west and the safety of their territory.

As he moved slowly, he noticed something down by the stream. A dark mound rose up amid a small copse of trees. It was almost covered with snow. It took a moment for Dennis's eye to make sense of the dark shape, but then he saw it: moredhel dead, several dozen of them and the picture began to fit together in Dennis's mind.

Clever bastards. They had carried off their dead to leave a puzzle, hiding them nearby. In another two hours, Dennis would have been looking at just another snow-covered bump in the earth. If that force was as large as Tinuva speculated, most of them might be heading up to visit the Tsurani now holding Mad Wayne's, but chances were the rest were lurking nearby, watching, most likely on the other side of the clearing.

Damn clever. Then a more obvious possibility occurred to him.

If we and the Tsurani were fighting a battle here, Dennis thought, *both sides would most likely be rushing up reinforcements even now. They'd reach the clearing and stop, the same way we did.* Dennis wondered if at this very second there were other eyes, Tsurani eyes, gazing at the fort and wondering what to do next. Curiosity, however, would lead most finally to venture in. Once out in the open the trap would be sprung. He realized with a cold certainty that the moredhel heading up the trail to Mad Wayne's were not a force heading out on an additional raid, or fleeing. They were an anvil, waiting for the trap to be sprung and for those fleeing the trap to run straight into them. It could be that they were less than a couple of hundred yards off, and no more than a quarter of a mile. As certain as he was of anything, Dennis knew that he was being watched by moredhel scouts. If they hadn't seen Tinuva or Gregory, they might think him an advance trailbreaker who would soon return the way he had come to carry word to his commander; they would wait until the Kingdom soldiers returned in force, then spring their trap.

Now what?

Trap the trappers most likely deployed on the far side of the clearing, go after the smaller group circling behind him, or get the hell out now?

Use caution when dealing with their kind, Jurgen had always said. His old friend would have told him to get the hell out. If Brendan and the Tsurani had been wiped out by them, there were undoubtedly enough moredhel nearby to annihilate Dennis's small command. Had the moredhel scout who was surely watching him known that a short distance down the trail sixty-odd cold, tired, and hungry Kingdom soldiers waited, he would be carrying word at this moment. Dennis knew what he must do.

Get out, circle around, then warn off any Kingdom troops that might be approaching from the south. He knew he would have to stand up, glance around as if satisfied that no danger lingered and move quickly back to where his command waited. Let the moredhel think him a solitary scout. Dennis would not be returning this way, and neither would any Kingdom force if he could intercept them. Let the Dark Brothers and the Tsurani fight with each other for a while. The moredhel would not linger to occupy a human stockade, and if the Tsurani managed to drive them away, Duke Brucal, Earl Vandros of LaMut, and Baron Moyet could decide how to drive them out of here and Mad Wayne's next spring.

Dennis and his scouts had signals to use in these situations. He would remove his heavy cloak, shaking it as if he was trying to rid it of excess water. That would let Tinuva and Gregory know he was under scrutiny and they needed to withdraw without being seen. Dennis was on the verge of standing up to do just this when he saw the enemy. Stepping out of the forest, down on the south-west side of the clearing, a lone Tsurani appeared, easily picked out by his bright blue lacquered armour.

Dennis grinned. Damned fool, typical of them. Make a big show of bravado. A new plan instantly formed in Dennis's mind. Except for a couple of their best units the Tsurani were blundering fools in the forest compared to his Marauders. The moredhel had to know additional Tsurani were here. In fact, it lessened the likelihood the moredhel knew that Dennis's unit was nearby. The trap was set for the Tsurani. *Let the two sides slaughter each other while we slip away, or with luck the Tsurani will so weaken the moredhel we might even finish them both off and reclaim the fort for ourselves. This might actually get amusing,* he thought with a wolfish smile, and then he heard the crack of a branch.

'It is a trap,' Force Leader Asayaga hissed, gesturing towards the smoking ruins of the stockade.

Sugama said nothing, but Asayaga could already read what his second-in-command was thinking, and what he would do.

The night march had been an exercise in stupidity and waste. Two hours of double-quick march in daylight could have brought them to this position, but instead they had endured a frigid, miserable night. His men were exhausted, shivering from the wretched cold, and the perverse gods of this world were sending down bucketful's of snow.

Now this damnable disaster. It was obvious that Force Leader Hagamaka of the Gineisa had launched the attack without waiting for the reinforcements Asayaga was bringing up. The thought of a Minwanabi ally failing so miserably, so publicly, might have brought Asayaga some pleasure, except for the sight of so many fine soldiers of the Empire dead, slaughtered in a futile battle. It was yet another tragic waste of good men. But why the urgent command for a night march through dangerous territory if Hagamaka wasn't going to wait?

He first suspected that Hagamaka had intended to embarrass him, to order reinforcements up, not wait and launch the attack, then accuse him of failing to arrive in a timely manner.

Yet, as he surveyed the carnage, he wondered: it was obvious the attack had turned into a rout, a pile of nearly two score dead were clumped on a low rise not a hundred paces into the clearing, and a trail of dead led all the way back to the fort.

No garrison of fifty Kingdom troops could have done this. Did they have more hidden inside the ruined fort, or a force waiting in the woods which had cut Hagamaka off? Then, if so, why the abandoned fort?

The Kingdom considered this a key link in their chain which guarded the shadowy northern front. From the Lake of the Sky's eastern shore down to the northernmost peak of the Grey Tower

34

Mountains, only the chains of stockades prevented the Tsurani from sweeping eastward, then south into Tyr-Sog and the other Kingdom cities of Yabon. Earlier in the year the forces of the Empire had taken Mad Wayne's fort to the north-west. If they could also hold Brendan's, they could control enough of this area to stage an invasion down into Yabon in the spring. With a second invasion pressing out of the Free Cities to the south-west, the Kingdom would lose Yabon inside a year. The Kingdom knew this, and were desperate to garrison and supplying these small fortresses. If they had destroyed Hagamaka they would, at this very moment, be barricading the shattered gate, making repairs ... and looting the dead. Messages would already have been sent south for more reinforcements.

Asayaga shook his head. No. Something was dreadfully wrong with this entire situation. He looked over at Sugama but knew there would be no sage advice. He was, after all, of House Tondora, allegedly assigned to Asayaga's force for training in anticipation of the Tondora joining the Warlord's host in the spring. It was an unusual but not unprecedented situation to have a junior officer train with the forces of an ally, but everyone knew that this was simply a charade. The Tondora – while publicly 'politically neutral', in the Great Council – were Clan Shonshoni and a client House of the Minwanabi, so everything they did was at Minwanabi bidding.

Though supposedly second-in-command, his bloodline and rank in the courts at home would have placed him far above what Asayaga could ever hope to aspire to. So there could only be one reason he was in a subordinate role now: to keep close watch on Asayaga. Asayaga was a son of the Kodeko, a minor house, but of Clan Kanazawai, and the Shinzawai were most likely next on the list of opponents to be crushed by the Minwanabi. The Minwanabi were far too clever to openly confront House Keda, the most powerful Kanazawai Clan family, and one of the Five Great Families of the Empire. But the Shinzawai, while an old and honourable family, with a venerated lord in Kamatsu, retired abruptly from the war with the other families in the Blue Wheel Party, dealing the Warlord a major setback. The move had actually helped the Minwanabi cause, but had also marked the Shinzawai as a political force to be reckoned with. And the Minwanabi never ignored such potential opponents.

By discrediting Clan Kanazawai, the Minwanabi would weaken the Keda and their allies. It was but another ploy in the Great Game.

Against that possibility, Asayaga of House Kodeko was ordered to remain in the war by the clan leaders. Ostensibly of the Yellow Flower Party – still allied with the Warlord – Asayaga was the logical choice to be left behind to keep an eye on the Minwanabi. Someone had to be, for their plots and schemes were unending.

Asayaga recalled the disgust he had felt when word of the loss of Lord Sezu of the Acoma had reached him; while of Clan Hadama, Lord Sezu was nevertheless an honourable man worthy of respect. His death had been the result of a manipulation of the Minwanabi sub-commander, who had reinforcements arrive 'too late' to save Sezu and his son Lanakota from death. Now only Mara, his daughter, was left to shepherd her house, though by rumours reaching the front, she seemed adept at doing so.

Asayaga kept his disquiet to himself; this late arrival smacked of the same sort of machinations as that betrayal of Sezu in the first year of the war, and that made him uneasy. Fighting the soldiers of the Kingdom was one thing, and even facing the Forest Demons, those known as Dark Brothers to the enemy, was simple warfare. But the treachery of the Great Game, reaching as it did through the rift from the home world to this distant and icy frontier, that was an enemy impossible to confront directly. Besides, even back home Asayaga never liked politics. He took after his father in that regard, and it was for that reason above all others why the Kodeko had remained a minor house in Clan Kanazawai.

Asayaga's gaze drifted to his senior Strike Leader, Tasemu, the true second-in-command, a veteran from the very start of the war. The one-eyed fighter nodded his understanding that they needed to talk in private, then motioned for them to pull back.

Sugama saw the interplay and cleared his throat. 'We must find out what happened, Force Commander. Perhaps both sides annihilated each other. We can take the fort now and hold it, gaining great glory. Think of what would be said if this kingdom fort was indeed abandoned and then we simply ran away. If we miss this opportunity the disgrace will be known throughout the army.'

And you would be certain to spread it, Asayaga thought. For that matter Sugama, by that mere statement, had forced his hand. The comment had been made as friendly advice, and if ignored, Sugama would be seen to have been in the right and have won his point in the Game. It was impossible now to withdraw without first sending someone up to the fort and thereby reveal his presence.

Asayaga silently cursed. He looked back at Tasemu who stared back impassively.

'What are you thinking, Strike Leader?' Asayaga asked.

The mere fact that a Force Commander asked a Strike Leader for an opinion obviously shocked Sugama; but, no matter which clan he belonged to, he had to learn to leave Tsurani rigidity behind if he was going to fight with Force Commander Asayaga. This was war on an alien world and you didn't live long if you held to forms and customs.

'A third force did this,' Tasemu announced.

'Who?'

But Asayaga already knew the answer: the idea was half-formed within minutes of him first creeping up to the edge of the clearing.

'The Forest Demons.'

'Demons? Creatures of myth! Impossible!' Sugama exclaimed.

'They are mortal,' Asayaga said, 'but those here first called them demons because they are most difficult to close with. They drift among the trees like the mist, and they can strike without warning. The Kingdom call them "the Dark Brotherhood". They are kin to those called "elves" we believe.'

Tasemu volunteered, 'And they do fight like demons when they wish, Force Leader. They are ... difficult.'

The mere mention of them had sent a shiver through more than one of Asayaga's men. They were a strange, unknown factor on this world. Logic would have dictated that these creatures should have allied themselves with the Kingdom in order to repel a foreign invader, as had the elves and the short men called 'dwarves'. Yet they obviously had not. They were often not seen for as long as a year, then suddenly a patrol would vanish or an outpost would be overrun; and when it was clear that the Kingdom had not had a hand, it was possible to conclude only one thing: it had been the Dark Brothers. This third player in the drama made every commander in the north uneasy, since the Forest Demons' actions were impossible to anticipate.

Yet it was not their unpredictability that disturbed his men. They were soldiers and expected to die if needs be; that was their place in the order of things. Yes, the war against the Kingdom – especially here on the northern frontier – was deadly, the fighting brutal. Often there was no time to care for wounded, who were given the honourable death of the blade lest they be taken prisoner and shame their houses by being made slaves or, worse, being hanged as one would a criminal or slave.

But at least the Kingdom soldiers were men. They fought with an honour that Asayaga found he had initially been surprised by in barbarians. There had been an unspoken truce at the siege of Crydee, where Kamatsu of the Shinzawai, Asayaga's cousin, had commanded. Both sides had calmly and silently collected their dead several times and had burned them on pyres of honour, before returning to their respective lines without incident, to resume the fighting the next day. The siege had ended with the withdrawal of the forces of the Blue Wheel Party.

Yet that siege had taught Asayaga what to expect from the Kingdom soldiers. With the Dark Brothers, however, the killing was different. More than once he had found bodies, Tsurani and Kingdom, butchered in horrible ways, the mutilation obviously done while the victim was still alive. Even the dead they disfigured: ears lopped off as trophies, heads placed on stakes. It was as if they loved to kill humans, and did so for the simple pleasure it gave them. And you could almost never see them coming. A superstition had come into being among the soldiers in the north, that if they died and were given funeral rites here on Midkemia, their spirits would be somehow sent back to their homeworld on Kelewan. But without speaking of it, the men had come to believe that should the Forest Demons butcher the dead and leave them for the carrion eaters, the spirits of the slaughtered Tsurani would wander this cold and alien landscape until the end of time. No priest of any order had been able to counter this belief. Asayaga, like every commander in the north, knew this superstition gave the Dark Brothers an advantage they scarcely needed.

He looked back at Sugama, hoping that Tasemu's words had registered some doubt.

'Shall I go to the fort, Force Commander, and lay claim to it?' Sugama asked evenly, as if Tasemu's words had merely been the whistling of the wind.

Asayaga was about to tell him to go to the devils of the underworld, but he held his tongue. He was trapped. A plan formed for a brief instant. He would order a retreat, hold Sugama back for a few minutes and slip a blade into his throat, thereby silencing him.

He knew his men would never ask what had become of Sugama when he caught up with them, but others back at the headquarters camp were not of House Kodeko, and they would almost certainly assume treachery if Sugama were the only casualty.

Send Sugama forward? No, damn it. If indeed the battle had been a mutual slaughter, or there was even the remote chance that the Kingdom troops had retreated after the fight, the shame of letting Sugama take the fort would be unbearable to his house. It would appear as well that he was a coward, ordering someone else to take the risk rather than set the proper example by doing it himself.

What was even more enraging was the realization that Sugama was following the same process of reasoning and thus dictating the rules of the game now being played.

Asayaga looked once more at Tasemu, but there was no need to say anything. Of the eighty men in his command most were new recruits; little more than boys called to serve by their blood ties to House Kodeko. They would obey without question, but they were untested. Asayaga would rely on his old core of twenty veterans, led by Tasemu, who knew the ways of this war. The Strike Leader nodded, raised a hand and gestured, Vashemi and Tarku, the most senior Patrol Leader and the wiliest old veteran without rank, respectively, half-stood and started back down the trail, checking to the rear as he went forward.

Asayaga shot a withering gaze at Sugama. 'Stay here.'

Taking a deep breath, he stood up and stepped out of the forest and into the clearing. He strode forward, acting as if he was out for a morning walk along a road on his family's estate, rather than advancing alone, fully exposed, heading towards a deserted, smoking ruin.

He passed the pile of bodies and as he drew closer he felt his heart constrict. All were dead, most from arrows, but the shafts had been snapped off by someone who wished to obscure the identity of the attackers. But the manner of death for some made it all too obvious. More than one of the warriors had been wounded first; but if it had been by Kingdom troops, the final dispatching would have been done with a certain professional respect for a worthy foe. A warrior from either side would often give the doomed a moment for final prayer and then cut his throat cleanly and quickly. He had done it often enough himself, both to Kingdom soldiers too injured to be taken back as slaves, and more than once to one of his own men whom he was forced to leave behind.

The dying had been murdered cruelly. Several had been decapitated. He slowed for a second, looking down at a face he vaguely recognized, an officer he had seen at times in camp. The mutilation was ghastly, the one most feared by any man. The agonized expression frozen on the dead man's face was evidence enough that he had still been alive when the carving up had started.

Asayaga swallowed hard and kept going. The fort was now less than a hundred paces away: he was coming into easy arrowshot range. The gate was off its hinges, the inside of the compound visible, bodies littered the interior. Several vultures were perched on the expansive stomach of one of the dead.

Perhaps the fort was abandoned after all?

And yet . . .

He slowed. Something wasn't right. The vultures, they weren't eating, they had stopped and were looking not towards him but instead at something within the fort that he couldn't see.

He stopped, and his hand went to the hilt of his sword.

Two things happened at nearly the same instant. The vultures, startled by something he couldn't see inside the fort flapped their wings, croaking obscenely, struggling to lift into the air: and a shout of warning came from behind. It was Tasemu.

'It's a trap!' Asayaga roared.

For the first few seconds he thought to rush the fort, but even as the vultures lifted off he knew someone was inside and if there was someone inside the smoking ruins of the barracks it meant there was most likely many of them, ready to hold the gate and riddle a charge with arrows.

He turned and sprinted back towards his men. Tasemu was standing out in the open, arms up, pointing back up the trail they had just come down.

'Behind us!' Tasemu cried, 'The Forest Demons are coming!'

Asayaga stopped half-way between the fort and the edge of the clearing.

Damn them! We walked straight into it. It was clear what would happen. Already Sugama was ordering the men to rush the fort and take refuge.

No! That's what the enemy want! They'll block the gate: then we get caught in the open and shot full of arrows.

He had to think. He looked back at the fort. It had been but a dozen heartbeats since he had turned back from it. The vultures were barely clear of the gate, wings flapping. The shelter of it looked inviting: too inviting.

His men were streaming out of the woods, running hard, Sugama in the lead. Then one of the men, just barely out of the forest, collapsed, blood fountaining, an arrow driven through his throat.

Sugama came on quickly.

'Hundreds of them!' he shouted, his voice edged with panic.

In spite of the chaos Asayaga could not suppress a grin. They might all die in the next few minutes, but it was good to see Sugama get a taste of the reality of this world first.

Asayaga waved his sword over his head as a rallying signal.

When the men were less than ten yards off he pointed away from the fort to the north-west corner of the clearing.

'Not the fort! Trap! Follow me!'

Sugama slowed for an instant, startled, as an arrow slashed past him. Then he turned to follow Asayaga.

Asayaga set off at a run. He had barely gone a dozen paces when he heard the blast of a horn echoing from the woods to the south. It was answered by another from within the fort!

He ran. The gate was no longer in view, and the west wall of the fort was now to his right and a hundred paces off. He led his column straight up the clearing, trying to keep an equal distance between the fort in the centre and the woods. An arrow skimmed past, kicking up a slushy spray of snow. He spared a quick glance at the fort. Dark forms lined the wall, bows raised. It was the Forest Demons, their distinctive visage clearly visible. Never had he seen so many of them and at such close quarters; before it had always been a furtive glance, a half-seeing as they drifted nightmarelike through the woods.

Asayaga had scouted this place several times over the last year and knew its layout. At the north-west corner a trail entered the clearing, leading to a fort taken by his command in the spring. It was four leagues to that place.

It would most likely be covered but it had to be tried. The east was Kingdom territory and impenetrable marshy ground for several leagues, a death trap. Straight north was the route to the realm of the Forest Demons, rocky game trails through high passes, a death trap as well.

Asayaga headed for the trail that might be either a trap, or a path to safety and then he saw someone stagger out from the trail clutching his chest, blood pulsing from between his clutching fingers. Stunned, he slowed to a stop as the dying person looked at him with blank eyes and then collapsed.

He stopped, not sure for an instant what to do next. He looked to his left, directly into the woods. Perhaps it was better to go that way rather than take the trail, for obviously something was covering that trail.

He started to run again, and his men following. Within seconds they were closing on the edge of the clearing and then a shower of arrows snapped out from the treeline, dropping half a dozen of his men.

Asayaga, sword held high, charged for the woods, praying that he could take one of his tormentors with him.

Dennis Hartraft stared into the eye of the archer poised not fifty paces away. The dark elf had his bow fully drawn and aimed. Remarkably, though, the moredhel had cracked a frozen branch when he stepped out from behind the tree to shoot – he must have been a relative youngster to make so basic a blunder.

It was, at best, a second of time since Dennis had heard that crack.

Time distorted and slowed; he saw the tips of the fingers relaxing, releasing the taut bowstring. Pushing off from the tree, he kicked backwards, eyes still fixed on his stalker. He saw the snap of mist breaking away from the bowstring, the blur of the arrow, the stinging brush of the feathers as the shaft creased his face.

He hit the ground, rolled across the trail, slammed up against a boulder. Two seconds, maybe three, had passed. He was on his feet, saw the elf flinging back his cloak, exposing a quiver.

Instinct drove him forward. In a single bound he vaulted the narrow stream, landed hard, slipping on the icy slope, then started up the rise, reaching for the dagger at his belt. The moredhel had the arrow drawn from the quiver, was reversing it, fitting the nock to the string.

Dennis sprinted forward, lost his footing on an ice-covered boulder, slipped and fell, nearly dropping his dagger, and came back up to his feet. The dark elf was drawing his bow and he knew he had lost the race.

Snakelike he lashed out with an underhand throw of the dagger. The spin was off, the dagger striking the elf in the chest, hilt first. But the impact startled him, he lost his grip on the bowstring and the arrow snapped off, missing Dennis.

Dennis leapt forward even as the dark elf dropped his bow and reached for his own dagger. Dennis dived in, catching the moredhel in the chest with his right shoulder. The pain to his old wound shocked him but he heard his foe grunt as well as the wind got knocked out of him.

The two fell together in a tangled heap, Dennis clutching at the dark elf's arm, preventing him from drawing his blade. They grappled, rolling on the ground. The moredhel attempted to cry out; Dennis clamped his hand over his mouth. The moredhel bit down and Dennis clamped his jaws together to cut off his own cry of pain.

The two rolled back and forth on the slushy ground, kicking and clawing in a primal fight for survival. He caught a glimpse of his foe's eyes – so strange, so like Tinuva's, yet different, filled with fury and murderous rage.

As if from a great distance he heard shouts, but all his world was now focused on the dark elf, who writhed like an enraged serpent as he sought to escape. They rolled again, Dennis on top, faces only inches apart. The moredhel head-butted Dennis in the face. The blow stunned Dennis, blurring his vision.

They rolled down the slope and crashed into the icy creek. Dennis lost his grip and felt the moredhel break free of his grasp and draw his dagger. The moredhel's arm snapped up. And then he moved with a spasmodic jerk. An arrow had slammed into the dark elf's chest, going clean through his body. A mist of blood exploded from the elf's back.

With a gurgling cry the moredhel staggered to his feet and started to run, blood pulsing out. Dennis gasped for breath and caught a glimpse of Tinuva standing up on the trail, already drawing a second arrow, tracking the moredhel, but then held his shot as the Dark Brother staggered into the clearing.

Tinuva relaxed his grip on his bow and looked down at Dennis. 'Move now!' Tinuva hissed.

Dennis, his heart pounding, shoulder aching, came to his feet and started up the slope to Tinuva's side.

'Trap, we're in a trap!' Tinuva announced.

As he gained the trail he caught a glimpse of the dying moredhel collapsing and confronting him, the column of Tsurani. There had been only one Tsurani, and now there was near on a hundred and he realized that his struggle with the moredhel must have dragged out for several dangerously long minutes.

Too much was happening too quickly and he leaned over, gasping for breath. The shock of his fight and near death was having its impact and he fought down an urge to vomit. Tinuva grabbed him by the shoulder and pushed him back off the trail.

'The moredhel net is wide,' Tinuva said quickly. 'They are waiting on the trail, two hundred yards from here. Ambush prepared. 'They didn't know we were near and the one you killed was one of their flanking scouts. They will find us in a few minutes, crossing the trail we made in the snow. Gregory sent me back to tell you.'

At that same instant he saw that the Tsurani were turning, shying away from the trail and heading straight into the woods in the direction where his own men were concealed. The move triggered a response: a shower of arrows snapped out from the forest.

Damn! Now we are revealed.

He sprinted up the slope, Tinuva bounding forward by his side. Ground that had taken minutes to cover before he crossed in seconds. He caught a glimpse of Alwin Barry and a dozen of his men poised around the boulders firing down on the Tsurani. Several of the Tsurani had their alien short-bows out and crouching behind the stumps of trees in the clearing, were shooting back.

Horns now echoed all around them. From the east side of the clearing he saw dark-cloaked forms, a hundred or more charging, while others poured out of the fort. More were coming up from the south. It was chaos. He needed to think clearly, but the smashing blow to his head from the dark moredhel still had him stunned. Looking down at the Tsurani he saw one of them barely a hundred feet away charging, sword held high. There was something vaguely familiar about him, an enemy he had faced before.

'Stop fighting!'

The booming cry echoed through the forest. It was Gregory, running hard, coming through the woods. He leapt onto the boulder they had hidden behind earlier and extended his arms wide so that even the Tsurani in the clearing could see him.

'Stop fighting! Dark Brothers are closing in!' Gregory shouted. 'We settle our differences later!' Then he said something else and Dennis recognized it as Tsurani. 'If we fight one another, we die! No honour in throwing our lives away!'

The Tsurani warrior leading the charge slowed, then came to a halt.

Gregory said something else and pointed back across the clearing. 'Those we call the Dark Brotherhood are upon us in strength.'

The leader turned and looked.

Gregory's words forced Dennis to focus his attention.

I am in command, he remembered, and he felt a flicker of anger towards Gregory overstepping his bounds yet again, and yet again being right. *If we and the Tsurani fight now, we all die.* He turned the anger on himself. *I should have grasped this immediately; Gregory realized it. Jurgen would have too.*

45

He turned about in a full circle, judging sound, distances, ignoring the Tsurani. He saw a line of horse-mounted warriors emerge from the trail that headed south, one of them holding a banner aloft – human renegades serving with their moredhel masters. Dennis felt his stomach knot; the only time the moredhel hired mercenary cavalry was when they were mounting an offensive; they had no use for humans otherwise.

A dozen or more trolls swarmed about the standard-bearer like dogs about to be unleashed for the hunt. Others on foot were pouring out of the forest from the far side of the clearing.

Main force there, he realized.

From behind, to the west and north-west he heard horns. The blocking force on the trail were spreading out and closing the net. *If they delay us even for a few minutes the mounted riders and other fell creatures accompanying them will close in for the kill.*

It was obvious they planned for a fleeing force to turn and go up the trail, and straight into their doom.

To the north, nothing, only a few sentries. Arrogant of them: it was the way back to moredhel territory and they had left it open.

North then, it was the only way out!

He looked back to the clearing again, and the Tsurani were already gone, moving rapidly to the north. All he could see were their retreating backs.

Damn them, they were suppose to be the diversion and now he was the diversion instead!

Furious with himself he held a hand up, circled it then snapped it down and set off at a run, his men following.

He bounded back towards the trail to Mad Wayne's, praying that perhaps the Tsurani had taken that turn and stumbled into the moredhel's trap.

He hit the edge of the trail and without hesitation jumped down. Within seconds his men were sliding down around him.

He looked down. No Tsurani tracks.

Damn! They had slipped out some other way.

A man next to him, Beragorn, was an old veteran. He grunted and turned, clutching at his stomach where an arrow with black feathers quivered.

Out of the mist he saw them coming, half-a-dozen moredhel. More filtering through the trees to either side of the trail. Instinctively he crouched, and an arrow snapped overhead. More men were sliding down onto the trail, turning, ready to fight.

No. In a minute those in the field will close in.

'Alwin! Block force. Then across creek!' he shouted. 'The rest of you, follow me north!'

He hesitated for a second, looking at Beragorn who was down on his knees. He reached for his dagger, to do the task any friend would do for a comrade when the moredhel were closing in.

Damn, his dagger was lost.

He glanced at Beragorn, whose eyes were glazing over as he fell backward against a bole. Taking a breath, Dennis seized the shaft sticking out of Beragorn's stomach, and with a single push, jammed it up into his old comrade's heart. The man stiffened and died.

Dennis sprinted off the trail, leaping the creek and running up the slope where he had fought the moredhel sentry.

This time his footing held. He looked back.

The tail end of his command were just now crossing the trail.

Alwin had heard him, calling out half a dozen men who stood to either side of the trail, their first volley of arrows slowing the dark elves' charge. A couple more men went down from a return volley. He caught a glimpse of Tinuva leaping the stream, landing, turning, bow drawn. He let fly, aiming back towards Brendan's Stockade. It was a long shot, yet it dropped a horse at the head of the trail, throwing the rider. Gregory sprinted past him, dodging through the trees.

'Follow Gregory!' Dennis shouted, pointing the way.

He waited a few more seconds, grabbing the shoulder of a man who started to slip back down the slope, pulling him up and over. It was the priest. He shoved him forward, screaming at him to run. He was about to shout for Alwin to break but the sergeant knew his business. The six men holding the trail leapt down to the stream and bounded across. Archers to either side of Dennis gave covering fire, killing two of the moredhel who tried to follow. Tinuva raced past, his retreat clear signal enough to withdraw. Riders were on the trail. Out in the clearing hundreds of the enemy were swarming in. But what of the other enemy,

47

the Tsurani? There was no time to think of that now. It was time to run.

Behind him, the bloodlusting cries of the moredhel echoed in the clearing and the forest.

The hunt was on.

THREE

Moredhel

Asayaga gasped for breath.

'Keep moving, keep moving, keep moving. . .'

The words were a chant, a prayer, blanking out his own agony.

One of his men was down, collapsed in the middle of the slushy trail. He slowed. Strike Leader Tasemu was standing over the man, struggling to pull him up.

'Keep moving,' Asayaga snapped, slapping the fallen warrior across the shoulder blades with the flat of his sword.

The warrior looked up. It was Sugama.

'Damn you. You are an officer!' Asayaga hissed at him so the men wouldn't overhear. 'Act like one. You were suppose to run lead with the scouts!' As much as he despised the Tondora dog, he would not undermine his authority in front of the men. Not for the first time, Asayaga cursed this war in which officers not of his own house were sent to serve with his men.

Sugama staggered to his feet and lurched forward. Tasemu gazed at Asayaga and shook his head. Asayaga said nothing.

He looked back over his shoulder. His command was strung out on the trail behind them. Those who were not totally preoccupied with their own pain had seen the exchange, the humiliation of an officer from one House by another. They would of course say nothing, for the behaviour of their Force Commander made it clear it was to be ignored. Yet, they would think on it, and some might mention it quietly while on guard duty or around a cook-fire to those who

49

had not witnessed it, and many of his men would dwell on one thing: that one whom they were expected to obey without question was obviously a flawed man, one who had been sent to the front for reasons having nothing to do with his competence as a soldier. He was either a man acting as a spy for the Minwanabi, an incompetent someone higher up in his clan wished to see conveniently dead, or both. That would give the men pause at critical moments, and Asayaga knew other men might die as a result.

If only there had been one more Kodeko officer left alive. Only one other Kodeko son remained on the homeworld, and should Asayaga be slain, the mantle of leadership would fall to his younger brother Tacumbe, but the last son of the House would never be sent here. Again he silently cursed a cruel destiny that left his house with no other competent officers at hand, and Minwanabi machinations that placed this fool at his right hand. If they survived this nightmare, he would name Tasemu his Force Leader, even though the man's talents were better suited for his present role. He would return Sugama to his own family and let him deal with his shame. Fatalistically, Asayaga allowed himself the thought he couldn't be more of an enemy to the House of Tondora than he already was. *They can only kill me once*, he thought as he again looked to see where his men were.

Motioning Sugama ahead he pressed on up the trail. Watching the back of the man as he hurried ahead, Asayaga wondered whether, if he fell, Tasemu would take commands from Sugama. *Another very good reason not to get killed any time soon*, he thought dryly.

The storm abated slightly as the day passed. As they turned a bend in the trail he could see a notch in the ridgeline ahead, the crests of the mountains to either side of the pass were concealed by the low grey clouds of the storm.

He paused for a moment, staring up the trail. He had never been this far north, for the ridgeline had always been a backdrop to his war, a distant mystery.

Hakaxa, his lead scout, was down on his knees, gasping for air, with Sugama bent double beside him. Hakaxa looked up as Asayaga approached.

'Crest of trail just ahead.'

Tasemu grunted. 'The crest. At the pass, they'll have something there.'

Asayaga nodded. He looked back again. His men were staggering forward, pressing stoically up the steep incline.

'Five minute rest here,' Asayaga announced. 'I'll scout ahead.'

Tasemu cocked his head slightly, gazing at him with his one good eye. 'No. Sugama with me.'

Tasemu gave him a bit of a hopeful gaze but Asayaga ignored it. No, there would be no knife in the back.

'Sugama,' Asayaga said quietly, and continued on. He could hear the ragged gasps for breath as Sugama struggled to stay up.

The storm was blowing straight into their faces from the north, and he could hear the moaning of the wind as it whistled through stunted trees in the pass just ahead.

He held his hand out, motioning for Sugama to stop, looked back and touched his nose, then flared his nostrils. Sugama stopped, looked at him curiously, and finally realized what Asayaga was signifying. He sniffed the air. His eyes grew wide.

Good, let him learn that he must use all senses out here.

Asayaga drifted to the side of the trail and moved forward cautiously. The trail turned and his heart froze. Sugama slipped up to his side and a sigh of anguish escaped him.

Asayaga found himself staring intently at a stockade wall. The pass over the top of the mountains went through a notch, the walls of the pass sloping up nearly vertically for a hundred or more feet to either side. The passage was barricaded by a stone wall a dozen feet high, with a crude wooden gate in the centre. Beyond the wall he saw the roof of what must be a garrison house. He sighed inwardly at the thought of the comfort that must lie within.

He saw no one, but the smoke gave it all away. This far north the garrison had to be moredhel.

'Can we go around it?' Sugama asked, whispering.

Asayaga shook his head. 'Not enough time. We don't know how close the pursuit is – those Kingdom soldiers may have bought us time, but we don't know how much. If we try to crawl our way over the mountain to either side, and the moredhel are still chasing us, we'll be destroyed. They'll go through the pass ahead, cut us off . . .'

'But if we attack and those behind us, Kingdom or moredhel, come up, we're doomed.'

Asayaga forced a grin. 'We take it quickly and hold it. Then let the bastards from the Kingdom sit on the outside while the Dark Brothers come up and finish them. With forty good men I could hold it against three to four hundred. 'And besides,' he added, 'it's warm in there. We need rest, hot food, and a place to dry out.'

His words trailed off as he caught a glimpse of movement. A sentry, cloak pulled up over his head, peered over the top of the wall for a moment. Asayaga sensed that the sentry was looking straight at him, he froze. Long seconds passed and the head disappeared.

Asayaga crept back from the tree and started down the trail, Sugama following.

'What you did back there, striking me,' Sugama hissed, trying to force the words out through ragged gasps for breath.

Asayaga slowed, fixing him with his gaze. 'If you are demanding a duel there's no damn time now. No time for Tsurani honour, no time even for the Great Game, you Minwanabi lapdog. There is time only for survival. If we die, I can't return home to see my younger brother grown, and you can't serve your masters. Dead, neither of us serves. Do you understand?'

Sugama's anger slowly subsided, and he looked around. Asayaga could almost see the comprehension dawning on the man as to just how alien this world was, how far from home they were, and how trivial matters of honour and politics were at this moment. Asayaga also knew that Sugama had never experienced cold like this in his life.

'It's going to get colder tonight, cold enough that if you sleep, you die.'

Sugama finally nodded.

Asayaga said, 'Good. I need you to help lead. If we are to survive, no man can question your orders. A man who hesitates, who looks to me or Tasemu to see if your order is to be obeyed may get all of us killed. I need you to follow me through this as if I were Ruling Lord of your House. If we survive to get home safely, then we resolve this matter as you like; I will publicly fight a duel, or you may return to the Minwanabi and ask them to send an assassin to kill me. Whatever your honour dictates. But I will let you return home freely and unencumbered if you serve the men who obey us now.'

Sugama looked straight at him, stunned by the bluntness of Asayaga's words.

'We have no time,' Asayaga repeated. 'Will you co-operate?'

Finally Sugama nodded. Without comment, Asayaga gave him a single nod in return, then moved back down the trail, rounding the bend. He knew Sugama was a Minwanabi spy, but he was also a Tsurani noble, and he would never violate this trust. Asayaga had nothing more to fear from him until they were safely behind their own lines. Then there would come a reckoning.

One of his archers tensed, then lowered his bow, arms trembling, as they approached. The cold, the exhaustion, the fact that everyone was soaked to the skin was taking its toll. He had to seize the stockade or none of his command would survive the night.

The last of his men came up, Asayaga looked at them inquiringly.

'Not sure, Force Commander,' one of them reported, 'several times I thought I heard something . . .' He shrugged. 'It was hard to tell with this wind.'

'They're close,' Tasemu interjected softly.

Asayaga looked over. The old Strike Leader was staring at him with his one good eye. Tasemu had 'the sense'.

Asayaga nodded, ordering the men to gather around.

'Good news,' Asayaga announced. The men looked at him, shivering, pushed to the final limit of exhaustion.

'I found a nice warm cabin ahead. A hot fire, dry bedding, plenty of cooked food, perhaps even some hot wine that will put the fire back in your bellies.'

Some of them looked up, a few allowed their Tsurani impassivity to break with slight smiles.

'We have to kill the owners first. Forest Demons.'

They huddled in close as he explained what had to be done, gazing into their eyes, trying to judge their strength, and also the desperation needed to charge a position not properly scouted.

The men formed up, the few carrying shields deployed to the front ranks, archers to the rear and flanks. As required by tradition he took the centre of the first rank of five.

53

There was no need to issue the command, he simply stepped forward, the tiny phalanx shuffled, stepping off to keep pace. He moved slowly at first, giving them a few extra minutes to get their wind even as they advanced up the steep slope.

Finally they turned the last bend in the trail and the stockade was directly ahead. He continued the walking pace for a few more seconds, perhaps the guard would be looking the other way, but even as the thought formed the high piercing wail of a horn echoed.

'Charge!'

They sprinted straight for the gate, Asayaga leading the way, stumpy legs churning through the slushy snow. The range closed, fifty paces, forty, down to thirty. The lone guard raised a bow, took aim, and released the string. Asayaga heard the snap of the arrow hit the shield of the man next to him.

The gate loomed up in front of them and Asayaga braced himself for the impact. Without slowing the phalanx crashed into the wooden barrier, over four tons of human flesh and armour acting as a battering ram.

He had hoped that the barrier log would not be in place, or would be so weak that they'd crash right in. He felt the log gate give inward, groaning, his men continuing to push, running in place, feet slipping, churning up the frozen ground beneath.

The gate held.

The warrior to his left collapsed without a sound. A rock the size of a human head had crushed his skull in. Asayaga looked up. Directly above were half a dozen moredhel, several throwing rocks, one aiming a bow straight down at them. Spears arced up, catching one, but the rest loosed their deadly loads and several more men dropped.

The effort at the gate was useless. He couldn't retreat now.

'Spread out along the wall!' Asayaga screamed, 'Stay against the wall. Archers! Keep them down!'

His men spread out. He caught a glimpse of Tasemu dragging a wounded recruit up against the wall. Pressed hard against the stones they were relatively safe; an archer would have to lean over to shoot and his own archers deployed to either side of the trail and back a couple of dozen yards were effective in keeping the enemy down.

Asayaga waited a couple of minutes, trying to judge just how many were on the other side. If a dozen or less, perhaps his own archers could take most of them out. Two more minutes passed slowly.

A few rocks arced over the wall but his men remained pressed against the side of the stockade and were safe. It was a stalemate.

'We can't stay here forever. I think our pursuers are close. If so they'll slaughter us out here.'

It was Tasemu.

Asayaga nodded. 'Pair up!' he shouted. 'Every other man vaults the wall. Get ready!'

Tasemu started to sheath his sword.

'No, I go first.'

Softly, the old warrior asked, 'Will you stop trying to get yourself killed?'

'It's my duty.'

'Suppose you get killed, then Sugama takes over?'

Asayaga shook his head and kept his eyes locked on Tasemu. 'I have no intention of dying, and if I do, you decide who takes over. Now, cup your hands.'

Tasemu grumbled but finally bent over and did as he was told.

'Ready!'

He looked along the wall. Most of his men had doubled up and were prepared, and there was no time to wait for the laggards.

'Now!'

He slammed his right foot into Tasemu's cupped hands and at the same instant grabbed hold of his shoulders. Tasemu stood up with a grunt.

Asayaga vaulted and grabbed the top of the barrier. He scrambled to pull himself over. He caught a glimpse of a moredhel, back turned, striking down with an axe, splitting open the skull of the man to Asayaga's right.

Asayaga rolled over the wall and landed on the rampart. The moredhel turned, letting go of the axe as his victim fell. He whipped out a dagger and with a snakelike hiss leapt on Asayaga. The two

55

clutched each other and rolled off the rampart, falling half a dozen feet to the ground.

The blow knocked the wind out of Asayaga but he hung on to his foe, blocking a slashing strike to his eyes with his cloak wrapped around his forearm.

With his left hand Asayaga drew his own short blade and rammed it straight up, catching the moredhel under the ribs. He kicked himself free, stood up and, reaching over his shoulder, drew his long sword.

What he saw made his heart freeze. At least thirty moredhel were deployed as a reserve, most of them armed with bows, ready to slaughter any who made it over the wall. Raising his sword he charged straight at the encircling foe.

Perched on top of a cliff, Dennis watched the slaughter down below.

'They're losing,' Gregory announced.

'I don't need you to tell me that,' Dennis replied calmly.

He couldn't help but admire the mad idea of storming the gate as a human battering ram. It had failed, however, and the element of surprise was lost.

He watched as the Tsurani spread out while on the inside of the pass the moredhel garrison poured out of the log barracks and formed up, ready to slaughter anyone who made it over the wall.

'Around thirty of them,' Gregory whispered.

Dennis nodded.

Damn.

This was old territory for him. His father had built the barrier down below as part of the outer line of the northern marches. The moredhel had obviously reversed the gate and wooden ramparts, and put in the cabin on the other side – the original barracks Dennis's father had built on this side of the wall had been burned down when Dennis had been a boy. Tactically it wasn't a sound position; anyone who knew the area could easily flank it by scaling the ridge on either side from old trails that smugglers and other weapons runners frequently used. It was why Dennis's father had eventually abandoned the position and built the small fortress that had become Brendan's Stockade.

It was just such a smuggler's route he had decided to take,

when they had closed to within spitting distance of the Tsurani a mile back.

Even as the Tsurani hesitated then formed up for their attack he and his men went to the east of the pass, scaling the steep slope. The storm had driven the garrison inside as he had hoped, so there were no patrols waiting to ambush them.

'Look.'

Gregory pointed back to the south. It was hard to see, since wisps of cloud cloaked them, then parted, but he caught a glimpse of the main trail as it crossed a low ridgeline a couple of miles back.

Riders, moving cautiously, but pressing forward. Then the clouds closed in again.

Dennis's men were coming up behind him. They were numb with exhaustion, soaked to the skin.

'I was hoping one side could slaughter the other,' Dennis muttered, 'then we finish off what's left. We need that shelter and the gate secured or we're all finished.'

Gregory nodded, staring at him, saying nothing.

'Oh damn it,' Dennis hissed, as he looked down. 'This is insane.'

The first of the moredhel archers fired, the arrow striking a glancing blow across Asayaga's helmet. He charged in blindly, hoping that at the very least a dying thrust would take one of the foes down with him.

And then he caught a glimpse of a moredhel staggering forward, the point of a spear sticking out of his chest. Another went down and then another.

A shrieking battle cry echoed on the wind, a spine-tingling scream that sounded like the baying of wolves closing in on their prey.

Looking up he saw Kingdom soldiers sliding down the near vertical wall of the pass. Several of them lost control on the icy slope and fell screaming, crashing to the ground, one of them landing directly on top of a moredhel, the blow killing both of them. Most of the soldiers managed to brake their fall by grabbing hold of stunted bushes that grew along the icy wall, stopping for a second, letting go, sliding again, braking, then finally alighting on the ground.

The first to land safely drew a heavy two-handed sword from a scabbard slung over his shoulder and with a murderous cry charged forward. A moredhel turned, backing up, swinging desperately, trying to use his bow as a shield. A single blow nearly cut him in half.

The leader spun around, catlike, ducking low as a moredhel charged in with levelled spear. In an amazing display of swordsmanship the leader delivered a backhanded blow while down on one knee, cutting the moredhel's leg off at mid-thigh as he charged past.

More and yet more Kingdom troops crashed down, some landing on the roof of the barracks, then leaping down from there.

Asayaga looked back up at the wall. A dozen of his men were struggling with the moredhel along the rampart, while others were still trying to get over, and several lay dead.

He turned his back on the Kingdom troops and sprinted to the gate. Two moredhel, swords raised, guarded it. It was over in seconds as he parried the first one, spun about, catching the second under the armpit as he raised his sword to strike, then reversed and swung back high, slashing the other across the face, blinding him. The moredhel went down, a quick blow across the back of the neck ended his agony.

Grabbing the end of the log which locked the gate he lifted it up and tossed it aside. The barrier immediately swung open and his men poured in, swords raised ...

At the sight of the Kingdom soldiers dispatching the last of the moredhel they slowed in confusion. Asayaga prepared himself.

Dennis, recovering from the back-handed blow which had taken off the leg of the moredhel came up, sword poised, looking for another foe. Another dark-elf, battle axe raised, charged and then pitched backwards, arrow in the throat. Then Tinuva was at his side, already nocking another arrow.

He caught a glimpse of Gregory crashing onto the roof of the barracks and leaping down to duck inside the door.

At this point, several of the moredhel turned and ran. Dennis whistled, catching Alwin's attention. He pointed. Alwin nodded, shouted a command and with half a dozen men set off in pursuit.

He turned, saw the gate swing open and was stunned at the sight of at least a score of Tsurani pouring in.

In a flash of memory he saw his father's estate falling at the start of the war, the Tsurani charging through the shattered gate, his father collapsing from an arrow which had caught him in the eye.

Dennis felt an icy chill, a cold, killing anger at the memory of that time, the memory of Jurgen, of all the dead.

He raised his sword and stepped forward, ready to meet the charge.

There was something vaguely familiar about one of the Tsurani, the one who had charged the gate and in a masterful display of swordsmanship dropped two moredhels in a matter of seconds. This Tsurani shouted something to the warriors around him, even as he stepped to the fore and raised his sword. Dennis immediately recognized the gesture, it was the chaka, the ritual position assumed by a combatant in a one-on-one duel, a two-handed hold, blade vertical, duellist turned sideways, blade poised behind the left shoulder. Dennis had seen it once before, when a Tsurani soldier had taken some occurrence along a picket line personally, and had challenged another to a duel. Two years later, a freed Tsurani slave had explained what he had seen to Dennis.

Dennis shook his head in disbelief. This damned bastard wanted to fight a duel! Several of his men chuckled and one of them started to raise a bow to drop the Tsurani, but in spite of his cynical attitude towards the entire show there was something about the gesture that caught him.

All this had taken but a matter of seconds and even as the Tsurani leader stepped forward to fight, his own men were deploying out after the slaughter of the moredhel, ready to riddle the Tsurani coming through the gate and along the wall. A quick glance revealed that the Tsurani had yet to bring any archers up from outside.

And yet . . . Dennis realized the man wasn't challenging him, but rather announcing that he was ready to fight him. It was only a duel if Dennis accepted the offer of combat. He looked at the Tsurani soldiers waiting calmly to see what occurred and realized they were the mirror image of his own men in misery and fatigue.

Dennis pointedly turned his back on the Tsurani commander.

'Close the gate,' Dennis shouted in the King's Tongue, then

struggled to form the words in Tsurani. His command of the language was limited, brief snatches learned from Gregory, but fortunately one of them was the command 'close'!

The Tsurani leader dropped his formal pose and growled an angry reply.

Dennis realized the leader had interpreted the command as an order to block off his warriors still outside. At that same instant a horn sounded from beyond the gate, echoing up from the south. A Tsurani, left eye a milky white, and features distorted by a twisted scar that ran from brow to chin, dashed through the gate and slid to a stop at the sight of the Kingdom troops moving in.

'Moredhel!' the runner shouted, the word the same in all languages, and he pointed back outside.

All froze. Dennis stared at the Tsurani and their eyes locked. He could sense Tinuva by his side and saw the elf lower his bow and turn it to one side.

Dennis felt the calculating gaze of the Tsurani upon him, knew that the hatred and distrust was mutual, and yet also sensed the deeper fear, not just of death, but of falling into the hands of the moredhel. That was not the professional hatred of one warrior for another in the heat of battle, in which even beneath the hatred there still existed a certain begrudging respect. This was a primal fear, a loathing, a realization that somehow the soul of a dark universe lurked in the hearts of the foe who was closing in.

Dennis lowered his sword, letting the point touch the ground.

'Truce,' Dennis shouted to his men. 'We fight the moredhel, then settle our differences with the Tsurani later.'

Several of his men muttered but most grunted a chorus of agreement. Blades, spear points and bows started to lower.

The Tsurani leader shouted something and Dennis detected a similar reaction from the other side. Dennis pointed to the wall east of the gate and then to himself. The Tsurani nodded, pointed to himself, then to the west side and barked out a command.

'Archers!' Dennis cried. 'Man the wall and keep low. Volley on command!'

He ran to the still-open gate. The last of the Tsurani were coming through. One of them, at the sight of Dennis, let out a roar, raised his sword and charged. The Tsurani leader, shouted, jumped in front of Dennis and parried the strike. The attacking Tsurani glared at Dennis and then pushed past him.

Two Tsurani, dragging a wounded comrade, came in last and their commander leaned into the gate. Dennis joined him. Together they slammed it shut, hoisted the log and dropped it into place.

Dennis peered out through a crack between the logs of the gate. Seconds later a renegade human, mounted, came around the bend in the trail, half a dozen wood trolls running beside him. He reined in hard. Dennis caught a glimpse of more riders stopping just around the bend in the trail. The lone rider started to turn about.

'Kill him!' Dennis shouted.

His archers stood up and within seconds the rider, his horse and all the trolls were down.

He caught a sidelong glance from the Tsurani commander and a grunt of approval.

Shouts of anger greeted the volley. There was a bark of command followed by silence. Dennis watched intently, hoping the scum would dare to mount a charge: if so it'd be a slaughter.

Several minutes passed.

Tinuva slipped off the wall and came up to Dennis's side. The Tsurani looked at the elf, wide-eyed. Tinuva nodded and said something in Tsurani. Caught by surprise the Tsurani made a quick reply.

'What did you say?' Dennis asked.

'"Honours to his House", the traditional Tsurani greeting. Then I complimented him on his swordsmanship. I don't know if you saw it, a masterful double kill.'

Dennis nodded.

'Where's Gregory?' Dennis asked.

'One of the men said he ran right into a roof support when he charged into the barracks: he was stunned for a moment, but is all right.'

'I'll find time to enjoy the humour of that if we live through the night,' Dennis said quietly.

Tinuva fell silent. He looked through a crack between the logs and then turned back to Dennis.

61

'They won't attack for a while. I think this is just an advance party. We laid enough traps along the trail to slow them down. They'll wait for the rest of their command to come up first then fan out and flank us.'

Dennis looked back at the pass. The mist was closing in, blanketing them, a cold wind slicing through the pass. The full fury of the storm was slashing against the other side of the mountain. Out of the mist he saw Alwin returning. The sergeant slowed at the sight of the Tsurani then came forward.

'Got them.'

Dennis let out a sigh of relief. At least one thing had gone right. No word of their presence had gone ahead.

He looked over at the Tsurani.

Damn, what a fix.

'This is what we do,' Dennis whispered to Alwin and Tinuva. 'Half the men stand down, get into the barracks. Get the fire in there roaring. Strip down, dry off, get some hot food. See what dry clothing we can take from the bastards that were here. Two hours, then we shift the other half in.'

He pointed to either side of the pass.

'Tinuva, I want you to detail a dozen archers, get them up on the flanks and keep the moredhel and their trolls back – I don't want them coming down on us the same way we came down on them. My guess is those scum are as exhausted as we are. Once they find out we hold the heights as well they'll give up for tonight. There's some old dwarven mine shafts a mile or so back down the slope. My bet is they pull in there, build fires to warm up, and wait till dawn to fan out and trap us. We'll get out a couple hours before dawn, dried and rested.'

'And our friends?' Tinuva asked, eyes flicking towards the Tsurani commander.

Damn, Dennis thought.

'I guess we settle it before we leave. The Broad River, you remember it?'

Tinuva smiled and nodded. The thought struck Dennis that a hundred years before he was even born Tinuva undoubtedly knew of the river. Again he realized just how ancient the elven race was and with it came the recognition of just how much they risked when facing battle: it wasn't just a score of years in the balance, it was a score of decades. An elven couple might have two children in a century. Each death was magnified far beyond what any human could understand in terms of loss to the race.

'With this storm the river should be up. We make for Garth's Ford. Get across and there we've got a position that a thousand Dark Brothers wouldn't dare to attack. There's a small stockade there, we stay warm, wait till they give up chasing us, then find a way home.'

'Good plan,' Tinuva whispered. He looked again at the Tsurani, nodded and went back up to the wall.

Men started to slip off from the wall, heading for the barracks, while Tinuva picked out the unfortunate ones who would have to climb up out of the pass to guard the flanks.

The Tsurani turned, shouted a command. The one-eyed warrior barked out an order, and half of the Tsurani started towards the barracks as well. Dennis watched as the one-eye stopped several of the men, whispered something and they nodded, returned to their posts, as the one-eye ordered others, who were obviously near final collapse, to head for shelter.

The two groups slowed as they drew near to each other, obviously torn between the desire to get inside versus the uneasiness of being so close to a sworn foe.

One of the Tsurani said something, pointing at the Kingdom troops and began to draw his sword. The one-eyed leader knocked the sword from his hand.

'It's warm in here, you bastards. Come on in!'

It was Gregory, standing in the open doorway, the glow of the fire behind him a cheery and welcome sight. He wondered if the Natalese Ranger had deliberately stoked up the fire within to lure the men inside.

The two groups still hung back, looking at each other.

Gregory said something else, this time in Tsurani, and made a formal gesture of welcome. The one-eyed warrior laughed gruffly and went through the doorway, his men pouring in behind him, followed by the Kingdom troops.

'His Tsurani is really quite good.'

Startled, Dennis turned. It was the Tsurani commander.

Dennis glared at him. 'I didn't know you spoke our language.'

'You didn't ask.'

'Damn you, you should have said something.'

'Really? Tell me, how far to this Broad River?'

'Find out yourself, if you outlive me.'

The Tsurani smiled. 'Let our men warm up, you and I too, then we can decide who shall outlive whom tomorrow.'

Dennis said nothing. He looked down at one of the two dead moredhel lying by the gate. Bending over, he tore the cloak off one and wrapped it around his shoulders.

The Tsurani did likewise and leaned against the gate not saying another word, his gaze fixed on Dennis as the darkness of night settled about them.

FOUR

Practicalities

The fire was soothing.

Richard Kevinsson sat by the corner of the fireplace, boots off, luxuriating in the near-painful sensation of his feet thawing out. Rubbing his hands, he extended them towards the flames.

Gregory and the Tsurani with the missing eye shouldered through the crush around the fireplace and heaved armfuls of logs into the roaring flames. Steam coiled up from a heavy iron kettle filled with stew, suspended in the fireplace. A few of the men, Richard included, had hesitated at first to eat it. It was, after all, a meal that the moredhel had been cooking and who knew what was in it – though Tinuva had reassured the Kingdom soldiers that stories of moredhel eating things indigestible to humans were myth only – but old beliefs were hard to ignore. Eventually, ravenous hunger won out over squeamishness and the men – both Kingdom and Tsurani – had gathered around, holding out tin cups and earthen mugs while the bubbling stew was dished out.

A freshly-killed stag had been found hanging outside the garrison house as well, and as fast as pieces of it were cooked in the open fire men snatched them out and devoured the venison, the first hot cooked meat both sides had tasted in days.

Many of the men were now fast asleep, curled up on the wooden planked floor. Of those awake, some were smoking, a few playing cards, others were just sitting about the fireplace.

Richard watched as two Tsurani played a game with intricately carved pieces of ivory on a small chequered piece of cloth. One of the players, as if sensing his gaze, looked up. Their eyes held for a second.

The Tsurani's hand drifted to his side, resting on the hilt of a dagger, his eyes locked with Richard's. The young soldier quickly averted his gaze and there was a gruff laugh, not from the Tsurani but from a Kingdom soldier sitting beside him who had been watching the silent interplay.

'He'll cut your throat from ear to ear, boy.'

It was Darvan, one of the 'old men', of the unit, recruited when Dennis and the others from Valinar formed the Marauders. He had his shirt off, and was hanging it up to dry, revealing a cross-hatching of battle scars on his forearms. One shoulder was slightly hunched from a broken collarbone that had not healed straight.

Darvan spat into the fire.

'You just lost face, boy. You lowered your eyes. In their lingo that means you are nothing but a cowering worm. Those bastards are laughing at you now.'

Richard spared a quick glance back at the two Tsurani, both of whom were leaning over their game, whispering to each other. Neither was laughing, but Richard wondered if they were talking about him.

'Bet they're saying how you don't have any manhood below your belt. I wouldn't let them get away with that, boy: it's bad for our company. You showed yourself a coward once before, are you going to do it in front of the Tsurani as well?'

Richard shifted uncomfortably.

Hearing him move, both of the Tsurani glanced up at him.

'Darvan!'

Alwin Barry stepped between them and the Tsurani. 'Shut the hell up,' he hissed, his voice barely a whisper.

Darvan grinned.

'We're in a bad enough fix as is without you egging the boy on to a fight.'

'They stink up this place,' Darvan growled. 'I say let's kill the bastards in here now, then go out and finish the rest.'

'Captain's orders. We stand down for the night.'

'The Captain –' Darvan started to say more but Alwin's hand shot out and grabbed Darvan by the throat, stilling his voice.

'You want to fight come morning?' Barry whispered, his voice filled with menace and his eyes boring into Darvan. 'Fine. We do it when the captain says so and not before. For now, leave this boy alone. Use him to start any trouble, and I'll kill you myself.'

Turning his back to the Tsurani, who were watching the exchange with open curiosity, Darvan could barely croak out words, with Alwin's hand around his throat. 'This boy?' he asked, pulling Alwin's hand from his throat. Still whispering, he added, 'We all know he's a coward. Jurgen died to save this piece of offal. And for what?'

Richard flushed, feeling as if every eye inside the room had suddenly shifted to him. Honour was now at stake.

His heart began to race, and though he was sitting next to a furnacelike fire, a cold chill swept through him. Then came the memory of all the dead in that cold frozen field, the angry gaze of the Captain, the eyes of Jurgen going dark and empty.

Knees trembling, he started to stand up, his hand going to dagger. Though terrified, he had to face the challenge.

'Not now!' Alwin snarled. 'Damn it boy, sit down before this place explodes!'

Richard caught a glimpse of the two Tsurani. They were both standing, one of them going for his own dagger and Richard instantly realized that somehow the Tsurani, not understanding the conversation, had assumed that the exchange of glances was turning into a challenge for a duel. Others, both Kingdom and Tsurani were moving, shifting apart into two groups, the room going silent.

As he shoved Richard back into his seat on the bench, Alwin rounded on Darvan. 'I'll personally flog you from one end of camp to the other if you get out of this alive!' With a back-handed blow he struck Darvan across the face, knocking the man backwards.

Darvan slammed into the wooden wall, his legs still hooked over the bench. Men were standing all over the cabin, weapons being drawn. Only the fact that it was two Kingdom men who were confronting one another made the Tsurani hesitate in attacking the nearest enemy. Darvan looked up, grinning, wiping the blood from his split lip. 'Afterwards, Barry. I'll remember this.'

Alwin half-turned to face the two Tsurani who were looking from Darvan to Richard, and extended his hands, palms out, in a calming gesture. The one-eyed Tsurani came up, saying something unintelligible. He pointed at Darvan and barked out a gruff laugh. The tension edged back down, the two sat and returned to their game. Other Tsurani around the room returned to their previous activities. Darvan rose slowly, and glared hatred at the Tsurani, whom he assumed to be a sergeant. The one eyed warrior spared him a mere glance, and turned away as if entirely unconcerned.

Alwin and the Tsurani Strike Leader looked at each other, but nothing was said, simply a nod of a head. Both understood the other and what had just played out . . . and what would eventually have to be played out. For the moment though, fire, a hot meal, drying out, and a few minutes of sleep were more important.

Richard, no longer comfortable in his corner by the fire, stood up and moved away. None of the other men in his company looked at him, or even acted as if they had noticed the encounter, but he could sense their indifference, or far worse, their contempt.

He looked around the crowded room. Cloaks, blankets, jerkins, boots, and footwrappings hung suspended from the low rafters, casting strange shadows in the firelight. Part of the ceiling, caved in by the assault, was roughly tacked over with a torn tent and a steady trickle of icy water puddled down from it onto the floor. Bunks of the former inhabitants had been looted for dry blankets, clothing, anything dry and warm. The room stank of wet wool, leather, sweat, the stew and – Darvan was indeed right, the Tsurani did smell different – a musky scent. Watching a pair of Tsurani take a small pouch out of their packs and add a pinch of a pungent spice to their bowls of stew, Richard decided that was where the scent came from, but it was disquieting, somehow emphasizing their alien nature.

Gregory, Alwin, and the man Richard thought of as 'the Tsurani sergeant' paced back and forth, keeping an eye on everyone, ready to quell any explosion before it ignited.

Richard spotted Father Corwin, kneeling in the far corner of the room where the wounded lay. A dozen men of the company had various injuries acquired over the last two days. Of the eight from the encounter in the forest clearing, not one was still alive. The four who had survived the long night march to Brendan's Stockade had been left behind in the retreat, their throats cut to spare them the agony of falling into the hands of the moredhel.

Richard moved over to the priest and looked down. He didn't know the name of the soldier the priest was treating, but he was young, features pale, sweat beading his face. He had suffered a broken leg in their crashing assault down into the stockade. Corwin had set the leg with the help of a couple of men and was tying off the splint, talking soothingly as if comforting a child.

'Will I be able to walk in the morning?' the soldier asked.

'We'll worry about that then, son.'

The young soldier looked up at Richard.

'I could help him,' Richard ventured.

'We'll ask the Captain,' the priest replied, but Richard could tell by his tone that the answer would be no. Either the boy walked on his own or died.

Corwin patted the soldier reassuringly on the shoulder, stood up, and looked over to where a Tsurani lay with a crossbow bolt buried deep in his upper thigh. A comrade was by his side, trying to get him to take a little food.

'Poor bastard,' Corwin sighed and without hesitation went over and knelt beside him. The two looked at Corwin, turning to him masklike visages on which there was no expression. They looked straight through Corwin and Richard as if they didn't even exist.

'Really got you,' Corwin said quietly, motioning to the arrow.

The two said nothing.

'Got to get it out sooner or later.'

Again no response.

'Damn it, don't they take care of their wounded?' Richard asked.

'It's obvious they don't have a chirugeon with them,' replied the Priest of Sung. 'This arrow's in deep. I guess they figure they'll just leave him here – no sense in putting him through the agony of trying to get it out. Richard, go fetch me some boiling water and I want you to take these two knives, stick one in the fire for a minute or so, the second one, leave it in the fire.'

As he spoke he drew two small daggers belted to his waist and handed them up. Richard followed the priest's orders and returned with a tin pot filled with boiling hot tea and the dagger which was shimmering with heat.

'No water, just the boiled tea.'

The priest chuckled. 'It'll do,' he said. He reached into his tunic, pulled out a small roll of white linen, tore off a piece and stuck it into the boiling liquid. Then he motioned at the arrow and made a gesture as if pulling it out.

The wounded man looked at him wide-eyed and shook his head, and his comrade said something and made a gesture, waving his hand over the arrow as if to block Corwin.

'He says they already tried to get it out, that it's snagged on the bone,' Gregory announced, coming up behind the group. 'Priest, just leave him alone, he's finished. You can't draw it without cutting the poor bastard to pieces. Those damned moredhel arrows are four-barbed.'

'Just shut up and stay out of my way,' Corwin growled. He reached into his tunic, pulled out a small leather case and unrolled it, drawing out several needles which already had threads attached, tweezers and tiny brass clamps.

He looked straight into the eyes of the Tsurani and began a low chant in a strange tongue. Those around him fell silent for the words carried a power, a sense of otherworldliness and Richard felt a cold shiver. The chanting continued for several minutes. Then Corwin slowly reached out, placing his right hand on the Tsurani's forehead and let it gently slip down to cover the man's eyes. Finally he drew his hand back. The Tsurani's eyes were still open but were now glazed.

Corwin gripped the arrow with his left hand and ever so slowly tried to pull it out. It didn't budge.

'Snagged on the bone, like he said,' the priest whispered. 'Richard, help roll him on to his side then hold him tight.'

Richard followed the priest's orders. The wounded man's eyes were still unfocused. Richard cradled the man on his lap and looked back down at the priest who was carefully examining the wound, running his fingers around the back of the man's leg.

Corwin picked up the still hot dagger with his right hand, positioned it underneath the wounded man's leg on the opposite side from the wound and drove the blade in half way to the hilt and rotated the blade.

A gasp escaped the wounded man. Richard looked into his eyes and saw that consciousness was returning: the Tsurani's pupils went wide.

'Hold him!' the priest snapped.

With his left hand he grabbed the arrow and started to push even as he pulled the dagger back out. A second latter the head of the arrow exploded out of the hole cut by the dagger.

The wounded Tsurani cried out, and began to struggle, but Richard grabbed hold of him, 'It's all right; you'll be all right,' he began to say over and over.

'Damn it, priest, he's bleeding to death!' Gregory cried.

'Just shut up and get the hot knife from the fire!'

The priest continued to push the arrow through the wound, finally pulling it out and flinging it aside. He picked his dagger back up, cut the exit wound wider and, using one of the brass clamps, pulled the wound apart. He motioned for the wounded man's comrade to hold the clamp. Taking a pair of tweezers from his kit he reached into the wound, drawing the artery which was spurting blood.

'Not the main one, thank the Goddess,' he muttered, even as Gregory knelt by his side, holding the now-glowing dagger fresh from the fire, the hilt wrapped with a piece of smouldering canvas.

The priest took the dagger, cursing when he singed his fingertips, then deftly touched the blade against the artery. A steamy cloud of boiling blood hissed up from the wound.

The man jerked, trying to kick, but Richard held him tight. He realized that for some strange reason he was beginning to cry.

This is a Tsurani, damn it. He felt a wave of anger for the man even as he held him tight and continued to try and reassure him.

'Almost done,' the priest announced.

He drew out the hot dagger, turned, and then cauterized the

entry wound. Finally he drew out the boiled bandages, stuffed both wounds, then tightly wrapped a compress around the leg.

'We'll stitch him up later, I want to keep it open so I can get in quick in case he starts to bleed again.'

The whole operation had taken no more than a couple of minutes. The priest sat back, then took the hand of the Tsurani who had been helping and guided it to a pressure point above the wound to help slow the bleeding.

'All right Richard, you did well, son.'

Richard, shaking, looked down at the Tsurani. There were tears in the corner of the man's eyes and he suddenly realized just how young his enemy was: about the same age as himself and the wounded Kingdom soldier with the broken leg. The Tsurani was obviously struggling for control, looking up at Richard in confusion, his emotions mixed between gratitude and hatred for an enemy.

The priest knelt, softly muttered a prayer and made a sign of blessing over the wound, finishing by lightly touching the man's forehead again.

Wiping the now-cooled daggers, he bundled up his kit and then picked up the arrow, which was covered with blood, and a hunk of flesh still on the barbs.

'Evil weapon,' he sighed, 'No bone splinters though; he just might make it.'

He tossed the arrow aside. The room was silent: all were staring at him.

'I'm pledged to healing,' the priest said, 'it doesn't matter who.' He looked back over at Richard. 'You're a brave lad for helping.'

The Tsurani Patrol Leader approached, bowed to the priest and said something.

Corwin looked over at Gregory.

'He said that the wounded man, Osami, now owes you a debt which the clan must honour. If we fight and they don't kill you, they must make you a slave. So if we fight, they'll let you leave before they kill all of us, so they won't have to capture or kill you.' Gregory explained.

Corwin said nothing for a moment and then began to chuckle softly. 'Hell, tell him I think you're all crazy,' Corwin replied. 'When you're done killing each other I'll take all your coins, and whatever the Tsurani use, and consider it a donation to the church.'

Gregory translated and now the Tsurani laughed. The tension in the room eased for a moment.

Gregory knelt next to Corwin. 'You a chirugeon?' He pointed to the small kit Corwin had used and was now cleaning ready to put away.

The priest shrugged. 'As a boy I apprenticed to one for a while.'

'What happened?' asked the Ranger. 'Get the calling?'

Putting away his medical tools, the priest said, 'No, that came later. I was a mercenary for a while.'

Remembering how frightened the priest had been when they had first met, Gregory could barely hide his surprise. 'A mercenary?'

Corwin nodded. 'Not all mercenaries are swordsmen, Ranger. I have no skill with blade or bow. I earned my living with a company of engineers building siege machines. Give me two men with axes and in less than a day I can turn a tree into a ram that would knock down that stone wall out there in under ten minutes. Throw in a pair of hammers and one bow saw, and I can do it in six hours.' He paused as if remembering. 'Saw most of my fighting from a distance, though I've had a few close calls under a wall or two, trying to collapse a foundation.' He smiled at Gregory's blank expression. 'I used to be a fair sapper, too.' He sighed and lost his smile. 'And I had more than my share of practice keeping other men alive, I can tell you.' He stood, and Gregory did as well. 'Then I got the calling and entered the temple.'

Gregory nodded. 'I though you priests used your magic to heal.'

Corwin shrugged. 'Like anything else, healing magic takes talent. Some brothers could heal every man here in a couple of days. A rare few can lay on hands and make a wound vanish or a bone heal in an hour. I have no such gift. I have to rely on my tools and prayer. The bit of "magic" I used to calm the boy is simply a healer's trick; anyone can learn it.'

Gregory didn't comment.

Sighing with fatigue, Corwin said, 'Besides, I never said I was a particularly good priest, did I?'

'Guard change, five minutes!'

Both Gregory and Corwin looked to see Dennis standing in the doorway, Asayaga by his side, shouting the same order in Tsurani. A chorus of curses and groans greeted the order.

Richard pushed through the press of men, reaching the place where he had hung up his outer coat, jerkin, boots and socks. They had yet to dry, and slipping on the damp woollen socks and sodden boots he grimaced. A Tsurani was sitting beside him, mumbling under his breath as he wrapped on his footcloths and then laced up the heavy sandals. Their eyes caught for a second and this time Richard did not lower his gaze.

Again the impenetrable stare. The one-eyed man came past the two, barked something at the Tsurani and continued on. There was a look in the man's eyes and Richard for the first time felt that he could understand something about these alien invaders, for he recognized the mixture of respect and hatred all soldiers hold for good sergeants. He almost smiled at the reaction. Again their eyes held and there seemed to be a brief instant in which the Tsurani was ready to smile as well.

And then both of them realized just who the other person was.

They turned away, stood up, belted on their swords, and formed up with their squads.

'Everyone listen.'

It was Dennis.

'It's quiet out there except for the damnable weather – it's slackening a bit, but it's still no spring evening. Squads one and two, on the wall, keep a sharp watch, and keep your fool heads down. They can see you more easily silhouetted up there than you can see them; and, remember, the moredhel have better eyes in the night than we do.

'Third squad, under Gregory, will secure the flank of the hill to our left. Gregory will detail several of you off to probe forward. Tinuva tracked the Dark Brothers. They've holed up in an abandoned mine a mile downslope but have patrols out.

'Two hours then we shift watches again. Those of you detailed to the flank and forward patrol will get an extra hour of rest when you come back in. The Tsurani have the same routine and will cover the right flank.'

'When do we fight them?' Darvan asked from the back of the room. Several men growled in agreement, while others mumbled for him to shut the hell up.

'When I tell you and not before, you damned fool,' Dennis snapped. 'Now get the hell outside!'

Richard fell in with his unit and followed the men out into the night. The storm still raged and he gasped as the cold wind hit. Filing past, rushing to get inside, were the miserable men who had been detailed to the first watch.

'Third squad.'

Gregory stepped in front of the group and motioned for them to follow. A narrow trail fifty yards further up the pass had been found, switchbacking its way up the icy slope. The men struggled to keep a footing, hanging on as gusts of wind roared through the pass, ready to snatch them off the icy precipice. The night was pitch-black, the men cursing, even the older veterans complaining that it was madness to be out on watch on a night like this.

The group pressed on. Struggling to the top of the pass they met Tinuva and several men. Gregory and the elf conferred briefly, then the first watch headed back down to the shelter below. Gregory motioned for the men to gather round.

'We seem to be lucky for once,' Gregory announced. 'The storm's driven them all back to the old mine but that's no reason to let our guard down. It might even be a trick. Space out, a man to every thirty paces, and don't get lost. Keep a sharp watch. I'm going forward and please don't kill me when I come back in.'

The men chuckled grimly.

'Move!'

The squad started into the woods, moving just below the top of the crest. Richard made to follow, but Gregory motioned him back.

'You're going forward with me.'

'Me?'

'Yes, you. Something wrong with your hearing, boy?'

Richard swallowed hard, saying nothing.

Without another word Gregory started down the slope, drifting from tree to tree, Richard struggling to keep pace. Looking to his right he caught a glimpse of the pass below, the glow of firelight shimmering from the top of the chimney, and wished he was back inside, sitting by the roaring fire, or better yet curled up and asleep by it.

He lost sight of Gregory for a moment and felt a surge of panic when he tore his gaze away from the fire and realized he couldn't see the Natalese Ranger. He blinked, trying to clear his vision, and stumbled forward, startled when the ice cracked beneath his feet. An instant later a hand snapped around his throat. He started to cry out, but then the hand released him and he found himself staring into Gregory's eyes.

'First lesson. Never lose contact with your partner when scouting at night,' Gregory whispered. His voice was calm, there was no reproach in it. It was as if the two of them were simply having a pleasant chat while strolling through the woods.

'You looked at the fire glowing, you were wishing you were inside, you forgot about me.'

Richard nodded, and suddenly realized that behind the calm words he could see a dagger in Gregory's other hand.

'Yes, I could have killed you as easily as a baby asleep in a cradle. Remember that, boy, for that's what they'll do to you.'

Not sure how to react, Richard could only nod.

'Second lesson: never look at a fire when you're on night patrol. It robs you of sight in the dark. Look to one side or the other. On watch, stand with your back to the fire. Blind yourself for even just a moment, and it can cost you your life. Now get your own dagger out. This isn't a night for archery or swordplay.'

Gregory turned and continued forward and this time Richard stayed close, trying to mimic his movements, the fluid glide to his steps, noticing a certain rhythm ... half a dozen quick steps, a pause, head turning, then forward, though at a slightly different angle; again, the pause. Once he stopped, pointing down and Richard looked, seeing footsteps in the frozen mud and a stain where someone had relieved himself.

'Troll,' Gregory whispered. 'You can tell by the smell.'

Richard nodded. The forest trolls of southern Yabon where he had been a boy were barely more than animals, without language and little more dangerous than a bear or lion. They were scarcely a nuisance to a party of armed men. Mountain trolls on the other hand had language and weapons and knew how to use them. And now they were in the woods around him. He gripped his dagger tightly.

'Night watchers,' Gregory whispered. 'The moredhel call them allies, but treat them like slaves; so do the human renegades who travel with this kind of group. They're all inside the mine staying warm while the trolls are out here freezing.' He was quiet for a moment, then softly he added, 'It's a stupid choice; trolls don't have the discipline needed for a night like this.'

Gregory pushed forward. They pressed down a low rise and then started to climb to the next ridge, moving parallel to the road they had run along earlier in the day. Richard even recognized the place where the group had broken off from the road, spotting the cleft boulder with a tree growing out of the middle that marked the spot.

Gregory stopped and held up his hand. He then pointed to the side of the boulder, the downwind side and held up his hand, two fingers extended.

Richard felt his heart trip over. Two forms were huddled beneath the downwind side of the boulder, hunched over a small flickering fire . . . two trolls.

Richard started to reach over his shoulder to pull out his bow and string it. Gregory shook his head. Motioning to the dagger in Richard's hand, he then drew a finger across his throat.

Richard felt his knees go weak. This madman was telling him they were going up to the trolls to cut their throats!

Gregory remained still for several minutes as if frozen to the earth. Richard crouched behind him, limbs trembling. To his disbelief Gregory stood up and ever so casually started forward, walking in the open. Richard didn't move. Gregory, without looking back, motioned for him to follow.

Richard, barely able to walk on shaky legs, followed. The trolls were a scant thirty paces away.

The two approached. One of the trolls finally stirred and raised its head. Richard suddenly realized that the two of them had been asleep and Gregory knew it. The first troll started to say something, Gregory responded in a guttural tongue, and then sprinted the last half dozen paces until he was on the troll, dagger flashing in the firelight.

'Come on boy!' he hissed. 'Kill the other!'

Richard remained frozen in place, watching, terrified as Gregory's dagger slashed down. The other troll started to stand up.

He was not even sure how he got there but suddenly the troll was in front of him, filling his world. Shorter than a man, the creature was wider at the shoulders by half again. Its misshapen forehead was dominated by a massive black brow, from under which tiny black eyes glinted. Its massive jaw jutted out and it displayed its teeth in a snarl, large pointed incisors extending beyond the upper and lower lips. A leather helmet was tightly pulled down, covering the large, pointed ears.

The troll slammed into Richard, pushing him up against the boulder, driving his dagger into the beast's stomach. There was a gasp of pain, fetid breath washing over him, claws tearing at his face. Richard tucked his own chin down and crouched and the lethal claws raked across the stone of the boulder behind him.

'The throat boy, the throat!'

Richard yanked his dagger free and tried for the throat, stabbing upward, but the troll, fighting in blind panic, blocked him. Instead he slashed at the beast's arms, cutting it again and again. Even as he tried to kill the troll he felt horrified, sickened, sensing the agony and terror of his victim.

'Die! Just die, damn you!' he cried, continuing to slash until the point of his dagger went in below the troll's chin and up into its brain. The beast sagged down with a groan and collapsed. Richard stepped back, sobbing, turned away, and vomited.

'Don't ever hesitate, boy.'

Richard, still bent double, looked up. Gregory was standing beside him, half-turned away, watchful gaze scanning the trail.

Richard realized that Gregory had finished his victim within seconds and rather than help had simply stood by, watching as he made his own kill. He felt a wave of anger and also of shame. He scooped up a handful of snow to wipe his mouth and hands clean. He was trembling, suddenly afraid that he might lose control completely and soil himself.

'It's all right,' Gregory whispered. 'Its one thing to kill in the heat of battle the way you did two days ago. This is different, even if it is a troll. It may be war, boy, but this is as close as a lawful man gets to black murder.' He put a reassuring hand on Richard's shoulder. 'You did just fine, son. More than one man's turned and run the other way.'

Even as he talked he continued to scan, carefully watching the trail and the surrounding forest. After a few moments of checking the signs to see if the struggle had alerted others, he said, 'Good. They're spread out too thin, hunched over fires and falling asleep from exhaustion. No one saw us. Come on.'

Gregory stepped back, picked up the feet of one of the trolls and dragged it away from the fire, hiding it on the far side of the boulder. Richard hesitated then finally reached down and dragged his own victim. The body was heavy, he could feel the warmth of it even through the foot wrappings. He laid the body down next to the other. Gregory had rolled the troll half over and was stripping off the heavy blanket wrapped around its shoulders.

'Take his too.'

Richard tried not to look at the body but did as he was ordered, imitating Gregory as he wrapped the blanket around his shoulders and over his head. They stepped around the boulder. Picking up a handful of broken branches he tossed them on the fire and sat down, pulling the troll cloak up over his head and face, motioning for Richard to do the same.

'No sense in blundering around any more. You can see the mine they're hiding in.'

He motioned across the trail and as the snow fall slackened, Richard caught a glimpse of a flickering glow, the entry way to the mine, several guards silhouetted at the opening.

'Might as well stay comfortable as we watch. The relief for those two will come up at some point and we'll deal with them the same way.'

Richard swallowed hard, nervously scanning the woods and trail. The storm continued to thunder around them, throwing down an

79

icy mix of rain and sleet. The trees creaked and groaned under the load. Occasionally a branch snapped, the crack echoing above the roar of the storm. At times the mist closed in, the glow from the mine disappearing, then lifted, revealing the encampment where the enemy waited out the storm.

'If we didn't have the Tsurani to worry about, I'd be tempted to try and turn the tables,' Gregory whispered, breaking the silence.

'How is that?'

'Set up an ambush. Tough thing to do, though.' He glanced around, as if seeing the hills in the blackness. 'Mines in this area are all the same – lots of veins of iron, silver, some gold – there are certain to be several other entrances to cover and they must have an inner circle of guards watching. Still, it would be good not to leave this nest of murderers alive.'

Gregory reached over to the pile of firewood, and tossed another branch on which flared up.

Richard stiffened.

'Don't worry, boy. Just keep that cloak up over your head, they'll think we're with them.'

Richard nodded.

'You'll do fine.'

'I don't know,' said the young man, barely above a whisper.

'It's difficult the first time you have to get close to kill another. You see their eyes, see the light in it go out. Even a troll's eyes have that light. I'd be worried if you didn't feel something after that. I don't like hunting with a man who's a killer without that feeling.'

'They're the enemy though,' Richard offered, trying to sound harder than he actually felt.

Gregory sounded thoughtful as he asked, 'Are they?'

'Trolls and moredhel? Of course; they're the enemy.'

Gregory nodded. 'Well, they were created by the gods, the same as we; that's a fact. Maybe if one was born in our towns or villages, raised with us, maybe they'd be our friends. I don't know.' He chuckled. 'Moredhel, maybe. Seem a lot like elves, though to say that aloud to Tinuva is to invite a cold reply. Trolls, though, I don't know. Can't imagine one taking the cows to market, if you see what I mean.' He poked at the fire with a stick. 'Some folks say their hate for us is in their hearts from birth. Either way, learned hate or instinct to hate, we sure have to fight them often enough. But never become like them, Richard. Never think taking a life is easy. Do that and in a way they win.'

Richard was startled. In his brief time with the company he had thought of Gregory as nothing more than a man of the woods, a scout who was respected for his skills and his seemingly inexhaustible strength; but a philosopher?

'You sound like my old mentor.'

'Brother Vasily?'

'You know him?'

Gregory chuckled.

'Remember lad, I know your family. Fought beside your father when the Emperor of Queg tried to capture Port Natal. Vasily and I raised many a glass together. Ah, now there was a rare fine thinker.'

Richard said nothing. His father. Gregory knew the Squire. And what would he say?

'Lad, if you don't mind me saying it, your father is one fine soldier, but I wouldn't want him as my sire. He's a hard man.'

Richard lowered his head. The beatings. That seemed to be the only way the old man knew how to treat his sons. If they did well, there was, at best, silence; but fail in anything and there would be a beating. As the eldest surviving son, he felt that the old man would never be satisfied. Too often there was mention of Quentin, twenty years older, from the Squire's first marriage, killed in the last war. Always the Squire spoke of him as the worthy son who should have inherited all, and that Richard was the weak second choice.

'Quentin was a good man,' Gregory said.

Again there was the disturbing sense that the Natalese scout somehow had the 'sense', the ability to read the thoughts of others. 'I see the same in you.'

Richard poked at the fire, saying nothing. 'I don't think our captain sees it that way,' he finally ventured.

Gregory chuckled. 'Dennis is a hard man on the surface, just like your father. He has to be out here not just to survive but to preserve those who serve with him. But underneath, he's very different. If he has a fault it's that he loves his men too much. Every death burns his soul. Jurgen was like his elder brother, the closest friend he has ever known. You just happened to be in the way.'

'I caused his death.'

'Don't ever say that again. Don't think it. War is cruel. Men die. Jurgen did what any man would do: he went to save a comrade.'

'I wish I had died instead.'

'Why?'

Richard looked over at him. 'Because,' he lowered his head, 'my life for his. Who was more worthy to live? Who did the company need more? I know the Captain wishes it had been the other way around.'

'Jurgen lived his life well. He had fifty years or more, you but eighteen. I think that's a fair trade. He gave you back years you never would have had. Just remember that and don't feel guilty. He didn't do it because you were the son of a squire. Remember that as well. He'd have done it for the son of a peasant or thief. So live every day after this as if it was a gift from him, and when the time comes some day, pay it back the same way he did.'

Richard looked over at Gregory, unable to speak. He realized now why the scout had wanted him out here on patrol, so that he could share these words with him.

He didn't know what to say in response.

Gregory stiffened and at nearly the same instant Richard noticed it as well, a sound, slush crunching, something moving on the trail.

'Lower your head,' Gregory whispered, 'then move when I do, and do what I do.'

Richard did as ordered, the troll's cloak pulled up over his head, his shoulders hunched forward, watching out of the corner of his eye. There were three of them, two trolls . . . and a moredhel.

Should we run? Richard wondered, but Gregory did nothing.

The three drew closer, slowed. The moredhel held out his hand, motioning for the trolls to stop. They stood less than ten feet away. He barked out a command.

Gregory grunted, head swaying as if coming awake. He growled a comment, and one of the trolls snorted as if in amusement.

A gust of wind swept the group, sparks flaring up from the fire. The moredhel took another step closer, snarling angrily, and then, to Richard's eyes, everything seemed to shift, as if time was slowing.

The moredhel's movement changed, as if he had suddenly realized that something was wrong, that he was not dealing with two trolls who had fallen asleep on watch.

Gregory started to stand, the cloak falling back, and at the same instant his hand snapped out, and his dagger was twirling over the firelight. A second later, the moredhel was dying, the dagger having slashed open his throat. Gregory was up, cloak flung back his sword drawn.

Richard stood, dagger in hand and leapt forward, following the scout. It was over in seconds, so complete was the surprise. Gregory split the skull of one of the trolls who stood gape-mouthed, staring down at the moredhel who was clasping at his throat, staggering backwards, trying to hold his lifeblood in as it sprayed out between his fingers.

Richard leapt for the second troll and this time he almost did it right, driving his dagger straight in, cutting the troll's throat, losing the blade when the troll jerked backwards, the dagger jammed into his lower jaw.

Richard stepped back and then leapt with surprise since he had stepped into the fire.

Gregory was bending over the moredhel, cutting down, ending his agony. Warily he looked up, then crouched low. Richard looked with him. Gregory pointed: there was more movement on the trail. From the entrance to the mine there was movement as well, shadows reflecting the flash of spear points from the fire within.

'Time to leave,' Gregory whispered, 'I think they're going to try a night attack, figure we're asleep. We've got to let Dennis know.'

Reaching into a pouch at his hip he pulled out several caltrops tossed them on the trail and kicked slush over them.

'Come on, lad, I think it's time to get moving again. What they find here might slow them a bit but we better pull out.' He glanced at the sky. 'Snow's lessening. It'll clear tomorrow. We'd better be somewhere else when it does.'

They turned away from the trail and as they did so Gregory patted Richard on the shoulder.

'We might make a scout out of you, yet, lad.'

Then the Natalese set off at speed, disappearing into the night. Richard was left struggling to keep up.

FIVE

Accommodation

The snow stopped.

Asayaga chanced a look over the wall. The mist was blowing clear; it was possible to see across the narrow clearing as the light of the middle moon illuminated the ice-covered forest. He could feel the temperature dropping as a cold wind lashed in from the north-west.

Good and bad, he thought. *We'll be drier but the ground will be icy, making footing difficult.* He had never seen 'frozen water' before coming to Midkemia, as his homeworld was a hot world compared to this one, but he had become as close to an expert on cold weather warfare as any Tsurani could after nine winters in the field; he didn't like it, but he understood it.

'Force Commander.'

He looked down. It was Tasemu. He had ordered the Strike Leader to stay in the barracks hall to keep watch, not trusting Sugama to maintain order.

Asayaga nodded, motioning for him to climb the ladder and join him on the wall.

Tasemu crouched down beside him.

'Force Commander, what are you going to do?'

Asayaga chuckled and sat down by the Strike Leader's side.

Do? At the moment he had no answer to that one. A dreaded enemy blocked the way back to their lines, and unbelievably he was sharing a meal and spending the night with nearly sixty Kingdom troops.

'May I venture to say that my Force Commander is not sure of the future path?' Tasemu announced, sounding quite formal but in so doing offering Asayaga a chance to ask for an opinion.

They'd been together since the start of this war and rank notwithstanding, he knew Tasemu to be a friend, and not just a loyal retainer. If they ever got back home they'd assume the old roles, but out here it was different.

'Speak your mind, Tasemu. What future do you see?' Asayaga asked, taking up his Strike Leader's offer of advice.

Tasemu sat back against the stockade wall and looked up. The low scudding clouds parted for a brief instant, revealing the stars. Tasemu rubbed the patch over his empty eye-socket, a habit of his when he was thinking hard.

'The black-skinned one, the Natalese, he is a deadly foe, as is their captain,' he replied finally. 'I have caught glimpses of them in battle several times. Only glimpses, but I know we have faced them before and lost. Killing those two would be a great coup, worthy in fact of the sacrifice of this entire unit. Later it would save the lives of many of our comrades.'

Asayaga snorted derisively. 'I never knew you to be worried about the skin of others, especially of the Clan Shonshoni. This does not sound like your thoughts. It is what Sugama is saying, not an old veteran like you.'

Tasemu smiled. 'It is what he is whispering at this very moment,' Tasemu acknowledged, nodding back towards the barracks, 'and more than one is listening in there.'

'And you? What do you think, Strike Leader Tasemu?'

Tasemu hesitated, then said, 'He's right you know.'

'If we were back at camp: and he was out here alone, I'd gladly shout such advice to him,' Asayaga replied heatedly. 'I'd shout for him to kill as many Kingdom warriors as he wants and die a glorious and honourable death himself in the process.

'But we are not in camp, we are here, stuck with these barbarians and those damned Dark Brothers waiting to kill us all.' He used the Kingdom words, rather than the Tsurani 'Forest Demons' as if doing so made them less fearful and more mortal. 'First we figure out how to survive, then we think about killing soldiers of the Kingdom. If we can combine those goals, so much the better. If not . . .'

He fell silent and like Tasemu leaned back, looking up at the stars, wondering, as so many soldiers of the Tsurani did, which one might be home. Or if they could even see the yellow-green star that was home to Kelewan.

'So, you are not planning then to kill the Kingdom soldiers, or try for their leaders?' Tasemu pressed.

'When it's worth it,' Asayaga replied sharply. 'When it's worth it to my family I will do it. But here? So what if we kill this Natalese and their captain. How many of us will survive when that fight starts?'

'Not many,' Tasemu answered. 'The cold, this damnable cold, too many of our men are already spent.'

'Even if we win, come morning . . .' Asayaga motioned to the other side of the wall and then drew a finger across his own throat. He paused, then shook his head. 'To those at home, we are already lost,' he continued, his voice barely a whisper.

'We're overdue. If word ever got back to the Warlord's camp that we all died in a futile battle, there would be no honour in it for our clan. Our House will be blamed for the loss of this command. If months from now a rumour comes back of our bleached bones being found in this gods-cursed place, thirty miles or more from where we were suppose to be, someone will seek to cast blame.

'It won't matter to me, I'll be dead, as will you. But it will matter to our house and clan. Sugama's family . . .' He shook his head. His face briefly showed disgust before his features resumed their passive expression. 'The Minwanabi, they win either way. He comes back alive from this, he's a hero. He disappears, they've got rid of a Tondora fool, but they'll cast him as the hero and vilify us. Clan Shonshoni rises. The Minwanabi rise. We gain nothing for our own.'

Tasemu asked, 'So then, you think the rumours from home are true: that the Minwanabi lord seeks to displace Almecho as Warlord?'

Asayaga let out a long, silent breath. 'Almecho would not be the first Warlord to be removed by a more ambitious rival. And the Minwanabi lord keeps his cousin Tasaio out here in this miserable weather for a reason.'

'But he's second-in-command, Force Commander.'

'That's the brilliance. If we are victorious, he shares the glory. But if we fail, he replaces a powerful rival ...' Asayaga stopped, then chuckled. 'Ever, we are Tsurani, Tasemu.' He motioned around him and said, 'We sit upon this wooden palisade, leaning against frozen stones, in this miserable cold, surrounded by enemies, hours away from almost certain death, on a world not our own, and what do we do? We discuss politics back home.'

'The Great Game is the Empire, Force Commander.'

Asayaga's demeanour turned suddenly stern. 'And the Empire is on another world! No. We must find a way out of here. A suicidal fight for honour may make sense back home, might help the family or clan in the Great Game, but to look for such a fight here, I would have to be an imbecile.'

Tasemu looked over at him and smiled. There was, for Asayaga a flash of memory then, a memory of nearly ten years ago when both of them were young soldiers, filled with dreams of glory and honour, ready to believe all they had been taught of Tsurani rules of proper behaviour in war.

Then had come the word of the failed invasion against the Thuril Confederation, and the cessation of hostilities in the highlands to the east of the Empire. Few dared openly call it a defeat, but for the first since the abandonment of Thubar – the Lost Lands across the Sea of Blood centuries earlier – the Empire of Tsuranuanni had been thwarted in its expansion.

The Party for War had been in turmoil, and the coalition of the Blue Wheel Party and the Party for Progress had been on the rise; then had come the discovery of the Rift Gate and the passage to this world, rich in metals and inhabited by barbarians. The Warlord Almecho had seized the opportunity to mount an expedition to bolster his falling stock in the Great Council and the war banners had flown and the battle call had sounded.

Young men had bravely marched before the Emperor's reviewing stand while drums and horns had sounded. The Light of Heaven himself had blessed the endeavour and Asayaga had felt certain a great victory would be swiftly coming. He was Force Commander of his House, but it was a minor house and in prestige he stood behind even a Patrol Leader of one of the Five Great Houses. But he would win glory, rise in importance, and bring honour to his House within his Clan.

War, however, had taught them something far different: reality.

Asayaga whispered, 'We must gain a position where if we do kill their captain and the scout word will somehow get back that it was us, that it was our Clan that did such a deed ; that it was our sacrifice, otherwise Sugama's family and Clan will create a different tale. Even at the cost of our entire company, to end the ravages of Hartraft's Marauders would bring glory to our house. But only if the Kodeko are given the credit.'

'Which would prove difficult with the Minwanabi relaying the word back to the home world,' Tasemu observed.

'A good reason, my friend,' Asayaga added wryly, 'to get us out of this alive. Then we can carry word home ourselves.'

'Alliance with the Kingdom troops, captain?' Tasemu asked. 'By all the gods if word of that ever gets back it will be just as bad as if word never gets back. You will be denounced as a coward for not taking their heads when you had the chance, or it will be seen as tantamount to surrender.' Tsurani soldiers didn't surrender; on their homeworld it meant slavery and dishonour. Better to die with a sword in one's hand than live a life of shame.

'Are you so eager to die, Strike Leader Tasemu?'

Tasemu looked as if he had been gravely insulted.

Asayaga chuckled and gripped his shoulder. 'We're alike,' he whispered, 'we want to get out of this with heads still on our shoulders as well. A dead man serves his house for a very limited time.'

Tasemu smiled and laughed softly, shaking his head. His friend had played the old game, indirectly leading in one direction, but in fact seeking the answer he had just received. 'True. I don't appreciate someone like Sugama urging me to get myself killed for honour's sake,' he replied, rubbing the patch that covered his blind eye. 'Given a choice, I'd rather defer such honours to him and lead a long life in obscurity.' His smile faded. 'But, he's got more than one lad ready to pull a blade and use it on any pretence. Whatever you do, you'd better do it soon, Force Commander.'

Asayaga sighed. 'Keep the watch.'

He slipped down the ladder and returned to the barracks. Though he would never admit it he was glad to have the errand, it would mean several minutes of warmth.

That was one thing about this damnable world he could never get used to. Of all the places to open a rift to, it had to be here, to a place where the water froze in the air. He resolved, as he had almost every night since the war had started, that the first thing he would do once it was over was to go home, find a sun-drenched beach on the Sea of Blood, and swim in the warm breakers, then lie on the sand, letting the heat soak into his weary bones. His family had a small home on the bluffs overlooking the ocean in Lash Province, near the city of Xula. He had not been there since entering training, but if he ever returned home, that is where he planned to travel first after seeing his younger brother.

As he reached the door to the barracks, he wondered if he would ever again experience the salt spray cutting through the hot dry winds, rich with the pungent, sweet aroma of jicanji blossoms, the brilliant orange flowers that bloomed on the floating kelp beyond the breakers for only a few days each year.

He pushed the door open and stepped in. The air was fetid with the stench of warm bodies and wet wool, boiling stew, stinking foot-wrappings and open wounds, banishing all memory of blossoms and salt spray. He cast a quick glance at the wounded lying in the corner. Osami, one of his youngest looked at him, trying to act stoic. He knelt down by the boy's side.

'Their robed one drew the arrow,' the boy said.

'I know.'

'Why would he do such a thing?'

'Perhaps they are crazy,' Asayaga offered.

'I'll walk, you know, Force Commander. I will keep up.'

Asayaga placed a reassuring hand on the boy's shoulder and squeezed it. He said nothing. It was not proper to offer false hopes and the boy should realize that. If he could not run then he must die. If he had sufficient courage he could wait for the enemy and try to kill one, but the chances of being captured, and the torture that awaited was more than any man could be asked to endure, let alone a boy. Or, he could close his eyes, bare his throat and let a comrade give him release.

If necessary Asayaga knew that task would fall upon him. The boy had friends, for many of the old veterans viewed him as something of a little brother, an eager youngster still desperate for glory. The fact that they cared so much for him would make cutting his throat difficult for them, though none would hesitate if asked; they were Tsurani. But no man would welcome the task, even if it spared the lad and his family shame. Asayaga pushed the thought away. Time enough before dawn to discuss with the boy a proper and fitting manner of death.

He caught a glimpse of Sugama, squatting by the fire, a knot of men around him, whispering. Occasionally one would look up, gazing over at the Kingdom troops. The rush for food and warmth had mingled them, but now the two sides had drawn apart and Asayaga could sense the mounting tension.

'It will explode soon.'

He had not noticed Dennis, who had been sitting on one of the bunks, sword drawn, blade resting on his knees. He was casually rubbing the sword down with an oiled rag, but that was a cover: he wanted his blade out, ready for instant use.

Asayaga hesitated, tempted to draw his own blade before approaching, but knew that such a gesture would cause the room to erupt. Would this man betray him? It could be a trap, once into strike range the captain, with one back-handed blow, could take him. These Mauraders were famed for such trickery.

He realized there was no way out. If he turned and run away it would be a signal of fear, or perhaps read as a sign that he was about to rally his own men on watch.

Dennis stared at him intently.

'When I take you, it will be in a fair and open fight,' the leader of the Kingdom troops said, his words loud enough so that all in the barracks hall fell silent, heads turned.

Some of Asayaga's men stood, not understanding the words, thinking that a challenge had been offered.

'Now,' Sugama hissed, 'our honour is at stake!'

'Tell your boy over there to calm down,' Dennis said, pitching his voice low, 'or my sergeant will silence him permanently.'

Asayaga spared a quick glance past Dennis. Leaning against the far wall was a short, stocky soldier, his appearance casual as he rested against the stone fireplace directly behind Sugama; but his right hand was behind his back, most likely holding a dagger.

Asayaga slowly raised his hand, giving the signal for silence. All of his men responded, except for Sugama who stood up.

Asayaga could see Dennis from the corner of his eye. The man tensed and Asayaga knew that a mere nod of the head, a single gesture and the sergeant behind Sugama would have his blade buried to the hilt in Sugama's back.

'Force Leader,' Asayaga hissed, looking straight at Sugama. The menace in his voice carried the warning and Sugama hesitated. 'Turn slowly and look behind you.'

Sugama's gaze broke away from Asayaga and he turned cautiously. The Kingdom sergeant nodded slightly, a flicker of a smile creasing his scarred face.

'Now sit down slowly, Sugama. If you try for him, he'll have that dagger behind his back buried in your stomach before you take another step.'

In spite of the game-within-games Asayaga knew he had made a mistake, but there was no way out of it. Sugama had just suffered another public humiliation. He had forestalled the encounter for the moment, but Sugama had to regain his honour. Sugama stood motionless, uncertain as to what to do next, while Alwin Barry slowly pulled his hand from behind his back, revealing a dagger with which he casually began to clean his fingernails.

After a painful moment, Sugama said, 'Yes, Force Commander,' and sat down.

Asayaga turned back to face Dennis who had not moved throughout the encounter.

'As I said before, it will be an open fight between us,' Dennis said again.

Asayaga grunted noncommittally and stepped closer, moving within the arc of Dennis's sword.

Dennis looked up at him. 'Walk with me a while, Tsurani.' He rose and, without waiting to see if Asayaga was following him, went outside. He regretted returning to the cold, but what he had to say was not for the ears of the men on either side.

Once outside, the door closed behind them, Dennis walked a short distance away, to an empty water-barrel near the wall. He sat upon it and looked up at the Tsurani leader. 'The second watch should be back in soon,' he said, speaking slowly so that Asayaga could understand.

'I know. The storm is lifting.'

'The Dark Brothers will try a night attack. They've had several hours to dry out, eat some warm food. With the weather lifting they won't wait. They know we're both in here and will figure we've murdered each other. They'll be eager for an easy kill.' As he said the last words he smiled slightly.

'Then we surprise them,' Asayaga replied. 'After that, you and I, we fight.'

Dennis shook his head. 'Typical Tsurani. Always ready to stand and fight without thought.'

'That is why we will win.'

Dennis held up his hand.

'Listen, Tsurani. Even together we can't hold this place. My father built this stockade, and he abandoned it for a reason.' He pointed upward in the dark. 'They get archers up on the sides of the pass it's a death trap.'

'So we put men up there.'

'To put enough men up there, we do not leave enough on the wall to repulse an attack. No, you can stay if you want. In fact, I encourage you to do so.'

'But you are running?'

Dennis nodded and gestured to the north. 'They have three hundred or more, at least twenty mounted. North is the only way out of here now.'

'And then where?'

Dennis grinned. 'Wouldn't you like to know.'

Asayaga studied him intently.

'You don't know yourself,' he said softly, speaking so quietly that the Kingdom troops on the wall above could not hear.

Dennis said nothing for a moment. 'I scouted it years ago,' he hesitated, 'before you came. Not since.'

'The black scout?'

'The Natalese scout,' Dennis replied evenly, 'Gregory. Same with him. It's land that no one claimed. Border marches separating our realms from the Dark Brothers and their allies – what we call the Northlands.'

'Then follow the ridge of this mountain and go west for a day. After that, turn south back to our lines.'

Dennis shook his head.

'They'll pin us up here. The ridges are piled high with snow and ice after this storm. We'll get trapped up there, they'll circle us in, block our escape and then drag us out.'

'So why are you telling me this?'

'Because, Tsurani, its one of two choices. We settle accounts now, or you come with us. I don't think you're fool enough to stay behind so I don't even offer that to you as a third alternative.'

'You offer me a choice?' Asayaga barked. 'Perhaps it should be the other way around, dog.'

Dennis's features clouded for an instant, hand gripping the hilt of his sword tightly. 'Who is the invader here?' he asked, his voice filled with menace. 'You dare call me a dog, you murderer?'

Asayaga started to speak, but then held his words. What answer was there? For a brief instant he understood the Kingdom soldier's anger. He inclined his head slightly. 'I offer no apology,' Asayaga said, holding up his hand, palm out, 'but I do offer to talk.'

'Well,' Dennis replied haughtily, 'that's something, coming from a Tsurani.'

Asayaga was silent for a moment, as if weighing his options. Finally he said, 'I heard one of your men speak your name. I know who you are, leader of Hartraft's Mauraders.'

'Yes,' and there was a sharp note of pride in Dennis's voice. 'What's left of the garrison of Squire Hartraft's estates, in service to my lord, the Baron of Tyr-Sog. So why is that important?'

'I have lost more than one man to you. Finding them in the morning, throats cut, no sign of an honourable fight. Slipping in like purse-thieves in an alleyway, then melting back into the forest.'

'Bothers you, doesn't it?' Dennis said, a cold grin lighting his scarred face.

'It is not war, it is murder.'

'Don't speak to me of murder!' Dennis hissed, barely containing his anger. 'Were you at the Siege of Valinar?'

Asayaga, even though he was unfamiliar with all the inflections of their language, could not mistake the tension in Hartraft's voice.

He nodded. 'No, I was serving with Clan Kanazawai under Kasumi of the Shinzawai against your Prince Arutha at Crydee. A hard fight, the first one I was in. But I have heard of Valinar; that was also a hard fight.'

'That was my family's estate.' Dennis made a sweeping gesture that took in the men up on the wall and those inside the barracks. 'This raiding company was formed around the few men who got out of Valinar. Less than twenty of us and those who remained behind, you killed them all. I am the only one left.' He fixed Asayaga with a look that could only be called murderous. 'My father, my mother, my younger brother and two sisters, and the woman to whom I was bethrothed, all were in residence at my father's estate the night you Tsurani attacked.' His voice fell to a whisper. 'It was the night of my wedding-day. It's been nine years, Tsurani, but I remember it as if it were yesterday. I held my wife in my arms when she died. I don't know if my brother and sisters are even alive.'

Asayaga tensed. The captured Kingdom soldiers had been taken to Kelewan and sold as slaves. They were labouring under the hot Tsurani sun if they still lived, in the fields or down reclaiming the land of the Great Swamp. The women . . . the old ones to the kitchens, the young ones, like Dennis's sisters . . . He thought it best not to mention that to Dennis. Then he remembered a story. 'You're the one who released the prisoner, aren't you?'

Dennis grinned, as evil an expression as Asayaga had seen on a mortal man. Early in the war a raid had taken a forward position, and every man there had been killed, save one. A young Tsurani soldier had been rendered unconscious and when he revived he found himself a prisoner. Rather than being enslaved as he had expected, he had been returned to his own lines, with a message: every man who had attacked Valinar would be hunted down and killed. It had been judged a hollow threat; but nine years later, only a handful of men who had been at Valinar were still alive to remember that fight.

'We are a raiding company, and we operate behind the lines. We serve at the pleasure of the Duke of Yabon, and under the command of the Earl of LaMut and my lord the Baron of Tyr-Sog, but the manner in which we serve is our own. Once behind your lines, I am free to act as I see fit. The Marauders are the thorn in your side, Tsurani.' He looked Asayaga directly in the eyes. 'We are here because we were on our way back from raiding one of your rear positions. So know I am not boasting when I tell you this thing: this is my world, Tsurani, not yours. But I am not ungenerous, and will give you a tiny bit if you'd like; just enough of it for your grave.'

Asayaga took a deep breath. 'We cannot settle this war here, at this moment, Hartraft,' he said quickly, as if these words were hard to say. 'Time is spinning out and you said they will soon attack.'

Dennis continued to smile without any hint of warmth. 'Yes. Maybe we should just sit here and argue till they come and kill you for me.'

Asayaga hesitated, wondering for a second if this man's hatred ran so deep that he would do such a thing. 'You are saying then that you command and we are to follow?' he asked finally.

'Something like that, at least till we are free of the damned moredhel. I need your swords in order for my men to survive, but not as much as you need my knowledge for your men to survive. Dying at the hands of the moredhel serves neither of us or our people. Will you serve?'

'Never. I command my men.' He said the words slowly, forcefully. This Kingdom soldier's ignorance of his foes was astonishing. Had he no sense of the proper order of things, of all that was implied by the acceptance of an order from a sworn enemy?

Dennis looked at him carefully and Asayaga could sense that Hartraft was studying him, trying to figure something out. Finally he grunted and nodded.

'A truce then. Call it whatever the hell you want to call it. We move together until we are certain we are free of the Dark Brothers.

Once that is accomplished we form ranks with our own comrades and then we fight.'

'I march the same path as you only because I order my men to do so,' Asayaga replied slowly. 'But you and I shall have an understanding. If you only pass along . . . suggestions, to me, I will consider them and perhaps agree to your suggestions. But order one of my men and you will as likely provoke a fight.'

Dennis looked at him, as if deciding.

Rapidly, Asayaga continued, 'In our world, enemy houses will serve together if ordered by their clans; but one of lower blood, of another house, is . . .' He fought for a concept. 'It is better if you just tell me what you wish. My men will likely not obey one of . . . inferior blood.'

'I won't start another argument with you about whose blood is better,' Dennis replied coolly. 'I've seen enough on both sides to know it's the same colour.' He nodded. 'All right. Suggestions. But if I say move, or deploy to a flank you'd better hear . . . my suggestion and act on it with haste. If it comes to a fight with the Dark Brothers, Tsurani honour be damned. If you want your men to survive, listen to what I say.'

'I will take no order from you. But I will consider suggestions.'

'Tsurani, call it what you want,' Dennis replied, a note of exasperation in his voice. 'Call it suggestions, advice, your mother's bedtime stories, I don't care what, but I know these woods, and I know the Dark Brothers in a way you will never learn if you are lucky. I'm taking you along because I see no way out of it, but I'll be damned if your blundering gets my men killed.'

'Blundering? I don't call the last nine years blundering. If we are blunderers why are we winning this war?'

Dennis wearily lowered his head and shook it. 'Maybe we should just settle it now,' he sighed. He stood up. 'By the Gods, either that or just give me a simple yes that we march together, and fight as a unit if attacked. Later we can argue all we want and cut each other's hearts out.' He looked back up at Asayaga. 'Or in your case, perhaps cut your throat so you'll shut up.'

'What was that?' Asayaga snapped, not sure of what Hartraft had said because he had spoken the last words softly and quickly.

'Nothing, Tsurani, nothing.'

'It is not "Tsurani". You say it as an oath. I am Force Commander Asayaga of the Kodeko, undercommander of the forces of the Warlord in the east, of the Clan Kanazawai, son of Lord Ginja of House Kodeko, brother to –'

'All right. Asay, then.'

'Asayaga.'

'Fine, Asayaga.' He cursed softly under his breath as he stood up. 'Let's go tell the men.'

Asayaga knew that all in the room had been watching as they had left. There would be some concern on the part of his own men that perhaps the Kingdom barbarian had attacked Asayaga in a treacherous act; he had no idea what might concern the Kingdom soldiers, but he knew that tensions would be mounting.

They entered the barracks and again were almost overwhelmed by the heat and stench compared to the icy clear air outside.

Asayaga looked around the room. 'We march tonight,' he announced. 'The Dark Ones will attack before dawn. The Kingdom soldiers are . . . allied to us until we are clear of the other enemy. You are not to speak to them, even to notice them, and you are forbidden to fight with them until I order otherwise. Once we've escaped from the Dark Ones, then there will be enough time for honour to be served.'

He could see more than one of his men relaxing with the announcement. Tasemu was right: the men, physically, were at their limit. Fighting was the last thing they wanted at this moment. If there was to be a fight, they wanted to save their strength, and as many as their comrades as possible, for the encounter with the Dark Brothers.

Sugama looked up at him, and fortunately had the good sense to keep his mouth shut and offer no challenge to what was a direct order.

'Captain.'

Asayaga looked over his shoulder, to see that it was the Natalese scout, who had spoken to Dennis. Neither he or Hartraft had seen the scout and his young companion return to the stockade, so intent had been their conversation.

'They're coming,' Dennis said quietly and Gregory nodded agreement.

Gregory started to explain, but Asayaga held up his hand, letting him know that he already understood.

'We have about an hour, maybe two,' Gregory said. 'They're slow forming up, but their flankers are already starting to climb the rocks to get above us. Tinuva is keeping an eye on them. We've killed a couple of their pickets on the way back, so the moredhel will be cautious on the advance, fearing a trap. We've got a little time, but we better pack up and get out of here now if it's going to do us any good.'

Dennis snapped a command to Alwin Barry, still standing behind Sugama, and instantly the room was bustling with activity as Kingdom troops started to don equipment. The order was passed outside, and within seconds more Kingdom troops streamed in, gathering around the fire to soak up a few minutes, warmth and wolf down the last of the stew.

Asayaga, shouting orders, began to gather his own men as well.

'I understand there is an arrangement,' Gregory asked, coming up to Asayaga's side and speaking in Tsurani.

Asayaga simply nodded.

'Smart move by both of you.'

'It doesn't mean the fight between us is over, Natalese.'

Gregory grinned. 'I never said it was. But I'm happy to see it postponed.'

Asayaga went over to where his four wounded laid. Two of them were putting on their gear and standing up; but the third, Ulgani, was barely conscious. Several of his comrades had gathered around him, heads bowed, hands placed upon his chest, whispering the prayer for the dying.

With all the bustle and turmoil in the room there seemed to be a ring of silence around this small group. Even the Kingdom soldiers, standing but a few feet away were silent. Ulgani's Patrol Leader placed a hand over his comrade's eyes, then drew his dagger.

It was over in seconds and the three stepped back, one of them draping a blanket over their dead comrade.

Asayaga looked down at Osami who had watched the ceremony, wide-eyed. He went to kneel by the boy's side. 'The march ahead, it is hard. Hard even on old veterans who are healthy. Remember, the chain is only as strong as the weakest link.'

The boy looked up at him, nodded, and then looked back at Ulgani. Blood was soaking through the blanket.

'I can run,' Osami whispered. He started to reach for his trousers, but they had been cut away and laid by his side, shredded and blood-soaked.

Panicked the boy looked around.

Someone tossed the boy a pair of trousers, tanned leather, most likely from a dead moredhel. It was the Kingdom priest.

'I'll keep an eye on him,' Brother Corwin said.

'Stay out of this, dark robe.'

'No. I put a lot of effort into that boy. He'll keep up, same as that other boy,' and the priest nodded to the Kingdom soldier with the broken leg. Grimacing, the boy was on his feet, supporting himself with a makeshift crutch.

'If it comes to running they're both dead.'

Dennis had come up to join the debate and was looking over coldly at Corwin.

Corwin grinned. 'We'll see when it comes time to run, won't we? For now, let them be my concern.'

'Be it on your head then, priest, but we slow for no one.'

Corwin waved him aside and bent over to help the Tsurani get dressed. Osami rejected the offer, even though it was obvious that he was in agony getting the trousers on.

'Everyone out!' Dennis shouted. 'Form up by unit!'

Asayaga, not wanting to let even the implication form that he was following Dennis shouted out his orders for his men to be outside first and ready to march.

There was a final frenzy of activity: men cutting off steaming slices from the haunch of stag still roasting in the fire, dipping earthen mugs into the bottom of the kettle for the last of the stew, snatching blankets from bunks to use as capes; while others filled skins with water, and tucked the skins under their tunics so they wouldn't freeze.

Asayaga headed for the door, Sugama falling in by his side.

'You know what will be said back home of this arrangement,' Sugama whispered.

'Why, what would you say of it?' Asayaga fixed him with his gaze. Sugama backed down.

'They are enemies, but we have a truce; that is sufficient for now,' Asayaga explained patiently. 'We are, as the Natalese Ranger puts it, only postponing our fight.'

The bitter wind cut off his words as he stepped out into the open ground in front of the barracks. His men were rapidly falling in. The last of those coming in from guarding the flank stumbled into line, grateful when a comrade offered them a warm piece of meat, or a dry blanket to throw over their shoulders.

He almost felt as if it was a race to see who could form up first, thus demonstrating their discipline. The last of the Kingdom troops came out of the barracks as Tasemu walked down the line and barked a command, the men snapping to attention.

Asayaga looked over at Hartraft's men who were standing in lines, half a dozen feet away. They did not come to attention as their captain passed. He paused with several of the men, checking their packs, slapping one of them on the shoulder, trading a comment with another that triggered a gruff laugh. Several of the men looked over at Asayaga and he wondered if they had made a joke about him.

'Order of march,' Gregory announced, stepping between the two groups.

'The trail is wide enough for the next few leagues that we move in twin lines. I'll bring up the rear, laying traps to slow them. I'd like several of the Tsurani to help.' He looked over at Asayaga and saw Dennis had crossed to stand next to him. Asayaga's eyebrow lifted in an unspoken question. 'I estimate an hour, two at most before they try to storm this place. By that time we've got to be three miles or more away, then we're off the trail and into the woods. You have more men, and they're fresher if we need to run like hell to catch up. If that is acceptable to you, Force Commander,' Gregory added, grinning.

Asayaga was surprised by the Natalese. He had given an order but offered it as a suggestion. His diplomacy was good. Asayaga nodded and repeated the suggestion of the scout, making it an order, and detailing off four of his best runners to bring up the rear.

Dennis looked over at Asayaga. 'Keep your men separate from mine. No weapons drawn except bows. If we hit an ambush you break to the left of the trail, I'll take the right. Make sure your men keep up.'

'Make sure yours keep up,' Asayaga snapped.

'We'll see.'

'All right, you bastards, let's get out of here!'

For a second Asayaga flared, ready to explode at the insult to his lineage, then realized that Hartraft was addressing his own men.

Strange, these Kingdom men, he thought. *The informality, the casualness of how they speak to each other, even the way they march.*

Asayaga started to move towards the head of the column. There was an explosion of curses behind him. Turning, he saw one of the Kingdom soldiers stepping out of the ranks, shouting, charging into his line of men, shoving a Patrol Leader, Fukizama, to the ground.

Asayaga could barely understand the words the Kingdom soldier was shouting, but it sounded like '. . . you thieving bastard!'

Fukizama rolled and came up, dagger drawn. He slashed out, slicing the man across the thigh. The Kingdom soldier, swearing, leapt back, drawing his sword.

Blades snapped out from scabbards on both sides and the two lines began to move towards each other, ready to fight.

Asayaga ran down the line, shouting, Dennis by his side, knocking swords up.

Fukizama had now tossed his dagger aside, and had his sword drawn.

'My name!' Fukizama screamed. 'My honour has been insulted!'

He started forward but Asayaga pushed him back.

'He struck me. Are we cowards, Force Commander? Are we dogs to be whipped without reply? I claim the right of honour.'

Asayaga froze. He saw Tasemu standing behind Fukizama. The sergeant was silent. He could hear the whispers of his men.

He turned and looked over at Hartraft who was standing in front of his men, blocking the enraged Kingdom soldier who was shouting obscenities at Fukizama.

'Your man there,' Dennis announced, pointing towards Fukizama. 'He stole Wilhelm's money-purse in the barracks. Wilhelm just now saw him slipping it into his pouch.'

Asayaga looked over at Fukizama and said nothing. It would be like him to do such a thing, most of his comrades did not trust him in any game of chance. He was crafty, and was part of the group gathered around Sugama.

He could see though that there was no chance of settling this, since Fukizama had already claimed his right to honour.

'It is a duel then,' Asayaga said, his voice cold. 'Your man struck mine first.' He then said the same in Tsurani.

'Damn all to hell,' Dennis snapped. 'The Dark Brothers are breathing down our necks.'

Asayaga turned to face Dennis. 'It is a duel,' he said, 'or we fight, here and now. Which shall it be, Captain?'

Gregory was between the two. His anger barely reined in, Dennis looked at Asayaga, then finally nodded his head in disgust. 'You god-cursed Tsurani. You and your damnable honour.'

Even as he spoke he stepped back.

Asayaga nodded to Fukizama. As he did so his own men stepped back, forming half a circle.

The two had their blades out, the Kingdom soldier a heavy bastard-sword, Fukizama a lighter one-handed weapon. Fukizama assumed the ritual stance, blade drawn back behind his left shoulder, both hands on the hilt.

The Kingdom soldier held his sword with two hands, then charged in, bringing the blade down in a flashing arc. It was over in seconds. Fukizama jumped deftly to one side, holding his footing on the icy ground. Before the Kingdom soldier could recover Fukizama was in on him and with a single blow brought his sword down in a slashing blow, nearly severing the man's head from his shoulders.

The soldier collapsed, dark blood spraying out. A cheer went up from the Tsurani.

Asayaga looked over at the other Kingdom soldiers. Blades were still out, angry mutters echoing. It had been closer to murder than a real fight. Asayaga looked back at his own men and it was all so clear. Fukizama had picked his opponent well, gauged him, looking for someone young, tired and obviously inexperienced and had then provoked him.

Fukizama turned to face the Kingdom troops, a taunt forming. The Kingdom troops were ready to charge.

'Fukizama!'

The triumphant soldier turned.

'Drop your weapon!' Asayaga shouted.

Tsurani-bred discipline caused instant obedience before the man realized something dire was about to happen to him. 'Force Commander?'

'Tasemu.'

The Strike Leader came forward, tore the pouch from the waist of the motionless man and opened it. He reached inside and pulled out a leather purse and held it up.

'That's Wilhelm's,' one of the Kingdom troops whispered.

Asayaga nodded, took the purse and opened it. There were half a dozen coppers inside – trivial wealth on Midkemia, but a year's earnings on metal-starved Kelewan. He looked at Fukizama and said, 'You dishonour your family and clan. You know the penalty for thieves.'

The man's eyes widened as Tasemu motioned to two other Tsurani who seized the man. Another pulled a rope from a backpack, walked to a tree next to the trail, and threw the rope over a high branch, knocking loose the accumulated snow.

In an instant it was done. The shaking, wide-eyed soldier was lifted and carried by four men, and the noose was placed around his neck. Another half-dozen Tsurani hauled away and Fukizama seemed to spring into the air, as if fetched heavenward by a giant's hand. His neck snapped audibly when the Tsurani let the rope drop a couple of feet then pulled it taut again and even battle-hardened Kingdom soldiers flinched at the sound. He hung twitching for a minute while the rope was tied off.

Asayaga threw the paltry coins on the ground.

'Anyone else?' Asayaga barked, glaring at his men.

No one spoke.

'I will tolerate neither a thief nor a disobedient man. Fukizama was both. Now form ranks.'

He looked back at Dennis. The men behind him stood silent, not sure how to react, startled by the swiftness of Asayaga's kill. He could see the wary looks in their eyes and the shock his actions had created.

'My man was wrong. He has paid with his life and I apologize. But Hartraft, tell your men not to come near mine again,' he snarled.

Dennis said nothing, looking down at the body sprawled on the slush-covered ground, then up at the twisting Tsurani. 'Your man stilled two of our swords,' Dennis finally hissed at last.

Asayaga said, 'At least your hothead died a warrior's death, by the blade. Fukizama died a dishonourable death and this is the last time any man of the Kodeko will say that name. His ancestors turn their eyes away from him.'

Dennis continued to look at the corpse in amazement, then at last he said, 'We waste time.'

Gregory stepped between the two leaders and overturned a large jar of stew on the road. 'You're both wasting time.' Tinuva was already dragging away the Kingdom soldier and would cut down the Tsurani. He would leave no signs for the Dark Brothers to know what had occurred here.

Dennis walked away, heading to the front of the men.

The twin columns started to move, Asayaga sprinting to the front of his own line.

They marched for a mile, then came to a small clearing, then halted.

Less than ten minutes later, Gregory came up the trail. He moved past the waiting men and pointed to a barely noticeable side trail leading off to the north-west. 'We must go that way,' he said. He then took a small jar out of his backpack and started splashing a steaming fluid around the clearing.

Dennis threw him a questioning look, and the Natalese Ranger said, 'The men are carrying enough hot food to start a small festival. The moredhel will be able to smell it a mile away. This will make it tough for them to determine which path we've taken.' He motioned for the four Tsurani who had come up the trail with him, behind the main body of men, and indicated they should rejoin their comrades. 'I'll wait here for Tinuva,' he said. 'He should be along shortly and we'll do what we can to mask your tracks.'

Asayaga and Dennis exchanged glances, then without comment both motioned for their men to move up the indicated trail.

The wind was at their backs, the frozen ground beneath their feet crunching. He looked up. The trees lining the tops of the ridges to either flank were swaying, cracking under their icy loads. The snow had ceased, the clouds were blowing away, and the stars were coming out. Moonlight illuminated the mountains and the trail ahead.

They headed north, fleeing into unknown lands.

SIX

Pursuit

Fog cloaked the pass.

Bovai dismounted, handing the reins of his horse to a human. Like most of his race he had little affection for horses and let the human renegades who brought them north care for them.

The moredhel scouts who had just rushed the stockade parted at his approach. Their uneasy manner and slight shifting of weight from one foot to the other – signs impossible for the human renegades who rode with Bovai to notice – signalled to the moredhel leader that something was dreadfully wrong even before he reached the gates of the fortification. He stopped inside the open gates.

His dark gaze swept the compound, taking in every detail: the bodies of his warriors lying where they had fallen, the stains of blood in the slush, the wisp of smoke still coiling from the chimney of the barracks hall and the fact that the place was empty. The enemy had fled.

The Lesser Chieftain of Clan Raven raised his head and sniffed the air. Nothing: just the scent of the raw wind, smoke, dead bodies, but nothing living, other than his own followers.

He walked to the open gate through which he had just ridden and knelt to examine the neck wounds of two headless corpses sprawled on the ground.

Clean blows, single strikes, the spray of frozen blood indicating that the killer had decapitated one, swirled around, blood flecking off his blade and then taken the second with a back-handed blow.

Masterful.

The fact that one of the dead was a nephew bothered him not at all. If the youth was so foolish as to be taken in such a manner then he was better off dead; besides, his father was a fool.

He absently nudged the body with the toe of his boot, it was unyielding, beginning to freeze into the icy slush, dead most likely since the evening before.

The troop of wood goblins coming up the road behind him approached the open gate. They slowed to a stop, grounding their spear staffs and battle clubs, heads lowered, eyes averted in fear. Their primitive minds knew that the moredhel did not take kindly to others seeing the bodies of their fallen.

He ignored them. In the shadowy mist he saw one of his riders coming back from his scouting ride to the far side of the pass, horse breathing heavily, plumes of steamy mist blowing from its nostrils. It was Tancred, his Master of the Hunt and he did not look pleased.

Dismounting, he approached, eyes as cold as the morning frost.

'They have joined together.' Tancred pointed out the bodies of both Kingdom soldiers and Tsurani warriors.

Bovai nodded. 'That is obvious,' he replied, speaking slowly, his voice barely a whisper, as was his fashion. He inclined his head slightly toward the carnage: thirty-two brothers dead, and only eleven bodies of the humans and the alien Tsurani left behind.

Golun, his second-in-command and leader of the scouts, was silent, arms folded, eyes darting back and forth, watching the exchange between the two. Bovai gave him a quick look, a warning. Golun nodded almost imperceptibly and turned away to continue his examination of the tracks in the slush.

'That they joined and attacked this post is most interesting,' Bovai continued. There was a flicker of a smile on his face. 'Their dread of us overcomes their own petty hatred of one another at the moment.'

'Hartraft is the human leader,' Tancred announced.

He could see several of his followers, standing at a respectful distance, look towards him now with interest. Golun, down on his knees running a fingertip along the edge of a footprint in the ice barely looked up, his intent stare indicating agreement.

'Are you certain?' Bovai asked, attention focused on Tancred.

'I thought I recognized him back at the fort, on the trail when we pursued them.'

'Thought, or know for certain?'

'I am certain, my chieftain. I know his track, his ways on the trail. I followed for nearly five miles.' Tancred nodded back to the crest of the mountain, the road disappearing into the swirling mists.

'They moved on opposite sides of the path, the Tsurani to one side, the Kingdom men to the other. Traps were laid, cunning was shown.'

'Where is Kavala?' Bovai asked, his tone casual. 'He went with you?'

Tancred hesitated.

'Go on.'

'You'll see his body when we renew the pursuit. It was an eledhel arrow that slew him.'

Bovai could sense the injured pride. So even his Master of the Hunt had been surprised and bested. Was there fear in his heart now as well?

He gazed intently at Tancred, probing his thoughts. A hunt leader could not show fear, or let it linger in his stomach, for others would sense it soon enough, taste that fear and become possessed by it. They would hesitate when an order was given, and uncertainty would claim their life as readily as the blade of the enemy.

Golun was behind him, eyes fixed on Tancred, waiting for a response.

'You want revenge, don't you? Your pride is injured because they surprised you and that one was killed.' He avoided using the name of the fallen moredhel.

Tancred nodded.

'Two tracks turned off from the trail and I dismounted to examine them. One was eledhel, the other heavy, I think the track of the dark-skinned companion of Hartraft, a Natalese Ranger. I should have sensed them; how I did not is difficult to understand.'

'And then your companion was killed.'

'If the one aiming at me had shot but a second earlier I would

109

not be here. I swung my mount around. Using it as a shield I was able to escape.'

'So they did surprise you?'

Tancred reluctantly grunted an assertion. 'The mist was heavy and the wind blowing through the trees made it impossible to hear other sounds.'

'I see. And what else did you observe?'

Tancred looked straight ahead, not daring to look into Bovai's eyes. 'I counted the tracks of sixty Kingdom soldiers, perhaps seventy of the aliens. Three, perhaps four wounded being carried, or helped.'

'Curious. Perhaps a soft hearted priest intervened.' Bovai laughed softly.

More of his band came in through the gate: moredhel, these, on foot, bows at the ready. The sight of the carnage within the stockade wall stunned them and several broke ranks to go to the body of a fallen, one drawing a blade, baring his arm to make the ritual cuts of mourning for the death of a father, sprinkling the blood on the eviscerated corpse.

A commander of twenty shouted an order for the bodies to be moved and a prayer-chanter began to sing, his eerie voice high-pitched as he sang to the spirits of the fallen, bidding them to go to the eternal land in the sky.

'You realize,' Bovai whispered, drawing closer to Tancred, 'that this should have been anticipated. Yet you assured me that those we left behind were sufficient in number to hold ten times their number.

'I left thirty-two of our brothers here to guard this pass while we raided and now they are dead. Kin of many who follow me are dead. This sours all that we have accomplished this last fortnight. The rejoicing over our kills is ended, and our victories will not be sung; instead, this is what will be remembered.'

'It is unheard of that forces of the Kingdom should ally with Tsurani,' Tancred replied hurriedly. He gazed warily at Bovai. 'You said that we would be able to play against their mutual hatred,' he retorted at last, 'to use it to our advantage.' His tone was accusatory.

Bovai could see his followers looking away, nervous. Tancred was speaking within his rights as a brother. He could not challenge him on that and besides, what he said was truth, which at this moment was dangerous. A seed of doubt was being planted and Bovai had to crush it before it grew.

'Things change. That is part of the reason we came here: to observe, to learn –' he paused '– and to kill them. You should have thought of it as well,' Bovai continued, dropping his voice to a faint whisper. 'You are the Master of the Hunt. What has happened here is a fiasco. What of those back there, what will they now say of seeing so many of our brothers dead? Soon, our Master will call the councils into meeting – less than a year from now if all goes as planned – and if we are to forge a grand alliance, we must not be weak, or we bring discredit to him.'

He paused as he considered the grand plan being forged up at the ancient city of Sar-Sargoth. While the moredhel chieftain knew two or three years more would pass before the plan took form, he felt a sense of urgency. Any mistake laid at his feet could prove disastrous. He looked at Tancred.

'Clans that have not seen one another in centuries gather soon on the Plain of Sar-Sargoth – word has reached us Liallan and her Snow Leopards will attend, and that she and her husband Delekhan would bear the sight of one another without a fight between them is significant.'

For a brief instant, Bovai remembered the almost-painful marriage ceremony when blood enemies wed to seal a truce neither side wished for. Delekhan and Liallan would happily cut the hearts out of one another, yet they were husband and wife. Then for an even briefer instant, Bovai admitted he'd prefer it to be Liallan who won that contest, as that would remove a rival Lesser Chieftain from Clan Counsel, and put himself that much closer to Murad, Grand Chieftain of the Clan. Murad himself was unassailable, now that he was Chosen of the Master, but should he fall . . .

Bovai forced his thoughts back to the present as he confronted Tancred. 'I hear that even Gorath will bring his Ardanien down from the icy mountains in the far north to see if these rumours about the Master's return are true.'

The Master had first revealed himself to a shaman during a ritual of vision one night when the man was alone upon a mountain top, appearing out of the gloom and stepping into the fire. He had borne the sacred mark and knew the secret ceremonies, and had fasted and chanted with the shaman for three days and nights. The shaman had reported the Master had said, 'I will return, soon,' then had vanished in smoke and flame. Word had spread like a prairie fire that the shaman had had a prophetic vision, hailing the return of the moredhel's greatest hero.

A month later the Master came to Murad, and in a dark and bloody ceremony had bound him to his service. As a pledge, Murad had cut out his own tongue, so that he would never forswear his oath to the Master. The Master had appeared before the Clan Raven Council of Chieftains with Murad at his side, and took the paramount seat, with Murad at his right hand, and a strange, robed creature with scaled hands and burning eyes at his left.

Now word was spreading that there was to be a huge gathering of clans the next Midsummer's Day, and the matter of a grand alliance to drive the humans out of the Kingdom was to be discussed under the holiest of truces.

Bovai kept his voice low. 'No, this shall be a gathering not seen in many lifetimes and if we fail here, Murad will not permit either of us to sit at the first circle of chieftains around the council fires; when the war against the humans comes, we shall be relegated to guarding baggage trains and herding goblins.'

He nodded back through the open gate to the column of wood goblins. They were obviously afraid, uneasy. What had been promised as an easy raid with plentiful booty had been marred. They were simple creatures, and their thoughts were filled with barely-suppressed terror. If they had been back in their homelands the column would be melting away, deserters running off to hide and spread word of this humiliation.

Bovai added, 'Assuming he lets us live. If we do not stop this fear growing within us, no honours will come to our families, no glory for our band, no sharing of spoils. We shall be forced to remain content to glean what we can from the debris left behind

112

by those in the van, those selected to stand with the Master and Murad.'

'We can change all this in a day,' Tancred replied hurriedly. 'Hartraft and the aliens are trapped north of the mountain passes. They must press up the trail to the bridge at Vacosa, it is the only way across the Broad River this time of year. Our garrison there is well fortified and will block them.'

'Ah, so now you know their strategy?'

Tancred gulped nervously. 'It is their only hope. Seize the bridge, destroy it, then swing eastward and outrun us. The garrison, however, will hold and we shall come upon them from the rear.'

'Thank you for that advice,' Bovai whispered.

He turned away from Tancred and walked into the barracks hall. The air within was thick with the stench of their bodies, their musky sweat, the strange scent of the spices the aliens were so fond of in their food. Half a dozen bodies were in the corner: five moredhel, and a Tsurani, his throat cut. The way his corpse was arranged indicated that he had been killed by his own comrades rather than being left alive. Bovai took a small measure of enjoyment from that. It amused some moredhel to torture humans to death, but he had little patience for it; he preferred a quick, artful kill in battle. Besides, they were in a hurry and he would have cut the warrior's throat in almost exactly the same fashion.

He walked over to the fireplace, taking off his gauntlets, extending his hands to warm them. It was an interesting dilemma and with all such dilemmas an opportunity might emerge. *How best to turn this setback into an advantage*, he wondered silently. Fear had driven two enemies into each other's arms and he smiled at that thought. *They fear me more than they do each other and that is good.*

This had started as nothing more than a raid, a training for things yet to come, to give his brothers a taste of blood and to bring home booty. Since the coming of the alien Tsurani all had changed along the frontier, the constant pressure of the humans, the dwarves and eledhel had dissipated, their attention focused instead on containing the invaders. If ever there was a moment to regain all that was lost, it was now. That was what his master had sent him to ascertain, and he knew that this was the moment to strike.

As he looked around the barracks he felt a twinge of doubt. Could Tsurani and Kingdom forces perhaps seek a permanent truce and turn against them? Doubtful, but then who would have believed only a day ago that thirty-two brothers of Clan Raven would fall in an ambush, that a Tsurani warrior could decapitate two of his finest, then unite with Kingdom troops and go marching off to the north? Only a genius might have foreseen such a turn; Bovai had a high opinion of his own skills and ability, but stopped short of considering himself a genius.

What will the humans' next move be? Now they were over the border marches and into lands which we have reclaimed. Whatever our mission was in this land, it is now changed, Bovai thought.

Taking the fire poker he tapped absently at the shimmering coals so that sparks swirled up. In the rising embers and dancing flames he sought some vision, an inspiration that would seize him and tell him what to do next. After a moment, he stopped disturbing the fire with the poker. The vision in flames was a shaman's gift, and he was no mutterer of holy words.

To seize victory from chaos, that was his challenge. All such challenges, no matter how grim, could be turned to advantage if met head on and conquered. Tsurani and Kingdom troops together. It had a certain amusing quality to it, and if it hadn't been over their border it would almost have been entertaining to follow, to watch and observe, waiting for the moment of the falling out.

He knew enough of Hartraft to understand that this alliance would be short-lived. Even beyond the border marches stories were told of the fall of the Hartraft Keep, of Dennis Hartraft's madness and his oath of revenge against the Tsurani. The vengeance visited upon the Tsurani by Hartraft's Marauders would do credit to a Lesser Chieftain of Clan Raven. Hartraft held Bovai's grudging admiration; he was a worthy foe just as his grandsire had been: Hartraft One-Eye, a fierce enemy. They had met in battle almost fifty years before, leaving Bovai with a scar on his left arm from a blow which had nearly severed the limb. The, 'One-Eye' was the gift given in return. The spawn of One-Eye had the same fiery blood and thus killing him would be a great honour, and a worthy vengeance for all the havoc wrought against his people.

He could hear orders being shouted outside the door by Golun. A small detachment would have to be left behind to carry the dead to one of the mines where their remains could be concealed.

If Hartraft was north of the mountains he must die. Honour demanded it and the Master would expect nothing less. It would be a good hunt. Killing him would still forever the fear his name engendered not only amongst the wood goblins, but even amongst the moredhel.

Golun entered. 'We are ready, master.'

Bovai nodded, but his retainer did not depart. He turned and looked at his loyal companion. 'What is it?'

Golun leaned over and said confidentially, 'Tancred would not tell you, but he is certain the Ranger with Hartraft is Gregory of Natal.'

Bovai stiffened, a difference in posture only one of his own race would notice. 'Gregory!' he whispered. If Gregory of Natal was with Hartraft, then Tinuva would be close by. He almost grimaced with suppressed rage.

Of any mortal on this world, Tinuva was foremost on Bovai's list of those who must die at his hands. His very existence was an affront to Bovai, a stain on the honour of his family and clan. Perhaps now would come the opportunity to confront him finally and to settle the blood feud which had burned in his soul across the centuries.

If it *was* Tinuva that Tancred had met on the trail ahead, then he knew why Tancred would not say the name. No member of Clan Raven would dare speak that name to Bovai, save Golun.

Bovai knew who had slain Kavala. The feud between Tinuva and Kavala was a long one, stretching over a century and had clearly been settled this morning. *But my feud is longer, deeper*, Bovai thought, *and I shall be the one to settle it.*

Three times over the years he had encountered Tinuva when Clan Raven had raided down across the moss-covered marshes of Yabon and had struck westward along the border of Elvandar. Three times Tinuva and he had spied one another across a river, a valley, and from the opposite sides of a ridged canyon. The last time they had faced one another, both had emptied quivers of arrows across the gorge, each coming close to death, but both leaving with empty quivers and only minor wounds. To present Hartraft's head to Murad would gain Bovai glory, but killing Tinuva was a matter of personal honour, and had nothing whatever to do with glory. Tinuva must die so that the darkest affront to Bovai's family could at last be forgotten.

Finally, Bovai forced himself from his reverie. To Golun he said, 'This changes nothing. If Tinuva is among them, that will come as it does. Right now, we must do as we planned, and bring them to heel before they can escape. Go.'

Golun left while Bovai stared into the fire for a moment longer. Then he stood. The time for fantasies of revenge were past; now was the time to act. He tossed the fire poker aside and left the barracks.

The dead had been moved to the side of the building and covered with blankets so that the goblins and human renegades would not see the remains as they marched through the gate. Already Golun was urging the column forward, half a dozen mounted men galloping to the fore while his own brothers stood to one side.

All eyes were upon him as he stood in silence, his black cape wrapped around his thin frame, watching as the column trotted past. The last of the goblins came through the gate and disappeared into the mist. They would push the pursuit: his own brothers had to have their moment of remembrance before moving on.

The circle of moredhel gathered around him, heads lowered, a mournful chant beginning – the singing of the dead, calling upon the spirits of the Old Ones to come down, to gather up the souls of the slain and return them to the Immortal Lands in the sky, taking them to reside with the Mothers and Fathers. Their voices were whispers, lost in the wind, drifting through the trees, muffled in the swirling mists.

The singers lowered their heads. One soldier, chosen from the band, let the cowl of his cape fall over his face so that none would hear as he whispered the names of the fallen, the sacred names that no one spoke aloud, his softly-spoken words drowned out by the murmured cries of those gathered around him. He bid them farewell on their journey, and henceforth no one would again say their names lest they call them back from their journey and condemn them to wander the world as restless spirits.

The chant fell away, until the only sound that could be heard was the crying of the wind and the creaking of the frozen trees bending beneath the cold morning gale.

Bovai raised his head. 'We came to hunt the enemy,' he said, 'and till this moment the hunt has been good.'

There were nods of agreement.

'Until this moment we rejoiced, we laughed as we pursued a foe who ran before us as the rabbit runs before the fox.'

'Until this moment,' several of his brothers responded, following his words and the ritual of the call for a 'savata', the hunt of blood-vengeance.

'Until this moment our hearts were filled with joy, the joy of the hunt, the slaying of our foes, and we drove them before us.'

'Until this moment!' More joined in.

He paused, slowly turning, looking at each of those gathered around him.

'Those who walk the mortal world for but a brief moment, who know not the touch of eternity, who have taken from us our lands, now have snatched our brothers from us, sending them into the dark lands from which no one returns. Even as our brothers leave us, their souls cry to us.'

His words struck into the hearts of those around him, for the shrieking of the wind through the pass had a demented, unworldly tone to it, like that of souls lost in the night and more than one of the brothers looked about nervously.

'Who was this who did such an infamy to our brothers?' the singer of the dead cried.

Bovai pointed up the trail, into the swirling mist where the goblins and humans had already disappeared. 'The Tsurani, and those who follow Hartraft.'

There was silence for a moment, for all knew his name.

'Tinuva, as always.'

'Tinuva.' The name was whispered, and heads lowered again. A few of the warriors glanced at one another, and some of the bolder among them cast a look at Bovai. He had mentioned the hated elf's name, which was the breaking of a silent, yet powerful, prohibition in Clan Raven.

117

'Hartraft and Tinuva I claim for myself for there is blood debt between us. The others I give to you, my brothers. Let us take their heads! Let us send their spirits to the dark world! Let us gain our vengeance and thus regain our honour! Swear this now with me.'

'We swear.'

The words were spoken softly, yet any who was not of their race, and had heard the two words spoken would have been filled with dread at the sound of the oath, as if a primal force out of an ancient time had stirred itself.

Suddenly Bovai was in motion. With a simple gesture he ordered his horse to be brought to him. He mounted with an ease that belied his distaste for riding and urged the animal forward. He would overtake the Master of the Hunt and the human outriders who served him, and he would lead the attack on Hartraft and his Tsurani allies.

The horse's hooves clattered on the stones and the sound of ice cracking under its iron shoes filled the cold day's air like a clarion of doom.

SEVEN

River

The river was flooded.

Tinuva, with Dennis and Asayaga behind him, slowly slipped out of the cover of the forest, crouching low, and slid down the muddy bank. Tinuva disappeared into the high tangle of dried rushes that were coated in a glistening sheen of ice.

Crawling through the tall brown foliage, he approached the trail that ran parallel to the river. He could remember a time, centuries ago, when he would walk openly on this trail, ambling along on warm summer evenings and hunting in the autumn, the trees ablaze with colour.

That had been centuries ago, and of the elves who had shared those moments, nearly all had gone to the Blessed Isles, dead in the bitter strife with the moredhel. Mortality was something he tried not to dwell on, but even so he suddenly felt old, and wondered if it was somehow a foreboding, a warning.

He thought of Kavala. The settling of an ancient debt had been achieved at last. Although he knew that the death of another was something in which to take no joy, still there had been a terrible moment of satisfaction when he had seen Kavala come out of the mists, unaware that death was closing in at last.

Now was not the time to dwell on that, to let such thoughts divert him from the dangers at hand. Alert to every nuance of sound and scent he lifted his head, looking towards the far bank of the river. The water was high and the rushes were bobbing and swaying as the icy current scoured the river bank.

A stag, standing at the edge of the far bank, raised his muzzle, sniffing the air. He looked Tinuva's way, then returned to drinking. Several does ambled out from the treeline on the far side to drink as well.

Good, nothing was waiting on the other side.

Dennis crawled past him for the last few feet, reaching the trail. It had once been a broad road, but was now weed-choked and abandoned. The coating of ice on the path was solid, showing no prints except for those of several deer that had come down for their morning drink. Dennis stood up cautiously, Tinuva by his side.

'In summer you could cross here and barely get your knees wet,' Tinuva said, shaking his head, watching as ice floes eddied past, swirling and tumbling in the current.

'You mean this is where we are to cross?' Asayaga asked and Tinuva could sense the trepidation in his voice.

'It's either here or we try and fight our way across the bridge,' Dennis snapped, pointing back downstream.

'We haven't looked there yet,' Asayaga replied. 'You drag us off a clear open trail, run us through a freezing stream for more than a mile, and we wind up here.'

'The bridge will be guarded,' Tinuva replied patiently. 'In the old times there was an entire moredhel village there; fishing was abundant, as was hunting in this region. Clan Raven once ruled this region; they were always cautious of enemies, from the south and the north. They erected barriers at both ends of the bridge, and constructed a blockhouse. Those who pursue us are Clan Raven, so we must assume the moredhel are back at the bridge, and they are up there in strength.'

'Then we attack and sweep them aside,' Asayaga announced. 'We did it last night.'

'That was evening, in the fog, and we had surprise on our side,' Dennis snarled. He gestured to the swirling clouds overhead. Coming out of the pass they had dropped below the storm, so there was no longer a concealing fog. 'There is no guarantee that someone didn't get out when we took the pass. They might have been warned. Even if it's open ground for bowshot's distance all around the bridge.' He fell silent, then added, 'And if Tinuva is correct, it won't be a small

120

company waiting for us, but a full war camp.' He looked at Asayaga. 'I know you Tsurani to be fearless, but even you wouldn't charge sixty warriors across an open field at a fortification of three hundred warriors who are waiting for you.'

'Then follow the trail up the river,' Asayaga argued.

'Why don't you want to cross here?' Dennis asked.

The Tsurani bristled. 'That water is freezing. You might be cold-blooded, but my men are not. It will kill them.'

'Then stay here,' Dennis retorted. 'Follow that trail up the river. It will give out above the falls half a day's march from here. Then jump off the damn falls for all I care, but my men are crossing here.'

'We threw them off our track only for a little while,' Tinuva interjected, 'but they will be back on it soon enough. Wait here and we are pinned. But if we get across here they'll have to back-track for at least ten miles or more to get over the bridge and by then we will be gone.'

'Madness,' Asayaga sighed.

Dennis grinned. 'Afraid, Tsurani?'

Asayaga turned, and his hand fell to the hilt of his sword.

Dennis said nothing but Tinuva could see his barely-suppressed desire to have it out.

'Asayaga. Would you let it be said that Kingdom troops dared something that the Tsurani could not do as well? I know you are made of sterner stuff,' said the elf.

Asayaga looked over at him, obviously not sure if the elvish scout was taunting him as well.

'I speak to you with respect for your prowess,' Tinuva went on. 'The crossing will be hard but it can be done. We run a rope across to hold on to. All men strip naked, bundle up their clothing and weapons, securing them to staves which they hold out of the water as they cross. The first across build a fire to warm the rest. Dennis and I shall go first, bearing the rope.'

Asayaga seemed to hesitate.

'It is the only way, Tsurani,' said Dennis in a calm tone, having suddenly lost the desire to taunt his enemy. Slowly, he repeated, 'It is the only way.'

At last Asayaga nodded reluctantly. 'I shall tell my men.'

He stood up and started back up the river bank to the edge of the forest where the two forces waited.

'Tsurani?' Dennis shouted.

Asayaga turned.

'Let me guess. You can't swim. Is that it?'

Asayaga turned away with an angry snarl and Dennis smiled. 'Perhaps we could drown them all,' Dennis whispered, even as he started to pull off his cloak, trousers, boots and tunic.

'We will still need them on the far side,' Tinuva replied. 'Sixty additional swords will be the difference between life and death in the days to come. We still have to outrun the moredhel and then circle around to an open pass. I doubt if we can achieve that without a fight.'

'And then what?'

'Worry about that later.'

Tinuva stripped down, drawing his short sword to hack a sapling and trim it into a staff to which he tied his bundle of clothing.

Sergeant Barry came down, looking a bit absurd in his nakedness, already shivering from the cold. He carried a heavy coil of rope, the thirty-foot lengths carried by every fifth man in Dennis's unit having been knotted together.

'I hope it's long enough. Got the end tied to that tree up there,' Barry said, as he tossed one end to Dennis, who tied it around his waist.

Tinuva looked over at Dennis. It was one of the few times Tinuva had seen him naked and once again he was astonished at just how many scars a human could acquire in such a short life. A nasty white slash traced across his chest and just below the left collarbone was a knot of pink flesh from the arrow he had taken in an ambush the summer before. Both arms were cross-hatched with lines and his left calf was twisted and gnarled from a blow that had nearly taken off his leg three summers past.

Without comment, Dennis waded into the river, staff over his shoulder, and Tinuva could hear his sharp intake of breath. Tinuva followed, closing his thoughts, silently chanting the 'Isluna', the meditation to block pain, to disconnect the flesh from the mind.

Nevertheless he could feel his heart constrict and thump over as the icy chill swirled around him. Within seconds he was up to his waist, angling his steps against the fast-moving current, pushing aside a chunk of ice that eddied around him. He leaned against the staff, bracing himself as he nearly lost his footing in a hole, the water going up to his chest.

Dennis was beside him, cursing with every step, damning the weather, the gods who sent it, the Tsurani, and the moredhel.

They reached mid-stream and Tinuva could sense that the river was beginning to rob him of his strength, as if it was a malevolent spirit that had sunk its fangs into his soul. He stumbled and nearly went under but Dennis reached out, grabbed him by the shoulder and pulled him back up.

'Come on,' Dennis gasped, teeth chattering.

The river finally shallowed out, and the steam rose from their bodies as they floundered up to the reed-covered bank. Stumbling, they gained the far shore. Dennis untied the rope from his waist and, pulling hard, managed to secure it to a stunted tree on the river bank.

Looking back, Tinuva saw dozens of men standing along the river, all of them naked. In spite of his pain he had to chuckle at the sight.

Dennis, himself still naked, threw his pack down and tore it open, reaching into his haversack for flint, steel and tinder. Tinuva tore up an armful of reeds and piled them high, busting open the dry, fluffy seedpods. Dennis quickly had a smouldering wisp of flame which he blew to life as Tinuva carefully fed in the fluff from the seedpods, then began to break up the hollow reeds, laying them on top of the tiny wisp of flame. Dennis ran to the nearest pine tree, broke off several dead branches and brought them back and soon the fire sparked to life. Finally, with the fire alight, they struggled clumsily to get their clothes back on.

Tinuva looked back to the river. The first men, all of them from Dennis's command were nearly across, spluttering and cursing, led by Sergeant Barry.

'Gregory just came in with the rearguard,' Barry blurted out. 'They're on to our trail.'

'Damn. How much time do we have?' Dennis gasped, teeth still chattering.

'An hour at most, half an hour more likely.'

'What's going on with those damn Tsurani?' Dennis snapped while wrestling with his boots.

Through chattering teeth, Sergeant Barry said, 'They're arguing back and forth. That damn squinty-looking one – their second-in-command – he's apparently against crossing. Honestly, I think the little bastards are afraid and won't admit it.'

'Fine, let them stay.'

'If too many of our men cross first,' Tinuva interjected, 'it might cause a problem.'

'And that is?'

'We get all our men across, they might fear to start over, figuring we might ambush them when they're in the middle of the river. Or, when we only have a few left over there, they turn on them.'

'Damn it all,' Dennis sighed. He reached out to help pull one of his men up the embankment.

'Get everyone coming in to start feeding the fire. Don't worry about the smoke, getting warm is more important,' Tinuva offered. 'Remember, we saw that stag and the does. They ran back into the woods. A good hunter might take one of them. The men need warm food as well.'

'Where are you going?' Dennis asked.

'Back.'

'What?'

'I think they might trust me.'

'What the hell for?' Dennis asked. 'If we shake them loose here, fine with me.'

'They might kill the last of our men still over there, and Gregory is one of them.'

'You're a fool to try and cross again,' Dennis replied, thinking of the icy river.

Tinuva did not bother to reply. Pulling off his cloak, the only article of clothing he had managed to put back on, he plunged back into the swollen river, hanging on to the rope, pulling himself hand over hand, passing more of Dennis's men holding onto the rope on

124

the downstream side. Twice, helping hands kept him up as he felt the strength in his muscles sucked out by the frigid water. At last he gained the far side of the river, glad for the helping hand extended by Gregory. He could barely walk, his legs completely numb.

'Why in the name of the gods did you come back?' Gregory asked.

'Someone had to. What is going on over here?' Tinuva whispered, his breath forming a white cloud in the air.

Gregory pulled off his own cloak and wrapped it around Tinuva's shoulders. 'There are mounted riders behind us. Men.'

'The moredhel?'

'Not yet. I guess they're still taking care of things at the pass.'

Tinuva said nothing.

'Something is brewing with the Tsurani,' Gregory whispered. 'We don't have time for this.'

Tinuva nodded, glad for the cloak Gregory wrapped around him.

As he approached the knot of Tsurani, he could sense the tension. Some had stripped down, but others were obviously hesitant. Asayaga drew back from his men.

'What is the problem?' Tinuva whispered.

Asayaga hesitated, head lowered, obviously ashamed.

'It's the fact that most of your men can't swim, isn't it?'

Asayaga nodded. 'My world. Those who live on the coast learn. The rest . . .' His voice trailed off for a moment. 'I have the power of command, but many think it suicide and demand the right to turn and fight.'

'You know there will be a fight between us if this continues.' Tinuva nodded to the thirty or so men of Dennis's command still to cross. They were eyeing the Tsurani with suspicion and several were whispering.

'Perhaps we should settle our differences now,' Asayaga said.

'And Gregory has undoubtedly told you that the moredhel's human renegades are closing in.'

'Are they?'

'I have no reason to lie to you. If anything I should be telling you that no one is coming and leave you here,' said Gregory in a calm, even tone.

'Then why tell me the truth?'

'Because for any of us to survive we still must travel together for now,' said the elf. 'We need you in order to live as much as you need us.' He locked gaze with Asayaga and calmly added, 'You know this is true.'

Asayaga reluctantly grunted his agreement.

Tinuva said, 'For the moment no more of Hartraft's troops will cross. Send half of yours over now. Then the rest can cross, alternating: one of yours, then one of Hartraft's – that way we can keep the forces balanced on both sides of the river. But we don't have any more time to waste.'

Asayaga, hands planted on his hips, looked up into Tinuva's eyes.

'I have never seen one of your race so close before,' Asayaga said. 'Is it true you are immortal?'

Gregory started to object to the digression, but Tinuva sensed something important was behind it. He gestured slightly with his hand and his old friend fell silent. The elf said, 'All of us are immortal. Our spirits never perish, no matter the length of our span in the flesh in this world. Mine is just longer a span than yours. We both live on in the next world, though our afterworld is different from yours, I think.

'In this world, though, I can die, the same as you, and trust my word, we shall both certainly die within the hour if you do not act now.'

'You came back. Why?'

How to explain? He could claim loyalty to his friend Gregory. That was true, but it was something beyond that. This entire war was one of madness: perhaps the Tsurani before him had slain some of his kin. And yet, he had a curiosity to see how this affair would play out and with that a sense that it was not destined to end here over this foolish squabble.

'Because I want to live and the best chance for that at this moment is for us to band together. Trust me. I know the moredhel in a way you do not and never will. They will not give up on the pursuit, for in their eyes we have wronged them grievously. Their honour demands that we be hunted down and killed no matter what the cost. Tsurani, I will tell you more later, but there is no time now. Order your men to go.'

Asayaga hesitated, then nodded. Issues of honour, no matter whose, he understood. He turned and said something in his own language which Tinuva sensed was a rueful curse. Then he pulled off his tunic and leggings, and barked out a string of commands. The others hesitated and then one of the older men, shaking his head and laughing began to strip as well. To his companions he shouted, 'My manhood is shrunken with the cold. What is your excuse?'

Minutes later Asayaga lead the column into the river.

'Go with them,' Gregory said, 'I'll bring up the rear.'

Tinuva nodded. Casting aside the cloak, he fell in behind Asayaga, oblivious to the curious stares of the Tsurani. Once their commander went into the river, the others began to follow, cursing and spluttering as they hit the icy water. Half-way across the man in front of Tinuva lost his grip and went under, dropping his staff. Reaching out, he grabbed the warrior and pulled him back, but his equipment had disappeared.

A shout went up from behind and he saw two more men lose their hold on the line, one of them bobbing back up and clumsily trying to swim, while the other simply vanished.

Reaching the shoreline again, Tinuva found he could barely move and was grateful for Barry's help in getting up the river bank. A blanket was spread out on the ground next to the roaring fire and he collapsed, shivering, oblivious for several minutes. Sergeant Barry held a cloak up to the fire for a moment to warm it, then lay it around Tinuva's shoulders. The contrast with the cold almost made him cry out, but the warmth was enough to revive him. He took a slow breath and willed his arms and legs to move, and at last he stood.

Naked men pressed in around him, all of them shaking, teeth chattering. A second fire was started, some of Dennis's men, now fully clothed, bringing up armloads of wood. The sound of axes rang in the woods. Soon there was even the scent of roasting meat. Tinuva saw that someone had found a stag and brought it down. Three men were butchering it, unceremoniously cutting hunks of meat and tossing them straight into the flames to be speared out with sharpened sticks.

His senses returning, Tinuva struggled back into his trousers, boots and tunic, the spasms of shivering finally passing.

Asayaga was standing by the edge of the water, still naked, reaching out and pulling each of his men in as they staggered to the shore, urging them up to the fires to dry out.

Brother Corwin started into the river, modesty demanding that he keep his habit on, though he did cinch it up around his waist. In spite of his portly build he was still strong enough to help two of the wounded, aided by young Richard.

Gregory was still on the far shore, fully clothed, bow out. A crow rose up from a tree on the far bank squawking loudly. Tinuva saw Gregory tense.

'They're here,' Tinuva hissed.

Dennis was at his side at once, tossing over a bow and quiver and Tinuva bent the weapon, notching the string which he had carefully wrapped up inside an oiled cloth before the crossing.

The last of the men were in mid-stream. Gregory suddenly cut the rope secured to the tree on his side of the river then sprinted for the water and dived in, still holding his bow. Surfacing, he started across, half-swimming, half-running clumsily through the chest-deep water.

Tinuva saw a flicker of reflected light, which resolved itself as a mounted man, burnished shield strapped to his left shoulder. Without hesitation, he drew and fired a shaft at the glint. Even if he didn't hit the target, he might hold the man away from the shore for an extra second or two, gaining those still in the water a safe crossing.

Another man, this one a mounted archer, came out of the woods, bow drawn, aiming at Gregory.

Tinuva raised his own weapon again, but this time he didn't fire as soon as the bow was fully drawn. He hesitated, feeling the breeze on his cheek, judging the range and the drift of the arrow, and then released. The mounted archer fired first. Gregory dived down and the shaft struck the spot where he had disappeared. Then Tinuva's arrow streaked in, hitting the rider's horse and the animal reared up, screaming with pain.

More riders emerged, spreading out along the river bank. Gregory was at mid-stream now, up with Brother Corwin, urging him on, arrows hissing about their ears. A crossbow bolt struck one of the wounded in the back and with a cry he collapsed. Richard tried to grab the fallen man but Gregory pushed him on, pulling Richard under as another bolt snaked in.

Dennis's most experienced archers positioned themselves along the river bank next to Tinuva, carefully took aim, and shot their bow-shafts high in the air.

With the rope on the far shore cut away, the men in the middle of the stream were gradually being swept down by the current. A Tsurani let go, disappearing into the torrent. Asayaga jumped into the river and started to wade back out and Dennis, cursing angrily, followed him in.

Together they reached Corwin, Richard, Gregory and several of the others. Another went under hit by a crossbow bolt.

Stepping into a hole, Dennis suddenly disappeared. Tinuva, who had been taking careful aim on what he suspected was one of the human leaders on the far shore, lowered his bow, ready to go into the water yet again. Cries of alarm rose up and half a dozen men jumped into the icy torrent, ready to flounder back out.

Dennis finally surfaced, held up by Asayaga, and the two regained the shore. His bow gone, Gregory, cursing and gasping, hauled in the priest and Richard.

Asayaga pushed Dennis up the embankment even as the Tsurani swarmed around their leader.

Looking around, Dennis cursed wearily, then half-crawled back up the icy slope.

'Noble gesture,' Tinuva offered.

Dennis held up a hand to silence him. 'Not another word,' he gasped, teeth chattering. He shouldered his way past Tinuva to stand by the fire.

A dozen mounted men were on the far shore, several of them venturing long shots, but the wind was brisk and the arrows arced down harmlessly. Taunts echoed back and forth across the river as the two sides glared at each other, unable to come to blows.

More fires had sprung up, and knots of men stood around

them, stamping their feet, dressing, wolfing down hunks of barely-cooked meat.

Gregory, clothes steaming, came up to join his friend. 'I had that bow for nearly half a score of years. I'll miss it.'

'For that you saved the priest.'

'I know. It still needs to be proven if it was a fair exchange.'

Tinuva looked at him quizzically.

'Nothing yet. Just wondering, that's all.'

'He's proven his value so far.'

'I know.'

Gregory nodded to the far shore.

'It'll take them an hour to get back to the main column. Two hours, more like three, to reach the bridge and then another couple hours to here. We leave a dozen archers to hold here, just in case they are crazy enough to try and rush across. I think we can get this lot moving in an hour or so.'

'Better dry yourself out first. The temperature will drop today now that the storm is past.'

Gregory, features turning blue, nodded and returned to the fire.

One of the riders had already turned about and disappeared back into the woods. The others drew back to the edge of the wood line and dismounted, and within minutes a fire had sprung to life.

He saw Asayaga standing by the fire, shivering violently, hands extended to the heat. Tinuva went to the second fire where the venison was charring in the flames, poked out a piece with a stick and went back to the Tsurani leader and offered him the meat, which he accepted without comment.

'Why did you do it?'

'I thought it was someone else, one of my men.'

Tinuva chuckled softly.

'Hard to mistake Hartraft for one of yours.'

'It was a mistake, I tell you.'

'A mistake to save him or a mistake in knowing who you were saving?'

Asayaga took a bite of half-cooked venison. 'He hates me.'

'Do you hate him?'

'It is my duty to kill him. And yes, he has been a thorn in our side for years. Killing him would bring honour to my clan.'

'Would you have let him drown?'

Asayaga hesitated.

'Would you?'

'No.'

'Why not?'

'When I kill him, I want it to be a fight of honour. Letting him drown would not bring honour to either of us. And it would be a waste. He's right. We need every sword if we are to survive.'

'Know this, Asayaga: Dennis is a brilliant warrior, among the finest of your race I think I have ever known. He, too, has honour, though perhaps not as your people define it. I think he would have done the same for you. In fact it will rankle with him now because he owes you a blood debt.' Tinuva chuckled softly. 'You've presented him with a paradox. In order to kill you he first must settle the blood debt of life.'

'There is nothing funny about it.'

Gregory approached them. 'Funny about what?' he asked.

'Dennis owes Asayaga his life, but wants to kill him.'

Gregory nodded, then observed, 'Elven-kind see the world slightly differently than we do.'

'Yes, there is much in this that is grim,' observed the elf. 'Yet, nevertheless I see humour in it. Your human gods love to present you with such riddles and challenges, or so it has seemed to me for most of my life. Long have I known humans like Gregory and I have even visited a human city, yet there are times when I wonder at the complexities of your thinking. You often seem to prefer difficult choices when simple alternatives are available; it is a constant source of amazement to my kind.' He glanced over to where Dennis stood. 'It will be interesting to see how the two of you solve this dilemma.'

Asayaga grunted, obviously not seeing anything of humour in the situation.

Dennis came up to join them, munching on a piece of meat. He tossed a stick with another piece of meat on it to Tinuva. He offered none to Asayaga.

'We rest here for an hour to dry out, warm up and eat. Tinuva,

131

I'll detail off some men, half a dozen, to stay behind here with you. I expect the Tsurani to leave a half dozen as well. That should dissuade them from trying to make a rush.'

'I will not take orders from you, Hartraft.'

'Fine then. Call it another of my bloody suggestions, Tsurani.'

'And then what?'

Dennis smiled and pointed to the next range of mountains to the north. 'We head up there, lose the bastards, then settle our differences.'

Without waiting for a reply he walked away.

'A hateful man,' Asayaga snapped and Tinuva could sense that the Tsurani had expected some sort of ritual to be played out, a formal exchange of acknowledgment of blood debt. He could tell, however, that Hartraft was uncomfortable with the entire incident and just wanted it dropped.

'War does that,' Tinuva replied finally.

'Does what?'

'It makes all of us hateful.' As he said the words he gazed intently at the far side of the river.

After a moment, Asayaga left to see to his men.

When they were alone, Gregory said, 'What is it?'

Tinuva knew what the question meant. Gregory understood his people well enough to know that sooner or later Tinuva would tell him what it was that had bothered him since the ambush. Quietly, Tinuva said, 'Of those the Tsurani and I ambushed, one was Kavala.'

Gregory swore. 'That means . . .'

Softly, Tinuva said, 'Bovai is near.'

Gregory said, 'Another of the gods' riddles and challenges?' He shook his head. For a human, he could mask his expression almost as well as an elf, yet to Tinuva, his distress was obvious.

'Hardly,' said Tinuva. 'A cruel fate, perhaps.'

'What will you do?'

Tinuva said, 'I will serve, and do what I can to help Dennis, you, and the Tsurani, survive. But if the chance comes to end this . . . blood debt, then I will take it.'

Gregory nodded. He knew what few humans knew of the truth

behind the relationship between the eledhel and the moredhel, and specifically between Tinuva and Bovai, and he would not speak of it to anyone without Tinuva's permission.

Finally, he said, 'Best not to let Dennis know about this until it is impossible to hide it. If he knew Bovai was there, he might just linger long enough to force a confrontation.'

Tinuva's mouth turned slightly upward, an open expression of humour. 'Dennis owes Bovai a blood debt, but he has more sense than that.'

Chuckling, Gregory said, 'I hope you're right.' He turned towards the fire and said again, 'I'm going to miss that bow.'

Looking at the fatigued men around the fire, Tinuva remarked, 'There will be extra weapons, soon enough.'

Gregory needed no explanation – he knew many of these men would be dead within days – and nodded once, then walked away, leaving the elf to his own thoughts.

Staring across the river, where the human mercenaries stood watching, judging what to do next, Tinuva wondered how long he would wait before seeking out Bovai.

Lost in his reverie he almost didn't notice the first command for the men to get ready to move out; then, sensing movement behind him as the activity in the camp quickened, he took one last look across the river, then turned and moved back towards the others.

EIGHT

Decisions

Twilight was deepening.

Dennis Hartraft turned away from the knot of soldiers, throwing up his hands in exasperation. 'You are all crazy,' he snapped angrily, looking back over his shoulder. 'Stopping now is madness.' He pointed to the pass in the next range of mountains, still ten miles away. 'Once over the Teeth of the World, we're in the clear. Then we rest.'

'And not one man in ten will make it that far,' Brother Corwin interjected. 'I suspect it's because neither you nor the Tsurani will admit in front of the other that you have to stop. This chase has been going on for three days. There's barely a man left who can fight, let alone march another mile.'

'Brother, I didn't know you were part of this council of war,' Dennis retorted. 'It's for any man who fights and wishes a fair say.'

'But I'll be heard nevertheless,' the monk snapped back without hesitation. 'Give these men a rest.'

Dennis, hands on his hips, stepped back into the circle of men. He caught the eye of Asayaga who was softly whispering, translating the conversation to the men of his command.

'The Tsurani here don't have councils of war,' Dennis replied. 'Their commander says go, and they go. I'm willing to bet they are ready to go over that mountain tonight and be clear of pursuit once and for all. You men called for a council and I must accept that, but I am telling you that to stop for rest now is madness.'

134

Asayaga, even as he translated, looked straight at Dennis without comment.

'Will you have it said that those –' the word 'bastard' almost slipped out but he held it '– these enemies of the Kingdom can do something we cannot do?'

Dennis's voice started off at a low pitch. 'I know it is our custom to ask for a council of war –' his voice started to rise '– the lowest in my command can ask for one if there is a serious question of my orders, but that is not the case in a time of crisis, or in the middle of a fight!' He ended on a shout.

'I see neither a fight, nor a crisis,' Corwin replied calmly. 'We've outrun pursuit. It's getting on to dusk. We have a clear view back across twenty miles and see nothing behind us.' He pointed back across the plains and low rolling hills which the men had wearily traversed. From their elevated position in the foothills, someone with a sharp enough eye could see clear back to the river they had forded that morning. Nothing moved upon it except for a few stags, the does that followed them, and a distant band of wolves.

'They can still flank along these mountains,' Dennis replied, pointing eastward to the forest-clad slopes which they had been approaching all afternoon.

'Someone would have to come behind us to where we crossed the river,' the monk argued, 'to make sure they picked up our trail. We haven't seen anyone behind us all afternoon.'

'So, you are a master of woodcraft and field tactics as well?' Dennis asked

'No, just a man who's spent a lot of time outdoors, and who knows how to apply logic; and logic demands that we rest. The ground ahead looks good: plenty of fir trees for fuel and making rough shelters, and game signs all around. Just rest tonight, then tomorrow we can push on. If you try a night march now, you won't have twenty men left come dawn.'

Dennis turned away from the priest, his gaze slowly sweeping the ranks of the men gathered round him. Then, for a brief instant an image flashed through his mind. He glanced back at the priest, and the image faded.

Corwin saw Dennis examining him and said, 'What?'

Dennis was silent for a moment, then, 'Nothing,' he said.

He looked at his men and saw precious little support amongst them. The priest was right, they were played out: fording the river had sapped the last of their strength and the forced march of the afternoon had been a final lunge of desperation. All were on the verge of collapse.

He shifted his gaze to Asayaga. It was hard to read the strange blankness the Tsurani can assume when they desired. He wondered if Asayaga was in agreement, or was filled with contempt for the weakness of his enemy.

'Rest would be good,' Asayaga ventured. 'Some have marched sixty of your miles or more without sleep for two days. Half my men will die before morning from the freezing sickness.'

Dennis was startled by the admission. He looked over at Tinuva and Gregory.

'My friend,' Gregory said softly, 'there are times when you forget that few can equal your endurance; it is your only fault as a leader.'

'But you would agree they might be close?'

Tinuva stood up and stepped away from the circle to the edge of the knoll where they had stopped for the meeting. All were silent as he carefully scanned the distant horizon, then raised his head, nostrils flaring as if smelling the cold wind.

'I've not walked this land in years,' he sighed, turning to look back at the expectant group. 'I've lost touch with its rhythms, its heart beat, the feel of its wind, the scent of the soil and the things that grow here.' He paused. 'I can tell you though that we are the first to disturb this place since the snows began to fall. But that does not mean we will be alone for long. I know who is pursuing us now, and that makes me cautious of lingering here.'

Several of Dennis's men asked him to explain, to say who was in pursuit but he would not answer. He slowly walked among the men, his searching glance assessing each of them in turn. He paused for a moment before Corwin, gazing deep into his eyes, then turned away.

'The brown robe is right, however. We try to march for another night and many will fall.' He turned and looked back at the knot

136

of Tsurani gathered behind Asayaga. 'Especially with you,' Tinuva continued, speaking now in Tsurani. 'The ice, the cold is alien to you. You, Asayaga, know that, even if your pride would have you march with us until the last of you collapsed into silent death.'

Asayaga, startled by the elf's skill in speaking Tsurani, simply nodded.

'The temperature will drop tonight now that the worst of the storm has passed. Come dawn it will be far colder.' As he spoke Tinuva turned back to Dennis, again speaking the King's tongue. 'Ice can kill as surely as an arrow or blade. Though I fear that we have yet to lose our foes, we must stop. Let us enter the forest ahead, dig in there before dark, build fires, make what shelter we can but we stay alert. That is what I suggest.'

Dennis sighed and slowly extended his hands in a gesture of submission. 'So be it then if that is what all of you wish.'

Murmurs of agreement and relief swept through the ranks and the group broke apart, slowly streaming up the hill and into the forest. Dennis insisted on pushing them another half a mile until he found ground to his liking, a steep overhanging cliff that blocked the north wind which was ringed with ancient firs.

His men knew their assignments: a half dozen of the best stalkers and archers set out to hunt for game, another half dozen were detailed to spread out and stand watch while the others hurriedly started to gather in wood for fires.

Asayaga approached Dennis, vainly struggling to control the shivering of his muscles and the chattering of his teeth that had troubled him ever since the river crossing.

'My men . . .' he hesitated, '. . . we will trade our labour for the food your hunters bring in.'

Dennis looked over at the Tsurani and for the briefest of moments almost felt pity, the way one would pity a wolf that had fallen out of the pack and was near death. Their agony was evident, half a dozen were being held up by their comrades, several obviously had frost-bitten cheeks, noses, and fingers.

Tinuva said I'd need these men, Dennis thought. *Hell, I could kill off half of them myself at this moment* . . . and he pushed aside the temptation.

'Go a little way back down the hill to the small pine trees, cut off the branches that are thick with needles. We'll use that for ground cover and to build up windbreaks. Any men with axes, get them chopping wood, lots of it.'

Asayaga nodded, too weary to raise any objections, and withdrew. A moment later, his men scattered to their tasks.

The overhang of the cliff formed a shallow V, but it was nowhere big enough to hold over a hundred and twenty men. Dennis went over to join a squad of men who were dragging up fallen logs to be wedged between the rocks edging the overhang and the trees further out, thus forming a rough stockade.

Within minutes fires had been started, the stockade walls on either side of the overhang were rising. Tsurani troops swarmed in bearing armloads of pine branches which were layered over the logs on the inside, while on the outside those men carrying field shovels packed snow into the cracks. More branches were laid in under the rocky overhang and those men too far gone to labour were bundled in, while Brother Corwin piled snow into a camp kettle and set it into the fire, and then threw in a handful of tea leaves once the water started to boil.

The first hunter came back in with a small doe over his shoulder and several men set to butchering it, everything but the offal going into the fire. Corwin claimed the liver and heart for the sick and wounded. Another hunter came in with a couple of hares, and yet another with a heavy dark-plumed bird that weighed near to twenty pounds. The Tsurani gazed at in wonder, since it did not range down into the lands where the war was being fought.

Soon the tantalizing smell of roasting meat cooked over a sweet-scented fire filled the air, driving the men to pause in their frantic labours and move closer to the flames until either Sergeant Barry or Strike Leader Tasemu set the men back to bringing in more wood.

A near-frenzy started to seize the group as more and yet more wood was piled on to the three fires that now roared at the base of the cliff. Dennis, finished with helping to build the rough stockade which was now nearly chest-high, stopped to look at the sparks swirling up into the evening sky.

Gregory, breathing hard, came into the encampment and joined him.

'A damned beacon,' Dennis sighed. 'A blind man will see its glow from five miles out and smell it a mile away.'

'Let it burn like this for a little while, till the men get the chill out. By then it will be completely dark, then let it simmer down a bit.'

'Anything up above?'

'Just the old trail. It's been long years since I've been up here, it's hard to remember.'

'Tinuva knows it, though.'

Gregory nodded.

'Something's really itching him,' Dennis said.

'You know who's following us don't you?'

'A whole moredhel army.'

'It's Bovai.'

Dennis looked away for a moment. He didn't want Gregory to sense the dread. Now he understood some of the strangeness in the way Tinuva had been acting, a feeling he had had that somehow the elven warrior was half-walking in another world.

'If it's Bovai and he knows who we are,' Dennis hissed, 'he'll come on no matter what, even if he kills half his troops doing it.'

'I know that, so do you.'

'So why the hell did Tinuva sway the argument for us to stay here? He knows how much Bovai hates my family; my grandfather almost killed him, and my father drove him away in shame the last time he came to Valinar.'

For an instant, something played across Gregory's face, as if he was going to say one thing, but then he said another. 'Because we are played out, Dennis. Tinuva was right, it is your one great failing as a commander: you seem to think everyone else is made as you, is as driven as you.'

'That is how I learned to stay alive,' Dennis snapped.

'Damn near every Tsurani would be dead by morning if we had pushed on.'

'Good. It would save us the work of butchering them.'

'I'm glad you feel that way, Hartraft.'

Startled, Dennis turned to see that Asayaga was standing behind him. 'I prefer to kill a foe whom I know hates me,' Asayaga continued, moving up to join them.

'Remember, Asayaga, the truce is temporary.'

'But for now we need you as much as you need us,' Gregory interjected, staring straight at Dennis who reluctantly nodded an agreement.

'I think your men were just as played out, Hartraft.'

'We are,' Gregory replied. 'We were coming back in from patrol, the place where we met three days ago, we expected to rest there and wait out the storm. The men were already worn. They're just as beat as yours.'

'Do you think your men are just as exhausted?' Asayaga asked, gaze locked on Dennis.

'What is this? Some sort of game of pride?'

'Yes, everything is a game,' Asayaga replied and Dennis could sense a note of bitterness in the Tsurani's voice. 'You are worried about staying here aren't you?'

'The enemy we face bears a deep hatred for my family. It will compel him to press forward against us.'

'Then we remain watchful and break camp before dawn.'

'If he comes he'll have the advantage.'

Asayaga nodded thoughtfully. 'Then fate is fate.'

'What?'

'Just that. We can go no further this evening, that is now a given. You believe the enemy will press forward and I will accept that as a given. So it is fate that decides, but for the moment it is senseless for us to stand here freezing while the warmth of the fire beckons.'

Without another word, Asayaga turned and walked around the flimsy stockade to join his men who were huddling around the fire.

Dennis looked over at Gregory who chuckled softly.

'He's right, you know, and the meat smells damn good.'

Dennis followed the Natalese scout reluctantly. Darkness was closing in. The last of the wood-gatherers came in with one more load and dumped it into the piles next to the roaring fires. The flames were so hot that many of the men had pulled off their heavy jackets, hats and gloves. Ropes were strung up to hang the wet clothing on to dry out.

Many of the Tsurani were sitting, unwrapping their foot-cloths, groaning with delight as they extended bare feet to the fires. The first slabs of venison were being speared out of the flames and pieces of meat were tossed about, laughter rippling through the group as more than one man swore and let the hot meat drop in order to suck scorched fingers, then gingerly picked the steaming treats back up.

The last Kingdom hunter came in with two marmots over his shoulder, both of them plump with early winter fat. The hunter was embarrassed with such paltry fare but the Tsurani cried aloud with delight, even as the disgusted hunter dumped the carcasses on the ground and apologized to his comrades.

There was a moment's hesitation as two Tsurani moved closer to the hunter.

'Go on, take the damn things,' he finally growled. 'I'll eat crow before I'd touch 'em. It's all I could find.'

His gesture of disdain was clear enough signal and the two Tsurani swept the marmots up and within seconds had them dangling from a tree limb. With expert cuts they sliced the skin around the necks, and then without making another cut they gradually pulled the skin off the bodies. The two seemed to be running a race and the conversations around the fires fell silent as the Kingdom troops watched what was being done.

Chattering amongst themselves, the Tsurani skinning the marmots finally had the skins completely pulled off and dangling from the rear legs of the giant rodents. Then with a quick jerk the skins were popped off and then with a snapping gesture turned from inside out, to right side in, so that each skin was now a bag with the fur again on the outside.

They now fell to carving the flesh and fat off the bones of the marmots and tossing them into the bags of fur. Next the bones were broken at the joints and stuffed in and finally all the guts as well. While the two laboured at their tasks other Tsurani had been gathering up small rocks and tossing them into the fires. Now they fished the red-hot rocks out of the flames and, laughing, tossed them bare-handed to the two butchers who grabbed the rocks and plopped them into the stuffed bags as well.

Finally a couple of pins, made from a Tsurani wood almost as hard as metal, were fished out of haversacks and used to stitch the neck holes shut. Broken sticks were used to plug the arrow-holes in the hides and the two bags were tossed into the flames.

Every Kingdom soldier had gone quiet and a bit wide-eyed, while the Tsurani seemed to be in near-celebratory mood, chattering amongst themselves, pushing in around the butchers, and obviously exclaiming over the strange feast being prepared.

Gregory watched the show, grinning slightly. 'I once slipped up on a Tsurani camp at night and saw this. Near as I can figure their lingo they got something like marmots on their world and they're considered a rare delicacy fit only for the nobility.'

The air was thick with the stench of fur burning off the carcasses. The two self-appointed cooks rolled the marmots back and forth in the flames and the marmots swelled up like balloons, reminding Dennis of nothing other than a dead body floating in the water, bloating up beneath a hot summer sun.

Finally it looked as if the marmots were ready to burst asunder when suddenly juice and steam started spraying out of holes in the bodies that nature had originally placed in the marmot and which had not been plugged shut. Loud shouts of laughter erupted from the Tsurani as the two marmots were rolled out of the flames. One of the cooks, hands now protected with gloves picked one of them up and with juice still squirting out approached Asayaga, who grinned and bowed ritualistically, then knelt down while the cook held the marmot over his head. A stream of juice shot into Asayaga's mouth. He licked his lips, and said something that caused a great burst of laughter.

The second cook held up his marmot and began to approach Asayaga, but the Tsurani commander said something and pointed towards Dennis. The laughter stopped and all looked over at Hartraft.

'The first juice of the marmot,' Asayaga announced in the common tongue, 'is reserved for nobles and leaders. You drink now.'

'Like hell I will,' Dennis grumbled under his breath, his words drowned out by the crackling roar of the fire.

The second cook, approached Dennis, grinning.

'Better do it,' Gregory whispered. 'It's obviously considered a sign of respect.'

'Damn it, I won't drink juice spraying out of a marmot's backside.'

'Do it!' Gregory hissed, 'or we might have a fight on our hands. This is the first sign they've given that they respect you as a leader; don't cock it up!'

Dennis spared a sidelong glance at his men. There was a mixture of reactions. Some were obviously disgusted with the entire affair, but more than one, especially the older hands, were grinning at the predicament Dennis was now in.

His angry glare killed most of the smiles. Then, cursing under his breath, he knelt down on one knee. The Tsurani cook held the marmot up, steam still spouting out of the marmot's rearend. The Tsurani squeezed the body and a stream of juice shot out.

Dennis managed to take a single gulp. The liquid was oily, thick, and scalding hot. He struggled to swallow and the cook turned away, shouting something. Laughter erupted from the Tsurani and was soon joined by the Kingdom troops, obviously delighted by the discomfort of their leader.

Asayaga approached Dennis, pulling a sac out from under his tunic and uncorking it. 'Here, drink this, to wash it down.'

Dennis looked at him coldly and Asayaga, smiling, tilted his head back and squeezed the sac. A stream of white fluid shooting into his mouth. He pointed the sack at Dennis and squeezed.

The sour bitterness hit Dennis's palate and this time he did gag.

'What in the name of all the devils is that?' he cried.

'Aureg.'

'What? It tastes like horse piss.'

'Ha! The wrong end of a horse, if it came from a horse. It's fermented needra milk.' The needra were the six-legged beasts of burden the Tsurani had imported from their homeworld. They served as oxen and draft-horses for the Tsurani, who had no horses on their world. 'Cools one in the summer heat and warms the stomach in winter.'

'Oh damn,' Dennis said.

As he spat out the rest, the Tsurani erupted in gales of laughter. Dennis looked over at Asayaga, wondering what the hell he was doing and the Tsurani drew closer.

'Respect forestalls the killing,' Asayaga said, his voice suddenly cool. 'My men will be more receptive to your "suggestions" in the future.'

He looked back at his men who were gathered around the two marmots which had been split open. Eager hands were reaching in, pulling out the steaming hot meat. One of the men came up respectfully to Asayaga and held out his hand. Resting on the palm were two steaming pieces of meat.

'The liver and heart,' Asayaga said, offering one of the curled up pieces of flesh to Dennis.

Dennis reluctantly took one and popped it into his mouth. In spite of his initial reaction he had to admit it tasted half-way good. He nodded.

A number of Kingdom troops, drawn by curiosity, were gathered into the crowd, several of them munching on bones and strings of meat, then turning back to their comrades, laughing and challenging them to join in.

'Laughter also forestalls the killing,' Asayaga said. 'From what I heard and what I sense, there will be fighting tomorrow. We must fight together, Hartraft: eating and drinking tonight will make that easier come dawn.'

Dennis found that he had to agree. He forced himself to take the sack of aureg and to drink. This time it didn't seem quite so bad, at least if he swallowed quickly, and though it wasn't brandy from Darkmoor, it did indeed bring a touch of warmth to his insides.

As they passed the sac back and forth, watching their men feast, Dennis suddenly felt a strange sadness. Stripped down as they were, laughing, gorging themselves, the moment struck him as tragic. He had long ago come to accept life as an unrelenting tragedy but somehow, this night it seemed more poignant than usual.

He was by no means falling into the maudlin thoughts that poets and ballad-makers spoke of – how enemies might share a moment of friendship. What he felt was sentimental foolishness: the war had done far too much to him. Looking over at Asayaga he knew he could kill him without hesitation and sensed that Asayaga felt the same.

And yet, if it wasn't for the dread closing in – the memory of what was occurring at this very moment but sixty miles to the south – he felt as if he could almost enjoy this evening. *Perhaps we are fey,* he thought. *We know we're doomed and have lived with terror these last three days and the break is a final grasping at a moment of laughter.*

He had shared many a campfire with strangers, and got drunk around many a fire as well, pledging friendships and then, come dawn, they had all gone their separate ways. He knew enough to place little weight on such things. Perhaps that was the reason for the melancholy. Or perhaps it was the sudden loneliness he felt with Jurgen not being here.

What would Jurgen say of this moment? He most likely would have smiled and stepped forward to share the juice, then clapped Asayaga on the shoulder.

But they had killed Jurgen, the same way they had killed my father . . . and her.

'Something troubling you?'

He looked down at Asayaga who was offering the sac of aureg and actually smiling.

'No more,' he said coldly.

Asayaga nodded, and in an instant his features were again the blank expressionless gaze of a Tsurani officer.

'Divide up your men. Once we are done eating, two sleep while one stands watch. I want the fires banked down. We'll keep them going but not the inferno we have now. Once past midnight, I want half on watch. We'll break camp the moment there is the first trace of dawn.'

'I take that as a suggestion only, Hartraft,' Asayaga said coldly.

'Take it any way you want, Tsurani.'

'You are a hard man.'

'That is how I stay alive, Tsurani.'

'Is it?'

'What do you mean?'

Asayaga shook his head and tucked the sac of aureg back under his tunic. 'Two sleep, one on watch till midnight. Then half watch while the other half sleep. We break at first light. I'll stand the first watch, Hartraft: you sleep.'

Asayaga stalked away, joining the circle around the fire and within seconds he started to laugh again, accepting a handful of steaming meat, but as he laughed he looked back at Dennis, eyes watchful and intent.

Dennis cursed softly. Picking up a stick, he speared a piece of venison out of the fire and walked into the woods to be alone.

NINE

Chances

The rising moon was blood-red.

Tinuva, all senses as taut as a bow-string took the colour of the large moon to be an omen, a warning from his ancestors, as it climbed over the forest behind him.

There was nothing direct to tell him of the danger, no sound of snow crunching, no scent on the frigid wind: the warning was deeper, coming from the core of what he was. He knew that humans, at times, could vaguely touch that sense, the feeling of being watched, or better yet the bond that twin brothers had, knowing what the other was thinking and feeling.

He felt hatred, an ancient hatred that stretched across centuries. He knew it as intimately as the presence of beloved friends, the memory of the sacred groves, the sight of the eternal heavens at night.

Bovai was close, very close. Stalking, reaching outward, trying to touch into his heart, and above all else calling to him.

He felt as if they were two serpents who had sighted each other at last, unblinking, staring, each trying to seek the first advantage before the lightning strike.

He was torn: the call of Bovai was like a deep longing, strangely almost like the whisper of a lover's voice that beckoned, seeking the release of passion, except that this was the passion of death.

Tinuva turned his head, gaze fixed, not seeing with his eyes, but with his soul, and the colour of the world shifted. It was no longer filled with the dark shadows of night, but instead was changing to a pale glimmer of light which settled over the frozen woods, sparkling and flashing. All was bathed in a lovely blue sheen and there were no shadows, though to a mortal standing next to him the night would seem unchanged.

He could see Bovai, advancing alone, moving without stealth, into the open, but still distant far beyond bowshot range. He knew that walk well: disdainful, bold with arrogance, confident in his power. There was more familiar about the moredhel chieftain, but he chose to not dwell on those familiar qualities. He knew the resemblances were the heart of the blood debt between them.

Each was aware of the other's presence. This was not like Kavala, who, preoccupied with other thoughts had only yesterday ridden to his well deserved doom. No, Bovai would never be so foolish, even if he were two hundred miles away, in the safety of his own dwelling, still he was always alert, always watching, for he knew that Tinuva would always be hunting.

Bovai stopped and turned his head slightly, looking straight at Tinuva.

Let it be now.

The words, of course, were not spoken, but sensed and Tinuva felt drawn by the power of them, but even as he was drawn he knew that Bovai was using all of his skills to shape the thoughts, to wing them into his soul and that there was concealed beneath them another purpose. Tinuva dared to let his attention shift for the briefest of moments and looked past Bovai.

Behind the dark elf there were others, hundreds, who thought themselves concealed, believing that the light of seeing would not reveal their presence, that all would be focused on Bovai. Amongst those of Bovai's blood there was skill and cunning, more than one moredhel staying cloaked, thoughts stilled, heads bowed so that the light which Tinuva projected in his mind would not catch their thoughts. But the simpler, darker creatures – the men, the wood goblins and trolls – in their clumsiness milled about, impatient in the freezing cold, wondering what it was that their master was about, why he had commanded them to wait while he advanced alone.

Tinuva focused his thoughts, remaining still, wishing that Bovai would come forward just another hundred paces, yet knowing that once in range their conflict would be joined and now was not yet the time. He had waited for hundreds of years: a few more days, when weighed against centuries, was nothing.

Tinuva's mind ranged out and he sensed more minds in the distance. It was expected that one day Tinuva would join the ranks of the Spellweavers, for his mind was showing more and more skill in using the native magic of his race. With bitter irony, he considered that Bovai would likely be his match in that ability, though he would never put aside the mantle of a chieftain for the ritual headdress of a shaman.

Tinuva's left hand dropped, brushing the edge of his long cloak. He swirled the cloak up, breaking the spell which in his inner eye had illuminated the forest and turned, running lightly in the way that only an elf could run, drifting through the forest like the whisper of a morning breeze, dodging from tree to tree, leaping fallen giants, startling up a doe hidden in the hollow beneath an upturned stump so that for a dozen strides they ran side by side until the frightened creature turned and bolted off in the opposite direction.

He blanked his mind, cloaking his thoughts, and he knew that even the most sensitive among the moredhel would not see him. To Bovai it would be as if he had simply vanished from the mortal realm. No Spellweaver yet, Tinuva had still cultivated their company when time permitted and had gleaned a skill or two that one his age should not yet know. Let Bovai try to work out what happened. It would gain them minutes, when they needed hours, but every minute gained got the men of the Kingdom and the Tsurani another minute further away from Bovai and his murderers.

As he ran he whistled softly, the cry an owl made when startled in the night by something that was stalking the stalker.

Gregory stepped out from behind an ancient of the forest, a fir tree so huge in girth that three men could have hidden behind it. Raising his horn, the Natalese scout blew four short notes, his personal signal which was now the warning that the enemy had been sighted and that it was time to abandon camp. He fell in beside Tinuva, running to keep up.

'He was there?' Gregory asked.

'Yes.'

They ran another fifty paces, vaulting over a fallen log, pausing for a second to look back, bows half-raised.

'Challenged you?'

'Yes. But his army was too close.'

They heard the distant thunder, horses galloping across the clearing, as Bovai sent riders to discover where the elf had fled. They listened, then heard the noise diminish as the riders were forced to move slowly through the woods.

Gregory raised his horn again and blew. There was a distant, answering blast, echoing in the cold, still air.

'Time to catch up,' Gregory said. He turned to run but Tinuva hissed softly, held up his hand, then pointed back.

The two of them slipped arrows out of their quivers, nocked them, and drew back the bowstrings.

Two riders, clearly visible in the moonlight, emerged, weaving though the trees, heads down as they dodged under the branches.

The two arrows sang out, speeding to their targets and one of the two tumbled backwards off his mount. The other cried out shrilly, his horse nearly rolling over as the dying rider tried to rein in and swing his mount around.

Within seconds Tinuva was up on the horse's haunches behind the rider, blade effortlessly drifting across the dying man's throat. He pushed him out of the saddle and scrambled to take his place.

Tinuva's whispered commands and gentle touch stilled the panicky animal, so that within seconds it was far more willing to obey the elf than it ever had been to heed the human he had replaced.

Tinuva looked over at Gregory who had gained the saddle of the second animal and was struggling to bring it under control, for both animals had been badly frightened by the scent of blood on the frigid air.

Tinuva trotted over to Gregory's side, as the animal finally obeyed the Ranger's firm hand.

'Why walk when we can ride?' Tinuva said calmly.

'Well, we better start riding and damn fast!' Gregory exclaimed, looking back over his shoulder.

Leading the way, Tinuva urged his mount to a measured gallop, weaving through the forest. Behind them they could hear the other riders approaching. They reached a low ridge and rode up to the crest. To his left Tinuva saw the encampment site and breathed a sigh of relief. The fires were still smouldering, but the camp had been abandoned. He caught a glimpse of the column beating a hasty retreat, moving up the trail, the first of the men already up past the top of the rocky outcropping.

He felt something brush past his face, plucking at the collar of his cloak and his heart froze. A hand's width lower and the arrow shot by one of Dennis's men would have killed him. His mind raced for a moment, wondering on the irony of it all, that after so long, he might die by the hand of an ally.

Gregory blew his horn again – the four-note recognition signal – and Tinuva heard Dennis's angry curses, shouting for his men to hold their arrows.

The two slid their mounts down the slope, charging past the empty encampment and up the trail. As they rounded a bend Tinuva was startled by the sight of half a dozen Tsurani blocking the way with blades drawn and he reined in hard, wondering if Dennis's warning and Gregory's horn blast was understood by them.

Asayaga was in the middle of the group. He barked an order and the swords were lowered.

Tinuva, heart still thumping, nodded his thanks.

'Tragic to kill a friend in battle by mistake when there are so many enemies to go around,' Asayaga announced in Tsurani.

The words were no sooner out of him than a startled expression clouded his face. Several of his men looked over at him in surprise.

Tinuva, equally surprised, took several seconds to respond. 'Old enemies must be friends when a greater evil looms.'

Asayaga grunted, not replying.

'Move quickly: their mounted warriors are closing. They aren't quite sure where we are but will figure it out soon enough,' Tinuva said quickly. He snapped the reins and rode forward up the trail, reaching the next turn on top of the rocky outcropping.

'Damn it. You could have been killed riding a horse like that!' Dennis cried, and then there was yet another surprise for Tinuva as Hartraft reached up and, as if to reassure himself, grabbed the elf by the forearm, squeezed tightly, then let his hand drop.

Dennis started to turn. 'I'm personally going to flay the idiot who shot that arrow.'

'No time,' Tinuva announced, trying to sound nonchalant about the whole affair. 'An honest mistake. I left on foot, you expected me to return that way. We'd better move. Gregory and I will ride ahead to make sure they don't have an advance unit up on the trail. I doubt it though. Bovai was out front with the mounted riders looking for you. The rest of his forces he ordered to follow. My little game worked: it gave us the warning we needed.'

Dennis nodded in agreement.

'You men dry, your stomachs full and your backsides warm?' Gregory asked.

There was a ripple of laughter.

He looked to the east. The large moon was two hand-spans above the horizon, a crescent, still blood red. Beneath it there was the first faint glow of approaching dawn.

'We've got a long run and a tough fight,' Dennis interjected, again assuming his usual role. 'They'll be on us soon enough. Now move!'

Tinuva urged his mount forward, up the long, sloping, ice-covered trail. 'And I think a storm is coming, so we need to be over the crest before it is full on, else we will die in the pass.'

Dennis and Asayaga gave commands and the men hurried ahead, following the trailbreakers' marks. The two scouts should already be into the pass itself, heading up into the high mountains. By late afternoon, they should be at the crest, then once over, let the storm fill the pass with snow. Then all thoughts of Bovai could be put aside for another time.

As the men moved out, Tinuva considered: within the space of half a dozen minutes death had whispered close three times, twice at the hands of friends, once from a foe that was closer to him than any who were mortal could ever guess.

He knew it was a portent and he breathed deeply, savouring the taste of this world.

'Come on, move your lazy asses, move it!'

Dennis Hartraft, gasping for breath, staggered to the top of the trail. Leaning over, he struggled against the urge to vomit, gulping down deep breaths of freezing air.

He stood up, and pushed back his helmet and wiped the sweat from his brow. Looking down the trail, he saw his men staggering forward, feet churning through the powdery snow.

'Archers to the flanks! Mark your targets carefully: don't waste your arrows on the goblins and men! Kill the trolls first, then the dark elves!'

More than one man had an empty quiver; they were running short.

He looked up at the sky. The noonday sun was riding low on the southern horizon. If it wasn't for the terror of the moment, he could have almost paused to take in the spectacular view. They had climbed several thousand feet throughout the cold morning and now the vast plain of the Broad River was spread out below them and he could easily trace out the distant road crossing up over the Yabonese Hills which they had traversed the day before. The air up here was pure and crystalline but unfortunately far too thin and it was affecting his men. Fortunately it was affecting their pursuers as well.

It had been a bitter running fight. Within a half hour of their fleeing the camp the first attack had swept up behind them and repeated assaults had hit throughout the day. There would be a break in the fighting, his men pulling back a few hundred more yards, weaving their way up the switchbacking trail, then another attack would come, there would be a pause, followed by a another pull back. Bovai's forces had paid a terrible price to press the fleeing humans. All of their human mercenaries were either dead or wounded, and the moredhel were now without any cavalry support.

Now that the switchbacks were behind them, all that was saving them was the fact that the path they were on was little more than a goat-track climbing straight up, reaching up past the tree-line. It was impossible for the enemy to flank or get ahead in such terrain as long as he slowly kept retreating: the trick was to disengage from the battle at the right moment and he could see that it was almost time to do it again.

He looked around. The mountain continued to soar upwards behind him for another half a thousand feet or more; the problem now was what he had feared for the last hour. The trail was giving out. It was all bare rock above – the thick tangle of stunted trees and bushes which had helped to secure their flanks had all but disappeared. With their backs to the top of the mountain the only tactic left was to deploy up into the boulders and make a final stand.

Looking around, he saw no sight of Tinuva or Gregory: it was as if they had simply vanished. He knew that Gregory had deliberately been keeping the elf away from the fight, pushing him forward to scout. It was strange, though, for them to have simply vanished at a time like this and it made him uneasy. He looked back down the trail and could see that the battle was again getting desperate: a column of goblins was forming up, shields forward and overhead, advancing from behind to charge past the beleaguered trolls and moredhel.

He slipped back down the trail, losing the hundred yards he had just so painfully climbed, dodging behind a boulder when several arrows came winging up from below, arcing up high and then plunging down.

The Tsurani were skilfully holding the path, deployed into squads of five-man units. Each unit would battle for several minutes, then they'd fall back, retiring to the rear and the next squad would engage. To either side of the trail, wherever it was possible to gain a foothold and a little concealment, Kingdom archers covered the approaches and acted as skirmishers to secure the flanks. Though he would never say it out loud, the two sides were working together seamlessly in this fight, both playing to their strengths, supporting each other, and several times he had seen a Kingdom or Tsurani soldier help pull someone from the other side out of a close scrape. The one-eyed Tsurani had even carried in a Kingdom soldier knocked senseless by a troll's club.

Within the first hour the moredhel had learned their bitter lesson and were now holding back after losing at least a dozen to the human archers who had every advantage of higher ground and a wind at their backs. Throughout most of the morning they had taken to driving their human and goblin allies forward for the bloody frontal assaults on the Tsurani infantry.

Not that the fight had been all one-sided: seven Kingdom and twelve Tsurani were dead, and a dozen more were wounded. As Dennis continued his slide down the path he passed Corwin who was marshalling the effort to keep the wounded moving, and given the nature of the fight on such a narrow front Dennis had finally agreed to detail off fifteen men to lend him assistance.

Slipping up behind Asayaga, who was in the second rank, Dennis grabbed him by the shoulder. 'You can't see it from here but around the corner of the trail a goblin column's getting set to charge,' he gasped. 'Get ready to pull everyone back.'

Asayaga grunted an acknowledgment.

His forward line was waiting with shields lowered. No one had approached through the switchback below them for several minutes. Asayaga barked a command.

No one moved.

Dennis, turned and started back up the path. The Tsurani knew what they were doing and Dennis realized it was best to get out of the way.

He heard a grunting moan, one of the guttural battle-chants of the goblins. The head of their column came around the bend in the trail, shields up.

Asayaga called out another command. Some of the men around him started to back up. Asayaga said a single word and more began to back up. The goblins nervously edged forward.

Suddenly the front rank of Tsurani broke completely, turned and bolted, a few of the men casting aside goblin shields they had picked up earlier in the fight. Soon the entire Tsurani unit was churning up the pathway, men shouting in alarm and panic.

The forward line of goblins cautiously lowered their shields, a few barked out taunts and began to come forward, and within seconds the entire goblin column was in hot pursuit, all semblance of order broken.

Dennis, legs trembling so that he felt he might collapse, pressed on up the path, the fleetest of the Tsurani already sprinting past him. He felt a hand grab him by the elbow as if to help pull him along and he shrugged it off. He caught glimpses of his own men falling back along either side of the narrow trail, more than one of them looking nervously at Dennis.

Straight ahead the trail all but gave out and Dennis reached the spot where he had stood only minutes before. This time he was down on his knees, gasping for air. His men had made this climb only once, but he had been up and down every step of the way, moving back and forth as the running battle ebbed and flowed. In spite of Asayaga's offer for him to sleep first, he had not laid his head down the entire night, but instead had stood watch, agreeing with Tinuva to the elf's plan to go forward as a scout and as a first warning, and then he had waited tensely for hours for the horn call that would be the alarm for them to move.

The world seemed to be out of focus. It was difficult to see, for fleeing Tsurani troops were all around him. Through a gap in their ranks he saw the swarm of goblins coming up the trail less than twenty yards away.

Asayaga shouted out a command and miraculously every Tsurani soldier fell into place, assuming his proper place in line and file. In an instant the Tsurani were charging and in spite of Dennis's orders several of his men slammed arrows into the disorganized goblin ranks, while his light skirmishers swarmed to either side of the trail.

The Tsurani hit the goblins like a battering ram, bowling over the forward ranks, sending their dying bodies crashing backwards, while Kingdom troops swarmed in on the flanks.

The slaughter was horrifying: within seconds a score of goblins were dead, or gasping out their last breaths and the rest were running in panic back down the hill.

Asayaga emerged from the ranks, a grin lighting his features as he staggered up the last few steps of the trail to stand before Dennis.

'Stupid creatures, you would think the same trick would not work twice.'

Dennis nodded in agreement.

Asayaga looked past him and his features dropped. 'The trail. What now?'

'We go up into the rocks.'

'I thought there was a pass?'

Dennis did not reply.

From further down the mountain it did indeed look as if there was a pass, but that had only led them though the first layer of the mountain range; this higher second barrier had been concealed beyond. It was territory he had never ventured into and even Gregory had seemed a bit off-balance at first when they had glimpsed the higher range beyond. Only Tinuva had pushed onward without comment.

'Where are the elf and the Natalese?'

'I don't know.'

'You don't know? So what are we to do?'

'I told you, we go up into the rocks.'

'And I thought the goblins were stupid. You lead us up here? Better we had never crossed the river.'

'I didn't ask you to come along on this,' Dennis snapped. 'You could have stayed on the other side of the damned river for all I care. We're here, this is it, so get used to it!'

'That is your answer, Hartraft? If we survive this day, tonight, at sunset, we settle things. I will not march another day with you if this is what your leadership brings us to.'

'Fine then, at sunset, damn you.'

'Might I interrupt?'

It was Gregory.

Dennis looked up at him, not sure if he should be glad or start swearing about the fix they were in.

'We have the trail.'

'Where does it go?' Dennis asked.

'That's just it,' Gregory replied. 'I'm not quite sure.'

'I thought you knew these mountains?'

'I never said that. You'll recall I said I might know a way, but I've never been up this far before. The one pass I was certain about was the road leading up from the bridge held by the Dark Brothers.'

Dennis stood up wearily. 'If this involves any more climbing . . .' he grumbled.

Gregory had already turned his horse, pausing to look back down the side of the mountain. 'We'd better move sharply. They're deploying out.'

Dennis looked over the edge of the steep slope and saw dark figures moving outward, all of them dismounted. There were hundreds of them, and this time the moredhel were joining in. *It is simple enough,* Dennis realized, *now that we are pinned down they simply spread out, don't attack frontally, and go to sweep around the flanks, then close in.*

Several of his men were throwing rocks and shouting angry taunts, but most were too far gone with exhaustion to react, simply falling in behind Gregory and Dennis because that was what they had always done. Gregory led the way, the trail running flat and parallel to the mountain for fifty yards then turning sharply around the flank of a massive boulder.

As they turned the side of the boulder Dennis felt a gust of cold wind and looking straight ahead he saw a narrow cleft. There were mountains several hundred yards beyond, but it appeared as if the slope ahead dropped straight down.

Once past the boulder Gregory stopped and dismounted, motioning for Dennis to follow. After another dozen yards the trail turned again and Dennis felt his stomach knot up. A few more paces and it was a vertical drop of five hundred feet or more. He had always hated heights and instinctively he backed up.

'Well that's just great,' he gasped. 'Now what, we jump?'

'Look,' Gregory said, pointing forward and to their left.

The trail, clinging to the north side of the canyon continued onward for a hundred yards, and then ended at a rope bridge that spanned the chasm.

'What in the name of the gods?' Dennis asked, for once caught completely off guard and willing to admit it.

'Tinuva remembered there had been a trail here, and long ago a bridge, but it was destroyed a hundred years or more ago. Someone's rebuilt it.'

'Where is Tinuva?'

'On the other side. He already signalled back that the trail continues on. This is the way out,' Gregory announced with a grin.

Dennis nodded, swallowing hard as he eyed the spindly-looking bridge which was nothing more than two ropes for hand-holds and two more beneath with uneven boards as a narrow walkway.

Asayaga was suddenly at his side, grinning. 'What are we waiting for?' he announced. 'Let's move.'

Dennis nodded, and without comment followed Gregory who continued to lead his horse.

'You're not going to try and get that beast across are you?'

'Tinuva got his across.' Even as he spoke, Gregory removed his cape and folded it over the horse's head, covering his eyes.

Dennis said nothing more as the Natalese scout reached the bridge and without hesitation stepped forward, the bridge sagging and groaning as the horse followed.

'Space the men about ten feet apart, I'm not quite sure how much this thing will hold.'

'You with a horse, we'll figure it out,' Dennis replied, watching as Gregory crossed the bridge, ambling along as if he didn't have a care in the world.

A cold wind whistled through the canyon, causing the bridge to rock. Backing up against the wall of the narrow trail, Dennis ordered the lead men to get across and one by one they started.

Gradually the two commands crossed, until finally there were only half a dozen men left by the boulder, one of them Asayaga's one-eyed Strike Leader who started shouting.

'They're closing in,' Asayaga announced. 'It will be tight.'

Asayaga shouted for his sergeant to move and the last of the men raced along the narrow, icy trail, Dennis watching nervously, expecting to see more than one slip and plummet to his doom.

Asayaga pushed the last of his men on to the bridge then turned to Dennis.

'After you, Hartraft.'

'You first,' Dennis growled.

'Afraid?' Asayaga asked with a grin and then his features changed in an instant, shield going up.

An arrow slammed into it and Dennis crouched down behind the barrier as two more arrows winged in.

'Now!' Asayaga cried and he jumped on to the bridge and started to run, urging the men ahead of him to move.

Dennis followed, making the first thirty feet without slowing.

Looking back over his shoulder he saw five black clad archers coming through the cleft by the boulder, and spreading out along the trail. Behind them were heavy infantry, shields raised.

The archers were already drawing their next flight of arrows and Dennis continued to run, oblivious to the swaying of the bridge.

An arrow painfully creased the back of his leg. The man in front of Asayaga shrieked, clutched at his side and pitched over. His motion caused the bridge to sway violently and for a second Dennis thought that one of the ropes had been severed and the structure was collapsing. The Tsurani soldier fell and Dennis watched in horror as the man tumbled head over heels, shrieking in pain and terror, his cries growing fainter until finally they were silenced, cut off by a sickening thud as the soldier's body burst on the sharp rocks five hundred feet below.

Dennis froze, clutching the ropes, feeling as if his legs were about to give way.

'Come on!'

He looked up. It was Asayaga.

Another arrow snapped past and he took one step, then another and was finally running again. Men on the far side of the gorge were shouting, cheering them on, the two captains running, arrows whispering to either side, the only thing saving them the gusty winds of the canyon which threw the arrows off their course.

He plunged the last dozen feet up the slippery path and gladly took the hand of Gregory who pulled him up the last few feet.

Turning, he looked back across the canyon. Black-clad troops swarmed on the other side but none were foolish enough to dare to venture on to the bridge in spite of the urging of their commanders to press the attack.

For several minutes the two sides traded insults and gestures, Dennis watching as the Tsurani made strange motions with their hands and fingers and shouted what were obviously the foulest of insults.

Finally, Gregory pulled out his hatchet and started to cut at the ropes. In another minute the bridge collapsed.

Asayaga came up to Dennis's side.

'Do you know where we are?'

'No.'

'Now what? If you don't know, why did you let him cut the bridge?'

'Do you honestly think we can go back that way?' Dennis asked wearily.

Asayaga looked across the gorge and finally shook his head.

Their men were already moving out, following the trail, having grown tired of taunting their tormentors. On this side of the chasm, the trail sloped downward and was well worn, a pleasure after the gut-straining climb. Turning a corner the chasm on their right disappeared as the trail weaved through a field of boulders and then dropped down into a broad open path. Dennis and Asayaga stopped in wonder.

Before them was a broad open valley, its upper slopes cloaked in heavy fir trees, a rich and fertile land which seemed to stretch onward for miles. Above the treeline high jagged peaks rose like guardians, hemming the valley in on all sides. Dennis sensed this valley had not been touched by war and that for the moment it meant safety and rest.

He looked over at Asayaga who stood as he did, in silent awe. Then their eyes met and both wondered what the other was thinking.

Bovai stood in silence, watching as the last of his foes disappeared.

He had heard rumours of this place but had never seen it. He turned to his tracker. 'How do we catch up to them?' he snapped.

'We can't.'

'What do you mean we can't?'

'This gorge cuts through the mountains for miles in either direction. Even if we go down into it, you can see it is vertical on the other side. They'll leave a watcher, one man alone could stop all of us.'

'So we ride around it.'

'That's just it, sire. It's miles or more around till we find another way, *if* we can find it. Another storm on the wind and even now the passes might be closed.'

'We find it!'

The tracker sighed inwardly, but let no expression betray his feelings. He looked at his master and nodded. 'First back to the bridge, my lord. That is the way.'

Bovai looked at the fallen span, as if willing it back into place. He knew that they were in alien lands. He stared at the mountains before him, as if committing them to memory forever. To the east, arching off along the northern side of the valley he saw below, he knew the Teeth of the World rose up, impassable for the most part. On the other side would be the great Edder Forest, home to the barbaric glamedhel. The moredhel of the Northlands were no less bold than his own clan, and they gave those woods wide berth. Bovai cast his eyes to the southern peaks that ringed the other side of the valley and realized that even if another pass existed from the Kingdom, the hills around it would be alive with stockades and castles garrisoned for the winter by men from Yabon and Tyr-Sog.

Back to the bridge, and along the Broad River, around the Edder Forest, and seek a pass in the mountains through the winter snow. Bovai knew it might take months to find another way into this valley.

One of the trackers said, 'My chieftain?'

Quietly, Bovai replied, 'Someone got into that valley, years ago, so that they could be on the other side of this gorge, and take the rope thrown from this side. That means there must be another way.'

The tracker nodded.

'Back to the bridge, and we start looking for that way.'

Bovai looked at his troops. He knew questions would be asked around the fires this night. Victory and vengeance had to be won, no matter how long it took, otherwise he knew with a grim certainty he would be dead at the hands of his master. Murad would brook no insult to his clan, and when he learned it was Tinuva who ran with the humans . . .

Bovai nodded once, and turned, leading his men back through the narrow gap in the rocks. Best not to think of Murad discovering Tinuva's part in this until the moment when he could present the Paramount Chieftain with both Hartraft's and Tinuva's heads.

Past freezing and injured goblins he strode, his mind lost in dreams of bloody vengeance, and none who saw his expression doubted for a moment that the chase was not over, but was merely postponed.

TEN

Valley

The valley was rich and fertile.

The high mountain peaks which surrounded it blocked off most of the snow so that the tall grass in the pastures was still exposed and stood nearly waist-high.

The stream they were following bubbled over rocks and swirled into eddying pools and more than one of his men exclaimed how they saw fish just waiting to be caught. Even for the unpractised eyes of the Tsurani, game signs were abundant and all were commenting on the fact, pointing out the does grazing in distant fields, wild mountain goats and the tracks of bear and elk.

Dennis asked, 'How can this place exist?'

Tinuva knelt at the edge of the stream and said, 'Feel the water.'

Dennis did as he was bid and exclaimed, 'It's warm!'

Asayaga knelt next to him and after he had plunged his hand into the water, said, 'I would not call this warm, but it lacks the icy bite I would expect from melted snow.'

'Exactly,' said Dennis.

Tinuva pointed to the north-west. 'Above us lies Akenkala, a volcano. In my youth she spewed liquid rock and filled the sky with smoke that lasted for more than a year.' He stood up, wiping his hand on his tunic. 'She sleeps now, but there is still fire within her.'

'Which heats the water running down into this valley,' said Asayaga.

Dennis looked around. 'The air here is warmer than it is to the south, in Yabon.'

Asayaga nodded. 'It is a wondrous place.'

'The bounty of this place is beyond anything I've seen,' said Tinuva. 'We passed orchards as we scouted.'

They resumed walking. The men were not lulled by the relative kindness of the environment. They were still in enemy territory, and it would be foolish to expect whoever lived here to be a friend.

For they knew *someone* live here.

They had yet to find a single person, but the valley was clearly inhabited. They had passed three farmsteads, constructed of heavy logs, all of them still intact. In the fireplace of one the fire was still smouldering and in the barn a dozen chickens were to be found in a coop.

As the afternoon progressed the men became more and more uneasy at the eerie silence, the sense that they were walking through a realm of ghosts.

Tinuva and Gregory had ridden ahead and Dennis finally called a halt, moving the men up towards the treeline to rest, but forbade them to light fires. The afternoon sun, however, was relatively warm and in the still air it was actually rather comfortable. Soon nearly all the men had drifted into an exhausted sleep, including Dennis.

Brother Corwin was quietly tending to the wounded, seeing to their comfort, working with skilled hands to clean an arrow-wound in the arm of one of Asayaga's men, who wandered over to watch.

The priest deftly bandaged the wound, laid out a blanket for the soldier to rest upon and stood up, wiping his hands. He saw Asayaga watching.

'All these men have been pushed beyond the limit,' Corwin said slowly, speaking in the manner one does when talking to a foreigner and is not yet sure of his skill with the language.

Asayaga grunted and said nothing in reply.

'Even the men without hurts need several days with a roof over their heads, plenty of hot food and sleep. If I could get the wounded into shelter I think I could save all of them as well.'

'Perhaps there is something ahead,' Asayaga ventured.

'This is a strange place. It's on no map.'

'You have a map?'

'Ones I saw in the monastery,' Corwin replied quickly. 'I studied them before coming up to join the army.'

'Where are you from?'

'Many places, but from Ran originally. Why?'

'Just curious. How far from here?'

'A month or more by caravan.'

'And this is your first time in battle?'

'No,' said the monk, obviously not wishing to repeat his personal history. 'I've seen a scuffle or two. I joined the order late, I was in my thirties when I got the calling to serve.'

'Why?'

'You are full of questions, Tsurani.'

Asayaga smiled. 'It is my job to learn. I understand there was some trouble regarding you. You didn't start with this unit, they found you and as a result a close friend of Hartraft was killed.'

'How do you know that?'

'I have ears, I listen when the Kingdom troops talk. They all speak of it.'

'Two of my brothers and I were coming up to join the army. We got lost. My brothers were captured by one of your units. I fled and stumbled into Hartraft's company. I ruined a surprise attack they were planning and in the chaos that followed Hartraft's closest friend and advisor was killed.'

Asayaga nodded thoughtfully. 'Which unit of my army?'

'How am I suppose to know? You all look alike to me.'

'You all look alike to me, except for the Natalese scout. Which unit?'

'I don't know. Why?'

'If Hartraft destroyed one of the units of my army I'm curious to know.'

'It all happened so quickly,' Corwin said slowly, as if the memory of the incident was still painful. 'One moment the forest was empty, the next Tsurani troops were everywhere and I ran.'

'Their helmets. Some are marked with feathered plumes, others with coloured cloth wrapped around the top,' and as he spoke Asayaga pointed to the strip of faded blue cloth tied to the back of his helmet.

'I don't remember.'

'Was it yellow? I know that Zugami's company was on patrol. Maybe pale green of Catuga, or the red feather of Wanutama?'

Corwin looked thoughtful. 'I think green. Who was this Catuga?'

'Was?'

'They were all killed; you know that don't you?'

Asayaga lowered his head. 'Green then.'

'Yes, I'm almost certain.'

'I see. The leader, Catuga, he had a spiked helmet and was tall for one of my race, as tall almost as Hartraft. He was an old friend of mine. Did Hartraft kill him?'

'Yes. I remember seeing that. I saw Hartraft kill him towards the end of the fight.'

Asayaga nodded and looked over to where Dennis slept.

'Scouts coming in!'

It was young Richard whom Dennis had detailed with an unfortunate half dozen others to stand watch while the rest of them slept.

Instantly men were awake, sitting up, looking to the west. Down along the brook which they had been following Asayaga could see the two riders slowing, turning aside, and coming up the hill to the edge of the woods.

At once Dennis was awake and on his feet and Asayaga fell in by his side. He could hear Dennis groaning softly as he walked, stretching, trying to shake off the exhaustion.

Gregory and Tinuva reined in and dismounted.

'Two miles ahead. A stockade. Fairly new from the looks of it, a good position, set on top of a hill, a dozen or so farmsteads surrounding it.'

'Occupied?' asked Dennis.

The scout nodded. 'Humans.'

'They know we're here?'

'Fair to assume so. The gate was closed, no one was in the fields or farmhouses outside the stockade.'

Dennis rubbed his chin as he thought.

'They undoubtedly had a watcher on the bridge,' Asayaga offered. 'Strange they didn't cut it.'

'Perhaps they didn't have time. Tinuva and I ran the risk of rushing it when we first saw it. We saw footprints but they were boy-size.'

'They know we're here,' Dennis mused aloud, head lowered. 'We need shelter. Do you think we could take it?'

'If they've got twenty men in there, armed with bows, they'll kill half of us.'

'A night attack then.'

'What I was thinking.'

'Why attack?' Asayaga asked.

'What?' and Dennis turned to look at him.

'We could talk, make an offer.'

'We are a good fifty miles beyond the frontier,' Dennis announced as if trying to explain something basic to a child. 'Anyone up here is outside the law and is to be treated as such.'

'The law?' Asayaga said with a bitter laugh. 'You call what we are doing to each other the law, and people up here are the lawless? Have we seen any sign of the presence of these Dark Brothers here?' And as he spoke the question he looked at Tinuva.

The elf slowly shook his head. 'Nothing. I've seen only human signs since we came to the valley floor. There is a chance, though, they could be allied to the moredhel.'

Asayaga looked sceptical. 'Do you think that? If they were allied to the Forest Demons they should have been waiting for us at the bridge. Surely those behind us would have sent one fast rider around us while we were down in the foothills, to gain their help in blocking the bridge. I think those who pursued us were as surprised by the bridge as we were. The way they attacked frontally tells me they had no knowledge of the terrain above us or what was at the top of the trail. Two archers could have stopped us from crossing. I think these people are hiding, had no idea of our approach and we are a very unwelcome surprise.'

Tinuva was silent for a moment as if deep in thought, and then finally nodded his head. 'You have a logical mind, Asayaga. And wisdom.'

'I see where this is going,' Dennis said wearily.

* * *

Dennis looked over at Asayaga as the two of them walked up the trail. They were in the open now, in the killing zone of open fields around the stockade. Tinuva, as always, was right in his observations: the wooden stockade was somewhat weathered, but was not more than several years old. Smoke coiled from a chimney of the long house inside the small fortress. Dennis could see faces peering over the wall, but it was hard to tell who they were.

'Women and old men, mostly,' Dennis said. 'Listen to me, the moment the first arrow flies we run and if you get hit, blood debt or not I'm leaving you. This scheme borders on outright stupidity. There is no way in hell they are going to swing open their gates to over a hundred armed men.'

'Blood debt?'

'You know damn well what I mean. Fishing me out of the river.'

Asayaga laughed softly.

'So you honour that, too.'

'I honour nothing, Asayaga. I think this idea is mad, but if we can capture this place intact, without losing any more men, or worse yet having it burn down around us, we just might survive the next few days. That's the only reason I'm coming along with you.'

'It's me coming along with you,' Asayaga growled. 'You're the Kingdom soldier, I'm the alien invader, as you put it when we discussed this idea.'

'I need you along to help explain what we want.'

'Not another step closer!'

The voice, clearly that of an old man, caused them to stop.

'Clear out of here right now, or my archers will riddle you with arrows.'

Dennis cautiously lowered the shield loaned to him by Asayaga's sergeant and raised his right hand. 'I wish to parley.'

'Clear out, I tell you.'

'I am Dennis Hartraft, of the House of Hartraft. My father and grandfather before him held the royal warrant as wardens of the marches before the coming of the Tsurani. I come without weapon drawn to talk.'

'Hartraft? They're all dead these nine years. Go away.'

168

Dennis lowered his shield, letting the butt rest on the ground. With his free hand he ever so slowly unbuttoned his cape and let it fall to the ground, revealing the faded colours of the Hartraft crest on his dirty tunic. It was not the tunic he usually wore on patrol, but Gregory had suggested that he pull it out of his pack and put it on.

'By these colours,' he pointed at his chest, 'you will see that I am who I claim to be. I am rightful warden of the marches.'

'Step closer.'

Dennis gave a sidelong glance at Asayaga and did as requested, stopping when he felt that to venture any closer was suicide. He carefully scanned the battlement, looking for the slightest movement that would indicate a bow being drawn.

Asayaga advanced with him, but kept his shield up.

'That short fellow beside you?'

'I am Force Commander Asayaga of House Tondora, of Clan Kanazawai.'

'Why would Tsurani and Kingdom soldiers march side by side? You are deserters and renegades. Clear out. You are liars: I heard that no Hartraft would tolerate a Tsurani to live.'

Again the sidelong glance from Asayaga.

'How do you know what a Hartraft would do?' Dennis asked.

'I just know,' the old man cried in a peevish voice. 'Now move it, you scum-eaters, you sons of drunken whores, you rump-kissing pasty-faced boys not fit to suck the pig-dung off my toes. No man who claims to be a Hartraft would walk with a damned Tsurani who looks like the offspring of a cretinous dwarf and a one-legged disease-addled harlot.'

Asayaga bristled, raised his shield slightly, obviously ready to respond to the insult to his lineage.

'Don't move,' Dennis hissed, and even as he spoke there was a puzzled look on his face as if trying to remember something.

Asayaga, features turning red with anger struggled to maintain control.

'The Tsurani by my side is indeed a sworn enemy,' Dennis replied. 'But there is a darker enemy afoot. Whoever it was you had watching the rope bridge will tell you that.'

'He saw only an elf and a Natalese before he fled to bring warning.'

'We are pursued by the Dark Brotherhood. Tsurani and Kingdom soldiers will always lower their swords against each other and join to fight such a foe.'

'Damn you,' and there was a tense shrillness to the challenging voice. 'If they are chasing you now you've brought them down upon us! Clear out! I'll grant you the rights of parley no longer. Clear out, you sons of a herder who sleeps with his goats because they remind him of his sister!'

'Damn foul-mouthed fool,' Asayaga hissed. 'Maybe you were right, Hartraft. Once it's dark we storm the place.'

Dennis, however, let his shield drop to the ground and stepped forward another pace.

It was the wonderful insults that had triggered something. A memory of long ago, of boyhood, a memory of hearing such phrases, cherishing them, and repeating them to his friends, until one day his father overheard him and washed his mouth out with soured milk.

'I know that voice. Wolfgar, is that you?'

The voice did not reply.

'Damn it. Wolfgar? I remember you now. When I was a boy you use to chant the old ballads for my grandfather. You were the finest of bards of the northern frontier.'

Dennis took another few steps forward and cleared his throat.

'Kinsmen die, cattle die, I myself shall die,
All that shall live after me,
When I go to the halls of my sires,
Are the songs that Wolfgar shall chant of the glory won
    in battle.'

He proclaimed the words in the old way, a deep baritone chant, his voice carrying far across the fields.

'You wrote those words,' Dennis said with a grin. 'I remember it well, you pox-eaten offspring of a pus-licking dog.'

There was no response until finally the gate cracked open and a wizened old man, leaning on a ornately carved and twisted staff slowly shuffled out.

It took more than a minute for him to cross the few dozen yards to where Dennis stood. He was so hunched over that the crown of his bald, liver-spotted head came barely to Dennis's shoulder. Like an ageing buzzard he craned his neck, twisting sideways so he could look up into Dennis's eyes.

'Oh, horse shit,' Wolfgar sighed. 'It *is* you.'

Dennis respectfully lowered his head in a formal bow. 'You were the greatest of bards ever to visit the Hartraft Keep.'

'Bountiful was the table of your grandsire,' Wolfgar said, his voice weak but suddenly revealing the richness of the training in his craft, 'for there is still fat at the root of my heart from the feasts he gave in my honour.' Bones creaking, he turned slightly to look at Asayaga. 'What in the name of all the devils is that? Is that little man typical of them, these Tsurani I hear of?'

'He is the captain of the band that joined my unit.'

Dennis could see Asayaga stiffen slightly and Wolfgar cackled.

'Proud as a peacock with a new feather sticking out of his ass, this Tsurani.'

'I did not join him,' Asayaga snapped. 'We have an alliance.'

'Oh, an alliance is it?' and Wolfgar's features clouded. 'Then you spoke the truth. The Dark Brothers are chasing you.'

'Yes.'

'Oh damn you,' Wolfgar sighed wearily. 'They suspected some of us were hiding hereabouts, but never bothered to look too hard, being troubled by other things. Now they'll be on us.'

'My men,' Dennis said and then he caught Asayaga's baleful gaze. 'Our men. We've been on the run for days. We need shelter, food, a place for our wounded to heal. I can offer you nothing in return but my bond one day to repay you. I ask this in memory of my father and grandfather who were honoured to call you their friend.'

'And if I refuse?'

Dennis drew closer, leaning over. 'I'll have to storm this place, Wolfgar and take it,' he whispered sadly. 'It's either that or my men will die. And you know the Hartrafts well enough to know we honour the pledge to our troops to see to their needs first. Don't make me fight you and your friends inside.'

Wolfgar sighed in the way only an old man could, the raspy whistle of his breath revealing an infinite weariness with the ways of the world. He craned his neck further around, his squinting gaze focused on the western sky. 'Storm coming again. Maybe it will block the passes for a while.'

Dennis followed his gaze and saw the wisps of high clouds beginning to darken the early evening sky. The old man was right, by morning it would be snowing again. 'I need shelter now,' he said and this time there was a cold insistence to his voice. 'I'll ask only one more time as a friend.' He paused and then shook his head. 'I'd prefer it if we clasped hands in memory of my sires who were your friends and patrons long ago. Once the storm is passed and my men rested we'll clear out and try to throw the Dark Brothers off from you.'

'No, it's too late for that now,' Wolfgar replied. 'The damage is done.'

He squinted, looking at Asayaga again.

'Someone as short as you most likely won't eat much anyhow. Come on, you bastards, bring your men inside.'

ELEVEN

Respite

The morning was cold.

Dennis Hartraft leaned against the wall of Wolfgar's stockade, cloak pulled tight around his shoulders, hood up to block out the cold wind sweeping down from the west.

He wondered if he'd ever really be warm again. The world was forever cold it seemed, seeping into his bones, and his heart. He knew it was a cold of the mind, not the body, for even though it was now winter in this valley, the cold he felt on the wind was nothing compared to the bitter freezing they had endured the last three days of their chase. Then Dennis reconsidered: not a cold of the mind, but a cold in his soul.

Perhaps it was Wolfgar who triggered it, memories better left dead . . .

A long-ago winter morning standing on the battlement wall, watching the first snow of winter drifting down, the wonder of it all for a child of seven, heavy flakes swirling, a bard kneeling by his side, laughing as he caught the flakes on his tongue or held out his mittens to catch one, then hold it up close to look at its intricate design until it melted away.

He remembered so clearly the sound of laughter, looking down into the courtyard below, a little girl running in circles, arms wide, shouting that she was a snowflake riding on the wind, the bard chuckling softly, telling him he knew a secret, that the little girl liked him.

Years later, again a snowfall and the little girl had grown, and they were to be married, standing arm in arm on the battlement, both of them sharing the memory of the bard, laughing, wondering if there was a way he could be found and invited to perform for their wedding.

And yet another snowfall, the flicker of fire, the screams . . .

He lowered his head, pushing that thought away. *Never let that back in, never.*

'Remind you of something?'

Dennis took a deep breath, blinking hard, his features falling back into the mask he presented to life. He turned.

Wolfgar was ever so slowly climbing the steps to the battlement, staff wobbling, the old man hanging on to it with both hands, taking one step at a time. Dennis almost reached out to help him, but knew better: old men had their pride, especially this one.

At last Wolfgar was at his side, hood drawn up over his head, frail body wrapped in heavy layers of furs. He looked up and smiled crookedly. His lips were blue and Dennis knew that wasn't from the cold, for his breath came in a raspy gurgle and his pale eyes were watery.

'You shouldn't be out in the cold like this,' Dennis offered.

'Damn you, it's a life covered in offal when I have to start taking advice from a lad who I once pushed off my lap because his swaddling clothes were leaking on me'. Wolfgar laughed and shook his head. 'I asked if standing up there reminded you of something, you seemed lost in thought.'

'Just waiting for Gregory and Tinuva to return.'

'There are some things that never change with a man – the boy still locked inside. Even when you were seven you use to stand like that, shoulders hunched, hands clasped in front of you, always watching. Reminded me of a snowy day, the two of us watching the first storm of the season, and I told you that Gwenynth liked you. How your eyes sparkled even though you were a proud lad of seven and would not admit that girls were of any interest yet.'

Dennis looked away.

'I heard what happened to her, to your father and grandfather.'

Dennis felt a hand on his shoulder. He wanted to shrug it off but couldn't.

'My heart was with you, lad. I wept for you. Your old grandfather always wanted to die in a damn good fight, and your father, well, he never had a chance to rule in his own right but I heard he died sword in hand. But for you, I wept.'

He fell silent, not mentioning her death. Dennis closed his eyes . . .

The begging, the pleading for her not to let go, his fumbling to stop the bleeding, to somehow force her soul back into her body and that smile that lit her features as she slipped away, as if she was trying to console a little boy who didn't understand, that it would work out in the end . . . but it never did.

'It was nine years ago,' Dennis whispered, using every ounce of effort to keep control of his voice.

'In some matters time is meaningless. For an elf like Tinuva, nine years is but a moment. Memory of loss can linger for an eternity. I know, I use to sing about it often enough.' Wolfgar hawked and spat noisily, removing his hand from Dennis's shoulder to wipe his mouth.

Dennis looked over at him. 'Let it drop,' he snapped. 'It was a long time ago. No song, not even yours can bring them back, except in memory, and I prefer those memories buried.'

Wolfgar nodded. 'My eyes are all but gone, young Hartraft. I didn't see Jurgen with you.'

Dennis sighed. 'Dead. Killed last week.'

'Ahh.' Wolfgar spat again. 'There was a man who could shake the dice.' There was a tremor to his voice. 'Is there anyone left from the old days?'

'The war took them all.' Dennis's tone indicated clearly enough that he didn't wish to say more.

There was a long silence of several moments. The two old friends watched as the heavy flakes gently swirled.

Dennis looked back at the long house where all the men were sleeping. Wolfgar's great hall was a heavy building of logs that stretched for over thirty paces. On the other side of the courtyard were stables, some workshops, and at the far end a detached kitchen, connected by a stone corridor to the long house so that if a fire started it would not destroy the entire dwelling. It was a fortress typical of the frontier, enough to keep a small band of marauders out, but against an army like Bovai's it would fall in a matter of hours.

It was, however, the difference between life and death for Dennis and the men with him.

After being allowed in, the men had built up roaring fires to warm the long house and all had collapsed into exhausted slumber. He had even managed a few hours' rest until he was awoken by Tinuva, who suggested that a scout should be sent back to the gorge, just to make sure that their pursuers had truly given up the chase for now and were not attempting to somehow get a party across so that the bridge could be rebuilt. So shortly after midnight Tinuva and Gregory had ridden back out. Unable to sleep, Dennis decided to keep watch until their return.

'They're all asleep in there, snoring and breaking wind,' Wolfgar announced. 'Gods' how they are stinking up the place! A hundred men in there, a tight fit, with a dozen more wounded packed into the blacksmith's shop. What in the name of Kahooli's Loins am I to do with them all?'

'Kicking us out now, I don't think my men would go along with it.'

'That Tsurani leader, Ass-you-gag.'

'Asayaga.'

'However you say the bastard's name. How by Astalon's Blood did you ever fall in with them?'

Dennis briefly recounted their tale and Wolfgar nodded appraisingly.

'Shrewd move. When do you plan to kill him?'

'Once this is over.'

'When is that?'

'I'm not sure now,' Dennis said. 'At first I figured it'd last a day at most. Now I just don't know.'

'Can you trust him not to stab you in the back?'

'Trust a Tsurani?' Dennis asked, incredulous.

The question had never been asked so directly since all this started. He realized he had been, in general, thinking minute by minute,

176

always keeping a watchful eye for the first false move which had yet to come, but not seriously contemplating that this arrangement could go on for weeks, even months.

'In their own way they're honourable I guess,' Dennis finally ventured. 'They don't torture prisoners, they kill the wounded cleanly as we do.'

'That's a mark on their side,' Wolfgar said quietly.

'He needs me more than I need him now.'

'How's that?'

'I know the way back, he doesn't.'

'Do you? The bridge is down. Do you know the way back?'

Dennis looked at his old friend, and then at the surrounding peaks brushed with the first light of dawn. Even as he looked at them the light blurred and softened. The overarching clouds sweeping in from the west blanketed what little blue sky was left on the eastern horizon. The flurries began to thicken.

'Like I said yesterday, a big storm coming,' Wolfgar announced. 'With luck it will close the last of the passes. Now answer my question, Hartraft. Do you know the way?'

Dennis shook his head. He had never ventured this far north before.

'Then you know nothing more than the Tsurani. But you still haven't answered the question, boy.'

'I was a boy twenty years ago, Wolfgar,' Dennis replied sharply.

Wolfgar threw back his head and cackled like a demented old bird. 'At my age, anyone who can still remember to button his trousers after making water is a boy. Now answer me: can you trust him not to stab you and your men in the back?'

'Yes, damn it,' Dennis snapped. 'They seem to have this thing, this code in how they fight duels. When the time comes he'll shout some sort of challenge first, the others will back up, and we will fight. Once that's settled I guess the general slaughter begins.'

'Can you take him?'

'In a fair fight?'

'Like the one you described. Not in the woods, not in the night, but deliberate, out in the open, one on one with only blades.'

Dennis hesitated.

177

'You're not sure, are you?'

Dennis shook his head. 'I've watched him,' He said. 'He's as swift as a cat – he cut two goblins in the flash of an eye, the head of the first had yet to even hit the ground and the guts of the second were already spilling. He's the fastest I've ever seen.' Dennis hesitated. 'Even Jurgen in his prime would have had a hard time taking him.'

'That's saying something,' Wolfgar replied. 'I bet on that old bastard more than once and won – bar-room brawl, duel of honour, nothing could touch him.'

'Something finally did,' Dennis said, his gaze distant.

'What will you do?' Wolfgar pressed.

'Fight him when the time comes.'

'That will be a show,' Wolfgar snorted. 'Tell me, do you want to beat him?'

'What the hell kind of question is that?'

'Some men, when they've lost too much become fey. They don't know it, but already the gods of the dead have touched them. Their memories dwell so much with those who have crossed over that in their inner heart they wish to cross as well and therefore place themselves upon the path unknowingly. Dennis, have you become fey?'

Dennis shook his head. 'That's madness.'

Wolfgar laughed. 'The whole world is mad right now. Not fifty miles south of here the Kingdom and the Tsurani are fighting over gods know what when I half suspect if the damn royals of both sides sat down and drained a keg together it'd soon be straightened out. Fifty miles north of here moredhel hack one another up for sport, and you sit here and talk about madness. Dennis, you haven't answered me, do you want to win?'

'Of course I want to win, to live. My men – if I'm killed in the opening move it might destroy their chance. I'm pledged to get my men back. I've done half a hundred patrols since the war started and always we get back.'

'We. What about *you*, do you always come back? How much of you stays behind with each of these patrols of yours?'

'You speak in riddles, Wolfgar.'

'I'm a bard, that's part of the trade at times. Do you like this Ass-you?'

'Asayaga.'

'Do you like him?'

Dennis looked at Wolfgar in surprise. 'Your questions are addled.' He regretted the word even as he said it.

Wolfgar, however, chuckled. Then, coughing, he leaned over, gasping until he finally caught his breath. 'You respect the way they fight, I know that. I heard some of your men speak of it last night before they settled in – grudging praise for the Tsurani skill in battle.'

'They're good. At least they're good in a stand-up fight in the open. Catch them by surprise in the woods and you have them every time, but a stand-up infantry against infantry and you'd pay a terrible price. I think we'd have been overwhelmed retreating up here if it hadn't been for them. There weren't fifty arrows left in my entire command, my men were collapsing from the cold and exhaustion.'

'I dare say the Tsurani are saying the same about you right now. They know they'd all be dead back at poor old Brendan's Stockade if you hadn't wandered in. They know as well your skill in the woods: they respect it, and deep down they fear it. So we have two sides here who both respect and fear each other.' Wolfgar laughed. 'Damn, how the gods love to play jokes. I've seen marriages like this – hell my third one was damn near identical to what you now got. So now you're stuck with each other.'

Dennis nodded. 'If I can keep the peace.'

'You will. That Ass You, or whatever it is he calls himself, you could find worse allies out here. Hell, better an enemy you can trust than a friend you aren't sure of. Try and extend your agreement. But damn my soul, if you can't, take your argument somewhere else: I don't want my long house turned into a slaughter pen.' He hesitated and looked over at Dennis with a calculating smile. 'But then again, your rotting bodies piled up outside my gate might buy off the Dark Brothers when they finally show up.'

Dennis started to reply but Wolfgar held up his hand.

'I might be a renegade bard with a price on my head, but I honour old memories, Dennis Hartraft.'

Dennis said nothing for a moment then finally he looked up.

'Your story? I haven't heard a damn thing about you since the King's warrant for your head was handed to my grandfather. Hell, I was still just a stripling then.'

Wolfgar laughed. 'Twenty years. That's what I get for composing bad verse about the pustulating sores on the royal buttocks.'

'Well it never would have started if you hadn't been seen jumping out of the window of the favourite royal consort,' Dennis replied. 'Prince Rodrick, now our King, is as you may have noticed, mad, or so they say. That woman was his favourite. Of all the women to stoke your lust.'

'I'd prefer to think that my troubles arose from art rather that lust.'

'I remember the day a squadron of royal troops arrived, angry as hornets, figuring our place would be where you'd choose to hide out.'

'I don't bring trouble on to friends.'

'My grandfather laughed so damn hard when he heard the story he swore he'd fight the prince himself if you came to us.'

'Like I said, I don't bring trouble on to friends.'

'So what happened then?'

'I decided it was wise to make my precious body scarce. I have an aversion to hangings, drawings and quarterings, and worst of all the litigators – if you can afford one – you have to put up with first before they get around to the punishments. Damn leeches, drain the last copper out of your coffer with their fees and you wind up dead anyhow. I couldn't work. That fornicating son of a dung-eating proprietor of a knocking-shop who calls himself a King these days had his agents everywhere. So there I was, a victim of me own fame, unable to work, and all because of a beautiful doxy, and a sore on the royal backside she had told me about.'

Dennis laughed. 'You brought it on yourself. He might have let it pass, I mean the tumbling of his consort. He threw her out of the palace the following day. Admitting the truth – that he had been cuckolded – would have been embarrassing. Oh, you'd have been dodging assassins for a while, but it would have finally blown over. But to compose that epic poem, dedicated to all the prince's failings in bed and the sores on his backside was more than anyone could stand.'

Wolfgar chuckled. 'It was a good piece of verse.'

'They still sing it,' Dennis said with a smile, 'though far from the King's Palace in Rillanon.'

'Well, after that little fiasco I figured it was time to go to a land where royal warrants couldn't find me. I tried to take ship to the southern lands but the dockyards were crawling with royal agents and snitches that would sell me for a few pieces of silver so I headed north instead. 'That is where I met my precious Roxanne, on the road not far from here.' As he said the name the old man smiled wistfully. 'Had my heart on the spot she did. She was a fortune-teller, a true wizard with the picture cards, the reading of entrails and cracked bones. She was travelling with a merry band of vagabonds and thieves, and there was always room for a minstrel in their company.

'Said I'd be hanged if I didn't stay with her, and so I did. Ahh, there was a time in my sin sodden youth when I thought I'd never worry for the companionship of a lovely woman, but at that age, to find just one more like her was a blessing. So we jumped the fire-pit together as they say, and soon thereafter she smiles and says we need to find a place to raise our family.'

Again he laughed wistfully until a coughing fit doubled him over. The seizure passed and he wiped the spittle from his chin.

'It was Roxanne who knew of this valley. Her little band of performers had found it years before: it was one of their secret hideouts and she led me here. We settled in; our two daughters came, and life continued, free, I might add, of any royal warrants and grasping lawyers looking for their fees. Free as well of the asinine wars that kings just love to get their people slaughtered in while they hide out in their palaces.'

'Daughters?'

Wolfgar smiled. 'Two lovelies they are.'

'Where?'

Wolfgar laughed. 'With a hundred hungry wolves at my gate last night, do you think I'd show my most precious treasures? I had them hide in the woods till things were settled. They came in with the other woman and children after your men bedded down for the night and slept in the servants' quarters. When the boy on watch came in reporting your arrival I knew we couldn't hold out against a hundred heavily-armed troops and was expecting the worst. We have a couple of small stockades up in the forests in case of trouble. This place is deliberately, out in the open. Bait, almost.'

'Why didn't all of you go up in the woods and hide?'

'Would you? Too many signs that we were here. Someone had to stay behind and lead you to believe that all of us had been taken.'

Dennis nodded. 'Where are the men?' he asked. 'I didn't see a dozen here capable of bearing arms. All the rest are oldsters like yourself.'

'The men?' and Wolfgar shook his head. 'Roxanne's people are wanderers. If they're in trouble, a warrant on their heads, they'll come here for a year or two to hide out, then they move on. One year we might have less than thirty living here, another year it might be a hundred. Most of the performers found ample riches working the army in the west. Those lads brighten up a great deal at the sight of a pretty woman dancing to the songs of a talented bard. The jugglers and acrobats get a copper or two also.'

'And a couple of purses vanish from the crowd, as well, I warrant,' suggested Dennis.

Wolfgar shrugged. 'Even when most of the performers are gone for months, we have a score of men around – too much work to be done by just women and children.' His expression darkened. 'A couple of months back, twenty of the men and most of their women went out of here to trade. Furs for salt, tools, a few trinkets and baubles for the children.'

'And they never came back,' Dennis replied.

Wolfgar nodded.

'They most likely ran into the same trouble we did,' Dennis said. 'Don't know what's up, but a lot of Dark Brothers are moving through the region just over that bridge.'

'Figured it was something like that,' Wolfgar grumbled. 'Never much cared for Roxanne's people. Pack of thieving scoundrels, but fair enough if you married into the clan. I guess with all them gone, I'm the leader here now.' He looked back at the long house. 'We've got around twenty children here to look after now. As for the women who lost their men, they've mourned. Practical people though, and with a hundred men to choose from with your party, they'll get over it soon enough.'

'What about the Dark Brotherhood?' Dennis asked.

'Them bastards? Remember this is the between-lands. Until the war started your border marches only came up to the Broad River. The moredhel rarely ventured beyond the next range twenty miles to the north of here.'

'You had an understanding with them, is that it?'

'They never knew about this place.' He paused, glaring at Dennis. 'At least until yesterday. We stayed out of each other's way. I guess all that's changed.

'You hear rumours and gossip. This isn't the only human community north of the King's law. I've heard stories of . . . well, some are pretty far-fetched. Lost cities and ancient gods. Mostly scams to sell lost treasure maps to the gullible, I suspect. But there are those rumours that seem to have a gleam of truth in them. The Dark Brothers don't get close to the other side of those mountains, for a reason. Something keeps them away. I'm just as content not knowing what it is, rather than climbing over those icy crags to find out.

'But until yesterday no Dark Brother ever stumbled across that entrance to the valley. How much trouble that's going to bring, I don't know. I guess it depends on how badly they want to dig you out of here. You could be safe for the winter, or maybe only for a few hours. I just don't know.'

A gust of wind caused the snow to swirl back into their faces so that they turned, facing back towards the long house.

Men were beginning to stir, a few were out in the courtyard relieving themselves, a coil of smoke puffed up from the kitchen house carrying with it the scent of roasting meat.

'How long are you staying?' Wolfgar grumbled.

'Depends – on what the Dark Brotherhood is doing, the weather. I don't know.'

'This storm keeps up you'll be here a while. Damn, a hundred mouths to feed, I wasn't planning on it.'

'We can take care of ourselves. I'll get hunting parties out before this storm really hits. I saw a lot of game signs; the valley seems rich.'

'Best damn place in the world right now. At least it was till yesterday.'

Dennis saw Sergeant Barry coming out of the long house, a dozen men following him, bows slung over their shoulder, and with them, several local boys to act as guides. With a nod to Dennis they ventured out and started up the slope to the treeline, spreading out as they advanced until they were lost to view in the snow.

As he watched them leave he experienced another flash of memory: days like this, heading out with his father to hunt, the fresh snow helping them to track. His father was not the type to go out with a fanfare and a score of beaters to stir up the game for him, he much preferred the solitude and the opportunity to teach his son the ways of the woods on his own. If the weather was fair they'd go for as long as a fortnight, taking enough game to eat well, but no more, many times just tracking an elk for the pleasure of it, then leaving him alone.

He swung his gaze back to the trail. The light snow had lifted for a moment and a quarter of a mile off he caught a glimpse of Gregory and Tinuva, riding slowly, coming back in.

'Good. They gave up the chase back at the canyon,' Dennis said.

Wolfgar nodded, hawked, and spat again over the stockade wall. 'That elf. Tinuva's his name isn't it?'

'Yes. Why?'

'Just I've heard a few rumours, that's all.'

'Such as?'

Wolfgar smiled knowingly. 'Remember the old saying, "never gossip about elves, for their ears are long and they hear all"?'

Dennis nodded.

'It doesn't bode well, that's all.'

'Tell me.'

'Do you trust him?'

'Yes,' said Dennis.

'Then he'll tell you if it's important for you to know.'

Dennis seemed unsatisfied by the answer.

'You're surrounded by death, Hartraft. But then again, your family usually was.'

The old man hawked and spat again. Pulling his fur cape tight, he turned and slowly hobbled down the steps, leaving Dennis alone with his thoughts.

Leaning back in his seat, Asayaga groaned and slapped his stomach.

He had never been one to pay particular notice to food the way some did, especially the effete lords who would spend hours debating the merits of a particular year's vintage, or pay hundreds of gems, even thousands, for a slave that could create a unique sauce. Food was for the stopping of hunger, and the giving of strength so that one could continue to live.

This meal, however, would stay forever in his memory, for it was, without a doubt, the most satisfying and varied he had encountered since arriving in this gods-forsaken world.

The previous night all of them had been more concerned with sleep than anything else, but come dawn hunting parties had gone out in every direction. Hartraft had insisted that they provide their own food as much as possible so as not to burden their hosts and by mid-afternoon the Kingdom soldiers had yet again proven their skills in the forest: all of the hunting parties came back in heavily burdened, exclaiming about the unspoiled lands they had stalked through.

Asayaga's men, as well, had contributed to the pot, spreading out along the streams, bringing in dozens of fish caught in makeshift nets, speared or simply grabbed and tossed out of the water, while others had laid traps for marmots and snagged half a dozen of them. Those who had not skills with either fishing or hunting had laboured throughout the day to bring in extra wood to heat the long house, worked in the kitchen butchering the meat, or helped tend to their wounded comrades resting quietly in the warm blacksmith's shop.

By midday Wolfgar's prediction of a rising storm had come to pass, and the last of the hunting and fishing parties had staggered in covered with snow. By late in the afternoon a blizzard was howling outside the long house and the mere thought of it made Asayaga shudder with dread. If they had been caught out in the storm all of them would be dead. Instead he was safe inside, a roaring blaze crackled in the two great fireplaces that warmed the feasting hall and all was well with the world.

As darkness settled, the first courses had emerged from the

cook-house to be placed upon the great table. The hall was cramped with more than a hundred men jammed around the table, squeezed in together side by side, Wolfgar insisting that the two groups mix in.

By mutual agreement any who came into the hall had to set aside all weapons, even daggers, and at first the men had looked warily at each other, feeling naked without a trusted blade at their side or hidden in a boot top. It was one thing to march side by side with a dreaded enemy in close pursuit, or to lie side by side in exhausted sleep, but another once strength had returned, and with it a realization of just who might be sitting to your left or right – an enemy that might have killed an old comrade or kin.

Then the first platters had come out, heaped with steaming slabs of meat – venison, elk, wild boar – warm grease splattering on to the table, accompanied by bowls heaped with fried livers, tongues, roasted brains mixed with bread crumbs and delicious kidney pies followed by baked fish.

The marmots came last, stuffed and roasted in the manner the Tsurani adored, and though most of the Kingdom troops turned up their noses at this fare the Tsurani cried out with joy, and friendly squabbles broke out over who had the honour of consuming the hearts and livers.

More platters were spread out upon the table, laden with dried fruits, roasted potatoes, half a dozen different kinds of bread and even boiled eggs which the men greedily devoured.

At first Wolfgar had been tight-fisted with his drink but as the room heated up with the scent of cooked meat and warm bodies he finally relented and called for extra kegs of beer to be brought in and tapped. Foaming goblets, drinking horns, and leather flagons were quickly filled and passed around to eager hands, the men laughing and cheering, downing the frothy brew and leaning back to belch with comfortable delight.

As appropriate for such an occasion Dennis and Asayaga sat at one end of the long table, with Wolfgar between them, the scrunched-up old bard watching the proceedings with a jaundiced eye, mumbling about the expense, the noise, and the alien smell of the Tsurani. But after several beers he began to relax as well, and even accepted a platter of boar's ribs which one of the young women who had mysteriously appeared shortly after dawn personally brought to his side.

'Thank you, daughter,' he whispered, reaching up to stroke her cheek as she put the plate before him.

Asayaga had noticed her within minutes after awaking in the morning. She was short for her race, nearly at his own eye-level, but that was the only aspect that might make him think she was a woman of his homeland. Her hair was blonde, the palest of blondes so that her long twin braids seemed like cascades of spun gold thread. Such hair was not unknown in his homeland, but far to the north of Coltair province, and rarely seen in his home city. Her figure was full, the tightness of her calf-length leather dress sufficient to show off every detail. Her eyes were a shimmering blue and her skin a soft delicate pink.

'Daughter?' Dennis asked, putting down his flagon of beer and staring straight at her.

Wolfgar laughed, a warm and lascivious grin wrinkling his pitted and leathery face. 'Ahh, not my grand-daughter, or great-grand-daughter, though I'll wager there's more than one of them around.' He reached out affectionately and pulled her to his side and the young woman planted a warm kiss on the top of his balding head. 'Her mother, may she rest in the Blessed Lands, she was a rare lass. Two of them she bore for me. Alyssa here, who will break any man's heart with a glance is the oldest.'

Asayaga immediately rose, his gaze locked on hers and bowed formally. 'I am honoured to meet the daughter of our generous host,' he said. 'My sword will always be at your service.'

Dennis, watching Asayaga's show, rose and stepped between the Tsurani captain and Alyssa. 'Your father was always an honoured guest in my family's keep. A daughter of his shall always have my protection.'

'Protection?' Wolfgar laughed. 'I think the two of you need protection from her.'

Alyssa blushed but there was a light in her eyes as she stepped back slightly and looked from one captain to the other. 'My father shames me,' she said, and her voice was soft and whispery. 'I thank you, Dennis Hartraft, for the kindness of your protection and you too, Asayaga of the Tsurani. I must retire to see to the serving of the food.'

'All is well tended to,' Wolfgar laughed, 'come sit by my side, it's safe here,' and he slapped the side of his wide chair and slid over.

Alyssa demurely sat down on the side closer to Dennis.

'Roxanne, join us!' Wolfgar cried, looking back over his shoulder.

Asayaga was startled to see the second daughter standing behind her father's feasting chair. When she had appeared was a mystery, and even now she was barely visible, standing in the dark shadows.

This one had the same hair as Alyssa but was taller and she had a lean, muscular look to her bare arms, and high-cheekboned face. Like her sister she wore a simple leather dress of calf length, the only feminine vanity to it a pale blue scarf tied around the waist as a belt, revealing just the slightest of curves beneath.

She didn't move at her father's call but simply folded her arms. 'I prefer to remain standing,' she replied, her voice deep and clear.

'I told her you think the men are dead,' Wolfgar said, looking over at Dennis. He lowered his voice. 'The one she had a preference for was one of them. '

'He meant nothing to me,' she replied, 'other than his friendship.'

Wolfgar threw a dark look over his shoulder at his daughter, then raised his voice. 'Pimply-faced, with the brain of a drunken hare. Typical of her mother's kin, and like a hare always fumbling after her. I was half-contemplating killing him myself.'

'As if you're an example of model behaviour,' Roxanne replied coolly, and Wolfgar laughed at her response.

'Roxanne, named after her mother,' Wolfgar said, nodding back. 'She took the name because her mother died giving her life.'

Again Asayaga stood, bowed and offered his formal greeting as did Dennis. Roxanne accepted both without comment.

Sitting back down, Asayaga found his gaze lingering on Alyssa who was leaning over and whispering something into her father's ear. He laughed uproariously and slapped her on the thigh.

Mindful again of his duty, Asayaga tore his attention away from her charms and carefully gazed around the room, chiding himself for his momentary lapse before the barbarian and his daughter. *Too many years in the field*, he thought. Too many months since last he had known a woman.

He studied the condition of his men. Almost all them were still concentrating on gorging themselves, hands reaching for food and drink. The noise was slowly rising, conversations starting, punctuated by ripples of laughter. In places he saw where Kingdom troops and his own were even trying to talk to one another. He caught a glimpse of two soldiers moving their hands about in pantomime and from their gestures he guessed they were talking about women. One of them laughed as the other, grinning, made a universal gesture.

He caught Tasemu's eye. The Strike Leader was at the far end of the table, flagon in hand, leaning back, watching carefully. Interestingly, the Kingdom sergeant – whose name he had learned was Barry, sat beside Tasemu, flagon in hand as well, the two of them almost like mirror-images of each other. Both were doing their jobs, silently watching. Barry nudged Tasemu and nodded to where several Tsurani seemed to be in a heated argument. In fact they were debating the merits of who was the best wrestler in the army. Tasemu merely grunted and smiled, the gesture enough to reassure Barry.

To one side Asayaga saw Sugama who was eating quietly, delicately, carefully taking each piece of fish with only his thumb and forefinger in the proper noble manner, while talking quietly with a few of Asayaga's men. Asayaga felt a moment's disquiet. In only a few days could this minor son of a rival house have gained a following? He studied the faces of the four men who were with him and realized that all were younger sons and brothers, men whose destiny was to linger as soldiers in a minor house until they were granted leave to wed and start families, living on a small parcel of land granted them by the Lord of the Tondora. It was just this sort of man who might be lured to betray his oath for promises of a higher station through adoption into a new house.

Then when Sugama turned to take an offered flagon of ale from one of the local boys, two of Asayaga's men exchanged a smirk and a silently-mouthed word, and Asayaga realized they were mocking Sugama behind his back, enduring his company for the sake of entertainment. Asayaga let out a silent sigh and allowed the tension to flow from his body. Even here, as remote as any Tsurani had ever been from the Empire, he worried over the Great Game and the loyalty of men of his own household.

A Kingdom soldier pushed a platter of roasted boar over Sugama's way, and one of Sugama's companions pushed it back, his comment lost in the general uproar, but Asayaga could read lips well enough to know that one of the worst of insults had been spoken softly, words that the Kingdom soldier did not understand and therefore let pass. Asayaga marked the man and made a note to have Tasemu speak with him later; he might be loyal, but he was also stupid to provoke needlessly a man who might save his life in the days to come.

A roar of laughter erupted and Asayaga saw where two soldiers, one from each side were standing, full flagons in hand. Someone slapped the table hard and the two started to drain their flagons, gulping down the contents, the Kingdom soldier winning handily. Again laughter and a few coins were traded, a Tsurani having shrewdly bet against his own comrade and thus gaining a rare and precious piece of silver that was worth more than an entire suit of armour. When the loser realized what his comrade had done a heated argument ensued to the delight of the Kingdom soldiers around them.

A platter containing a half-consumed marmot was pushed down to Asayaga and in spite of feeling bloated he reached into the body, pulled out a leg-bone and sucked the meat off.

'Hey, Ass-you. Just how the hell can you eat that?'

Asayaga looked over at Wolfgar and started to bristle. Then he caught Alyssa's bemused stare. Without comment he pushed the platter to Wolfgar. 'Try it.'

Wolfgar belched loudly and shook his head. 'I'd sooner eat horse dung that was still warm. And tell me, why do you Tsurani smell funny? By the gods, I think you were a bunch of temple harlots.'

The conversation around them drifted off, though Asayaga's men did not understand the words, they knew enough of Wolfgar after one day to sense that their leader was being baited.

'It's because we don't smell,' Asayaga replied.

'How is that? You speak in riddles.'

'Because we bathe the way all civilized men do. You're smelling someone who is clean, which is more than I can say for you. I think the butt end of a she bear in heat smells better in comparison to you.'

He said the words calmly, but there was the slightest flicker of a smile at the corners of lips.

Wolfgar stared at him intently and then threw back his head and roared with laughter. 'By the gods you and I shall have a game of insults some night. You strike me as a civilized man who knows something beyond half a dozen of the crudest words which any idiot can let dribble out of his face.'

'An honour,' Asayaga replied. 'But the name is Asayaga, not Ass-you.' The flicker of a smile had disappeared and he spoke the words with intensity.

Wolfgar nodded and said nothing. Finally he leant over and reached into the marmot to pull out a piece of meat. His gesture elicited a scattering of applause from the men who had been watching the interchange.

'Daughters!' Wolfgar cried, changing the subject and waving expansively to the men gathered around the table. 'Take your choice of one of these. Better breeding-stock than what was stabled here before. One of them might be man enough to put up with your evil tempers and barbed tongues.'

Alyssa laughed coyly and lowered her eyes, raising them again for a second to gaze at Asayaga. Dennis, noticing the exchange of glances, muttered into his cup and then gazed straight ahead.

'Virginity is preferable,' Roxanne replied coolly, hands resting on her slender hips.

Wolfgar, laughing, picked up a flagon and handed it back to her and she took it, drained what was left and then tossed it aside. Then the flicker of a smile creased her face, and Wolfgar reached up and patted her on the cheek.

'You always did have more of my blood in you than your mother's.'

'Look out for her, Hartraft,' Wolfgar announced. 'She can drop a stag on the run at fifty paces with her bow, or with her bare hands claw out the eyes of a man who tries to touch her!'

Asayaga looked at Roxanne intently, but her gaze was not on him;

rather it was fixed appraisingly on Dennis, who did not seem to notice her, his attention fixed suddenly on the far corner of the room. Dennis nodded to Asayaga and made a subtle hand gesture.

Asayaga looked around and saw that Sugama and his companions were in a small knot around one of the tapped kegs of beer. As they spoke one of them kept looking back over his shoulder at several Kingdom soldiers who were eyeing them with equal distrust. Words were being exchanged by both groups: it was obvious that both sides were half-drunk, and insulting each other in their own tongues. Then one of the Kingdom soldiers stood up, fists clenched, and men to either side began to back up.

What happened next caught Asayaga completely by surprise. From the corner of his eye he saw Roxanne reach down behind her father's chair and then stand back up a few seconds later with a crossbow. She shouldered the weapon, aimed it and squeezed the trigger.

The bolt hissed across the room, brushing past the Kingdom soldier and buried itself in the side of the keg not a hand's-span away from Sugama.

The hall fell instantly silent, everyone looking from the quivering bolt and then to Roxanne.

'In my father's hall,' she said coldly, 'there is no brawling. Take it outside: I hate cleaning spilled blood off the table I must eat from.'

The silence reigned for several long seconds. Alwin Barry, still sitting by Tasemu's side, stood up, raised his flagon to Roxanne and then drained it. Putting the flagon back down he began to laugh, a soft chuckle at first, shaking his head as the laughter built. Tasemu, following Alwin's gesture, stood and did likewise, the two laughing together until finally they were slapping each other on the back, pointing at Roxanne and then to the thoroughly discomfited knot of men around the keg. Within seconds the entire hall was roaring.

Roxanne looked around the room and then with a gesture of disdain, placed the front of the crossbow on the floor, recocked it, loaded another bolt in and slipped the weapon back under the seat. This gesture caused a redoubling of laughter and finally, looking a bit irritated, she stalked out of the hall.

'Ahh, that's my blood!' Wolfgar roared. 'That's the type of women

I can sire. By all the gods, I can still do it, I can, if only I could find a wench blind enough to let me!'

His comment caused a hearty round of toasts and cheers, Asayaga translating the boast to one of the soldiers sitting by his side so that it shot around the room, the laughter increasing as it spread to the other Tsurani. The few women in the room were also laughing, shaking their heads and holding their hands up in mock horror.

Wolfgar stood up, and with a groan somehow managed to step up on to the feasting table, knocking over a platter of meat. Raising his feasting cup, he drained it to the dregs, tossed it aside and slowly walked down the length of the table, acknowledging the upraised flagons and goblets and the lusty cheers of the men. A number of the Kingdom troops started into an obscene ditty about a blacksmith who had five daughters, and the fate that befell each of their midnight visitors who were dragged out to face the hot tongs and anvil. The Tsurani were singing as well. Somehow they had understood the nature of Wolfgar's boasting, and Asayaga was intrigued that the song they started to sing in counterpoint had almost the identical plot.

Finally Wolfgar held out his hands for the men to be silent and the room fell quiet. As he stood the years seemed to fall from his shoulders. Dennis watched with approval, knowing that before them stood one of the Kingdom's finest singers of sagas, even if he was a reprobate, liar, and thief.

Softly at first, but with firm control, the old man began a very old song:

> 'Fare thee well, my sweet Kingdom lassie,
> Fare thee well, and I bid you goodbye,
> For I'm off with the dawning to cold northern mountains,
> Off to the north, where for King shall I die . . .'

Dennis sat back and looked over at Asayaga, who seemed intrigued by the old song of a soldier knowing he was sent to face the Dark Brothers in a campaign doomed from the start. Dennis closed his eyes and remembered when he had first heard the song as a boy. He had sat by his father's side, silently listening to Wolfgar, while tears had flowed unchecked down his cheeks. The song was about duty, honour, and sacrifice, and Dennis wondered at Wolfgar's choice. For if any Kingdom men were doomed to the fate of the hero of that song, it was the men in this room.

Asayaga saw Dennis's expression, and realized the song had some meaning for him. He listened to the story in the song, ignoring its odd rhythm and strange tonal qualities. The story was heroic, about a man who put honour above common sense. Asayaga was torn, because on one hand, it was a very Tsurani attitude, yet on the other, no Tsurani would even raise the question of failure and debate it, even within himself. To die for honour was a great thing.

'I've spent too much time on this world,' he muttered to himself, as Wolfgar finished to a deeply appreciative round of applause. Asayaga saw that some of his own men had translated for the others, and more than one soldier on both sides sat with eyes rimmed with moisture.

Yes, thought the Tsurani Force Commander, *it is a powerful tale.*

He left the room, ignoring the bitter cold outside, and went to the slit trench he had ordered dug earlier in the day. The men had used the common area in the centre of the stockade when first arising, and he had put a stop to that as soon as he realized there were no latrine facilities inside the stockade. No soldier with any field experience would let his men foul their own camp. Disease came too quickly on the heels of filth, a point that seemed to be lost on the barbarians. He reached the trench and started to relieve himself, a sense of relief flooding through him.

'They're happy in there.'

Startled, Asayaga saw that Dennis was by his side, relieving himself as well. Finished, the two stood silent for a moment, the blizzard driving the snow around them. The lanterns hanging on the outside of the long house swayed in the wind, casting dim shadows, barely visible as a heavy gust of snow swept across the narrow courtyard.

'We're going to be stuck here for a while,' Dennis said. 'The only way out now is through the high passes and they'll be blocked by morning.'

'It keeps the Dark Brothers out, though, even as it keeps us in.'

'Yes. The chase is over.'

'For now at least. I doubt if they will give up. We've injured them.

If it was reversed, Hartraft, if they were trapped in here . . .' His voice trailed off.

'No. If it was me and my men trapped in here and you were on the far side of the mountains, what would you do?'

'Wait you out.'

'I see.'

Again they were silent for a moment.

'You are a hard man. A hard opponent, Hartraft. Were you this way before the war?'

'That's not your concern. What we face now is my concern.'

'Our pledge to fight, is that it?'

'Like I said, the chase is over. We agreed to a truce until we escaped, and for the moment we have.'

Asayaga turned and stepped closer until they were only inches apart. He looked up into Dennis's eyes. 'What do you want? Come dawn should we roust our men out from in there, line up, draw weapons and commence slaughtering one another?'

Even as he said the words both could hear the laughter and the start of another song from within the long house.

'We both know what is in there is not real,' Dennis replied, waving vaguely towards Wolfgar's long house. 'We're outside our world for the moment, but sooner or later reality will come crashing back in. Less than a hundred miles from here, this night, Kingdom troops and Tsurani troops are sitting in their camps, waiting out the weather, and when the blizzard passes, they will be out hunting each other, and the war will go on. Are we any different, are we excused?'

'We could kill each other tomorrow down to the last man and it won't change what happens back there. I am as honour-bound as you, Hartraft, but killing you tonight will not change the war. It is as if we are both dead and gone from it. Tell me, is it honour, a sense of duty or vengeance which drives you now?'

Dennis did not reply.

'Is it dawn then? If so, I'd better go in and tell my men to stop drinking and prepare. You'd better do the same.'

He snapped out the words, struggling to control his anger and stepped back. Then he bowed formally, and started to turn away.

'Wait.'

'For what?'

'Just wait a moment,' Dennis said, his voice heavy, distant. 'There must come a day, we both know that. Once back into our lines, yours or mine, we have to face that.'

'So why not now?'

'Don't press me, Tsurani: the ice we tread on is thin.'

'Go on then, say what you want.'

'We'll still need each other once the passes clear. The Dark Brothers will be waiting, perhaps even bringing up reinforcements. We stand a better chance of surviving if we work together.'

'Is that the real reason?'

'Like I said, the ice is thin: don't press me.'

Asayaga finally nodded.

'A truce, then, till we return to our lines,' Dennis said haltingly. 'We command our own men, and keep the peace between them. If any break that peace, you and I agree to sit in judgement together.'

'With Wolfgar.'

'Why?'

'I suspect he might be the most impartial of all.'

'You're right,' Dennis replied slowly. 'He will judge as well. We share all rations, lodgings and work.'

'Of course.'

Asayaga looked back at the long house. 'And the daughter – Alyssa, what of her?'

'I don't know what you are talking about!' Dennis snapped.

'Fine then.'

Dennis hesitated then extended his hand. Asayaga took it.

Neither noticed the intent presence that lingered in the doorway of the stable and had heard every word.

TWELVE

Blood Debts

The blade was sharp.

The tip of the knife punctured his skin effortlessly, drawing forth a drop of blood. He watched the tiny pearl of crimson well up on his skin, and turned his arm so that the drop might fall free. He watched as it stained the icy whiteness beside his boots. The daily ritual complete, Bovai sheathed the blade.

His left arm was scarred from elbow to wrist by tens of thousands punctures he had inflicted upon himself over the years so that the limb was now a mass of twisted scars.

Soon, he thought, *I shall be done with this ritualistic self-mutilation. Soon the stain on the honour of my family and clan will be finally ended.*

On the night he had heard for certain that Tinuva had gone over to the eledhel he had vowed thus, to draw his own blood in atonement, day upon endless day, until the blood of the traitor was spilled.

For Tinuva, the traitor, was also his brother of birth.

Lowering his arm, he leaned back against a tree and looked down at the fortress guarding the river crossing. They had been camped there for nearly a fortnight, over three hundred of his brothers, the remaining humans and goblins crammed into the stockade, waiting for the weather to change and for his scouts to report that the northern passes into the valley were clear enough for his force to attack. The swirling snow lifted for a moment so that he caught glimpses of men coming back in from the forest, guiding a cart loaded with wood. He absently rubbed his scarred and bleeding arm and closed his eyes. There was a time, a time so long ago it seemed he could hardly remember it, when Tinuva had been his beloved brother, Morvai, spoken of by many as the one who would one day be the Paramount Chieftain of Clan Raven. Some even whispered that perhaps he would even be the one to unite all the clans in holy war, so that the exile in the northern bitterness would end and the plague of humans and the traitorous eledhel would be driven into the sea.

How he remembered those days, when together they would go out into the forests to hunt, to talk, to dream: two brothers still in their youth, side by side, planning for all that would come . . .

Morvai was fair to behold. Some would later say that from birth his heart was already calling him to join the eledhel. There had been a gentleness to him, rare in moredhel warriors, save when with their mates and young. Yet all would admit that none could match him in the hunt, in the skill he showed with blade or bow, in fleetness of foot, or even in the charm of his voice. And there was no doubt as to his fierceness and courage in battle. No small number of humans had died at Morvai's hands, and a number of the eledhel, as well, before he had felt the unnatural tug of their queen's dark magic.

As he remembered Bovai lowered his head, for he had loved his brother – idolized him – and would have gladly served him. His loyalty was remarked upon by all, and the sight of one brother without the other by his side was considered rare. Bovai knew that Morvai had abilities he lacked: a quickness of mind and a nimble wit. So he attempted to achieve what his brother had with different tools: strength and cunning, ruthlessness and an unhesitating willingness to kill. Together they were a perfect pair, the blade and the hammer. What Morvai could not achieve with guile, wit, and charm, Bovai could achieve with brute strength and terror.

So they had been for the seemingly timeless years of their youth. They had faced a hundred battles together against rival clans, renegade humans, even venturing beneath the earth to take the riches of the burrowing dwarves. Each had saved the life of the other more than once, and as he contemplated the memory Bovai's hand drifted to his chest, to the wound he had taken leaping in front of Morvai so that the arrow had struck him instead of his brother.

How Morvai had wept that night, sitting by his brother's side as the bolt was withdrawn. He had pledged his undying devotion and had cut his own arm, letting his blood drip into the wound so that their bond was seen by all to be eternal.

There are few things that could break such a bond, but at last they had encountered it and her name was Anleah. Bovai remembered as if it were days before instead of years . . .

The brothers had watched in open admiration as Gaduin, their father and second most powerful chieftain of the clan, returned in triumph. The warriors following him carried booty and led half a dozen prisoners with their hands tied behind their backs. One of them instantly commanded attention.

She was beautiful and proud, and no warrior looking at her for a moment would fail to recognize her for what she was: the daughter of a chieftain. Bovai and Morvai stood before the entrance to their father's home, their faces stoic masks, but their eyes shining with pride.

'My sons!' Gaduin had called to them. 'See what I have fetched home. She is the daughter of our old enemy, Vergalus of Clan Badger, and she will be our guest for a while.'

Their father had given her over to the women of the lodge to be cleaned up and made presentable, and she had dined as a guest at their table that first night.

She gave her parole not to attempt escape, or accept rescue, and was therefore allowed to live under their roof, and was given the freedom of their village. Both brothers were taken by her beauty, the soft charm of her voice and sharp intellect. She had seemed perfect to Bovai . . .

From the moment he had laid eyes upon Anleah, Bovai was smitten, though he had no tongue to tell her, or his father. It was Morvai, the elder brother, who had always had the knack for smooth words and finely-turned phrases, who had pressed his suit.

Morvai spent as much time with Anleah as was possible, and Bovai retreated deeper into his silent longing for the girl, until the night when Morvai had asked their father to intercede with Murad, not to return the girl to her clan, but rather to send gifts and seek permission of her father for Morvai to take Anleah for his wife.

Gaduin had laughed and revealed his true intent in leading the raid and taking her prisoner. The bitter rivalry with Clan Badger had consumed the two clans for decades and scores of the best warriors on both sides had died. It had always been Gaduin's hope that Morvai would find her becoming, and take her as wife.

She was too young to rule and had no brother, and no chieftain in Clan Badger held enough power to hold that clan together once her father joined the Mothers and Fathers in the next world. Murad had no offspring, though he had numbered three wives over the years. Gaduin saw his eldest son as the logical inheritor of the Paramount Chieftain's mantle some day, and knew that with Anleah as his wife, the two clans would eventually be joined. Thus peace would be established, and the strength of Clan Raven doubled by the alliance, with the possibility of Clan Raven eventually absorbing Clan Badger under the rule of Morvai, and after him the children of his union to Anleah. With two of the greatest clans in Yabon united, the process could begin for the taking of the others.

And it was clear at that moment to Bovai that he must stand aside and remain silent. He feigned delight at his brother's happiness, and said nothing when his father dispatched an embassy to Clan Badger proposing the truce and to negotiate a bride price.

Bovai accepted this out of love for his brother, though it burned his heart. What burned even more was that Morvai was so taken with Anleah's charms that he never realized the anguish this caused his brother. So Bovai forced his gaze to look elsewhere when Anleah walked past, averting his eyes when she ate at their table, struggling not to notice the scent of her hair, the dark flicker of her eyes, the power of her voice.

Less and less did Morvai go to the hunt with his brother and a strain developed between them. Days would pass when they barely spoke and he tried to believe that it was because Morvai had begun his courtship: a series of rituals that could take years before he and Anleah could come together at last. Bovai feared that his brother suspected Bovai's hidden longings, and so the estrangement became mutual. Later, Bovai realized the odd distraction Morvai had shown had nothing to do with his betrothal to Anleah or to any concern over his brother: rather it was the first stirring of that cursed pull from Elvandar – what the eledhel called 'the Returning'.

Days passed into weeks, and Bovai lived on a diet of pain and longing. Then one day, Gaduin announced the betrothal of Morvai and Anleah with the plan that they would be married on Midsummer's Day.

Six days before Midsummer's Day, the entirety of Anleah's family, complete with retainers and warriors of note, arrived for the wedding rites. Bovai found it strange to be surrounded by warriors of Clan Badger, since he recognized more than one from fights of old. In their midst was a warrior whose countenance bore bitterness and gloom, and his name was Kavala. While others in his clan seemed pleased at the marriage and the forging of a bond between the clans, Bovai knew that this warrior regarded his brother with a special hatred. For if any warrior in Clan Badger was likely to follow Vergalus as Chieftain of Clan Badger, it would be Kavala. Yet he saw the future as clearly as a hunter saw a buck in a clearing. Should this wedding go forward, he would some day have to bend a knee to Morvai and swear allegiance.

In addition, years before, in one of the many skirmishes between Badger and Raven, Morvai had killed Kavala's brother. Bovai knew that Kavala had one more reason than he needed to hate Morvai.

The reception of the Clan Badger warriors and the family of Anleah was cool at first, but by the end of the evening toasts were raised by both sides, pledging the end of hostilities, and both Gaduin and Vergalus were open-handed in the paying of blood-debt gifts to the fathers, brothers and sons of warriors slain in battles of old, those who had not yet been avenged. Kavala had been tight-lipped, but he had uttered the ritual words as Morvai presented him with a finely-fashioned bow of yew and bone as a debt-payment for killing Kavala's brother. No hint of forgiveness was evident, but he observed the formalities. Thus was the feud ended.

While this ritual was going on there came a moment when Bovai saw Morvai alone and he approached his brother's side.

The look in Morvai's eyes was one of warning.

'If you come to tell me that you love her, I know,' Morvai said evenly.

Stunned Bovai could not reply.

Morvai put his hand upon his brother's arm. 'You have acted with honour.' Then he spoke softly. 'The heart wants what it wants. Always remember that, no matter what else happens.'

Bovai found he could not speak. And then Morvai turned away, broke into a smile and extended a hand to his bride's father, and the two of them clasped hands firmly, then shared a drink from the same goblet.

Bovai had looked over at Anleah, seated at the feasting table and, seeing her aglow with love for Morvai, had felt his heart might shatter within his chest, for he knew that he would never see her look at him in that way.

Throughout the ceremony he had stood by his brother's side, heart filled – at first – with pain, but when he had seen his brother kiss her, he had forced his mind away from his pain, and willed his heart to ice. He would never love again, if love meant such pain.

He had seen something else at that ceremony: the look she gave to Kavala. It had been warm – a friend's smile – yet the look Kavala had returned to her told Bovai that now Kavala had three reasons to hate Morvai. He saw a reflection of his own longing mirrored in Kavala's expression, just for an instant, only a brief flicker; but Bovai had seen it.

When, at long last, protocol permitted, Bovai fled, leaving the feast for fear that his stomach would rebel and that he would vomit. His pain drove him from the camp. He took his bow and told a sentry he was going hunting.

For five days he absented himself from his father's compound.

For a year and a month, Bovai and his brother lived without comment. Anleah grew more beautiful, happy in her marriage. Every smile and laugh was a dagger in Bovai's heart, for he knew the laughter and the smiles were for Morvai. She loved him with an intensity only a few of the moredhel ever knew, and even the most reticent among the warriors would smile at the sight of her singing on her way to the stream to clean clothing, or as she tended the garden.

But Morvai grew more reflective, more thoughtful, and disappeared alone in the forest for days at a time, often returning without game. There were days when he would suddenly become distracted while in conversations, as if he were listening to some distant call.

One day Morvai called Bovai to his side and said something that troubled his brother for months to come. 'Should I fall, brother, should anything happen to me ... will you look after Anleah?'

Bovai said, 'Of course, but nothing will happen.'

Morvai smiled and said, 'Fate is fickle, brother. Rest assured, something will happen.' He put his hand on his younger brother's arm. 'See to her needs. Take her back to the lodge of her father, should that be her wish.'

'I will,' said Bovai.

Months fled, the seasons passed, and Morvai became ever more distracted. Gaduin asked Bovai if he knew what troubled his eldest son, but Bovai could think of nothing. Yet Bovai also sensed a deepening unease within his brother's soul.

Then, in late summer of the third year following the marriage, Morvai finally changed. No moredhel needed to be told when a family member made the change, known by the eledhel as the Returning. Bovai awoke an hour before dawn one day with a dread sense that something was terribly wrong. He was already out of his bed and in the courtyard of the compound, buckling his sword-belt, when he heard Anleah scream.

He had raced with his father and other warriors to Morvai's lodge, and inside found Anleah standing before an empty bed.

'What is it, woman?' Gaduin shouted.

Softly, with tears flowing down her cheeks, Anleah spoke. 'I awoke to find a stranger in this room, father of my ...' Her voice broke. 'My husband is no more.'

A cold more frigid than ice stabbed through Bovai's stomach. He glanced at his father and saw the old warrior's implacability. While his mask remained in place, all colour had drained from his cheeks.

Softly, Gaduin said, 'We must find the traitor. He must die.'

Bovai felt the same pent-up rage and fear that his father was suppressing. Their beloved brother and son had changed. He was no longer of their blood. The evil Queen of Elvandar's black arts had lured away another of their people: even as they stood there, the being who had once been Morvai was making his way southward, toward the haven of Elvandar.

Bovai signalled and warriors hurried back to their own lodges to get weapons. Within minutes, fifty moredhel had made their way into the forest, after Morvai.

The chase had been brutal, with no respite for either prey or hunters. In the memory of their race, there had been no greater affront to a clan than this. Even those renegades who had been banished by their own people and who lived in communities of humans and goblins might some day redeem their honour. But one who fled to Elvandar was a betrayer of everything that made one a member of the People, a moredhel.

For six days they ran through the forests, swamps and bogs of Yabon. At last they came to the river marking the boundary of Elvandar.

Bovai had glimpsed his brother three times in the chase; once upon the crest of a hill, another time moving into distant trees on the other side of a valley; and there at the river's edge.

Bovai had unleashed an arrow which had arched high into the sky only to strike futilely mere yards behind his brother as he splashed through the water.

Figures in tunics with bows waited on the far bank, watching to see how close Bovai and the others would approach their border. Bovai's rage overcame his caution and he ran forward to try to kill the traitor before he reached the shelter of the trees on the other side of the river. He nocked an arrow as he ran, then quickly planted his feet and sighted, forcing himself to accuracy, for this would be his final shot.

As he drew, so did those behind him, and they were answered by the enemy across the river. His own arrow had left the bowstring a scant moment before others, and with a howl of frustration he had seen the shaft fall inches short. Then his shout of rage had turned to pain as an elven arrow struck him in the thigh.

Two of his companions had had to drag him to safety, for even wounded, Bovai was ready to charge across the river.

The last he saw of the creature who had once been his brother was his back as he disappeared into the darkness of Elvandar.

'Bovai?'

He stirred from his painful memories.

It was Golun, leader of his scouts.

'Yes?'

Golun saw that Bovai's arm was still bared in spite of the icy cold.

'Remembering?'

Bovai nodded. Golun had been at the wedding feast and knew of all the dishonour that had followed. Clan Badger had proclaimed the shame of Clan Raven unbearable and disavowed the peace between them. Anleah's return was demanded by her father. Bovai told Gaduin of his promise to Morvai – to take the girl home – but his father had lashed out and struck his son at the very mention of the traitor's name.

Rather than let Anleah return to her people, Gaduin had forced Anleah to marry Bovai against her will. Bovai had fought six battles over four years with Clan Badger, before forcing them to yield after the death of Vergalus. Kavala had been forced to bow before Murad, and Clan Badger had been absorbed into Clan Raven.

Ten years of struggle had followed, as other clans in Yabon sought to displace Raven. The bitterness of what all saw as a base betrayal by Clan Raven of Clan Badger had taken years to quell.

Golun had stood by Bovai's side throughout and in the years that followed Bovai had proven himself worthy of command, his mind cold, calculated, and filled with cunning. He was remorseless in the hunting down of his clan's enemies, gaining the reputation of being the darkest of warriors and one never to be crossed, for vengeance was all that he lived for. He had partially redeemed himself in Murad's eyes, and now he was poised to regain the seat on the Council denied him after his father's death, the seat at Murad's right hand. His rage had served Bovai well.

None outside the clan, and few within, understood the rage that was stoked every day as he lived with a woman who loved a memory. Anleah was a dutiful wife and allowed Bovai the pleasures of the marriage bed, but she evidenced no joy in being with him. She endured his touch, and each time desire drove him to take her, he left their bed feeling bitter pain instead of joy.

Many days he would see her gazing out of the window of their lodge, or working quietly in their garden, and he knew her mind was turned to the past, to a night with another whom she still loved, despite his profound betrayal of his race. Gone were the happy songs, the laughter, and the smile. Anleah, most beautiful of women among Clan Raven, was now a figure of melancholy. Her smiles for Bovai were always tinged with sadness, and she never laughed.

More than anything else, Golun understood these things, and why Bovai had become such a terrible figure on the battlefield. He understood that Bovai could never, truly, have the woman he loved, even though she shared his home and bed; and that scar on his heart, soul and honour haunted him.

Over the years Golun had heard rumours that Morvai's new elven name was Tinuva; that he had skirmished along the frontier with warriors from other clans. Three times Bovai had glimpsed his one-time brother, and yet had been unable to close with him. It was clear to him that Bovai knew that would be his last opportunity to find and destroy his brother.

Golun unclasped his cloak and threw it over Bovai's shoulders and Bovai nodded his thanks. He had forgotten just how long he had been standing there in the cold, alone, in just a tunic.

'At least Kavala is dead,' Bovai said, and Golun grunted in reply. 'Strange, across all the years I could not slay him. He desired Anleah as much as I, and if I had fallen in battle, I know he would have courted her. But his hatred for Tinuva matched my own – he blamed him for Clan Badger's destruction. He was ambitious and would have displaced me if he thought he could, yet I endured his envy and hatred; a day did not go by that he did not wish to drive a dagger into my heart.'

'His death frees you of the need to kill him, and it has also revealed the presence of your brother for certain. It is ironic that in removing an avowed enemy, Tinuva did you a service.'

'Yes,' Bovai replied, drawing the cloak tight around his shoulders to ward off the chill. 'At the fort we took, I sensed his presence, yet after all these years it was almost hard to believe that finally we were coming to the conclusion of all events.'

'Slay him and your honour is fully restored,' said Golun. 'With your honour intact at the Great Council next summer no one will dare to speak against your name. Who could deny one who would slay his own brother in order to restore the family name?'

Bovai nodded. Golun was his friend, but Golun was also ambitious. He knew what it was that Bovai sought.

Bovai looked over at him.

'Delekhan,' Bovai whispered. 'He has always used my brother's betrayal against me in Council.'

'It would be far better that you, rather than he, should rule the entire clan if Murad should fall. The death of your father left the way open for your ambitious cousin to seize control, when it should have been you sitting at Murad's right hand.'

Bovai glanced over at Golun and wondered for a second if there was some veiled insult in his words. If the tragedy had not played out as it had, it would have been Morvai bringing together Raven and Badger, Morvai who would now be ruling both clans, their combined strength thus making him Murad's most trusted captain.

'Kill Tinuva: but you will still have to contend with the problems down there,' Golun said, nodding back to the stockade by the river.

'Now what?'

'Another fight between the humans and goblins. Two dead on both sides.'

'Damn.' Bovai sighed. Following Golun's lead, he started back down the hill.

Garrisoning all of them together to sit out the storms was proving to be a nightmare. Half a dozen heads were already staked above the gate, executions undertaken in order to maintain order.

It had been nearly a fortnight since they had lost the chase and their prey had escaped. He knew they would hole up in the valley. Several of the humans with the party had heard rumours of the place and one claimed to know a pass to the north of the mountains that would bring them into the valley from the other side. That pass was a march of at least thirty miles, once the Edder Forest was circled, and until the storms abated and the thaw that often came at midwinter melted off some of the snow and compacted the rest, the march would be impossible.

He knew he had to do three things now. The first was to keep his force together. He had promised to get them back safely to their homeland before winter. If it had not been for the diversion of the chase they would have gained the final pass before the storms. Having failed in that he now had to succeed in the other two. To satisfy the men and goblins, Hartraft's Marauders had to be annihilated. The glory derived from such an act would assuage their anger and they would return home to boast of what they had achieved. And finally the death of Tinuva would settle a dispute that had lasted for centuries. It would afford him little pleasure, he knew, and Anleah would love him not one whit more when the traitor was dead, but it would remove a canker from his heart, and come summer it would place him in a position to challenge Delekhan himself for a prominent place in the clan Council. He might never have Morvai's love, but he would some day have glory his former brother had only dreamed of.

As the snow swirled he returned to the fortress and for several minutes loud arguments ensued. Some moments later there was the ringing of steel, and six more heads were placed upon the battlement wall.

Gregory refilled Tinuva's mug with tea and passed it over to him, pouring another cup for himself. Moving the small kettle off the flames, he tossed another log on the fire and settled back. The two of them were sitting inside the rotted-out remains of a massive tree stump. Tearing away the south side of the stump to gain entrance, they had settled in after a morning of hunting. The thin outer wall that engulfed them on three sides formed a natural shelter against the wind and snow: the two of them were able to stretch out comfortably on the sawdust-dry inner remains of the great tree.

'You never told me about her before,' Gregory said, his friend having fallen silent, after speaking, for the first time, of the story of his wife, Anleah.

Gregory kept his voice soft, trying not to show the slightest shock over the tale that his companion of so many years had just related. He knew Tinuva had been of the moredhel, but had never questioned him about that, or the reason for his 'Returning', to the eledhel. One did not question elves on such secretive matters and the mere fact that Tinuva had just discussed Anleah with him was startling, and a bit worrisome.

Tinuva nodded. 'No reason before. It was long ago.'

'Not so long ago that the memory doesn't hurt.'

Tinuva, gaze fixed on the fire, again fell silent. An acceptance of the elf's silences was one thing Gregory had learned early on in his friendship with Tinuva. Elves understood time differently. Perhaps it was because the span of humans was so short that they had to cram each moment with something. An elf could go for days, weeks even, without speaking and in fact be completely unaware of it. It was one of the reasons they seldom chose humans as friends, for humans clouded the air with too much talk and too frenzied a pace of living.

The small log he had tossed on the fire burned down and Gregory replaced it with another.

Finally Tinuva stirred. 'Yes, it hurts,' he whispered. 'It will always hurt. I love her still.' He sighed, and the anguish of the sound cut into Gregory's heart. 'And I loved my brother as well.'

Gregory wanted to ask the question but knew he couldn't; he would have to wait.

More than an hour passed before Tinuva spoke again.

'I'll never know if she wed my brother willingly, or if my father forced her. I guess it doesn't matter, in any event.'

Startled, Gregory fought to keep his features composed, his eyes fixed on the flames. 'I find it difficult to understand much of what you've told me, my friend.'

Tinuva laughed sadly. 'You have no idea of the struggle within my soul, of the great divide between moredhel and eledhel. You have no idea of what it was to be a moredhel. Yes there is a darkness to it, but ah, the passion, the power of it is intoxicating beyond my ability to describe. My father's people are a unique and difficult race, yet they have their own honour and glory.

'There are few outside our race who know of the Returning,

Gregory. You and a few others among the Rangers. Even Martin Longbow, Prince Calin's friend and hunting companion, is ignorant of the Returning, I think. To some among us, it is a difficult thing, for it speaks of an ancient lore and mysteries even the wisest among us can hardly fathom.

'Some believe once we were a single race, serving the Ancient Ones.'

Gregory nodded, for much of that lore had been hidden before the arrival in Elvandar of a white-clad warrior called Tomas. Rumour was he had once been a keep-boy in Crydee, but now he was a swordsman unmatched in ferocity and power. It was said he harboured an ancient magic within him, and Gregory knew there was some truth to this, for he had seen his friend and other elves when they spoke of Tomas. He had heard the whispers of Valheru, the Ancient Ones.

'It is said that when the Ancient Ones departed this world, they named us a free people, and we divided, some clinging to the ways of our ancestors, while others sought out power for the sake of power.

'It is from that division that the moredhel and the eledhel arose. We have grown so different that our language, customs, and beliefs have changed.' Tinuva looked at Gregory. 'Did you know that the union between a moredhel and an eledhel can produce no offspring?'

Gregory said nothing, but silently gazed at his friend.

'Some say this proves we are a different race from the Dark Ones. Yet, those of us who were once of the moredhel, who have Returned, can take wives and father children.'

Gregory said, 'It's passing strange.'

'There are mysteries even more difficult to plumb,' said Tinuva. 'Such as the heart of another.' He paused. 'I told you that even before we were married I suspected Bovai loved Anleah. At the wedding feast, I told him there was no shame in it, for who could know her and not love her?

'Bovai was not the only one. Kavala hated me for the betrayal he saw as the cause of his clan's destruction. But most of all, he hated me for wedding Anleah.'

'He was the one you slew on the road,' Gregory interjected.

Tinuva nodded.

They had heard the two approaching moredhel and had laid the ambush, and then at the very last second Tinuva had shifted aim, going for the one on the right, the same target Gregory was aiming at. It had thrown the ambush off and one had escaped, but now he understood why.

'A moment I have dreamed of for centuries,' Tinuva whispered.

'I understand.'

'Bovai hates me for what he sees as a betrayal of everything he holds sacred in his life: his clan's honour, his blood, and his shame. Kavala hated me because of personal jealousy and envy as much as because I killed his brother. Kavala made a practice of hunting close to the boundaries of Elvandar, and when he could, he'd stalk our sentries. He killed four over the years, leaving his mark on them, so that I knew it was his doing, his way of reminding me he was out there, and more. It was he who left a message on the first corpse that Anleah had been wed to my brother.'

Gregory said nothing, waiting for Tinuva to continue, but the elf paused and sipped his tea before continuing.

'I feel shame, and no little fear that my moredhel blood still lingers in my veins, for I will tell you what I will tell no other, Gregory: I enjoyed killing Kavala.' He rose as he said it.

Gregory looked up at his friend, not certain how to respond. He would never have imagined his friend capable of taking pleasure in the death of another.

Tinuva kicked at the coals of the fire and then tossed another log on which crackled and hissed as the flames took. Then he squatted and held his hands out to the growing flames, warming the palms. 'The madness of it all taints me. My father kidnapped Anleah to fulfil his own plans and my joy blinded me to the reality that my happiness was never a factor in my father's choices. I ignored the pain my brother's love for her must have caused him, distracted already by the call of the Returning. A clan destroyed and brothers hunting brothers in the name of honour. Madness, all of it madness.'

Another silence fell, but this one was shorter.

'That realization came at the moment I knew I was no longer of the moredhel. I left my life behind and went on the journey to be reborn.'

'And yet you slew Kavala without hesitation, taking the shot rather than letting me do it.'

Tinuva smiled. 'I am of the eledhel, but that does not mean I am without flaw.'

Gregory shook his head. 'No mortal being is without flaw.'

'You know that my brother and I shall settle this thing soon,' Tinuva said, looking up at the sky, which was darkening with the approach of night.

'Is that why you tell me these things now? You feel fate closing in?'

Tinuva smiled. 'So that someone will know. So that if I do not survive, you may tell Dennis what the truth of this hunt was, and some day tell those in Elvandar what has transpired. 'I was always better with the blade than my brother, but that is no guarantee of my success. Fate is bringing us together to finish this tragedy, but I may be the one to travel to the Blessed Isle, and not my brother.'

Gregory nodded, saying nothing.

'Bovai's honour demands it. I am an apostate; I have abandoned all that he is. The shame to my clan is all but unbearable in a way that it is hard for anyone not of the moredhel to understand.'

'And of what he now has, that once was yours?'

'Yes,' Tinuva sighed. 'I have never loved another as I once loved her. I know now that it is in the past, but still, at times I remember . . .'

His voice trailed off and again a silence lingered until darkness concealed the cold woods around them. Then the elf sighed and Gregory was startled beyond words to realize that Tinuva was silently weeping.

The tears of an elf were said to be the rarest of all things, and that but a single drop could restore the life of a dying man. Gregory knew the later was but an old wives' tale, but in all the years he had known elves, he had never seen one weep. He remained motionless, hardly daring to breathe and the darkness of night closed in, the fire flickering down and dying before Tinuva spoke again.

'My brother and I shall soon meet again,' and his voice was a

212

shadow moving on the night wind, 'and it will come to a bloody end.' He looked at his friend. 'For the only thing that will keep me from killing him is my own death.'

Gregory remained silent. He listened to the wind, and silently thanked the gods that he was spared the burden that was crushing his friend.

THIRTEEN

Accord

The woods were silent.

Asayaga, bow raised and partially drawn, waited. The stag was half-concealed behind a fallen log, only its antlers and the upper arc of its back visible. It had been there for some minutes, peeling bark from a low-hanging branch, head down.

Asayaga remained motionless, barely daring to breathe, a slight trickle of sweat creasing down his forehead.

The stag raised its head, seemed to look straight at him. *Don't look in its eyes*, Asayaga remembered, *they can sense that*. He let his gaze drift away. A moment later the stag stepped out from behind the overturned log. With a steady, fluid motion, as relaxed as if he were a branch stirring in the breeze, Asayaga drew back, sighted down the shaft and let his fingers slip off the string.

The arrow winged in, the stag leapt into the air and then collapsed.

Asayaga started forward.

'Don't move.'

Asayaga froze and looked over his shoulder. Dennis was leaning against the tree beside him, bow in one hand.

'Remember, I told you this before. The sound of your shooting, the impact of the arrow, the death struggle of the animal –' and as he spoke he nodded to the stag which was feebly thrashing on the ground, '– if anyone else is near, it will draw them. I told you, if you are in hostile woods, after you shoot you should draw back in to your cover and wait a moment.'

'But the animal?'

'If you didn't make a clean kill, that is your own damn fault. But you must wait. Look around you, listen carefully. Usually if someone who is unskilled hears the shot he'll immediately start towards you, expecting to catch you off-guard butchering your kill, and you get an arrow in the back.'

He smiled, a smile that held no warmth.

'I know, I've done it more than once.'

'To Tsurani?'

'Do you want to know?'

Asayaga did not reply, his gaze going past Dennis to the snow-covered glade and the stag struggling in its death agony. It was something he had never quite understood about himself. He had seen thousands of men die in nearly ten years of war and could look on it at times with a near-total detachment, but an animal suffering – be it a horse or needra injured in battle, or the stag now dying – moved him deeply. He tried to shut out the look in the animal's eyes.

So strange to be out here like this with Hartraft, he thought. They had taken to the habit of going for a walk together each morning. For the first few days the walks had clearly been defined as a meeting to discuss what had to be done that day.

Dennis always went forth with his bow and more often than not returned with something for the pot, and finally Asayaga had borrowed a bow from Wolfgar.

Dennis had first met Asayaga's efforts with barely-concealed disdain, but after several days, he announced that if Asayaga was to hunt by his side he had to learn to do it right or leave the bow behind.

Now, at last, Asayaga had made his first kill and he felt a touch of bitterness. The Tsurani had accepted Dennis's lessons and admonishments in silence. He was willing to defer to Hartraft's superior skills, and besides, he was learning, how Hartraft worked in the woods: a valuable lesson worth the humiliations. At this moment, however, he half-expected a nod, an acknowledgment of a difficult shot through the woods on game they had stalked for nearly an hour.

The mere fact that he expected some sort of praise from Hartraft made him angry with himself. He now did as ordered, carefully scanning the woods, watching as the branches slowly swayed in the afternoon breeze, trying to catch a movement that was not in rhythm, listening for a sound that was out of the ordinary. He caught the distant sound of a horse, and looked back to Dennis, who had heard it as well and simply shook his head. Of course it was all an exercise, for they were still safe in the valley, but he played out the game.

'Nothing.'

'Are you certain?'

'Why? Is this still a drill or do you have someone hidden in the woods waiting to kill me?'

Dennis's features clouded. 'Some day soon it will again be real between us, but until then, you are safe in my company. But while marching with my command in the woods I expect you to be of some help, at least.'

'Who held the centre of the trail in our final retreat, Hartraft?'

'The next fight might be different – a running battle through the forest – and there it's archery and stealth that counts.'

Asayaga held up his hand motioning Dennis to silence. 'This argument is ridiculous,' he hissed. Drawing his blade, he turned and went to the stag, which was still kicking weakly, and knelt by its side.

He lowered his head, whispered a prayer and then drew the blade across the dying beast's throat. Its kicking weakened and then finally stopped.

'A dumb beast suffering needlessly tends to divert me,' Asayaga said coldly, looking up at Dennis.

Dennis knelt beside Asayaga without comment, and started to gut the animal.

'Why have you taught me this?' Asayaga asked.

'What?'

'How to hunt.'

'We need food, and also, when we face the Dark Brotherhood again, I need you to understand our tactics.'

'No. I see it as foolish of you.'

'Why?'

'I am your enemy, Hartraft. In the month that we've been here I've observed you. You have taught me skills I never knew before. It makes me even more dangerous to you now.'

Dennis leaned back, his hands covered in blood, and laughed. 'You, dangerous? I'll give you a half hour to go hide, then we can have our fight. You'll be dead before the hour is finished.'

'When we fight it will be in challenge, as you agreed, in the open, before our men.'

'Why? That gives you the advantage. Let's do it in the woods instead.'

'And give you the advantage?' Asayaga replied with a laugh. 'We agreed to an open challenge, blade on blade.'

'I don't quite remember it that way.'

'Are you calling me a liar?' Asayaga barked, and he stood up, reaching to his side, but his sword was back in the long house, with all the rest.

Dennis shook his head. 'No, I am not calling you a liar, Asayaga.' He motioned for the Tsurani to sit back down. 'We have to settle how this will be fought.'

'Our pledge is binding, it is to be a duel in the open.'

'All right then,' Dennis replied wearily, 'let it be swords, in the open, witnessed by all our men.'

Asayaga, gave an angry grunt. He watched as Dennis effortlessly gutted the animal. 'You've lived all your life in the woods, haven't you?' he asked at last.

Dennis nodded, saying nothing.

Asayaga leaned back, looking past him. It had been clear for over a week and there was even a hint of warmth in the afternoon air, sunlight sparkling though the trees, catching the snow still clinging to the branches so that it seemed as if the trees were garlanded with baskets of diamonds. 'Where I lived the woods were dank jungle. I always hated them, they seemed so dangerous, foreboding. The sunlight never shone there, and deadly serpents and stalkers lurked within.'

'Stalkers lurk here too,' said Dennis.

'Such as you.'

'Yes.'

Asayaga nodded. 'Yes, but it's different. If there was no war, this would be a good place. Sheltered in winter, the fields look fertile, the game is rich. It could be a good life here.'

'If there was no war . . .' Dennis hesitated. 'Yes, it could be.'

'Was your home like this before the war?'

'Don't ask me about my home, Asayaga.'

'Sorry. I did not mean to bring the return of unpleasant memories.'

There was silence for several minutes as Dennis finished his job, putting the heart and liver back inside the hollowed-out carcass, then washed his blade and hands with snow. 'It was like this place,' he said softly, almost as if speaking to himself. 'Our valley had good land, by midsummer the grain stood waist-high and there was more than enough for all: even the poorest of my father's tenants ate well, had a dry roof over his head, and a warm fire in the winter.' He sat back, absently wiping his hands on his stained trousers. 'The great forest was thick with game. My father – and when he still was able, my grandfather as well – we would go hunting together and when we returned there would be a feast and all in the keep joined us. The feasting would last for days, especially the great Midwinter festival like the one we celebrated two weeks ago. My grandfather had an old retainer named Jocomo who would dress up as Father Winter and come riding into the courtyard with a bag of sweets for the children.' With a faint smile Dennis added, 'He always said that the wolves who pulled his sleigh were ill, which is why he had to borrow one of grandfather's horses and each year when I was a child I would believe him. Anyone who came to our door was given a place at our table and my grandfather would insist that before we of title ate, those who served or were visitors must eat first.'

'Your people loved him, then?'

'Who could not?' Dennis said wistfully. 'He always distrusted the high nobles in the great halls to the east, far away in Rillanon and Salador, where it was safe, saying that they had forgotten why we existed, that our duty was first and foremost to protect those in our charge, and not the other way around.'

Asayaga sat silent, saying nothing, and after a while Dennis went on.

'Yes, he was loved. I remember when I was a boy, maybe eight summers old. I told a stable boy to polish the silver trim on my saddle and came out to find him asleep, the silver still unpolished and in my childlike rage I struck him.' Dennis shook his head. 'My grandfather saw this.'

'And he beat you?'

'No,' and Dennis. 'He said nothing, but the following morning, hours before dawn, he dragged me out of my bed, pushed me down the stairs and threw me into the stable and told me to muck it out.

'How I cried bitter tears, with him standing there glaring at me, not saying a word. After I mucked out the stables, I fed all the horses, then had to walk them, then oil the harnesses, before I could eat breakfast. Then I had to groom every horse, help the blacksmith with shodding, then help to bring in the hay; and thus I worked the whole day, and every day like that for a week. I ate in the stables and collapsed into exhausted sleep in the stables. The humiliation was the hardest part to bear, for all in the keep knew, and all treated me no longer as if I was the grandson of the Baron, but was just a common stable boy.' He smiled. 'The boy I struck secretly helped me in spite of my grandfather's orders for him to take the time off and go hunting and use my horse. Lars was his name and he became one of my closest friends after that.'

Dennis sighed and looked over at Asayaga. 'Lars was killed the night the keep fell, standing by my grandfather's side.'

He turned away from Asayaga, not wanting the Tsurani to see his emotion. 'There was a story how a new man-at-arms –' he whispered, his voice distant and haunting, '– just a boy, fell asleep on watch one night. He awoke to find my grandfather standing above him, in the driving snow, having taken his place in the sentry-box.'

'Did he hang him?' Asayaga asked. 'That is our punishment.'

'It is ours as well, but not that night. The terrified boy begged forgiveness and my grandfather raised him to his feet. "You not only failed me," my grandfather said, "you failed your family whom I nevertheless protected while you slept. You were all that stood between your mother and danger this night and you failed her far more than you failed me. Now go back to your mother and when you are finally man enough to take the responsibilities of a man you may return to the service of our people. I will serve out the remainder of your watch."'

Asayaga smiled.

'That boy, years later, was my trainer and the sergeant of this company.'

'Jurgen?'

Dennis simply nodded and looked away. 'It was a good place, our valley. The border marches were quiet: sometimes a year or more would pass without a single clash with renegades. At times we would see an eledhel or even a dwarf come to our keep for a night's shelter and a place by the fire.' There was a long pause. Then: 'Old Wolfgar,' and Dennis smiled, chuckling softly, 'before he had his run-in with the king, was often at our table. He favoured my grandfather more than any other duke or baron though they would pay him more for a song in their honour than grandfather would. 'You see a bit of my grandfather in Wolfgar.'

Asayaga looked at him surprise.

'Beneath that obscene tongue there's his zest for life, his joy in watching a sunrise after a stormy night, his trading of a jest between friends, and his love of a good song: all things he shared with my family.' Dennis looked off as if Asayaga was not even there. 'The night my grandfather died, there was not a man among us who would not have died in his place. I wish I had . . .'

His voice trailed off for a moment.

'It was my wedding day, the assault coming just before dusk. Everyone from the village and the keep was in the great hall when one of the sentries came rushing in, screaming that an enemy host was attacking. Before we could even pick up our arms your men were already scaling the walls. Within minutes we lost the gate and the assault on the great hall began. We blocked the entryway, but you set the roof afire.'

Again there was a long silence.

'I should have died that night.'

'You didn't, though.'

Dennis looked over suspiciously at Asayaga.

'No insult, Hartraft. Fate decreed differently is all I mean.'

'My father and grandfather barricaded the main door, then both ordered Gwenynth and me to flee through the escape-way, saying that someone had to get help. I refused.' He stopped for a moment, looking up at the tree tops. 'Something struck me from behind. I always suspected it was Jurgen, although right up till his death he never admitted to the deed. I awoke outside the keep, with Jurgen and a few dozen of our men.'

'And Gwenynth?'

'She was kneeling over me, wiping my face when a bolt winged in from the dark.' He lowered his head. 'She died in my arms.'

'Hartraft, though my words might ring hollow, I am sorry. War should be an honourable affair between men who chose to fight.'

Dennis, head still lowered, snorted derisively. 'Tsurani, when was the last time you saw a city burn, or a village overrun by starving troops, or the body of a girl lying in the snow, the crossbow bolt in her back a blessed release from her agony?'

'I know,' Asayaga whispered. 'I know.'

'We knew that you, the Tsurani, were coming, but thought you were still days away. Gwenynth and I were pledged to marry and we changed the date to the night before my departure for the wars. My grandfather had patrols ranging forward to guard the passes into our valley and to give warning of any approach, but no warning ever came. How and why the patrol guarding the pass failed us I don't know.'

Asayaga stirred uncomfortably. 'I was not there, I have sworn that to you, Hartraft.'

Dennis nodded.

'And yet I heard something about it.'

'What?' Now his gaze was firmly locked on Asayaga.

'The attack-column found four of your men dead in the pass leading to your valley. I remember one of the Strike Leaders talking about it. He said one had a dagger in his back, the others no wounds, and he suspected poison.'

'I never heard this,' Dennis said coldly.

'I only tell you what I heard around a campfire long afterwards.'

Dennis sat wrapped in silence and Asayaga could see that this bit of news, which had waited for eight long years to be delivered, came as a profound shock.

221

'And this Strike Leader? Is he still alive?'

Asayaga shook his head. 'Dead. It's believed you killed him in one of your ambushes three years ago.'

'Good.' The single word was spoken with a cold icy satisfaction.

'It doesn't change what happened,' Asayaga said, and he struggled to control his own anger, for the commander of a hundred had been of his clan.

'To me it does.'

'And when you've killed the last Tsurani who was in that battle, then what? By the gods, they're likely all dead by now anyhow. Dead in battle, dead from the coughing sickness, frozen, drowned; or gone mad and wandered off into the forests. This war has claimed thousands of my people, Hartraft. When will you be satisfied that you are finished?'

'When we bury the last of you, or you finally flee.'

'We can't leave.'

'Why? The portal is open: just go.'

'Can you leave?'

'You're on our land, damn it!'

'Not because I want to be. Like you I have rulers above me. I'm here because my clan ordered it. Do you think I want to be here? You Kingdom soldiers do not even have the faintest glimmer of an idea about all that is behind this. You have no idea of the clans, of the rivalry, of what some call the Great Game, which is behind all of this madness. It goes far beyond you, me, our men, or even this war itself. Only an idealist would be stupid enough to believe that the purpose of this war is simply for us to conquer you. And I dare say that on your side there is more than one prince who would sell his own brother and the thousands who serve beneath him, if it could advance his own position in the game of kings.' Asayaga looked over at the stag, its eyes blank, the warmth already leaking from its body. 'We are all pawns, Hartraft, all of us.' And as he spoke, Asayaga felt shame for allowing his bitterness to show.

Dennis looked at him and then slowly nodded his head. 'But your family is safe while mine is dead, my land occupied, my keep in ruins: that is the difference between us, Tsurani.'

'And are you dead as well, Hartraft?'

222

Dennis stared at him. 'Don't try to get into my soul, Asayaga. You are not my friend, I do not seek your advice. The last one I would allow near me died last month, a Tsurani spear tearing out his heart.'

'I heard Jurgen was a fine warrior: I heard how he saved that young soldier, the one who helps the priest.'

'Not much of an exchange.'

'For the boy it was. He'll carry that for the rest of his life.'

'I hope so.'

'Three times I've had men step in front of me to take an arrow, or a blade that would have killed me. I carry their souls with me.' Asayaga's voice was heavy. 'That is the nature of war, and the love men have for each other in war. In the retreat to this place I saw one of your men risk his life to save one of mine.'

'That does not mean anything. The heat of battle, nothing more.'

'I wonder.'

'I dislike idealists as much as you do, Asayaga. Don't read more into it than that. I sit beside you now because I must.'

'I don't want to be your friend either, Hartraft. I don't befriend those without souls. We are men and as men we admit that vengeance has its place, but to live for that and nothing else? It's not much of a life, Hartraft, not one that I want any part of.'

He said the last words sharply, staring directly into Dennis's eyes and for once he sensed he had hit a mark with this man, for Dennis lowered his gaze. There was a moment of awkward silence between the two men, which was broken at last by the sound of approaching horses. Dennis tensed, hand instinctively reaching to his bow, but Asayaga had already caught a glimpse of the party riding towards them and he stood up.

Alyssa, long white cape flowing, reined in, a moment later followed by Roxanne with her father riding beside her.

Asayaga saw the flicker in Alyssa's eyes and in spite of his struggle for reserve he knew that his tension in her presence showed. The game between them had been going on for weeks, barely a word spoken, but always the veiled glances, the momentary smile, and then almost a studied indifference.

'Your first stag?' Roxanne asked as she dismounted and walked up to the animal to study it.

'How did you know it was me?'

'Both of you left with a dozen arrows in your quivers and, Tsurani, you now have eleven.'

Wolfgar laughed. 'Times I think she should have been born a man!'

She looked back at her father disdainfully.

'A good kill,' Roxanne observed, 'put him on my horse.'

Without comment, Dennis hoisted the animal and laid it across the haunches of the horse which pranced nervously at the scent of blood until Roxanne went back and with a firm hand on the bridle, stilled the animal.

'You should not be out riding,' Dennis said, looking over at Wolfgar.

The old man coughed, leaned over in his saddle and spat. 'The day is warm enough. I can't stay cooped up forever. Damn me, if the ride is the end of my life here, well I can only think of a couple of better ways to die, and the preferred method of my leaving is one I will not discuss in front of my daughters, so shut up and stop trying to nurse an old man.'

He leaned over and gently swatted Dennis across the back of the head.

Asayaga watched the exchange and saw the look in Dennis's eyes, a momentary warmth for an old lost friend, an absent reaching out to pat Wolfgar on the knee. He could also see Roxanne watching the two of them, but Dennis did not notice, his gaze had shifted instead to Alyssa.

Asayaga felt a surge of jealousy and it bothered him. Alyssa had, throughout their stay, remained aloof, bearing herself like a princess of the court, required to entertain guests, but obviously feeling that one worthy of her attention had yet to arrive. But at this moment, as she gazed upon him, he wondered. She wore the hint of a smile at Dennis's attention and then she edged her horse away. She turned as she did so, and looked down at Asayaga.

'A feast tonight, Asayaga, in honour of your first kill. That is an old tradition.'

224

He bowed formally. 'We cannot tonight, my lady. The fasting for the Day of Atonement begins at sundown and lasts till sundown tomorrow.'

'What is this?' Wolfgar asked.

'Our tradition on the feast day of the god Hilio, the Judge of Life. It is a day set aside for fasting, meditation, and the seeking of atonement for the wrongs committed over the last year.' He ventured a slight smile at Alyssa. 'I'm not entirely sure this is the right day, for I have lost some count of time since we encountered Dennis's forces, but I believe it to be close enough. On our world, it is celebrated with the first rising of the new moon after midwinter. I think the god will be tolerant.'

'Then when your fasting is done,' Alyssa offered.

'I thank you, my lady.'

'You may choose who shall sit by your side.'

He smiled. 'Then of course, my lady, I will ask that it be you.'

She laughed softly. 'I am honoured.'

She turned away, but as she did so, her eyes stayed on him and he felt his heart freeze. It was the subtle sign he had heard poets speak of, the gaze of a woman over her shoulder, the looking back with eyes half-lowered, the indicator that she was indeed interested in him.

In the nine long years he had been trapped on this world not once had he known such a moment. Like any of the men of his unit he had turned more than once to the camp followers, but that was a deed of the moment, something without meaning. This was different and he wondered if here was someone who could touch his heart after so many years of loneliness.

The moment vanished like smoke as she slowly trotted away, nonchalantly calling for her father to ride back to the stockade.

'I'll come back when I'm damn good and ready,' Wolfgar growled, but even as he spoke his gaze was on Asayaga.

Asayaga looked around, wondering if Dennis and Roxanne had sensed the moment as well and knew that they had. And then he wondered if Alyssa was simply playing a game of flirtation and that he was reading far too much into what had just happened. Yet he could sense coolness on the part of Dennis, and an almost amused disdain from Roxanne as she lightly sprang into the saddle and set off after her sister, leaving the three men alone.

Wolfgar watched as the two girls wove through the trees and down the slope, disappearing from view. Asayaga could sense the intense love the old man felt, for a bit of a wistful smile lit his features as if he were remembering something from long ago. He sighed and looked back to see that the two men were watching him and that he had been caught off guard.

'A favour to ask,' the old man sighed.

'Anything,' Dennis replied.

'Keep an eye on them.'

'Of course.'

'No, I don't think you fully understand. We both know what will happen here soon. Your foes will not leave you here in peace. I would suspect that even now they have watchers on the northern passes.' As he spoke he pointed to where, through the trees, the distant peaks that rimmed in the valley were clearly visible. The tallest of the pinnacles trailed a wispy streamer of clouds. 'If they don't today, they will have them there by the time you're ready to leave.'

'I have my patrols out,' Dennis replied. 'The approaches you told me to picket are watched.'

'Even your patrols will not see everything,' Wolfgar replied.

'It could be weeks yet, perhaps not until spring,' Asayaga ventured.

'Let's hope so,' Wolfgar replied. 'I'd like things here to last a bit longer. I've had nearly twenty good years in this valley. A strange place for me, who was once the toast of the royal court, to spin out his days.' He laughed and shook his head. 'The first few years hiding here, I thought I'd go mad with it. A bunch of drunken louts to sing my ballads to. Oh, they thought me amusing enough – if they hadn't, someone would have slipped a dagger between my ribs, in-laws are like that. But the years spun out, my two little ones grew, became young ladies and now . . .'

His voice trailed off and he lowered his head. Asayaga was startled to see tears in the old man's eyes.

'You don't realize just how quickly the years pass until it happens to you. Someone of your years still thinks there's all the time in the world. Then one day you awake and you see the first wisps of grey in your beard, but you still feel strong enough, you can still tumble a wench and make her laugh come morning, you still think you have the entire world.

'Then, one day, the girls you once so eagerly pursued, why, they are off chasing boys who seem like children to you, for in fact they are children compared to you!'

'You still have the fire in you,' Asayaga offered, smiling.

Wolfgar held out a trembling hand. 'I can barely hold my feasting cup without it slopping over me: it's been years since I could curl these fingers around a lute, let alone around the plump backside of any of the serving-girls. So don't lie to me, lad, though I bless you for trying.'

Wolfgar's gaze lingered on the mountain tops.

'They'll come over that pass. It's hard to defend, too broad at the top. When they hit, take the pass to the west; I doubt if they know of it. Roxanne can guide you. Take everyone with you.'

'You'll guide us,' Dennis offered, a note of concern in his voice.

Wolfgar shook his head. 'My last wife is buried here. My happiest memories are of this place. No, I think I'll stay.'

'No.' Dennis snapped the one word out, his voice filled with bitterness.

Wolfgar leaned back over, his trembling hand resting on Dennis's shoulder. Asayaga could see the sudden anguish in Dennis and understood. Here was a man who had no one, who thought himself completely alone, and then by the pure randomness of fate had rediscovered a long-lost friend from his childhood. It would be even harder to lose him again.

'You know it must be,' Wolfgar offered. 'I would only slow you down and the first night in the cold would most likely kill me anyhow. I'd prefer to die in my own feasting hall, my written ballads spread on the table before me, a good cup of mead in my hand.'

Dennis, sensing Asayaga's gaze, turned away, head lowered. 'Yes,' he whispered. 'You're right, damn it. I'm sorry we ever found this place.'

'I'm not. The war is spreading this way. Things in the north are stirring. It would have only been a matter of time before they came here. I think it a blessing. I know my girls will be safe, the other women and children as well. That was what I have been worried about ever since the men of this place disappeared.' Wolfgar patted him on the shoulder. 'That's why I ask you to protect my girls. I know what happens with girls who march with soldiers. I want better for them than that.'

He looked over at Asayaga.

'No offence meant.'

'And none taken. You speak as any father would and I swear my oath to you that I shall protect their honour with my sword and life.'

As he spoke, Asayaga drew his hunting dagger and turned it so that the hilt was pointed towards the old man, thus showing his pledge-bond. Wolfgar smiled and bowed formally from the saddle, revealing for a moment the training and breeding of old when he had performed in the courts of kings.

'I know what the two of you intend to do once you're free of pursuit: to take up your old war again. If the two of you are fate doomed to do that, I ask that you pledge before each other now that whoever survives will see my girls to safety, to somewhere beyond the wars.'

Dennis's eyes which had softened for a moment, now glazed over again into hardness.

'I pledge it,' Dennis said without enthusiasm and Asayaga did likewise.

Wolfgar noisily cleared his throat and wiped his eyes. 'Foolish tears of an old man,' he said huskily.

He reined his mount around and motioned for the two to fall in by his side. Together they started down the slope to the stockade walking in silence.

The afternoon was getting late, the sun starting to slip behind the western mountains, the long shadows of the peaks spreading out across the valley. Off to his left Asayaga could see another hunting party coming in, several Kingdom archers followed by half a dozen Tsurani, a couple of his men armed with bows as well.

The gates of the stockade were open and the bath-house constructed by Asayaga's men within days after their arrival was a hive of activity, smoke billowing from the chimney, a swarm of naked men spilling out of the doorway, laughing, jumping into the slushy snow

– Gregory, who looked almost bear like in their midst, bellowing from the shock. The Kingdom men were all from the north and the ritual of a snow roll after a midwinter's bath had caught on with the Tsurani. The Kingdom men seemed to be on the verge of addiction to the Tsurani tubs. Unlike Kingdom bathing, where you'd sit in a tub while someone else poured water over your head – often cold – the Tsurani had built large round wooden tubs, large enough to hold half a dozen people each. The water was warmed ingeniously, by heating up large rocks and lowering them into the water in a metal cage, over and over, until the water seemed to be on the verge of scalding. Dennis had almost ordered the project halted when a few of the rocks had exploded upon heating, but Asayaga had insisted it was a common problem on his homeworld and that no one would be in danger once the rock had survived the first heating.

Dennis felt no pleasure at the sight of the cavorting men. The Tsurani had no shame, he had come to learn, and bathed openly in front of others, men or women, and his Marauders were becoming equally uninhibited. He did not consider this a good thing.

Other men piled into the bath-house, hanging up their tunics on pegs hammered into the outside wall, then sitting on the steps to pull off their foot-wrappings or boots before venturing in.

'I still say it's dangerous,' Wolfgar grumbled. 'All that hot water opens up the skin so evil vapours can get in and make you sick.'

'How many of your men have boils?' Asayaga asked, looking over at Dennis.

'I don't know. A dozen or so.'

'Diseases of the skin, you Kingdom soldiers are riddled with it. You're the filthiest people I've ever laid eyes on. How often do you bathe? Once a year whether you need it or not?'

'Like Wolfgar said, it's unhealthy. It's fine for women but they're different.'

Asayaga laughed and shook his head. 'Try it with me.'

'What?'

'The bath. Yes, you, Hartraft: or are you afraid?'

Wolfgar threw back his head and laughed. 'He's got you.'

'We don't have much time before evening parade, so will you?'

'Getting the dirt off you might make Alyssa notice you,' Wolfgar interjected with a grin, 'or even Roxanne.'

As if the mention of their names was a summons, the two daughters, along with several of the women of the stockade, came out of the gate wrapped in heavy towels, laughing and pointing at the men cavorting in the slush. The sight of them caused the Kingdom soldiers to scramble, running up to grab their tunics and pull them on, a sight which made Asayaga burst into laughter since the short jackets barely covered their backsides. Gregory, grinning, took his time, waving casually to the girls. The Tsurani nodded politely, but made no attempt to hide their nakedness.

Wolfgar urged his mount forward and rode up to his daughters, but it was obvious within seconds that whatever his objections the women were going into the sauna.

'If it wasn't his daughters going in there,' Asayaga ventured, 'I dare say that old man would go in as well, and it wouldn't be so he could get clean.'

Dennis actually smiled.

'Well, Hartraft,' Asayaga asked, 'are you going in?'

'What? Now?' He looked over at Alyssa who was sitting on the steps, pulling off her boots.

'Yes, now. Back home men and women bathe together all the time.'

'I don't know. These are respectable girls, they're my friend's daughters.'

'The others aren't?' Asayaga laughed at Dennis's discomfort.

'The women here have been doing this since we built the bath. They understand the customs.'

'Still.'

The serving-girls led the group in, Roxanne and Alyssa following, and as the door closed again Alyssa gave him that backward glance.

'Well, if you aren't, I am,' Asayaga announced, and heading over to the rough-hewn platform in front of the sauna he casually started to disrobe.

Dennis slowly walked over.

'If I hear of anything going on in there –' Wolfgar announced.

'It won't be your daughters,' Asayaga replied. 'I made my pledge. But as for the others, old man, think of all that you are missing.'

Wolfgar grinned slyly. 'Oh, you don't know if I've missed it or not!' Laughing, he reined his horse around and rode back into the stockade.

Stripping naked, Asayaga hung up his tunic, trousers and foot-wrappings and leaned his bow and quiver against the log wall. Even as he did so he had a sudden sharp memory of home, of the bath-house in his village, a beautiful place for the baths were the centre of any town and as such a place of pride for the villagers. It was built of the best stone, fine grained marble offset with lovely blue tiles, with hot and cold baths, hot-air rooms and steam, then afterwards you could lounge on the deck overlooking the sea and sip warm tea. His father's estate had large bathing tubs, of course, but as a boy Asayaga had preferred bathing in the village. Men and women might bathe without modesty, but a adolescent boy was an adolescent boy, he remembered with mild amusement. He had met his first lover at the bath, a girl who regarded him boldly, even though he was the son of a noble.

He looked around, aware again of just how alien this world was: the forest, snow-capped mountains; the marble and tiles replaced by logs with the bark still on them, the cracks between them chinked with dried mud and straw.

And yet, if given a choice at this moment, he wondered if he could return. In spite of all that he knew would transpire in the days ahead, at this moment he felt completely free. The Great Game, at least for now, was far away. Granted there was still his lieutenant Sugama to contend with, but ever since their arrival in Wolfgar's valley, Sugama had been relatively quiet, his embarrassment on the first night's feast having silenced him. There was no commander above him, no one from another clan manoeuvring to get him killed or humiliated. He was free.

He looked over at Dennis who was slowly, and none too eagerly, removing his jacket to reveal a sweat-stained undershirt that was ragged and grey with filth. Yes, Hartraft was the enemy, and in the ways of war and killing with stealth he was indeed frightful and unrelenting. But he was also straightforward and without guile in his dealings. He would find the Great Game inconceivable. There was no hidden meaning within meanings, no subtlety within him; if he planned to kill someone he said so, then did it. He did it remorselessly, and without feeling, but he did it while looking his opponent in the eye.

As Dennis pulled off his shirt Asayaga was surprised by the scars that laced Hartraft's slender frame. A pink knot just below his left collarbone, from either an arrow or a rapier wound looked barely healed. As he pulled off his trousers Asayaga could see where his left calf had been sliced nearly in half, most likely a blow from someone down on the ground, and there was another wound on the thigh, a bolt apparently having gone clear through his leg.

'You've been cut up as well,' Dennis said, as if reading Asayaga's thoughts, and pointed to the white knot of a scar on the Tsurani's chest.

Asayaga nodded. 'An arrow at the Battle of Walinor. Went clean through me,' and he half-turned to show the exit wound.

'Better when they do, digging an arrow out of the chest, it usually kills a man. You're lucky to have survived it.'

'We have some good healers, better than the priest even.'

'Corwin? He's all right, or at least I think he is.'

Asayaga sensed something. 'You think he is?'

'Nothing, at least not for now.'

Asayaga nodded. From inside the bath-house laughter echoed.

'Ready for this, Hartraft?'

Dennis seemed unsure of himself and Asayaga felt a momentary pleasure in that. It was good to see the legendary Hartraft off balance, even if it was over nothing more than walking naked into a steamy room with women present.

'Don't worry,' he offered finally. 'The custom when women are present is for everyone to keep a small towel on for modesty. You'll find them inside the door. So let's go.'

Leading the way, Asayaga stepped inside and then broke into a grin. His men had constructed this bath-house, and had introduced the locals to the custom . . . but they had obviously not instructed anyone on the finer points of etiquette.

This should be interesting, he thought with a grin as he found a bench close to the steaming rocks then settled back to watch Hartraft's reaction. It was obvious, the moment the Kingdom soldier came through the door and reached for the small towel that wasn't there that Dennis would have been far more comfortable in the middle of a battle.

Sitting back, all Asayaga could do was to shake his head in amusement. He motioned to a corner where towels and clothes had been piled, and Hartraft hurriedly grabbed one and covered himself.

Dennis's discomfort had allowed the Tsurani Force Commander a momentary distraction. Now as he settled down to bathe himself, Asayaga had to fight to maintain his composure. Alyssa sat back in the nearest tub, her arms resting on the sides of the wooden tub, regarding Asayaga with a clear gaze and a slight smile on her lips. Struggling to remember his pledge, he used a bucket and tepid water to soap up and clean himself off.

To Dennis, Asayaga said, 'It is easier when someone else scrubs your back. I will show you.' He made Dennis turn around, and he rubbed at the man's back, appalled at the dirt that was washed away. When he was done, he handed Dennis a clean cloth. Dennis returned the courtesy, though Asayaga thought Dennis's prior experience in giving a bath must have been to his favourite hound or a horse. Still, Tsurani impassivity prevented complaint.

When they were both clean, Asayaga said, 'It is best to enter the water quickly. It will seem hotter than it is, because we have been cold so long.'

With that, he dropped his towel, and boldly climbed into the tub to settle in with a deep sigh of contentment opposite Alyssa. He had seen naked women many times before, and the lure of a woman had not struck him with such force since he had been a very young man. Her breasts were neither small nor large, but rather they seemed in balance for her size, and he had a great deal of trouble not staring at them.

He was saved from disgracing himself when Dennis entered the water. Then, with a yelp like a scalded dog, he leapt out of the tub. 'Are you mad? That water's near to boiling!'

Roxanne looked at Dennis with open amusement. 'Yes, hero. We are all being finely boiled.'

Alyssa laughed. 'You're too hard on the man, sister.'

'Oh, I like a hard man, well enough, but I don't think our captain is quite what I had in mind.' She stared openly at Dennis's crotch while her sister covered her mouth and tried to hide her laughter.

Dennis's pride was injured. He realized that if these two girls and the other women of the compound could endure the heat, so could he. He ignored Roxanne's barb and moved to the edge of the tub. With jaws clenched he stepped back into the tub and for a moment it seemed he would leap out again. Beads of perspiration appeared on his brow, then ran down his face as he sat back next to the Tsurani.

He felt tense at first, but as the minutes passed he seemed to gradually relax, stretching his legs out, and letting the heat sink into his bones. The two sisters had their heads together, whispering, and Asayaga seemed to be looking everywhere in the room except at Alyssa. Dennis let his mind wander and after a moment found himself startled by the rattle of metal. He looked around in surprise to find one of Asayaga's men loading red-hot stones into a basket. He watched as the soldier pulled out a basket on a chain, then lowered the fresh one in, the red rocks filling the room with yet more steam.

'This strikes me as a bit strange,' Dennis finally said, 'but it's not . . . unpleasant.'

Asayaga laughed. 'You barbarians.'

'Us barbarians?' There was a defensive note in his voice.

'Please, Hartraft. We have a custom in steam-houses.'

'Like the towels for modesty?' Dennis whispered pointedly.

Asayaga could see just the slightest flicker of a grin. 'Well, I think my men forgot about that. But as I was saying, the custom is that all arguments must be left at the door of the baths. Even the bitterest of foes will swim in the same pool and breathe the same steam and be allowed to do so in peace.'

Dennis leaned back and closed his eyes, breathing deeply.

'A good custom,' he whispered at last and Asayaga smiled.

'Tell me, Hartraft,' said Roxanne. 'Have you anyone waiting for you back at your camp?'

Dennis's eyes narrowed and he said bitterly, 'No.'

Roxanne studied his face and appeared on the verge of saying something. Her mouth turned up at the corner in a slight smirk he had seen before in advance of a caustic remark, but as it appeared she was about to speak, she sat back, remaining silent. She continued to stare at him for another minute, then softly she said, 'I'm sorry for your loss.'

Dennis didn't know what to say. He stared back at her, their eyes locking for a moment. *Something about this woman irritates me*, he thought, and in an attempt to put aside that irritation, he sank back against the side of the tub and closed his eyes.

Against every expectation, Dennis discovered after a few minutes of sitting there with his eyes closed that he was enjoying the hot soak. Relaxing further, he realized with a start some time later he had dozed off.

The girls had departed and Asayaga said, 'Are you rested?'

Dennis wiped his hand over his face and said, 'As it stands, yes.' He seemed surprised.

'See, there are things you can learn from us, Hartraft.'

Dennis stood up and grabbed a towel. After the hot water, the room felt chilled. 'You do this a lot?'

'Every chance I get,' said Asayaga, as he also dried himself off.

The last two Tsurani soldiers were leaving and as Dennis followed, he said, 'I think I might like to try this again.'

Outside, they dressed quickly, for if the hot bath-house had felt chilled, the freezing snow was brutal to Dennis. As he donned his tunic he said, 'What's that smell?'

Asayaga laughed. 'That's the stink you carried around with you. Now that you're clean, you notice it.'

Dennis stopped putting on his tunic. 'I have another in my field kit,' he said. Refusing to acknowledge his discomfort at being bare-chested, he said, 'I guess I should have these washed.'

Asayaga nodded. 'You'll find your men take ill less often if they keep clean. I do not know why this is so, but it is.'

As he moved away from the bath-house, Dennis saw four Tsurani erecting poles in the compound, each forming the corner of a square. Others were bringing wood and piling it in the centre of the square. He glanced at Asayaga.

'The rite of Atonement is tonight.'

As if that explained it, thought Dennis, now anxious to put on his clean tunic. He hurried to the building where he housed with Sergeant Barry and a half dozen other men, and found his kit bag. He pulled a tunic out and noticed with disappointment that it was barely cleaner than the one he wore, but he put it on anyway, and decided he would ask one of the women to wash his remaining clothing in the morning.

He thought back with some bitterness to his childhood, for clean clothing had always been provided. And despite what Asayaga said, his family bathed every week during the winter, more often in the hot months. To himself he admitted that years in the field had made him a coarse and dirty man.

Outside, he heard the sound of chanting and realized it must be the Tsurani. He decided to go and sort out his clothing now, rather than watch this rite.

Tinuva watched with interest as the Tsurani first built a small fire and then lined up for their ceremony. Asayaga, followed by Sugama and the other Tsurani were formed up in a line, weapons conspicuously absent. They watched the sun lower in the west, and chanted softly. When at last the sun was behind the western mountains, Asayaga moved forward to the first pole, which Tinuva noted was the easternmost, bowed his head, and said something softly. He moved to the northern pole and repeated the gestures. The western and southern poles followed; then he paused before the fire. He held out his hand and let a piece of material fall into the flames. He bowed once more then came to stand next to Tinuva.

Without taking his eyes off the ceremony, Tinuva asked, 'What is it you ask your god?'

Asayaga said, 'We ask Hilio, who judges men in life, to forgive us our shortcomings. Each man will repeat the request, at each of the poles, representing the four directions, for no man knows where Hilio may be. It is hoped that when we are free of this mortal life, Hilio will intercede with Silbi, She who is Death, to look upon us with mercy. We also ask Hilio to give us the strength to forgive those who have wronged us in the past year, to let others make atonement to us.'

236

Tinuva said nothing for a while, then: 'A friend once said no mortal being is without flaw.'

Asayaga said, 'This is true. And there is wisdom in knowing this. It will be a quiet night, for meditation and fasting. No man may touch food or wine until the sun sets tomorrow night.'

Tinuva said, 'A feast?'

Asayaga nodded. 'Always.'

'Then come hunting with me after your Day of Atonement, Asayaga.'

'I went hunting with Hartraft today.'

'So I have been told.' With a slight smile, Tinuva said, 'I shall be a far more patient teacher, and I will show you things even Dennis doesn't know.'

Asayaga allowed himself a rare smile. 'It would be good to know some things Dennis doesn't know.'

The elf returned the smile, briefly then leaned back against the support post and watched the rest of the ceremony.

A few minutes later Alwin Barry called for parade, and the Kingdom soldiers fell into formation. There was little military ceremony associated with the Marauders, but while in camp, Dennis insisted on morning muster and evening parade in order to keep some pretence of military discipline among the men.

Asayaga had answered by having his men join the parade every night and held a separate muster every morning. As the ceremony ended, the last of his men hurried to their positions under the watchful eye of Strike Leader Tasemu.

Barry glanced at his opposite number, and the two men began inspecting their respective commands. Asayaga said to Tinuva, 'Where is Hartraft? He has never missed a parade.'

He got his answer when Dennis came striding out of his quarters, his arms heavy with clothing, marching purposefully towards the washing hut. Both the Tsurani and Tinuva stood in stunned silence, then as the Captain of the Marauders vanished from sight, both broke out in open laughter.

FOURTEEN

Betrayal

Dawn was breaking.

'Form ranks!'

Dennis passed the order as he always did, his voice almost soft, disdainful of the parade ground bellowing typical of too many officers serving in the Kingdom armies. The last of his men came out of the long hall, slinging on their equipment. Tsurani soldiers mingled amongst them, heading to the opposite side of the narrow street to fall into ranks as well, Strike Leader Tasemu, like Dennis, passing the order in a calm even voice.

Tinuva, Gregory by his side, leaned against the open gate, watching the show and it struck him as fascinating how both companies had basically the same rituals, the turn-out before dawn, the evening inspection, even the mannerism of the sergeants, who combined a certain gruffness with some and a touch of fatherly help with others.

The Tsurani snapped to attention as Asayaga came out of the long hall, dressed in full armour and accepted the salute of Tasemu. He then proceeded to walk slowly down the line, pausing to draw a sword from a scabbard to see that it was properly sharpened, stopping to adjust the buckles on a young soldier's armour, opening several backpacks to make sure all the equipment was properly stowed.

Dennis followed the ritual as well, though his men stood at ease, but at his approach they were watchful and respectful. He ordered one man to string his bow, then chewed him out over the fact that the string was not properly waxed and the ends were frayed; another man received a dressing down because his backpack was missing a blanket.

'If we had to pull out now, this minute,' Dennis snapped, 'you'd freeze to death the first night out and I'd forbid any man to share his blanket with you, damn it. Three days cleaning the jakes.'

After Dennis stepped past, Sergeant Barry gave the unfortunate a withering gaze and made a point of nodding towards the privies outside the stockade gate. They had replaced the slit trench Dennis had ordered dug the first day, but the privies needed cleaning whereas the trenches had not.

Inspection finished, Dennis turned to face the Tsurani who were standing less than a dozen feet away. Asayaga finished at nearly the same time and the two officers stood looking at each other, Dennis obviously uncomfortable with the Tsurani's insistence of standing at attention, thus forcing Dennis to do likewise.

'All equipment is in order. All my men are accounted for,' Asayaga announced.

'All accounted for,' Dennis replied, 'save for four on the north pass. Patrol to the eastern gorge reports no sign of the enemy.'

Asayaga nodded his thanks. The Kingdom soldiers had assumed the burden of patrols and watches so the Tsurani might observe their Day of Atonement. Tsurani soldiers would take extra watches and patrols to compensate the Kingdom soldiers over the next few days.

'I have no incidents to report,' Asayaga stated.

'Nor I,' Dennis replied yet again.

There was a moment of awkward silence then Dennis finally turned to look back at his men. 'The Tsurani, as you know, are observing a holy day that will last till sunset. Some of you saw the ritual begin last night. As I understand this ritual we may not speak to them unless they speak to us first. They will fast for the entire day and I ask that we refrain from eating in front of them. We'll stand their watches for them today so they may meditate and pray, and they will make up the difference tomorrow. I don't want to hear any damn comments about anything you see them

239

do. They participated in our midwinter feast and showed proper respect.'

'And drank more than the rest of us,' a wag quipped from the back rank, his comment greeted by a ripple of laughter.

'Well, there will be a feast tonight, after sundown and we are invited. So be respectful and let's keep it peaceful.'

He turned back to Asayaga and the two saluted.

The Tsurani broke ranks, stacked their gear inside the long house and then came back out. Several of the warriors saluted as they passed Dennis, their action causing him to respond with a confused nod.

'My men are grateful that you are respecting our Day of Atonement,' Asayaga said. 'When the subject first came up many thought you would refuse.'

'Why?'

'Just because, no reason was needed.'

'That's ridiculous. The request was reasonable.'

'Are you saying I am being ridiculous?'

'Are you saying I am being unreasonable?' Dennis snapped.

The two stalked off down the length of the street, arguing vehemently.

'Must they always seek a reason to argue?' Tinuva whispered, looking over at Gregory.

'You know Dennis, we've fought alongside him long enough. Besides, I think they almost like it.'

Tinuva nodded, turning away from the disagreement in the middle of the narrow street to watch as the Tsurani filed out of the gate of the stockade and formed up to face the eastern horizon.

The sun had yet to break over the mountains to the east, but the tops of the mountains to the north and west were already aglow, bathed in a radiant pink that glimmered off the snow capped heights. Over head the clouds shone in the reflected light of dawn, shifting rapidly in color, changing to a brilliant gold and at last the sun broke the horizon, casting long shadows across the snow covered valley.

Asayaga, who had finally come out to join his men, removed his helmet, placed it at his feet, then knelt down on the slushy ground, bowing low until his forehead touched the earth. Then he began a sing-song chant.

More than one Kingdom soldier, out of curiosity, stood by the open gate, watching.

For several minutes the Tsurani continued their chant, occasionally rising, then kneeling back down. Two of the men, standing behind the line, had lit a small brazier and the sweet scent of incense drifted on the wind as they brought it before the group and set it down.

From across the field to the north the last of the Tsurani guards returned from their watch atop the pass and hurried to fall in with the group, removing their helmets and quickly bowing before joining in with the prayers.

'Who's replaced the watch up there?' Tinuva asked, looking over at Dennis who had come up to his side to watch the ritual.

'I've sent up young Richard and Hanson this morning to join Luthar and Corporal Bewin.'

Tinuva nodded. 'Richard?'

'It's about time the boy did his share of duties around here,' Dennis said, his tone indicating that there was nothing more to be said about the lad.

'Shouldn't be too bad up there today,' Gregory interjected.

'Another few days of warmth and we might have problems. I want a forward patrol over the pass to check things out once this Tsurani holy day is finished.'

'We already reckoned on that,' Gregory said.

Tinuva looked around at the Kingdom soldiers who had gathered at the gate. 'Where's Corwin?' he asked.

'I don't know,' Dennis replied. 'Off meditating or getting herbs I guess. Why?'

'Just he's been gone a lot this last week.'

Dennis looked back at the group. 'Next time he heads out, trail him.'

The chanting began again.

'Just what the hell are they wailing about?' Dennis asked.

Tinuva cocked his head and listened. What little command he had of the language of the Tsurani had improved tremendously in the last

241

few weeks. Like nearly all of his race, his sense of hearing was far more acute to the finer nuances of sounds, the subtleties of pronunciation, combined as usual with a near-perfect recall.

He nodded slowly, deeply moved by what was being said, and began to whisper a translation:

'Hear, O Hilio,

'Hear, O Judge of the Living, for we call out to thy distant dwelling places,

'Lost in the wilderness we call to thee,

'Standing at the threshold of eternity, before the gods of all, we bow our heads in submission,

'For we are but dust, and to dust we shall return.

'We come into this world with nothing,

'And must depart from it bearing the burden of the sins we have committed.

'Forgive us those sins, Lord Hilio,

'Forgive us our sins as we must forgive.'

Asayaga's voice trailed off into silence and again he bowed low, striking his forehead upon the ground. Then the chanting began again:

'Hear our cry from out of the wilderness, out of the strangeness of this world we call to thee,

'For though we step across the eternity of the universe, still we are within thy sight and within thy hand.

'Though lost in the wilderness, we shall not lose faith in thee.'

Asayaga stood up and turned to the smoking brazier. Reaching into his tunic he pulled out a small scroll of paper and reverently placed it onto the hot coals, so that the paper flared up.

'What's that?' Dennis asked.

Tinuva motioned him to silence.

'Receive our comrades who have fallen this year,' Asayaga said, bowing to the brazier. 'Gather them into thy gardens of paradise so that they shall know peace and comfort.'

'Names of the fallen from his company most likely,' Tinuva whispered. 'Last night it was a prayer for forgiveness. They believe the smoke carries the message to the heavens, and to their god.'

Asayaga hesitated for a moment, eyes darting over to Dennis and then he continued.

'What is he saying?' Dennis asked as the chant continued.

'I'm not sure if he wants you to know.'

'Tell me.'

'He said: "and our foes who fight us with honour, and whom we have slain, may they know peace in the realm of their gods."'

Dennis, startled, stared at Tinuva.

'It's what he said,' Gregory interjected.

Dennis said nothing. Asayaga caught his gaze for a brief instant but then turned away. In the shadows Dennis could see the Tsurani rising one by one to stand over the brazier and then a blade would flash across a finger and a hiss of steam would rise up from the blood-offering.

And so the Day of Atonement began, and more and yet more men of the Kingdom stood silent, watching, whispering comments as to what the Tsurani were doing, and what the chanting meant.

The early morning was cold as Richard trudged up the pass. His breath formed steam before his lips as he climbed up the path from the valley below. Eventually, he reached the hut which the guards used to warm themselves while they ate.

Hanson, Richard's companion, stamped his feet to get some life back in them, as Richard looked inside the hut. The fire was burning low, so Richard tossed a log onto it and poked it back to life. Stepping out from the shelter of the hut which housed the watchers at the pass, he said, 'You wait here and warm up a little, and get the soup hot, while I go tell the others we're here.'

Hanson gave him no argument, and went inside while Richard went forward to relieve Luthar and Bewin, from their position on top of the cliff that overlooked the northern pass.

Both men were huddled up, their heavy capes over their shoulders, but they were alert, turning with drawn weapons at the sound of his approach over the crunchy snow.

'Anything?' Richard asked.

The two stood up, stretching, Bewin absently rubbing his shoulder which had given him trouble ever since a Tsurani had put a spear through it the year before.

'Silent except for the wolves,' Luthar said, yawning.

This was Richard's first time on watch in the mountains and though he would not admit it, he was excited by the prospect and responsibility it offered. Not a word had passed between him and Hartraft, except for orders and the usual chewing-outs since the day of Jurgen's death and he secretly hoped that this assignment of trust meant that somehow the commander was finally showing some signs of forgiveness.

The view from the cliff was magnificent, the mountain sweeping down across the open rocky slopes to the treeline more than a thousand feet below. Far beyond the trees were distant plains and in the still morning air he could see what appeared to be a herd of wild horses grazing. The next range of mountains, more than a dozen leagues away, stood out stark and clear, so close it seemed that he felt he could touch them.

All of it was snow-covered, the dawn light illuminating the mountain slope and ice-clad trees so that it seemed as if the gods had carpeted the world in diamonds and rubies.

'Food ready?' Corporal Bewin asked.

'Hanson's with me and has the pot of soup simmering.'

'I'd prefer some ale myself,' Luthar sighed.

'Well, our relief will be up tonight,' Richard answered.

'Damn Tsurani and their holy rantings. I should have been relieved last night.'

'They stood watch the night of Midwinter feast,' Richard offered.

'It wasn't my watch then damn them. I've been up here four days without a drink.'

'Stop your whining,' Bewin replied. 'It all works out. Let's go get warm.'

Luthar, grumbling, carefully worked his way down the rocky outcropping to the hut hidden at the edge of the treeline behind them.

'Keep a sharp watch, son,' Bewin said.

Richard smiled. 'I will.'

'I'll send Hanson up at noon to relieve you. Remember lad, stay low, don't move around a lot, and keep alert. Keep watching along the flank of the mountains as well as the plains below. They could

244

try to work a few scouts over the tops of the peaks to swing in behind us.'

'Yes, corporal.'

'It's hard to tell but out there, below the treeline, it looks like something beat down a trail, it could just be those wild horses, but I want you to keep a close watch on it. If you hear anything strange, see birds kicking up out of the forest, or if something just doesn't feel right, you come back and get me.'

'Yes, corporal.'

'Fine, son. Now off for some soup and sleep for me.'

Richard smiled. There was almost a touch of warmth in Bewin's voice and it did his heart good. Bewin had been the only one to take him under his wing and show him some of the tricks of survival after Jurgen's death: the rest of the company had pretty well cut him off.

Settling down into the cleft between two boulders Richard sat on the furs vacated by Bewin and Luthar, then pulled his white cloak up over his shoulders and head. From a hundred feet away he would be all but invisible and after several minutes he actually felt comfortable, as well as excited by the responsibility given to him. All the men of Hartraft's command, and for that matter the Tsurani as well, were now depending on him and he swelled with a touch of pride at the thought of it, standing watch while his comrades slept, or celebrated their ritual.

In the weeks they had been together in the valley he had become fascinated by the Tsurani. Having been assigned to Brother Corwin, he had spent hours helping to nurse the four wounded Tsurani and three Kingdom soldiers who had survived the bitter march to the valley. One from each group had died, but the boy he had argued about saving had actually managed to live, his leg now almost healed, and though Osami would walk with a limp for the rest of his life, at least he was alive.

The two had struggled to teach each other their tongues, and though the conversation carried little beyond food, the mastery of the Tsurani game of dice, and clumsy, laughing comments about some of the serving-girls, he felt he could call Osami a friend.

When the talk in the barracks at night turned to whispered

conversations about what was to be done regarding the Tsurani once they left the valley, he felt confused. Some of the men talked coldly of simply slaughtering the lot once they were free and clear, doing it by surprise in the night. Others declared that given all that happened perhaps an open and fair fight was best after all, and that maybe it could even be settled by a duel between Asayaga and Dennis, and then the two groups could go their separate ways. And finally there were a few who said the whole thing was crazy and once out of the valley they should just back away from each other and call it a draw. Richard whole-heartedly was behind that opinion, but given his position in the company with the death of Jurgen, he knew better than to offer any comment.

The nightmare of the moment of Jurgen's death came back to him whenever he slept – the way Jurgen seemed to hang in the air above him, the spear covered with his heart's blood, the eyes looking into his, his strange, detached smile as the light fled from his eyes.

And Hartraft. The way the commander looked at him, the coldness which had not broken once in the past month, that tortured him, too.

The lazy hours passed. Occasionally he would stand to stretch then sit back down. Towards mid-morning he thought he saw something moving down on the plains. He shaded his eyes, straining to see. It almost looked like a horseman, briefly glimpsed for a moment, apparently chasing a second horse, then the trees on the lower slope, several miles away, blocked his view.

Should he call Bewin?

He decided to wait, to remain still and watch, but the long minutes passed, and he wondered if his eyes were playing tricks, that it was just two horses with no one astride the second. The two horses turned and disappeared back under the trees. With nothing to point out he knew he'd look foolish.

He settled back. Strange how this all had turned out. He had expected the war to be far different – armies arrayed, valiant lancers to the fore in full armour, trumpets blaring, banners flying, the chance to fulfil all the childhood dreams of glory.

And yet, in the past month, he had seen instead a savage murder-match in the forest, men grappling like animals in the driving rain and snow, long, exhausting hours of running with terror at one's heels, the brutal killing of the troll which squealed in terror as its life slipped away; then the final mind-numbing march up the mountain slope.

No trumpets, no mentioning of his name in a dispatch back to the King, no jovial brotherhood around the campfire. And as for the enemy, that was the boy Osami, his own age, just as frightened as he was, the two of them secretly sharing a stolen bottle of brandy, shaking dice together and gambling over a few coins which Osami treasured as if they were jewels. And then there was the boring endless tedium of inspections, bringing in firewood, or toting the kills that the hunters made back to the compound.

He heard voices behind him and looked back. He couldn't see anything because the camp was well hidden on the reverse slope, but it sounded like Brother Corwin, – he heard a booming laugh, a snatch of a comment from Bewin rejoicing that the monk, having climbed all this way, had thought to bring along a skin filled with brandy. He started to move, then thought it best to remain diligent and to keep careful watch. Looking up at the sun, he judged that in another hour at most it would be time for his relief and then he could sit with the monk and have a sip of brandy.

Strange that Brother Corwin would come up this far, but the monk had taken to disappearing for days at a time, out to gather herbs hidden beneath the snows which might help to heal the half-dozen men down with the flux and the few wounded who were slow to mend.

An hour or more passed and Richard wondered if Bewin knew just how carefully he was doing his job, not drifting back to seek a few minutes' warmth by the fire, but staying, instead, at his post no matter what the temptations Corwin had brought along.

Again he caught a glimpse of movement – the herd of horses which had been out in the middle of the valley had been edging closer towards the woods which flanked the slope, then shied back, breaking into a run for several hundred yards before settling back down.

'A beautiful day, isn't it young Richard?'

He turned. It was Brother Corwin, laboriously coming up the slope, his heavy breathing making clouds of steam before his face, holding the hem of his monk's robe up as he kicked through the icy crust of snow.

Richard smiled. If he had had any friend in this last month it had been Corwin. The monk had shown him many of his secrets of healing: how to stitch a wound, pull an arrow and to staunch bleeding, his compassion shared equally on both sides and he had praised Richard for his own gentle touch and friendliness to young Osami.

Richard half-stood but the monk motioned for him to be seated. 'Don't show yourself, lad, one never knows who is watching below.'

'I haven't seen anything this morning, Brother, other than a few horses.'

'Still, the woods always have eyes.'

Corwin sat down by his side.

'Why? Do you think they are down there?'

'It's fair to think so. They know we are here.'

'Then why not attack us?'

'Because as long as there are watchers up here you can give sufficient warning. Three or four archers could tie them up for hours while a messenger was sent back. This is the only pass from the northern valley. I know, I've walked these woods for weeks.'

'Its so peaceful,' Richard sighed. 'One would almost think there is no war.'

'Oh there is war, young Richard.'

The way he said it caused Richard to turn and look into the monk's eyes.

And at that same instant Richard felt the blow of the dagger plunging into his side.

It struck with a violence he could never have imagined, an agonizing pain that drove the breath out of his lungs and he fell backwards, gasping.

Even as he fell back he could not believe what had just happened.

Corwin stood up, dagger in his hand and smiled.

Richard, terrified, trying to breathe and yet unable to do so, looked at him, wide-eyed.

'Why?' he gasped.

There was almost a hint of sadness and pity in Corwin's eyes. 'I'm sorry, my son. I actually like you. Too bad, you were such a handsome young lad. Such a waste it seems.'

'Bewin!' He gasped the cry out, clutching his side, struggling to stand.

'No sense in calling for him. They're all dead.'

'What?'

'Poison in the brandy. Easy enough. I don't think they even realized they were dying, just a quiet drifting off to sleep. Quite peaceful actually. Then I cut their throats to make sure.'

'Bewin!'

A cross look clouded the rotund brother's features. 'They're dead, Richard. It's an old trick, I've used it a number of times.'

'Who are you?' Richard sobbed.

Corwin smiled again. 'Hartraft should have figured it out. I've been hunting him for quite some time. Years ago I was sent to his stinking little village to kill him, his father and grandfather but couldn't get close enough to poison their drink.' Corwin laughed and shook his head. 'Besides, I realized a better plan to punish the Hartraft clan. Strange he didn't remember me when I came across you all out in the forest, but then again I've put on a few pounds since, and no longer looked like the holy relic merchant I once posed as.'

Richard leaned over, coughing, frothy droplets of blood spraying on to the snow.

'I opened the pass the night his village fell. Just like here, poisoned the guards and stabbed the one still on watch, then sat back and watched the Tsurani storm in. Far more amusing to let one foe kill another. I followed the attack, knowing where the escape-hole was to get out of the keep. Too bad about the girl – the bolt was actually meant for Dennis, but in a way it was far more delightful in its results. It was kinder to her to kill her, rather than have her mourning her husband, and far crueller to have him watch her die, don't you think?'

'Who are you?' Richard gasped again.

'A servant of Murmandamus,' Corwin announced coldly. 'Long ago I was told to kill the Hartrafts. His father's estates were a vital key in my master's plans. Oh, I've stalked Dennis on and off over the years, but this cursed war made it damn difficult to close in on him.'

Corwin smiled, using the hem of his robe to wipe Richard's blood off his dagger.

'I was back with Bovai and his attacking column when we caught a Kingdom scout who, after some persuasion, said you Marauders were nearby. My mission was to get south, but the wonderful thing about the moredhel is they think in terms of years and decades rather than days and months. So Bovai sent me out to find you, infiltrate your ranks, but to leave Hartraft alive. With final revenge so close, Bovai must be half-mad to have Dennis's blood on his own dagger, not mine. After you're all dead, I'll return to my original mission.' He laughed. 'Actually it was quite masterful the way I ruined that trap you were setting for the Tsurani. In fact, they were about to head off in the opposite direction when I led them back to you and triggered a nice little slaughter.

'But as for Hartraft, believe me young Richard, it would have been easy enough to poison him this last month, but Bovai wants the pleasure of that kill. Besides, I only had enough poison hidden on me for one more job, and figured I'd need that to help with my escape when the time came to lead Bovai through this pass.'

'You bastard!' Richard cried, feeling at last for his dagger.

'Oh lad, it's a sin to curse a holy brother.' Corwin snickered at the joke. 'Bovai's waiting down in those woods, boy. I just saw signs of him yesterday. Once you and your friends are dead he will attack. I'm sorry son, but it's time to die. Since I like you, let's make this easy. Just lie back and close your eyes. I promise it won't hurt.'

Richard, soul filled with terror, fumbled with his dagger, and held it up, gasping in agony with every movement.

'All right then,' Corwin whispered coldly. 'Now I'm afraid it will hurt, lad. I don't like defiance. Have you ever seen a man have his tongue carved out and then listened to him drown on his own blood? It's really quite interesting.'

Corwin sprung, but his bulk played against him as Richard staggered to one side. Richard felt a hot slash across his arm even as his own blade cut across Corwin's face, laying open his cheek to the bone.

Corwin, bellowing in rage, dived back in, blade flashing. Richard backed up, left hand clasped to his side, strength draining away and then the world seemed to spin around as he fell off the outcrop of rock. He fell, world tumbling end over end and then there was darkness.

He awoke to agony, the salty taste of blood in his mouth, and experienced a moment of terror, as he expected to see Corwin above him, having already cut out his tongue.

He waited for a moment, cautiously looking around, and then tried to sit up, but the slightest movement sent a wave of agony through him. Coughing, he spat up a foam of blood.

He tried to make sense of his surroundings, for the ground seemed to rise up beside him. He blinked and realized he was not where he had fought Corwin, but on a ledge a few feet below his hiding spot. He must have fallen over the edge when Corwin struck him. He wondered why he was still alive, then considered the drop. The fat false-priest could hardly have climbed down to finish him off, and probably thought him already dead, or close enough that the cold would complete the task. And the slash he had given him to his face probably had him off somewhere trying to staunch the flow of blood.

With hazy vision he looked around and then, ever so slowly, stood up, with every muscle crying out in pain. He saw a small rock at knee level protruding from the face of the bank and stepped upon it. Heaving himself upward, he almost fainted as he gripped the ledge above. Knowing he had but one chance, he forced himself to take a deep breath and pulled himself over. Then he collapsed on the ground and passed out.

Consciousness returned some time later and Richard sat up slowly. He looked at the angle of the sun and realized no more than an hour had passed. He got to his unsteady feet and looked around.

The monk was nowhere to be seen. Stumbling, he wove his way back down to the camp. The fire still snapped and crackled in the hut, and there, lying around the fire, were Bewin, Hanson and Luthar. Poisoned by Corwin.

The realization filled him with rage. He leaned over, gasping and coughing and specks of blood splattered onto the snow.

I'm bleeding inside, I'm dying, he thought.

He looked back over his shoulder, wondering if he heard horses approaching. Were they coming already?

Looking up at the sun, he judged that it was well past noon. Corwin must have left him for dead more than an hour ago. Already they could be on the move.

Another spasm of coughing overtook him and he sat down, feeling such an infinite weariness that he was tempted to lie down by the fire and sleep. He fought it off, knowing that it was the dark shadow. Absently, he picked up the sack of brandy lying by Bewin, then remembered what it contained and threw it aside.

Crawling over to the corporal he slowly worked the waist-belt off of the dead man then opened his own tunic. Reaching into Bewin's haversack, he pulled out the field-dressing that Hartraft insisted all of his men carry. For the first time he looked at the puncture wound on his right side between his two lowest ribs. A thin trickle of blood seeped out and with each breath he could almost feel the air leaking away. He pressed the bandage up against the wound then ever so slowly wrapped Bewin's belt around his chest and cinched it in tight to hold the bandage in place. The effort caused him to cry out in anguish. Unable to button his tunic, he left it open and stood up.

Amazingly Corwin had not thought to take the horse tied off behind the hut. It was an old nag, used to haul extra supplies up to the watchers, and was there in case a messenger ever had to get back quickly. Richard knew that the monk didn't like horses, but still he should have taken the beast along – or killed it.

It wasn't even saddled, but the effort of doing that now was beyond him. He led the horse around to the side of a rough-hewn table set in front of the cabin. Richard crawled up on to the table and then clawed his way onto the back of the horse.

Facing down the mountain, back towards Wolfgar's Stockade, he set off. He knew in his soul that it was now a race, twenty miles against death. Who would win the race he wasn't sure. To gallop the old horse would have her wheezing in minutes and probably kill him with bloodloss. To walk would mean a half-day's ride back to the garrison.

He gritted his teeth and urged the horse into a canter, settling in with a rocking motion that caused him more pain than he thought he could endure. He held onto the reins and vowed to remain conscious until he reached the Captain.

Throughout the day, except for the brief outdoor ceremony at sunrise, the Tsurani had remained inside the long house, but now, with the setting of the sun, the door had been opened and Asayaga stepped out. Dennis had just completed the sunset parade inspection and his men had stayed in place, talking quietly about the Tsurani.

Asayaga, dressed in full armour approached Dennis and saluted. 'It is the custom to have a feast at the end of the Atonement Day. We request your presence as guests.'

Dennis simply nodded, not sure what to say.

'Will you and your men please follow me?'

Asayaga led the way into the long hall. The great table had been scrubbed clean, plates were laid out, fresh rushes were on the floor, the room was filled with a sweet cloud of incense. The Tsurani were arrayed around the table, an open place between each of them and Asayaga motioned for Dennis's men to take the empty places.

Wolfgar, his daughters, and the other members of the household were already present down to the smallest child. Dennis accepted the place pointed out by Asayaga which placed him between the Tsurani captain and Wolfgar. The Kingdom soldiers were silent, looking around curiously.

Asayaga raised his cup, looking towards Strike Leader Tasemu who stood by the door. He stood at rigid attention and the minutes passed.

Finally Tasemu turned, faced the group and started a sing-song chant, and the other Tsurani joined in. The chant lasted for several minutes and then ended with lowered heads, the chant eerily drifting off into silence. The Tsurani solemnly raised their cups and flagons, drained them, and then slammed the cups down with a loud cheer.

Asayaga turned and bowed to Wolfgar. 'It is custom, that when the Day of Atonement has ended, a man brings into his home any wayfarers upon the road and feasts them. Tonight we are the wayfarers upon the road and we thank you.'

The cups were refilled from great bowls of ale set around the table and all the Tsurani raised a salute to Wolfgar, who stood up smiling, nodding his head in thanks.

Next Asayaga turned to Dennis. 'It is the custom, as well, for a man to then seek one towards whom he feels anger and to extend his hand, clasp his forearm, and to pledge that the year to come shall be free of that anger.'

As he spoke in the language of the Kingdom the other Tsurani fell silent, but from their expressions Dennis sensed they knew what their captain was saying.

'You and I are pledged to a king and an emperor who are at war, Hartraft. We must obey that pledge first. But I ask tonight that we will sit together without rancour, or thought of what we must still decide between each other. We are enemies, Hartraft, but at least tonight let us sit as honoured enemies and share this meal in peace.'

Asayaga started to extend his hand and Dennis did not know how he would react. Actually clasping the hand of a Tsurani in a formal ceremony was something beyond anything he had ever dreamed of doing.

Asayaga hesitated, looking into his eyes, and all in the room fell silent. A flicker of a smile crossed Asayaga's face and, turning aside, he picked up his own cup, filled it, and offered it to Dennis instead.

Caught off guard Dennis took the cup without even thinking and a ripple of laughter echoed in the great hall followed by a flurry of activity as the Tsurani soldiers took their own cups, filled them again and offered them to the Kingdom soldiers.

Dennis, nodding, raised his cup, tipped it slightly in salute to Asayaga and then drained it. A cheer resounded throughout the long hall. He put the cup back down.

'There are times, Asayaga,' Dennis whispered, 'when I almost forget that you are Tsurani.'

'And there are times I forget you are Hartraft of the Marauders, Dennis,' Asayaga replied.

Dennis could not help but offer a grudging smile and picking up his own cup, which had yet to be touched, he offered it to Asayaga, who drained it.

Tsurani soldiers who had been sitting at the back of the hall left the table and returned seconds later with steaming platters piled high with cold slices of roasted meats, which had been prepared the day before and soon all were sitting, eating their fill, the room abuzz with conversation, the men finding it amusing to fill each other's drinking cups and then press the cups into the hands of their neighbours, forcing them to drink.

'Your ritual was deeply moving,' Alyssa said, leaving her seat to come over and stand between Asayaga and Dennis.

'I thank you, my lady,' Asayaga replied.

'It is a shame that this pledge between you two could not be kept till the next year's Atonement Day.'

Asayaga nodded. 'War is war, my lady. Hartraft must obey as I do. If ordered to fight we must do so. The only question then is what is in our hearts.'

'And what is in your heart, Hartraft?' Alyssa asked, looking over at Dennis.

'I do my duty, my lady.'

'Is it just duty? Father has told me of what happened to you, your family. Is it just duty?'

'You have not seen this hall burn, your father dead, your beloved spouse dying in your arms.'

The words spilled out of him and, embarrassed, he turned away. She put a hand on his shoulder and he looked back.

'I know my father will not survive this winter,' she whispered. 'Your coming was the harbinger of that, and this hall will burn too.'

'And won't you hate the moredhel for that?'

'Yes, the ones who might do it. Yes.'

Dennis looked back over at Asayaga. 'Why do you even try?' he asked.

'What do you mean?' the Tsurani replied.

'This. All this,' Dennis said, a note of confusion and frustration in his voice. 'The feast, that prayer yesterday about the spirits of my dead comrades, the drink just offered. Why the hell do you even try?'

'Because I am Tsurani,' Asayaga replied in a sharp whisper.

Dennis, stunned by the intensity in Asayaga's response, said nothing.

'I don't want to be here, Hartraft. I wish by all the gods I was home, miserable as it was with the intrigue, the damnable Game of the Council. I am a retainer to Lord Ugasa, and his son who will rule after him, and have achieved the highest rank I may hope to achieve. I gained my rank through twenty-five years of dutiful service, doing what was ordered without hesitation. And ten years of that service has been here, on your world, Hartraft.

'I was ordered to this place, this war. Of the fifty of my clan who originally came with me there's only Sergeant Tasemu and three others left. The others are the younger brothers and the sons of those who have fallen here.'

Dennis nodded, and said nothing when Alyssa's hand slipped onto Asayaga's shoulder.

'I wish the men of Clan Minwanabi had never come to your keep, that you were living out your days there, that you and I had never met.' He spat out the last words sharply, so that several of the men sitting to either side fell silent, turning their attention to the two captains. 'But we have met, your family is dead, my comrades dead, and all that we have left is what is to come of our lives, brief might they be.'

He looked back up and Dennis was stunned to see tears in Asayaga's eyes.

'I just wish I could find peace and learn to forget.'

Then Asayaga stood up abruptly and turned his back to the table. More men were falling silent and Dennis looked around the room. The Tsurani were watching their captain, wondering what had just transpired.

Dennis saw Gregory and Tinuva looking at him curiously, Gregory giving the subtle hand signal to ask if there was trouble.

Time seemed to stretch out. He looked the other way. Wolfgar was silent, as if lost in thought. Roxanne, by her father's side, staring at Dennis, but there was no sarcasm in her gaze this time, but a look of pity and sadness.

Dennis stood up awkwardly, and took his feasting cup. He

approached Asayaga, and held out the cup. 'If I have caused sad memories tonight,' he said, 'I apologize.'

Asayaga stared at him and said nothing in return.

'The men are watching us,' Dennis whispered. 'They think we are arguing.'

'Always the men are watching,' Asayaga sighed, 'and we must act accordingly.'

Dennis shook his head. 'Take the cup, Asayaga: you need a drink.'

There was the flicker of a smile. Asayaga took the cup and drained it. Instantly conversation in the room returned.

'I suspect, Hartraft, that I've just received the most friendly gesture you will ever give to a Tsurani.'

Dennis said nothing. His gaze caught Alyssa's for a second and he could see the relief in her eyes. He knew as well, at that same instant, that whatever feelings she might have kindled in him were worse than useless. Her attention was fixed on Asayaga and there it would stay.

He returned to his chair, Asayaga sitting beside him, and the two ate in silence, the room around them echoing with laughter, bursts of songs, and a wild eruption of cheers when one of the Tsurani, with a throw of the dice, won a dagger from a Kingdom soldier who grinned when he handed the blade over.

'Made this bugger as wealthy as a prince in their home lands,' the soldier laughed. 'Them with no metal.'

Another soldier simply pulled out his dagger and tossed it to the Tsurani next to him and within seconds an exchange of gifts had ensued – Kingdom troops offering daggers that were far more precious than gold to the Tsurani, who in turn offered back equally precious gems and polished lacquer bracelets.

This exchange caused an almost wild hilarity to set in, and cups were raised, in many cases simply to be upended over the upraised face and open mouth of a nearby companion. Even Dennis had to smile at the foolishness and old Wolfgar stood up, slopping his drink, and began to declaim a ballad, but few if any listened.

And then it happened so fast Dennis barely caught the flash of the blade and spray of blood that exploded.

Sergeant Barry stood up, staggering, holding his right armpit which had been flayed open, arterial blood spurting out.

Dennis and Asayaga leapt out of their seats and raced around either side of the table but could not push their way through the men who were up, backing away, shouting, some still thinking that a joke was being played, others beginning to realize that the two sub-commanders – Barry and Sugama – were fighting.

Sugama stood crouched, a Kingdom dagger in his hand. Barry had snatched a knife from the table and held it in his left hand; poised to pounce, ignoring the rush of blood from inside his armpit.

'Sugama!'

Asayaga was moving up behind him, but Sugama ignored his commander. Instead he hissed something in Tsurani and several men started to move to join him.

'The son of a bitch stabbed me!' Barry roared, and a number of Kingdom soldiers grabbed their weapons as well.

'Damn it, Barry, don't move!' Dennis cried.

'You drink with these bastards!' Barry screamed. 'I even started to trust them and look at what you get in the end!'

He half-lifted his right arm, while still warily holding his fighter's crouch, blade up in his left hand.

Dennis looked over at Asayaga, at the men around him, and he leapt for Barry, trying to pin his arms. He knew Barry was almost as strong as himself, and when moved to a fighting rage, as he now was, he was all but unstoppable.

Barry tried to throw him off and Dennis saw that more than one of his men was standing by, not moving, just watching. And then he saw Sugama make his move, coming in low, realizing that Barry's arms were pinned. Asayaga was behind Sugama but out of reach. Dennis tried to push Barry out of the way, never anticipating that Sugama would make such a desperate and cowardly attack.

The blade sank to the hilt into Barry's stomach, even as Dennis tried to push the sergeant out of the way. Barry gasped, doubling up in Dennis's arms.

Dennis dropped Barry, reaching down to scoop up the blade which the sergeant had let slip. Sugama was backing up with a look Dennis had seen all too many times in a man's eyes, the realization that death was closing in and that he was the one to deliver it.

'Hartraft, no!'

It was Asayaga trying to move between them but Dennis ignored his cry. He drove Barry's dagger into Sugama's stomach, and letting go, stepped back.

Sugama, with a gasp, collapsed against the side of the feasting table, wide eyes looking down at the dagger in his gut and then he stared accusingly at Asayaga and said something in Tsurani.

'This is your fault, Asayaga –' Dennis half-heard Tinuva whispering a translation '– you dishonour our ancestors by drinking with our foes. I curse you and all who follow you.'

Dennis turned back to Barry and knelt down by his side. It was obvious that the wound was fatal, and already Barry's features were taking on the sickly pallor of death.

'So much for trusting the bastards,' Barry whispered.

'I'm sorry,' Dennis gasped.

'Stabbed me with my own knife,' Barry sighed, his words drifting off and then he was still.

Dennis stood up slowly. The room was in deadly silence. Sugama lay on the table, curled up, looking back bitterly at Dennis, several men gathered by his side. In a cold rage, Dennis swept up a knife still on the table and started towards him.

Asayaga moved to get between them.

'Let me finish the bastard,' Dennis said coldly.

'He's dying already. You've given him a warrior's death.' Whispering, he quickly added, 'If you had not struck, I would have hanged him in dishonour, and my men would have come to heel, but now I fear we are beyond that. I cannot let you finish him while he can't defend himself. Let him die quietly.'

'To hell with that, he murdered one of my men! Step aside, Tsurani.'

'No.'

Dennis raised his knife and went into a fighting crouch, and as he did so all the men around them started to back up. He ignored the screams of Alyssa, the hoarse cries of Wolfgar.

'You could have stopped him but you didn't,' Dennis accused.

'He's as quick as a viper.' Asayaga said, 'I was waiting for the moment to grab him. I didn't think he'd strike again.'

'Step aside.'

'No. I can't, Hartraft, not with him already dying!' Asayaga cried. 'He was unarmed when you stabbed him and if I let you finish him I will lose my men. You must understand that.'

'Then take a blade, Tsurani.'

Asayaga didn't move.

'Take a blade!'

Asayaga, eyes fixed on Dennis, held a hand out to his side, and one of his men gave him a dagger.

It was Tinuva who finally moved between them, his back to Asayaga, eyes fixed on Dennis.

'Out of the way!' Dennis cried.

'Look past Asayaga, to the door,' Tinuva said quietly.

Dennis shifted his gaze and saw that Roxanne was standing by the doorway. Leaning against her was young Richard. For a second he thought that the boy had been injured in the fight as well, then realized that his assigned post for the day was at the northern pass.

All eyes in the room shifted to Roxanne as she helped Richard into the room, leading him around Asayaga, to stand in front of Dennis, and Dennis slowly rose from his fighting crouch.

The boy stiffened, as if trying to come to attention. 'The moredhel,' Richard whispered. 'Sir, the moredhel are through the pass.'

There was stunned silence. Tinuva tried to take the boy from Roxanne, but he refused, struggling to stand alone.

'Sir –' His eyes closed for a moment and he collapsed.

Dennis caught him in his arms. Richard opened his eyes again. 'Sir, I'm sorry about Jurgen. I'm so sorry.'

'That's all right, boy,' Dennis replied. 'Now tell me what happened.'

'Jurgen, sir, I'm sorry.'

'That's all right boy. Now tell me.'

Richard coughed, bright blood flecking his lips. 'It was Corwin. Poisoned the others, stabbed me. Sir, he was a spy for the moredhel.'

A murmur ran through the room.

'Around noon. He stabbed me in the back and left me for dead.'

'Noon. They could be here any minute,' Gregory hissed.

Dennis looked up at Gregory who instantly barked a command for the Kingdom troops to get their weapons. An explosion of activity swept the room. Asayaga shouted and his men ran for their gear as well but Dennis stayed with Richard, still holding him.

'I'm sorry about Jurgen.'

'That's all right son,' Dennis said again softly. 'He'd have done it for any man.'

'He rode with me back here,' Richard said with a soft smile lighting his face. 'I fell off my horse and wanted to sleep and he woke me up. Said I had to warn you and he would ride with me. He's waiting outside for me now.'

Dennis could feel the hair rise on the back of his neck and he looked to the open doorway.

'And sir, I was to tell you –' Richard closed his eyes again for a moment.

'Yes?'

The boy stirred. 'It was Corwin who betrayed your keep.'

'What?'

'He murdered the watchers guarding the pass. Bovai sent him to kill you. He couldn't do that, so he killed the guards, letting the Tsurani in on the night you were married. He was the one who did it. He was the one who fired the bolt that killed your wife as well, though the shot was meant for you.'

Stunned, Dennis leaned back, still holding Richard. His mind flashed back to the night at the keep, and now he realized why Corwin had looked familiar. For the briefest of moments, across from the tunnel exit, he had seen a man at the woodline, holding a crossbow, illuminated by the flickering light of the burning keep. He had been younger, and thinner, but it had been Corwin he had glimpsed as the man turned to flee.

Someone was crying and Dennis looked up to see young Osami kneeling down, reaching out and taking Richard's hand.

Richard smiled. 'My friend,' Richard whispered in Tsurani. He turned his head to look out the open door. 'Jurgen said for you to live ...' and then he closed his eyes and his spirit slipped away.

261

'He's gone.'

Dennis looked up. It was Roxanne.

'You must act, Hartraft: the boy is gone,' she said. 'There is nothing more to be done for him, poor lad.'

Dennis nodded and released his grasp on the still body. Osami took the burden from him, gently smoothing the tangle of hair from Richard's brow and weeping.

Dennis stood up. Asayaga was before him. He looked past Asayaga to the body lying on the table. Sugama was dead. Dennis looked back at Barry who was dead as well. Several of his men had ignored the command to gather their weapons and were crouching by the side of the sergeant, eyes filled with hatred for Asayaga.

'We settle this later, Hartraft,' Asayaga said coldly.

Dennis nodded.

Tinuva was standing in the doorway.

'I can hear their horses outside the stockade,' the elf said. 'They're still on the side of the mountain, a half hour, maybe an hour away at most.'

'We leave now,' Dennis said.

'Now?' Asayaga cried. 'It's night. They've caught us by surprise. We should barricade and hold this place.'

'I was caught in a keep once before,' Dennis replied. 'I won't be again. They'll shower us with fire arrows and burn us out before dawn. We run. It's our only chance.' He looked over at Roxanne. 'Can you guide us to the west pass at night?'

She hesitated, glancing back to her father.

'She'll guide you,' Wolfgar said and Dennis realized he wasn't talking of her ability, but rather giving her an order.

There was a look of anguish in her eyes. The old man reached out and gathered her into his arms. 'Child, all mortals must face this day and we knew it was coming. Life has been good to me, for in the end I was given you and your sister.' He kissed her on the forehead. 'You can be as sharp-tongued as a viper, but you can also be as sweet as wild clover honey. I love you and your sister more than my own life. I'd trade all the years with kings for but one more hour with you.' He squeezed her slightly, then gently pushed her away. 'Now lead my friends here to safety.'

As he spoke he looked past her to Dennis and Asayaga.

'Settle your differences later, you two. It was a drunken brawl and men get killed in drunken brawls. Leave the dead here.'

Dennis said nothing.

'You are a Hartraft, boy,' Wolfgar admonished. 'Either command or step aside.'

The words were his grandfather's and Wolfgar spoke them with a voice that rang with the remembered power of long ago.

Dennis nodded. He shouted for his men to form ranks and prepare to march.

The column headed out of the gate of the stockade and turned south up into the forest where it would eventually pick up the trail that led to the western pass. In the middle of the column were the horses carrying the children and several of the older women. Half a dozen of the old men and women, however, had announced that they would stay behind with Wolfgar, and the partings from their children and grandchildren were bitter.

Torches flickered on top of the stockade gate and along the wall, revealing where several straw dummies had been set up, crowned with helmets. Wolfgar and the others remaining behind would move along the palisades, making as much noise as they could to try to convince Bovai the stockade was still fully manned. The ruse might delay the moredhel for a time as they stopped and deployed out before attempting to storm the stockade.

Tinuva, who had ridden out to scout, came in and urged the group to move, for in a matter of minutes the lead scouts of the enemy would be close enough to see what was transpiring.

The rear of the column passed and Dennis stood watching them. Wolfgar stood by the gate where his daughters were already mounted. They both leaned over, arms around their father, sobbing quietly. He reached up, patted each on the check, then slapped the rumps of their horses, sending them on their way.

Dennis waited for the last to leave, Asayaga standing silently beside him. Looking into the long hall, he saw the three bodies lying on the table amidst upended cups and over-turned platters. It would be their funeral pyre soon and again he thought of Jurgen, picturing him standing within, waiting for the boy to join him on the journey. Somehow he wondered if in a way the boy was a replacement for himself and for a reason beyond his understanding his eyes filled with tears.

He felt a gentle hand on his shoulder. It was Wolfgar.

'Along with you now, young Hartraft. Take care of my girls.'

Dennis nodded, unable to speak.

'And you, Tsurani. Marry Alyssa. Grandsons of your blood would bring me honour.'

Asayaga bowed low. 'Your request honours me, Wolfgar.' Then he said, 'And if it were possible, I would ask for she is . . .' He let the sentence go unfinished. 'But on my world she would be a slave, and there is nothing I could do to save her. I will see her safely to Kingdom lines, with my life if needs be.'

Wolfgar said, 'I thought it might be something like that. Very well. She'll get over you. Now, hurry along before the bastards catch up with you. And don't kill each other: it would be a waste of a good friendship.'

The two said nothing.

'Now go. An actor should know when to leave the stage, a poet when the lay is finished, and a bard when it is time to put aside the lute.'

Asayaga saluted and then hesitated. He reached out and touched the old man lightly on the face and then ran for the gate to catch up with the column. Only Tinuva and Gregory were left, waiting for Dennis.

'Goodbye, Wolfgar.'

Wolfgar laughed softly. 'It'd have been nice to have had one more night. I was planning on trying for that lovely redheaded girl, the one that's taken to the Tsurani lad who's wounded. Ahh well . . .' Still laughing, he patted Dennis affectionately and said, 'If you had the brains of a sack of rocks you'd marry my Roxanne. She can be a hard one at times, but she has strength and she can love. She would be good for you, lad. She'd heal that wound you've been nursing all these years.'

Dennis's face flushed, and he seemed too embarrassed to speak. He let Wolfgar accompany him to the gate, softly whispering his famous ballad about the shortcomings of the King and the memories it stirred caused Dennis to smile. Wolfgar's hand slipped away from Dennis's shoulder.

Before he even quite realized what was happening, Dennis was outside the gate, Wolfgar and the other old ones slowly swinging it shut behind him, then throwing the lock bar in place.

Dennis looked behind him, but the way back in, back to all that was, had been closed off.

'Come on, my friend,' Gregory said, 'it's time we moved on.'

Dennis set his face in a mask of determination. He nodded once and said nothing more.

FIFTEEN

Flight

The morning was cold.

Leaning against a stunted tree to catch his breath, Tinuva turned to look back. In the early morning light it was easy enough to see Wolfgar's Stockade, for it was burning now, a distant smudge of smoke rising up and spreading out in the still morning air. The smoke hung low, an indicator of bad weather to come. Raising his gaze, he swept the sky. To the east it was still clear, but to the west a fingerlike spread of clouds was drifting. By early evening it would be snowing again.

The column staggered slowly past, heads lowered against the icy breeze which swept the top of the pass. The Tsurani, stoic as ever, marched uncomplaining. Most of them were now wearing heavy felt boots and wool trousers: in fact, except for the lacquered armour emerging from beneath the white-and-grey camouflage cloaks it was hard to tell the difference between them and the Kingdom troops, that and their shorter stature. All the men were wearing crudely-made snowshoes, fashioned while passing the peaceful days with Wolfgar, but more than one pair had already broken and the unfortunate men without such gear had to labour through the drifts like a swimmer breasting an icy surf.

Without the horses, the column never would have made it to the top of the pass for in places the drifts were higher than a man's head and the animals had to be used as rams to batter down the icy walls so that the column could pass. He could see where a week ago it would have been impossible to traverse the pass. What was so frustrating was that the delays and exhausting work to get through the notch in the mountains served to make an easy path for those in pursuit.

The men were silent and Tinuva could sense the tension between the two bands. Throughout the night, in spite of the dread that followed them, the whispered conversations had been about the fight between Barry and Sugama and the near-duel of Dennis and Asayaga. Some of the Tsurani even blamed Dennis for the betrayal by Corwin, thinking that as captain he had failed to uncover the traitor and was thus dishonoured.

If it had not been for the unfortunate young Richard, the truce would have disintegrated into a general slaughter with the moredhel simply having to finish off the survivors. Tinuva wondered how the two sides would manage to fight together when the time came, for surely they would indeed be fighting within the next day, or two days at most.

Even from this great distance Tinuva could see that Bovai's army had dozens of mounted troops formed up outside the burning stockade, with at least another two hundred or more on foot, and that the column was already on the move. The combined command troops of Tsurani and Kingdom soldiers would be outnumbered at least two to one, if not more.

'They're coming?'

Gregory was by his side, shading his eyes against the early morning sunrise, looking back to the valley.

'Just setting out.'

'Arrogant bastards, took the stockade and slept the night while we cut the trail for them to follow.'

'Why not? We can't throw off their tracking. They'll catch up before we can reach safety.'

Gregory squatted down, rubbing his hands together and eyed the notch through which they were passing.

'Already thought of that,' Tinuva said. 'It's too wide here, and there's no cover. We'd be flanked in minutes and cut off.'

'Wish we didn't have the children and women. Without them we could push the pace.'

'Should we have left them behind then?' Tinuva asked.

Gregory smiled and shook his head. 'Being honourable has its drawbacks at times and this is one of them.'

'Yes it does,' Tinuva whispered.

The last of the column trudged past, followed by Dennis and Asayaga who walked in silence. The two slowed and joined Tinuva, and they all looked back to the valley.

Tinuva could see the sadness in Dennis's eyes at the sight of the burning stockade.

'A good ending,' Gregory said softly. 'I bet the old man was singing that song of his, sword in hand. He'd prefer that to the slow wasting of the heart which was killing him anyhow.'

Dennis said nothing for a long minute. 'Any defendable positions?' he asked finally.

Tinuva shook his head and nodded back to the south-west. The slope of the mountain swept down into a vast impenetrable forest, another range of mountains rising up more than twenty miles away. 'I trekked this place long ago,' he said, his voice distant. How long ago was something these men would barely understand. 'Beyond the next range I remember a dwarven road used by their miners for the hauling of ore down to a mill along the river.' As he spoke he pointed to the wooded crest. 'The dwarves from Stone Mountain abandoned the mill and mine years ago when it played out.'

'And the Broad River?' Dennis asked. 'Do we try to circle round back to the ford we used or make a run for the bridge?'

It had been a topic of speculation almost every night after their arrival at Wolfgar's: how to get out. In general they had agreed upon the bridge. Tinuva had been there long ago, but Wolfgar and Roxanne had made a trek to it less than half a dozen years back. The span had still been intact then.

Twice Dennis had attempted to lead a patrol out to check but both times they had turned back, the pass simply impenetrable and one of the men had been lost in an avalanche. So now they would have to make the decision blind. Ten miles past the next range, then on to the road and south to the bridge. All their planning, however, had been predicated on the hope that there would be sufficient warning of Bovai's approach giving them a lead of a day or more to get out.

'If the span is still there and undefended we cross, destroy it, and are home free,' Dennis said, but there was an ironic tone to his voice. 'If he put a blocking force onto the bridge, however, or worst yet destroyed the span, we are trapped.'

Dennis looked at his companions.

'The ford is in the opposite direction,' Gregory replied, 'heading back into territory the moredhel control now. Plus, it's another sixty miles or more. They'll swarm over us long before then.'

'To run a blocking force around to the bridge is an extra thirty miles or more,' Tinuva interjected. 'If Bovai came up only within the last few days, we can still outrace them.'

'You don't think they did it?' Dennis asked.

'I didn't say that.'

Dennis nodded. A shower of sparks swirled up from the long house a dozen miles away in the valley below as it collapsed in on itself. It was plainly visible to all and he heard a muffled sob. Alyssa and Roxanne had come back from the head of the column and were sitting astride their mounts, watching as the only home they knew was destroyed. Asayaga turned away from the group and went up to Alyssa's side. Reaching up, he touched her gently on the leg.

'Make for the bridge then, and hope it's there,' Dennis stated in the detached voice he assumed when giving a command.

Tinuva nodded.

'We'd better keep moving,' Dennis said. 'It'll have to be straight out. No stopping until we're across the river.'

'You're talking two days' march with children and women, and a storm brewing,' Gregory interjected. 'Do you see an alternative?'

Dennis looked back at Tinuva who said nothing, his gaze locked on the valley below.

He's there.

Bovai reined his mount about, looking up to the distant pass highlighted by the brilliant light of dawn. He could see the antlike column disappearing over the notch, but far more powerful than what he could see with his eyes was what he could sense in his soul.

Tinuva was looking at him.

The long house and the entire stockade was an inferno. It had served its purpose for the night as shelter after the long march of the previous day – there was even food to be found and a few of the old ones foolish enough to be taken alive had provided entertainment for the goblins.

He had vague recollections of old Wolfgar and the stories about his defiance of the King. It was a shame, in a different time and place he might have even suffered him to live, but any friend of his brother was a sworn enemy and besides, the old man had decided to go down fighting.

'Did you send for me?'

It was Corwin.

Bovai nodded, barely looking down at the man who was still wearing the robes of a monk. 'I expect you to get mounted and guide us.'

'The path they've left, I don't think you need a guide.'

Bovai could sense the fear. It would be just like Hartraft and Tinuva to have laid traps to slow the advance; there might even be a few left behind and this fat one was afraid of an ambush.

'Nevertheless, mount and go forward.'

'I think my services to you could be better rendered in other ways.'

Bovai finally looked down and fixed him with his gaze. 'You should have cut the boy's throat to make sure.'

Corwin had told him the boy had fallen to his death, but they had seen Richard's body lying on one of the tables in the long hall.

Corwin had cursed himself for having blurted out the young soldier's name upon seeing him. Had he kept silent, Bovai would never have known his error in judgment, but with the boy having fallen down the side of the path onto the rocks, Corwin had been convinced he was dead.

Bovai continued, 'If you had finished him, this chase would be finished. Hartraft and . . .' his voice trailed off, for the subject of his brother was not something to be shared.

'Tinuva,' Corwin whispered and gave the flicker of a smile.

Bovai's backhand caught Corwin across the cheek flayed open by Richard's dagger and the man staggered back.

'You have no right to dare mention his name in my presence,' Bovai snarled. 'I gave you a task and you failed. You failed to lure them into Brendan's Stockade, you failed to drive a wedge between them, you allowed the boy to escape and warn them.'

'I've served you for ten years,' Corwin said coldly, hand cupped over the side of his face, a trickle of blood leaking out between his fingers.

'And?'

Corwin hesitated.

'Go on.'

Corwin's eyes narrowed, his gaze sharp and crafty, like a cornered rat's.

'Your men have been whispering during the night. They are angry, exhausted. They know Tinuva is with Hartraft and they fear him. Many whisper that you are more interested in settling the affairs of your vendetta rather than finishing off Hartraft so they can go home.'

'Always the ferret, aren't you?'

'It is how I survive. The beauty of my betrayals are that men, even those of your race, trust me up till the moment I slip the dagger between their ribs or serve them a flagon of brandy. Don't waste that talent lightly. Our master has plans for me.'

'And you would betray me in a heartbeat if it furthered whatever dark goals you sought.'

Corwin smiled. 'Only should it serve our master. Otherwise, our paths are the same.'

Bovai snorted derisively. 'Nevertheless, ride forward.'

Corwin hesitated then bowed low in acknowledgment and turned away.

Golun rode up to join Bovai, his gaze locked on Corwin who was stalking away. 'I'd kill him now and be done with it,' he announced.

'Our master has need of him. He is to go south and prepare the way for an invasion in the next three or four years. Until I sit at Murad's right hand, or replace him, I cannot risk displeasing the Master.'

Golun seemed unconvinced. 'A traitor is always a traitor.'

'Like my brother up there?' Bovai whispered, nodding to the high pass.

The morning air was so clear that he still felt as if he could see him, in a small knot of several men, where the flicker of light from the dawning sun flashed off a bit of metal.

'Finish off the Marauders, that is what will give you glory, and reunite those who follow you now. Then worry about Tinuva.'

Bovai said nothing and merely nodded, his attention still focused on the crest of the mountain and the flicker of light.

The snow drifted down gently and when Dennis stopped walking it was the only sound, the whispering of the flakes as they came to rest on the overhanging branches and the forest floor.

He heard the snicker of a horse and turned, bow coming up instinctively, arrow already nocked. Then he lowered his weapon.

Roxanne, following his track, ducked low under a heavily-laden branch and came up to his side.

'I told you to stay back with the main column,' he said softly.

'I hunted here with my father for years. I can help.'

'Not now, not this kind of hunting,' he hissed. 'Go back.'

He set off again at the double, moving swiftly, daring to stay on the narrow trail. Throughout the morning and into the afternoon he had been haunted by the fear that Bovai would have sent a blocking force around to cut off this avenue of escape. Corwin knew the plan – he must have passed it along – and to run blindly forward with the hope that Bovai had not been able to set up a trap in time was a quick way to a certain death. If they were going to block the bridge, they'd have scouts out forward as well.

Down in the forest in the broad open valley the snow was not so deep, but now that they were ascending the next ridgeline the passage was getting difficult again. He had long ago taken off his cloak and slung it around his pack, but nevertheless he was breathing heavily, and sweat was soaking through his tunic. Drenched as he was he knew he'd have problems with the cold once night settled.

He pressed on, inwardly cursing as the girl doggedly followed, at one point moving ahead of him, breaking the trail.

He finally came up by her side and grabbed hold of her reins. 'Damn you, go back.'

'You're ready to drop from exhaustion, Hartraft. Let someone mounted break the trail.'

'A mounted rider is a dead target in these woods,' he hissed. 'We do it on foot. Now go back.'

'The women and children back with the column need rest, a fire.'

'We don't stop.'

'What?'

'You heard me. We don't stop till we reach the bridge.'

Though his men knew the routine he had decided not to tell Wolfgar's people of his plan to keep marching: there was no sense in their anticipating the agony of a night march in a storm until they were already into it.

'That's still fifteen or more miles off – half of them will be dead by then,' she snapped. 'You can't push these people on a night march.'

Dennis reached up and grabbed her by the arm. 'Your father understood this and I would expect his daughter too. This is not some leisurely hike. They caught us by surprise and either we run them into exhaustion and they stop, or they catch us and slaughter us. We march through the night. Those that can't keep up, we give them a bow, a few arrows and hope they slow the moredhel down a bit, then finish themselves off.'

'Including the children?' she asked, her voice as cold as the evening chill.

He was tempted to give her a bitter response but then shook his head. 'No,' he whispered, 'of course not. Get some of the women to double up on the horses with them, they can hold a child if it falls asleep, but we keep moving.' He hesitated. 'I've ordered my men not to carry anyone who falls behind – if they do, I lose both the straggler and a good soldier. Everyone marches or they die.'

She nodded, eyes not on Dennis, but still surveying the forest. 'They didn't get ahead of you. I know this way. The moredhel would have to make a march of sixty miles or more to swing around the valley and come back out here to cut us off. Besides, there's half a dozen trails like this over this ridge. If there was a trap it would have been just on the far side of the pass back into the valley. You're free of them.'

'I don't survive by living on assumptions,' Dennis replied.

'Break the trail with my horse, otherwise it will be you who's left behind by tomorrow morning.'

He scanned the woods yet again. Already the shadows had deepened so that he could barely see more than half a bowshot away. Throughout the day the snow had been unbroken except for the tracks of animals.

All his instincts were against her suggestion but he knew she was right. He could not keep up this pace of running point throughout the night and still be ready for a fight. He reached down and unclipped his snowshoes. 'Take my shoes, then wait for the column to come up. Tell Asayaga to keep them moving.'

'No.'

'What?'

'This old horse is big enough for both of us. Like I said, I know this ground. I'll ride behind you.'

He was tempted to reach up and simply pull her out of the saddle but the look of defiance in her eyes sparked a memory and finally he shook his head. He clipped his snowshoes to the side of the saddle, pulled out his cloak, put it back on then scrambled up, Roxanne sliding back. She hesitated, then finally put her arms around his waist.

The horse looked back at him, and he knew if it had a voice it would cry out in protest. The poor dumb beast was exhausted. He leaned over, patted it on the neck and whispered a few words of encouragement, then nudged it forward. Though he would not admit it, the feel of the warm saddle under him was a blessed relief. The horse ambled along slowly, needing just an occasional nudge to guide it along the trail.

As the darkness settled and deepened the snow increased, heavy thick flakes coming straight down, then gradually shifting to lighter and drier flakes that began to dance and eddy as a light breeze picked up.

He caught a glimpse of a darker shadow in the snow and reined in. A stag, caught by surprise, struggled to its feet, a curtain of snow falling from its back. The two gazed at each other for an instant and then it clumsily bounded off.

'A good sign,' Roxanne whispered. 'No one is about.'

He nodded and they rode on in silence for several minutes.

'You hunted here before?' he asked.

'Before the shortness of breath began to afflict my father he took me over the pass several times. I think it was more just to see some new country: there was always more than enough game in our own valley. We'd ride like this, with me behind him, and he'd tell me stories of kings, princes, cities with a hundred tall spiralling towers and of the great ships that sailed on warm seas.'

He spared a look back over his shoulder. There was a sad smile on her face as she remembered a happier time.

'I think that's the most I've heard you say since I've met you.'

'And this is the most you've spoken to me since I met you.'

Again there was a long silence. The snow came down harder again, at times obscuring the view so that he could barely see a dozen feet in front of them. They crossed a narrow stream, the horse nearly losing its footing on the ice-covered rocks on the far bank. It was barely calf-deep but it was, nevertheless, a major barrier. Men would get wet, then have to keep on marching, their boots freezing, the cold sapping their strength. Chances were at least one would lose his footing in the stream and get soaked, a virtual death-sentence for what in other times would be seen as a source of levity and a good laugh.

He waited for a moment, not sure how far back the column was.

'How come you never talk, Hartraft?'

'Talk? To who?'

'Me.'

'There was never much to say.'

'You like Alyssa, don't you?'

The branch of a tree, overburdened with the newly-fallen snow groaned and cracked, and a cascade of snow tumbled down near them, sending up a swirl of flakes.

'Asayaga is better at such things than I am. He has the courtly touch.'

'Father told me about your Gwenynth. I'm sorry.'

'If only I had known it was Corwin,' he said coldly. 'I should have known, sensed it. And he was within my grasp for weeks.'

'Is that all you think of?'

'What?'

'Vengeance?'

'It's a start,' he replied, the tone in his voice indicating that the conversation was finished.

'I lost my father last night. If we do have to fight the moredhel I hope to do my part, but to spend my life hunting them down . . . father would want different for me.'

Dennis did not reply.

'He was worried about you.'

'Keep an eye on the woods.'

'He remembered you as a boy who had a fire in his eyes, a love of adventure, and even a touch of the poet. He said the two of you would make up funny little verses together. That you loved to watch sunsets, to sing, and would clamour for books to read.'

'I was a boy.'

'No, that was the same you, just long ago.'

'I don't need someone else to tell me to get over what happened,' Dennis whispered. 'Now do your job and keep an eye on the woods.'

'No one can see thirty feet in this,' she said.

'I didn't survive nine years of war thinking like that.'

Even as he spoke he caught a glimpse of a hooded lantern at the head of the column. He wanted to swear at the fool who had lit it, but realized that in a way the girl was right. There was no one out here other than this desperate column.

Asayaga was in the lead, holding the lantern. Reaching the edge of the stream he hesitated.

'Just cross it,' Dennis hissed.

'We need to rest, we're carrying many of the children.'

'Put all of them on the horses and keep moving.'

He turned his mount and pressed on up the slope, leaving the party behind to negotiate the frigid water.

The hours passed and the snow thickened to a heavy all-consuming fall that muffled the world, deadening all sound except for the laboured breathing of the horse. An hour after sunset they crested the ridge and paused for a few minutes, then dismounted to let the tired animal rest. He explored both sides of the trail, hoping to find that the pass was narrow enough to make it defendable. The ground, however, was open – just a shallow depression – . Dejected, he came back to find one of his corporals, Alfred, bent double, gasping, Roxanne down by his side offering him a drink from her wine-sack.

'Captain Asayaga sent me up to find you,' he reported, leaning against the sweat-soaked and shivering horse for support. 'Gregory came up from the rearguard: they've had several skirmishes, killing two human scouts. We lost two as well, both Tsurani who were wounded and stayed behind.'

Dennis nodded.

Just below the top of the pass they had spied an abandoned cabin, Roxanne stating that it belonged to an old hermit. He had hoped to let the party rest for half an hour, to build a fire for the children to warm up, but that was impossible now.

'How far to the dwarf road?' Dennis asked, looking over at Roxanne.

'In fair weather, not more than two hours on horse. The bridge beyond, a half hour in good conditions.'

Dennis sighed and shook his head.

If the road was overgrown it would help, but dwarven roads were usually well built, straight and well paved – no one could match the dwarves for stonework. It would prove a disadvantage now. Once on it Bovai would send his whole column of cavalry off in hot pursuit rather than simply probing.

'Tell Asayaga we must move faster,' Dennis said. 'Keep them moving.'

He mounted, Roxanne sliding back to give him room.

Alfred saluted and started back.

'No, wait here until they catch up with you, Corporal. No sense you running up and down this hill twice.'

'Thank you, sir,' Alfred gasped.

Dennis nudged his tired mount, but the horse refused to budge for a moment and finally he had to kick hard with his heels to get it moving.

He was throwing caution aside now. If they were not blocking this point it should be an open run down to the road. Once on the road he could check for signs. It gave him a terrible naked feeling, riding hard like this in the middle of the night, abandoning the careful routine of years of moving, waiting, listening, then covering as your companion leapfrogged forward.

Several times his mount nearly lost its footing. Once he lost the trail completely and had to slowly backtrack, barely able to pick out the pathway as the snow continued to fall.

The third moon had risen an hour before and there was ample light by which to navigate if he kept to a slow and steady pace. He fought back the urge to pick up speed, but galloping down a mountain trail through the woods at night would be folly of the worst sort.

He could sense Roxanne falling asleep, her arms around his waist going slack, her head lolling on his shoulder, her warm breath on the back of his neck. He let her rest for a few minutes then slapped her lightly on the thigh.

'Stay awake, I need your eyes.'

She sighed, mumbled something and then sat upright.

'Where are we?'

'I don't know,' she whispered.

He sensed a narrow clearing ahead before actually seeing it where the trees thinned out slightly. He reined in and slipped out of the saddle, taking his bow, which had been resting across the pommel, and removing the oil-cloth draped over the string. Nocking an arrow he slipped forward, paused, then slowly dropped down onto the road. Even in the darkness he could discern its lines, a straight cut through the forest, wide enough for two carts to pass each other. Bent low, he crept to the middle of it, crouched and carefully scanned the path. After several minutes he started to brush aside the powdery snow, probing down through the foot-deep fresh fall until he hit the hard crust below. He cursed silently. It was hard to tell in the darkness, especially by touch, but there were footprints: goblins and at least one horse. He reached into his haversack, pulled out some tinder and a precious springlock sparker, a gift from Wolfgar on midwinter's night, wound it up and held it close to the tinder, his cloak draped over his shoulders and head to shield himself. He pressed the trigger and a shower of sparks came spinning out, striking the tinder. Cupping the fluffy down and thin white bark shavings he blew them to life so that a tiny curl of a flame flared up – not much more than the light from a candle about to flicker out – but after hours of darkness the light seemed nearly as bright as day. Keeping one eye closed in order not to destroy his night vision, he scanned the footprints, kicking back more of the powder and then let the flame wink out. Catlike he straightened up, opened his other eye and carefully scanned both ways: nothing moved.

'Roxanne,' he hissed and she came out of the edge of the woods and down to the road, leading their horse. 'He's sent someone around – at least four goblins and one rider. They passed here just before the storm started.'

'The bridge,' she whispered.

He stood up, brushing the snow off his trousers. 'Either hold it, or destroy it,' he sighed. He weighed the odds. Go back, get a few men, then come back again. An hour or more to do that. It was hard to tell how long before dawn. One man, in the dark, however, might catch them by surprise. 'I'm going,' he said. 'You wait here, guide the column onto this trail and tell Asayaga I've gone ahead and what's happening. Make sure he puts out scouts as he comes up to the bridge in case it doesn't work out.'

'I'm going with you.'

'Like hell you are.'

'What are you going to do, just gallop in on this old nag?' she snapped. 'You don't even know the ground before the bridge.'

'Then tell me now, girl, what will I see before approaching the bridge.'

'Like hell. You'll need someone to cover your back.'

He wanted to laugh but was too exhausted even to make the effort.

'I go, or you can just stumble into the trap on your own. There's no room for all that nonsense about protecting Wolfgar's daughter, Hartraft. If you fail here, we all die. I can put an arrow through a man at fifty yards. My father was a bard but he was also a damn good bowman and taught me well.'

Dennis sighed and shook his head. 'You do exactly what I tell you to do.' He mounted, fighting down the temptation to rake the flanks of the horse and simply gallop off. No, she was right. It was a blind attack – surprise and speed was everything, but an extra arrow might make all the difference. He pulled her up behind him. He urged the horse up to all that it could give, which was, at best, a laborious trot. The poor animal gasped for air, legs rubbery, barely able to hold its footing. She protested once, begging him to let the dying beast rest for just a few minutes, but he pressed on. He had no idea as to the size of the bridge – even if it was still there – but if it was, and the centre span was wood, it might still be standing, especially if the goblins, arriving at dark and typical of their breed, had decided to settle down for the night and do their job come dawn.

They rode in silence for a while then finally Roxanne's head came up, and she looked off to the side of the trail. 'I remember that,' she hissed into his ear, and pointed. 'It's a side trail up to an old quarry. My father took me there to see the marble. The bridge is only a few minutes' ride ahead.'

Even as she spoke, he could feel that their horse was ready to give way. He tried to kick it forward but the animal simply stopped, its flanks shaking, and with a groan it settled to its knees. Cursing, he slipped off the saddle and uncovered his bow. 'We go in on foot.'

Roxanne dismounted, unslung her own bow and strung it. He waited impatiently and was about to speak when she reached out and gently scratched the horse's ear. 'I'm sorry old friend,' she whispered. 'Rest now.' She looked back up at Dennis and he could see that her eyes were bright with tears and that she was shaking, though whether from cold or fear he couldn't tell.

'Take the right side of the road, stay a dozen paces behind me: I'll be on the left. If I fall, you get the hell out. No heroics, just turn and run until you meet up with Asayaga.' She nodded. He realized that it was beginning to get lighter, that dawn was not far off. He patted her on the shoulder, a clumsy gesture, then withdrew his hand. 'Remember: get out.' Then he turned and set off at a lopping trot, not looking back.

The road turned in a long gentle curve to the right, cutting down and clinging to the flank of the hill. Off to his left he could now hear a low rushing thunder: the river cascading over a falls. *Good, the sound would cover his approach.* He could see nearly a hundred feet now: if not for the snow it would be a clear view all the way down to his goal. And then he saw it – a dull, pulsing glow of light. He picked up his pace, arrow nocked and bow half-drawn, the glow of light turning the falling snow ahead into a pool of pink. He could see a glowing swirl rising up as well and spreading out; then there was a flash of fire, an explosion of light, and dark demonic figures dancing and waving their arms as one of them hurled another pot of oil into the conflagration consuming the centre span of the bridge. He ran, powdery snow churning up, his sprint so quick that he nearly lost his footing on the ice underneath. He reached the edge of the bridge, the stone span arching up to the centre section of wood that was blazing from end to end. His first arrow caught a goblin in the middle of its back from not fifty feet away. The goblin pitched forward, shrieking, staggering out on to the burning beams. For a few precious seconds the dying goblin's four companions thought he was drunk, which he indeed was, and broke into gales of laughter at their companion's antics, until a second one spun around, an arrow protruding from his body. The other three finally began to turn, one of them pointing at Dennis. They were perfect targets, silhouetted by the fire and his next arrow gutted yet another, who sank down to his knees shrieking in agony, his cries heard above the roar of the fire. One of them began to charge, but the second hesitated and looked around for a way to escape. Another arrow streaked in, piercing the charging goblin's heart, but he continued forward for a dozen paces, almost reaching Dennis before collapsing. The last survivor began to squeal and run frantically back and forth at the edge of the inferno, looking for a way out. Dennis, with cold brutality drew another arrow, carefully nocked it, and raised his bow.

'Hartraft!' He heard an arrow hiss past his cheek and then he was down, something ramming into him from behind, a dagger flashing into the snow within inches of his throat. He kicked out, rolled over and then his attacker was on top of him, blade poised, the flash of it coming down yet again, narrowly missing his eyes. His assailant was a moredhel, strong and sinewy. He pinned Dennis's right hand to the ground with his left, even as he raised his right for another

281

strike. Dennis tried to kick his legs up, to catch him in the back of the head, but the response was a knee to the groin which caused Dennis to gasp. And then he barely saw the shadow of Roxanne coming up from behind, her dagger glinting as she leapt in, cutting the moredhel across the throat.

Silently, the moredhel staggered to his feet, the dagger slipping from his grasp. Both hands went to his throat and arterial blood squirted out from between his fingers. He looked back at the woman, astonishment in his eyes, as if she had broken some rule and played a cruel and unfair joke. Then he sank to his knees.

Dennis rolled away, a hazy sheen of pain consuming his world. *The other goblin. . .*

He looked up. Roxanne had Dennis's bow in her hand. He watched her reach into her quiver, pull out an arrow, nock it and raise the bow. It was a heavy weapon and she struggled to draw the arrow back. The goblin still at the edge of the fire was shrieking, hands raised imploringly. She hesitated for a second then released the shot. The bolt brought the creature down, but didn't kill it. Trembling, she took a second arrow, and advanced towards the goblin.

'Be careful,' Dennis gasped, coming to his knees, eyes still on the dying moredhel.

Roxanne stopped a dozen paces away and the goblin kicked and thrashed, trying to roll out of the way. 'Be still and let me finish it,' she cried.

The second shot missed completely. She started to scream at the goblin even as she drew a third arrow, stepping closer, aiming almost straight down.

Hands raised, it continued to beg for mercy in the common tongue. She released the arrow, and the screaming stopped, changing to a gurgling cry, almost like that of a wounded rabbit. She started to fumble for a fourth arrow but the goblin finally curled up and was still.

She came back to Dennis and knelt down by his side, looking warily at the moredhel whose throat she had cut. Blood leaked from the wound, but it was not yet dead. The dark elf stared at her. 'And to think, a human woman slew me,' he whispered. 'Tell my brothers it was Hartraft, then Bovai will have more reason for vengeance.'

She nodded.

'Tell Tinuva his cousin Vakar will await him on the far shore.' Still kneeling, he lowered his head and was still.

Roxanne, sobbing, leaned over and vomited, gasping for air.

Dennis, legs wobbly, stood up and gently rubbed her shoulders as she cried.

'I'm sorry. I saw him coming up, I shot and missed, almost hit you.'

'It's all right, it's your first fight. It's alright.'

'And the way he kept shrieking, I didn't want him to suffer, I just wanted him to die.'

'Its alright,' he said woodenly, looking at the bridge. The entire centre span was a crackling hell. It was obvious that the moredhel had not let his goblins sleep through the night. They had shovelled the wooden section clean, then piled brush and dried timber torn from the side of the mill above the bridge onto the span. Even as he watched, the flooring gave way, crashing down to reveal one of the two support spans underneath. The goblins had been at work there too, having cut through both beams with an axe. The support spans gave way and the entire structure crashed down into the thundering river below in an explosion of steam and hissing embers. He sighed, barely noticing that Roxanne was standing, leaning against him, still crying, her arm around his waist.

'I'm sorry,' she sobbed.

He held her tighter and gently wiped the tears from her face. 'It will be all right, you did just fine.'

He looked back at the bridge. They were trapped.

SIXTEEN

Confrontation

The dawn was beautiful.

Tinuva, gaze turned towards the east, could sense that the sun had risen above the mountains. The world around him was grey, all of it grey, the snow swirling about him in drifting eddies. He remembered how his father had told him that when it snowed even humans could see the wind, and it was so. He watched as gusty eddies danced and flickered, a single flake pausing for a moment to hover before his eyes, a twirling crystal of light, the exhale of his warm breath causing it to dance away even as it melted.

'It is a good morning,' Tinuva whispered.

'What?'

He looked over at Gregory and smiled. 'A beautiful morning.'

'My friend, you must be addled,' Gregory sighed.

Tinuva reached out and lightly touched Gregory on the shoulder and the gesture caught his mortal friend off-guard for a moment. The elf said nothing. The voice within his heart, the whispering of the forest had already told him enough.

They waited a few more minutes, but no pursuer closed.

'They must have stopped to rest,' Gregory finally whispered.

Tinuva nodded in agreement and the two scrambled down from the low outcropping, remounted on the single horse spared for the rearguard and rode back half a mile, Gregory hooting like an owl to signal Hartraft's men of their approach.

The reserve was well concealed behind an upturned tree and they reined in. The six men stood up, pulling back their cloaks. Three were Tsurani, led by a Kingdom corporal.

'Nothing,' Gregory said. 'Fall back.'

'The road is just a few hundred yards beyond,' one of the men said. 'And there's hard news.'

'What is it?' Gregory asked.

'The bridge. A rider just came up. Dennis took it, but the span is down. Goblins led by a moredhel were burning it when he came up.'

Gregory and Tinuva dismounted. Tinuva said nothing as he reached into his saddlebag, scooped out a handful of oats and fed the horse, gently stroking its nose and whispering apologies for having driven it so hard through the night.

'We make a rearguard here,' the corporal said, his voice flat. 'Buy time for them to run a span across.'

'What about the mill there? We could pull out some of the beams,' said Gregory.

'The mill is ancient. The timbers are all rot and dust,' Tinuva said quietly, his attention still fixed on the horse. 'They'll have to cut down some trees, build a rough hoist and swing a span across. It'll take hours.'

'Then climb down into the gorge and ford the damn river,' Gregory replied.

Tinuva shook his head. 'Maybe you and I can do it, but the children, the old women?'

Gregory sat down heavily and cursed.

The corporal looked at the two. 'How much time do we have?'

'I don't know,' Gregory sighed.

'Not long,' Tinuva replied. 'They're coming.'

'Dennis sent just you back here?' Gregory asked, looking at the six men.

The corporal nodded. 'Hartraft wants us to slow them down as long as possible: every man is needed to cut down the trees, build the hoist and defences if we don't get the bridge up in time. One of us is to ride back when contact is made to give warning.'

'All of you go back,' Tinuva said quietly.

Gregory looked up and Tinuva smiled. He opened a small leather bucket, emptied the last of his water into it and offered the drink to the horse.

'You heard me, go back.'

The corporal hesitated.

'Six more men back there might make all the difference in getting that span across. We can handle this.'

The corporal looked to Gregory who nodded his head.

Tinuva said, 'Corporal, go. Take my horse – he's a gentle creature – fighting is not in his blood so be kind to him.'

'Sir?'

Tinuva patted the corporal on the shoulder and then pushed him towards his mount. The corporal reluctantly nodded and then climbed into the saddle.

'Don't stay too long, sir.'

'I'll be along soon enough.'

The corporal motioned for his men to move out and they quickly disappeared into the snow.

'You go too, Gregory.'

'Not likely.'

'One more against two hundred won't matter. You know what I need to do.'

Gregory stood up.

'You've been my friend, Tinuva, since I was a boy. I'll not leave you now.'

'It is between my brother and me now. I know him, Gregory: he has thirsted for this across the centuries. I will go back and he will know I am waiting. His pride and his lust will consume him and he will stop to face me. If I win, perhaps the others will stop, if not . . .' His voice trailed off. Then he said: 'Well, if not, at least the rest of you will be free and that is good enough.'

'I stand by you.'

'You'll be killed out of hand, Gregory, and it will divert me from what I have to do. They will not tolerate a human witness to what will happen.'

'No, I go with you, Tinuva.'

Tinuva stepped closer and as he did so he knew that somehow

his countenance was changing, becoming something that he had left behind in these woods long ago.

'Go!' His voice was dark, filled with power.

'I won't. No!'

The blade flashed out as if it had leapt from its scabbard. The cut was a clean one and hissing with pain and shock Gregory backed up, holding his right hand, blood dripping from his fingers.

'Natalese, try and draw a bow now,' Tinuva snarled, voice full of menace.

'Damn you,' Gregory cried, shaking his injured hand. He tried to flex his fingers and blood dripped onto the snow.

'Go!' Tinuva raised his dagger. 'It'll be the other hand next time, and I'll cut so that you never draw again.'

Stunned, Gregory backed away, fumbling for his own dagger with his left hand. Again Tinuva leapt in and Gregory's dagger went spinning off, disappearing into the snow.

'Then the hell with you,' Gregory snarled. He backed up, trembling, his voice near to breaking. 'The hell with you.'

Tinuva smiled. The sense he had within was like a distant memory. It was almost frightful, this look of shock, disbelief, and rage in another's eyes. It almost brought him joy and he struggled against it, finally lowering his own blade.

'I want you to live,' he whispered. 'If you stay, you die. This is between Bovai and me, and you can do nothing. Tell Hartraft to build the bridge, get across, then destroy it. If it all works out, I'll find another way back.'

'You're going to die.'

'Even those who are long-lived must face that,' Tinuva said softly. 'From our birth we are all dying, but some of us finish sooner than others.'

Gregory lowered his head, and his shoulders began to shake. Tinuva stepped forward, putting a hand on his friend's shoulder, though he still kept his dagger poised.

'Of men, you were the one true friend I have found in this world,' Tinuva whispered. 'A day will come when we shall hunt again, the wind in our hair as we track game through Yabon. Now, go my friend.' And he kissed the Natalese lightly on the forehead.

Startled Gregory looked up to see tears in the eyes of his friend. Tinuva, smiling, brushed a tear from his face and dabbed it into Gregory's bleeding hand.

After a moment, Gregory laughed softly. 'Nothing's changed,' he sighed. 'So that lore about the healing properties of elf tears is just a tale.'

'Yes, just a tale.'

The two stood silent for a moment. Then Tinuva raised his head, turned and listened. 'They're coming. Go and tell Hartraft. Now go!'

His final words were again filled with command and a dark power.

Gregory stood as if frozen for a moment then finally raised his head. 'Till our next hunt my friend.'

But Tinuva was already gone, having disappeared into the storm.

'He's here.'

'What, my chieftain?'

Bovai raised his hand, signalling for the column to halt. Golun looked over at him in confusion.

'Tinuva: he's close. He's waiting for me alone.'

Golun drew his mount around in front of Bovai.

'Then ride him down,' Golun hissed. 'We don't know if Vakar reached the bridge and destroyed it. If he failed they'll be across and destroying it even now. We had to stop so the damnable goblins could rest, but now we are closing in. Push in now, my chieftain.'

'Vakar succeeded. They're trapped.'

'You might sense that sire, but I don't.'

'Bovai!'

The voice drifted on the wind, unearthly, floating on the breeze. Bovai stiffened. Even Golun turned, dropping his reins, reaching to unsling his bow. Bovai extended his hand, motioning for him to stop.

'Bovai!'

Again the echoing cry, more felt than heard; even so the column of riders behind Bovai stirred, bows rising up.

'Hold, all of you,' Bovai hissed, turning to look back at his fellow moredhel. 'It is Tinuva; the time has come for the matter to be decided.'

'He's delaying us, buying time,' Golun hissed. 'Then he'll slip away.'

Bovai looked back and shook his head. 'He's with them now. Despite the evil of their queen and their Spellweavers, the eledhel have honour. He will not run this time.'

Golun sighed and lowered his head. 'Then upon you shall it rest if they escape.'

'We'll have Hartraft and all of them before the day is half done.' As Bovai spoke he looked back at his followers. 'It shall be but a little undertaking, my brothers, then honour for me, and glory for all of us. Which we shall tell Murad of upon our return, with the honour of our clan restored and the heads of Hartraft and Tinuva in a basket to present to him.'

Several nodded their heads.

'All of it, all my share of the loot, of the glory, I give to you, for what I shall do next I have waited an eternity for.'

Golun leaned closer. 'Then fight him, if you must, but let me lead this column around to the road to finish Hartraft.'

Bovai looked at him in surprise. 'A few minutes only,' he whispered, 'and I want all of them to see. All of them.'

Golun cursed silently.

'Order the goblins and humans to move back: they are not to see this. They can rest on the far side of the hill we just crossed.'

Golun reluctantly grunted an acknowledgment, then barked out the command for a squad to direct the goblins and humans to their designated place. Those so tasked muttered in disappointment and Bovai knew he had just won his point, for the rest now felt privileged and would not miss the honour of bearing witness to the confrontation about to take place. It was one which had been speculated about in the long houses across hundreds of winters. At last Bovai would face his renegade brother Morvai, now called Tinuva.

'No one intervenes,' Bovai said. 'No matter what. Anyone who raises a bow or unsheaths a blade, let him be struck down.'

There was a chorus of agreement even as the unfortunates given the task of herding the goblins and humans broke away from the ranks and headed back down the column.

Bovai dismounted, pulling his bow out from its case, testing the draw. Some of his followers rode up, reaching into their quivers and drawing out arrows.

'Take this: this is the shaft that killed Uvanta at two hundred paces,' one of them said.

'This shaft came from the hand of Govina the master fletcher,' another said.

Bovai, deeply moved, bowed his thanks to each and carefully placed the two arrows in his quiver. It meant that these members of his clan now fought with him and the gesture filled him with pride. His fight had become theirs. He stepped away from the group and raised his head.

'Tinuva!'

His cry echoed out. If a mortal had heard it, a chill would have coursed down his spine, for the cry was a whisper from another world, high-pitched, unearthly, filled with a fell power.

He moved silently, drifting with the wind, feeling its touch, sensing that never had he been so alive as he now felt at this moment. The shadow which had darkened his world was about to be lifted forever, and again he could walk in the sunlight and beneath the moon without shame.

'Bovai.'

The voice was close, very close. He tensed, turning . . . and then he saw him, standing in a clearing, his bow down, the world around him a swirl of white snow, the only sound the gentle hissing as the icy sparkles struck the ground.

'Tinuva.'

He stepped closer. The wind swirled up and for an instant he felt a touch of panic, imagining that it was all illusion, that his brother had disappeared. The snow parted like a curtain being drawn back and he was still there, not a dozen paces away. He took another step, then Tinuva slowly raised his right hand.

'Close enough.'

Bovai nodded in agreement.

Tinuva sighed, a sigh that was filled with an infinite sadness and for the briefest of moments Bovai felt a stab of pain. Here before him was his brother, whom he had once loved as no other. Though now of the despised eledhel he could sense all that he once was.

'So how are you, brother?' Tinuva asked and Bovai felt a flash of hot anger.

'I am not your brother. My brother Morvai died the night you were created, eledhel. And you know all that I have been since the day you left, as I know all that you have been.'

Tinuva nodded. 'I slew Kavala.'

Bovai shrugged. 'He was too ambitious for his own good. If you had not killed him, once you were dead I would have cut his heart out.'

'I didn't need to go that far. Killing him was enough.'

'As I shall now kill you,' Bovai said softly.

'That is what you want?'

Bovai hesitated and Tinuva took a step closer, bow still down. Bovai half-raised his bow and he stopped, tensing. 'You were once of the People. You know that what you've become is an abomination to us all. You are a traitor to your race. Honour demands that you die. It is not what I *want*; it is what I *need*,' Bovai finally hissed.

Tinuva sighed again. 'Then there is no more to be said,' he replied, but now his voice was full with power, power as Bovai once remembered it and it sent a thrill through him. For this was the Morvai he had once loved, but whom he must now slay, and all the glory that had once been Tinuva's would now be his. Honour would be restored, the clan would again be whole, and Tinuva could be buried as a brother who had finally returned, through death, to his own blood.

'Then, "brother" let us begin,' Bovai snarled and he stepped back.

Another eddy of snow swirled up, as if the passion of the two had stirred the breeze. An arrow snapped past Bovai, missing him by inches. He raced from the clearing, one now with the wind, turned, caught a glimpse of a shadow, and released his bolt.

The hunt between the brothers had begun.

'Damn it, tie it off, tie it off!'

Dennis pushed his way in, tearing off his gloves, and helped to lash off a log. One of his men, swearing, pulled back bloodied hands that had been wrapped around the rope. Throwing another lash around the log, Dennis pulled hard, straining to keep it taut as two men behind him threw the end of the rope around one of the stone abutments and tied it off.

'Secured!'

Dennis stepped back, looking up at the two logs which had been raised to form an inverted V twenty feet high at the edge of the broken span. The whole contraption was wobbly: they simply didn't have enough rope, nor the time, to do it all right, but it would have to do. A double length of rope, flung over the top of the V, dangled down to the black, scorched stones.

He looked over the edge. It was nearly two hundred feet down to the river below. He caught a glimpse of two Tsurani far below. They had volunteered to try and get across the river. There had been three of them, but the third had lost his grip on the icy rocks and plummeted to his death. The two survivors were valiantly trying to make their way across the torrent below, jumping from icy rock to icy rock, with the hope of then climbing up the far side. If they succeeded a rope would be hurled across and they would help in the desperate task of trying to pull the timber across.

Leaving the bridge, Dennis went up the road a couple of hundred yards and then turned into the woods. A group of Tsurani were hurriedly cutting the branches off a tree which had just been dropped. He paced off the length.

'I already checked it, Hartraft – it's long enough.'

Asayaga looked up, sweat dripping from his brow, axe clutched tightly in his hand.

'The top looks too thin – it might just break when we drop it.'

'Tsurani are builders, Hartraft; we know what we are doing.'

'You'd better.'

Asayaga stood up. 'Don't try to order me any more, Hartraft. We know what we are doing. You're suppose to be handling the defences, leave this to me.'

'Once across we settle things. Tsurani.'

'Why do you think I'm working so hard?' Asayaga snapped.

Dennis was tempted to make a reply but knew they were wasting precious time. 'Just keep at it, damn it.'

He stalked back to the road and pressed on up to the crest. Half of his men were dragging in logs and throwing up a barricade. To either side men were dropping saplings, making a tangle that could stop a cavalry charge from cutting around the flanks. The position was impossible, however, and he knew it. The crest was too open. They might break up the initial charge, but eventually they'd be flanked and pushed back. Once off the crest, the ground below – around the bridge – was a death trap.

In the ruins of the mill he saw the old women and children huddled around a fire. He looked over at the corporal who had come in from the rearguard only minutes ago. They had already spoken but he felt compelled to do so again.

'You know what to do for them if the moredhel start to break through,' Dennis said, nodding back towards the mill.

The old corporal gulped and nodded. 'Trust me, sir. I'll see to it. The poor little lambs . . .' He looked at the tiny faces of the children and the frightened expressions on the women and his own visage softened for a moment, then with resolution in his voice, he said, 'I'll see it's done, sir.'

Dennis caught a glimpse of Roxanne, who had refused to stay in the mill, and was now helping with the defences. She noticed his gaze, nodded in his direction and continued with the work.

From back down on the road a gang of Tsurani emerged, half-carrying, half-dragging a sixty foot log. Dennis raced back down to join them.

'I have this, Hartraft,' Asayaga snapped and Dennis stepped back.

The men cursed and struggled for several minutes to swing the log out onto the road, but because it was twice as long as the road was wide, the heavy root-end snagged in the saplings at the edge. The tangle was finally cut away and the Tsurani, half-running, propelled forward by the weight of their burden, slipped down the road and up on to the bridge. Reaching the edge, they laid the log down under the inverted V.

Asayaga shouted for the ropes from the overhead hoist and the four men holding the cables lowered them down. The ropes were slung around the log like nooses, and tied off. Thirty Tsurani started to push the log forward. Dennis wanted to comment, but remained silent. Asayaga was in charge of this and the Tsurani were damn good engineers.

The log was soon nearly thirty feet across, the men at the front letting go as their section passed the edge, then coming around to the root-end, ready to throw their weight on if it started to tip. Finally it was balanced: another few feet and it would pitch over into the gorge. Asayaga detailed off the rest of his men to the cables going up over the inverted V, ordering them to pull and keep the forward end of the log up high. The far end of the log started to rise and after going up only half a dozen feet the root-end started to skid backwards.

'I need more men!' Asayaga shouted.

Dennis grabbed one of his soldiers and sent him up the hill to get those working on the barricade to come down. The women and children who had been watching from the mill instinctively came out and Asayaga directed them to the cables.

'We need to hoist the log, and push the root-end forward at the same time!' Asayaga shouted.

Kingdom troops came swarming down the road. Dennis had suggested that horses be used but Asayaga had refused because the ground was too slippery and if only one of them balked, or worse yet took off in the wrong direction, the whole enterprise would be lost.

Asayaga detailed men off to the two ropes and waited for a moment as several of them brought up a short length of log and set it across the butt of the span so that more men could press in on it.

A Tsurani, showing remarkable bravery, clawed his way up the inverted V, carrying a small bucket of butter carried out from Wolfgar's. It was all they had to use for grease where the ropes crossed over the top of the V. Dennis could see that with proper equipment like a simple block and tackle, the entire job could be done by a dozen men. Now it would have to be brute strength and a prayer that the ropes did not snap under the strain, that the log didn't hang up in the sling, and that the Tsurani had indeed made it long enough.

The men struggled on the ropes and gradually hoisted the front end higher, while at the other end the Tsurani pushed the span forward. The next twenty feet gained came fairly easily but there was still another eight to ten feet to go. A precarious balance was reached when the log was high at the far end, but was now so steeply angled that no more forward purchase could be gained.

'Another hour, damn it, and I could have made a pivoting sling and swung the whole damn thing over with twenty men!' Asayaga cried, looking over angrily at Dennis.

'We don't have an hour.'

Asayaga held up both hands. 'No one move!'

All fell silent.

'Men on the ropes, the angle is too steep now. As we push on the log, slowly give way and lower it back down.'

The men still leaning into the rope nodded. Asayaga slowly motioned with his hands and a few feet were surrendered. Then he barked a command and those pushing on the root-end gained a bit of ground. The log suddenly stopped and Dennis could see where one of the slings had slipped backwards several feet.

Asayaga saw it as well and cursed under his breath.

'Cut the supports for the hoist,' Dennis said, 'As it pitches forward run the log out.'

Asayaga looked over at Dennis with an icy glare. 'I'm running this.'

Dennis was ready to flare back but saw that all around the men were watching them, the tension ready to explode. He sensed that if the log tumbled over and went into the river a blood-bath would ensue.

He slowly extended his hands. 'You are the engineer, Asayaga, but if we are to save those children we have to do this now.'

Asayaga looked at the children manning the ropes and then back at the sling. He quickly stepped up to the edge, studied the log and the hoist, then stepped back. 'Get off from up there!' he shouted, and the man with the butter threw the bucket aside and slipped back down.

'All right, Hartraft, but if it all goes over the edge it's your decision.'

'Our decision, Tsurani.'

Dennis picked up an axe and went to one side of the hoist, Asayaga doing the same at the other side. Both ends of the hoist were resting on the bridge. If they cut them loose at the same time, he reasoned, the entire affair should pitch forward, dropping the log on the far side.

'Get ready,' Asayaga cried and raised his axe. 'When it starts to let go, you men on the log push forward. On the ropes, let go when you can't hold it any longer and don't get tangled.'

He looked over at Hartraft, then nodded and brought his axe down.

Dennis struck at nearly the same instant and the ropes snapped free, parting with an audible crack. Groaning, the hoist began to pitch forward, slowly at first and then in an instant crashing over. The men on the end of the log shouted and ran forward, throwing their weight in.

Dennis looked up and saw the far end of the log slam down on the opposite span, bounce, hold precariously and then roll, as if about to go over the edge. A groan rose up even as the men on the root-end continued to strain, driving forward. The log snagged against the side railing of the bridge, barely a foot of its length secured to the other side.

No one moved for a moment, as if all feared that an errant step, even a word spoken, would cause the log to roll and fall. The hoist, like a crudely-fashioned necklace hung to either side.

'We need a man across there,' Asayaga hissed. 'Someone light. Get Osami.'

The boy stepped forward, nodding as Asayaga explained what had to be done. He pulled off his cloak and tunic, looked at the log, then sat down and yanked off his boots as well. Barefoot, he took a long coil of rope and slung it over his shoulder while Asayaga tied another rope around his waist. Asayaga grasped the boy by the shoulders, then let him go.

The boy stepped up onto the log and everyone fell silent. He swallowed hard and looked over at Dennis. 'I save Richard friends,' he said calmly, and then he was out over the chasm, walking slowly, upright, arms extended.

No one spoke as he placed one foot in front of another. The log sagged in the middle and it shifted slightly and a gasp went up as the boy seemed to sway, then regained his footing. Reaching the middle, he climbed over the ends of the hoist, advanced half a dozen feet then stopped. The rope trailing behind him had snagged on the hoist. Gingerly he reached down and started to untie the rope around his waist.

'Go back and unsnag it, Osami!'

Osami shook his head, untied the safety line and let it drop.

Dennis looked over at Asayaga and could see the tension in him – not just for what had to be done, but for the boy. Loosened from the tether, Osami started up the final length, the angle of his climb steepening so that he had to lean forward. Again he almost lost his footing and this time a cry went up from everyone watching. Regaining his balance, he scrambled up the last six feet and flung himself onto the far side.

A wild cheer went up, and Dennis looked back to see more than one of his men slapping a Tsurani on the back, exclaiming over the bravery of the boy.

Osami did not hesitate. He deftly wrapped an end of rope over the log, moved back a way and flung it around a stone abutment, then ran the rope back, weaving half a dozen lengths back and forth, throwing what little weight he had into each weave then finally tying it off. Then he slid back down the log and grabbed hold of the end of the rope snagged on the hoist. Turning, he started back up, the men cheering him on.

He started to look back, smiling, and his feet slipped out from under him. Before Dennis could even react the boy plummeted, swinging in a long arc downward, desperately trying to hold on to the rope.

Asayaga braced himself, holding the other end, coiling it up over his shoulders and stepping back, screaming for Osami to hang on.

Still holding the rope, the boy swung down like a pendulum, arcing under the stone span until the rope snapped taut, nearly dragging Asayaga over the side. Dennis leapt on top of Asayaga as he lost his footing on the icy pavement and the two of them crashed down together, Dennis grabbing the rope as well.

He heard the sickening thump of the boy hitting the rocky slope under the bridge and then Osami swung back into view.

Half a dozen men were now on top of the two commanders, grabbing hold, helping to pull the boy up, and at last Dennis was able to reach over the side and grab Osami under the armpits even as the boy started to lose his grip. Other hands reached out, pulling Osami up over the side, a couple of men nearly plunging over into the precipice in their eagerness to help.

Eventually, the group collapsed back from the edge and Asayaga reached out and cradled Osami.

Gasping the boy looked up and smiled. 'I did it,' he whispered.

'Yes you did.'

Dennis could see he didn't have long to live. His face was a bloody pulp, his skull was fractured, blood pouring from his ears, and one shoulder was caved in. How the boy had managed to hang on was beyond him. He knelt down, fumbling in his haversack, and pulled out a piece of cloth to wipe the boy's face clean.

Osami's eyes were already going dark. He looked up again at Dennis and smiled. 'Saved friend, yes?'

'Yes boy, you saved us,' Dennis whispered, and then Osami was gone.

Dennis sat back as Asayaga held the boy, struggling to control himself. Then he stood up. Eyes distant he looked across the span.

'Another volunteer, take the rope across,' he said. 'Once secure, I want twenty men over to help haul the second log across: that should give us good enough footing.'

Another Tsurani already had the rope which Osami had clung to, and tying it around his waist he leapt up on to the log and started across.

Asayaga turned away. Going over to the railing, he looked over the side.

Dennis went up to join him. 'I'm sorry,' he said.

'He was my elder sister's boy. Joined us just before we set out on this insanity. It was his first mission.'

Stunned, Dennis said nothing. This was the same boy that Asayaga had been willing to kill back in the retreat long ago, the boy that

Richard had insisted on saving, and who the cursed Corwin had helped as well.

Dennis put a hand on Asayaga's shoulder. 'I didn't know.'

'There was no reason to tell you. In our way, we are all of the same family, all who serve our house, so his ties to me gained him no favouritism. Even Sugama would not have thought to go after the boy to strike at me.'

'Sugama?'

'Don't you understand, don't you see anything? Haven't you learned anything of us in all this time? Sugama was my enemy, as much as you are. His clan seeks to destroy my clan; he was sent here as much to spy on me as to replace the Tondora officer who had died.'

'But you were willing to defend him back at Wolfgar's.'

'To preserve my command. I could not let you kill him like a wounded pig when he was already dying. All of us would have lost face.'

Dennis turned away and saw that the volunteer was already across, securing the second rope as a handrail for the next man to follow, and that another Tsurani was already up on the log and stepping out.

'I never could thank your Richard for what he did in the way I wanted to, as an uncle and not just as Osami's commander. I wish I had.'

'He knows that now.'

Asayaga looked back to the open span. 'Once the second log is across we move the children and women, then the men. We should be across within the hour.' His face an impenetrable mask, he looked at Dennis.

'Asayaga, we still must settle what is between us, but I am truly sorry for Osami. He was a brave lad. I think Richard must be greeting him now in Lims-Kragma's Halls.'

'Remember, Hartraft, we go to different places when we die. I don't think your gods let Tsurani into their Hall of Judgment.'

'Still, I think Richard would want to greet him,' Dennis said. He hesitated, his voice dropping. 'And Jurgen would be there, too.'

Asayaga sighed, finally nodding his thanks.

'Dennis!'

He looked up and was stunned to see Gregory approaching, cradling his right hand, a bloody bandage wrapped around it. He felt a momentary panic. So damn close and now the damned moredhel were closing in.

He looked past Gregory. Tsurani and Kingdom soldiers were circling in behind the Natalese scout, but where was Tinuva? But even before Gregory spoke to tell him what had happened he knew what the eledhel was doing: he was sacrificing himself in order to buy them time.

As he heard Gregory's words a terrible rage began to build in him. So much of his anger had been shifting over the last month. For so long it had been aimed at the Tsurani, at those who had murdered his family, at the war, and in the end at Corwin. But now at last he understood and it was as if a curtain that had covered his soul across the years had been torn away.

He could see the same fire in Asayaga as well, for the elf had been the one who had always walked between the two sides, respected by all, trusted by all.

He saw Roxanne and Alyssa standing at the edge of the circle and the fire was in their eyes as well, for the one that Tinuva now faced had destroyed their home, and murdered their father as well.

He caught Roxanne's eye. She studied his face and something in her eyes told him she knew what he must do. A mixture of fear, regret, and faint hope played across her face in seconds, then she returned to her implacable expression.

'Figure out a way to get the children and women across,' he said to her. Without waiting for a response he looked over at Asayaga. 'Are you with me?' he asked.

'For what?'

'We go back and fight. I'm finished with running.'

A curtain of snow drifted down from an overhanging branch. It seemed to hover before him, each flake clearly defined in his mind, each one alive for an eternity, flowing with the gentle wind, cloaking him, touching his brow, cooling the fever of his rage.

Tinuva slipped away from the tree, moving low, almost one with the snow on the ground. He rolled in behind a fallen log that rose like a white hump-backed beast from the forest floor. Bracing himself, he grabbed hold of the arrow sticking out of his thigh and snapped the end off, chanting inwardly to block the pain. He knew he should push it through but there was no time and doing so might sever an artery. Time enough later. He dared a glance up over the side of the log, ducked, rolled, then came back up, bow drawn, arrow winging on its way. The distant shadow moved and collapsed and for a second he felt a disquieting thrill; and then there came a laugh.

'Well sent, brother, well sent.'

Tinuva reached around to his quiver, drew another arrow, started up, then rolled backwards and dodged off in the other direction, racing through a thicket of saplings. He caught a glimpse of others standing silent, arms folded, watching intently, backing away at his approach. There were faces there that he recognized – for how could he not recognize cousins, comrades of hunts from long ago, those with whom he had once laughed, and whom he had once fought alongside, slaying their enemies together?

A few even nodded gravely, for even though he was apostate and an abomination, they remembered hunting and going to war with Morvai.

He turned away from the outer edge of the circle, an instinct telling him to suddenly drop, an arrow singing past his ear, kicking up a plume of snow as it struck the ground by his side.

Sitting up, he drew, aimed, shot again and Bovai dodged back behind an ancient pine, the bolt tearing off a spray of bark.

Tinuva was back up and running, but the pain was registering, each step a flood of agony that would have caused a human to fall, screaming, but he pressed on. He spared a quick glance to the south-east. Though the storm continued, still he could sense the face of the sun beyond the clouds, far above the white mantle, hovering in a fierce blue sky. It had risen to mid-zenith; the duel had consumed hours. He could hear angry mutterings from beyond the next hill, the impatient cries of goblins, the hoarse voices of men in protest, but all the moredhels' attention was focused on this duel, a duel which Tinuva knew they would see as a hunt that would be spoken of into eternity, the hunt of brother against brother. Each knew the tricks of the other, the subtle movements, the way of thinking, the scent of the other on the wind, the feel of one's gaze upon the other even with the back turned.

He knew Bovai was breaking to the right, racing to cut across in front, rather than following the trail of blood dripping into the snow. He dodged behind a tree, a perfect position with a fallen log leaning against it, forming a small tunnel underneath. Crouching down, he drew and waited. Then he saw him.

He felt the brush of the fletching against his check and sighted down the shaft. The clouds parted for a second sending a gauzy shimmer of light racing across the clearing, highlighting Bovai, telling him as well that time was passing slowly, and that far away men were still labouring to escape.

Bovai slowed, as if his own inner voice was shouting a warning. He looked straight at Tinuva, eyes widening. Tinuva shifted ever so slightly and then released the arrow.

The bolt sang through the woods, spinning between trees and branches, and tore across Bovai's side, scraping his ribs. Bovai staggered, falling backwards, rolling for cover. A growl rose up from those circling the two, for though not all could see, they could hear and knew the sounds, were able to identify who had shot and who had fallen.

'Tinuva.'

It was the inner voice, a whisper.

'Brother?'

'You had me, didn't you?'

'No brother, I shot to kill.'

'You lie. You had me. Why?'

'It is not yet time, brother.'

There was a moment of silence.

'I have her, you know, brother,' Bovai's voice whispered.

Tinuva lowered his head, body trembling. He knew this was a ploy to goad him into rage and error. After a moment, Tinuva whispered, knowing his thoughts would carry on the wind, 'You have never had her. She will always be mine.'

'Silence!' Bovai's angry reply, a scream of rage, was loud enough for all the onlookers to hear.

Tinuva stood up, shooting blindly at the source of the scream, and was greeted by a taunting laugh. 'Waste of a good bolt, brother.'

Tinuva reached back to his quiver and felt that there were only half a dozen arrows left, but he did not care. It would only take one more to kill Bovai, just one more.

'Come for me brother, out in the open, blade to blade.'

Bovai stood up. 'Look into my eyes brother, come closer, look into the eyes that look into hers every night.'

'Damn you,' Tinuva hissed.

'Yes brother, we are all damned are we not?'

'No.'

'You are. You abandoned your blood. That shame can be erased only in blood. Let me send you to the far shore, brother. There you can see the Mothers and Fathers, if they will have you.'

Another flicker of sunlight dashed across the woods and clearing.

He wasn't sure how long had passed now, for together the two of them were drifting in another world, a world that only those of the eledhel and moredhel truly understood, where a second could stretch to eternity, or a hundred years could be but a flicker of an eye.

'Come to me, brother. One of us is fated to die this day, let his brother look into his eyes and be the last he shall ever see of this realm.'

Tinuva slowly let his bow drop; then reaching to his belt, he drew out his dagger and stepped into the clearing.

'Move it, keep moving!' Dennis cried. Stepping to the side of the road, he looked back.

The column was strung out, the rear of it barely visible in the drifting snow which came down in a hard squall, then in seconds lifted to a few flurries, then closed in again.

Men were gasping, staggering, legs pumping, all semblance of formation gone, the strongest to the fore, the weaker to the rear. No scouts were forward, all caution abandoned in this headlong rush, the column rushing along like a torrent of rage unleashed. No longer were they the hunted: now they stormed forward as the hunters.

Dennis turned to look up the road. How much further he wasn't sure, for the ride down this path with Roxanne had been in the dark.

Gregory had ridden forward, promising to wait at the turn-off into the woods and to give warning if the moredhel were advancing.

'How much further, Hartraft?'

Asayaga staggered up to his side, breathing hard, sword drawn, the blade catching a glint of sunlight when the sun showed through the clouds for an instant.

'I don't know.'

'Your plan?'

'What plan?'

Asayaga looked at him and smiled.

'Then let's go,' Asayaga cried and he pressed on, Dennis by his side.

It was an intricate dance, a ballet of death, the two leaping towards each other, blades flashing, the cold sound of steel striking steel and then a backing away, the dance to be repeated again and yet again.

The watchers of the clan had drawn closer, forming a circle to contain the fight, all silent, intent, more than one muttering bitter admiration for Tinuva, the Morvai of old whom they remembered as a comrade and friend. In their eyes he was again almost one of them. A dark fury shone in his regard, his jaw was stern, a pulsing radiance seemed to form around him.

Lightly he danced, oblivious to the pain, the blood that trickled down his leg, filling his boot so that he left a slushy pink footprint with each step.

Blood flowed from Bovai as well, dripping from his slashed side, from the cut of Tinuva's dagger to his left arm which had sliced nearly to the bone.

Again the two came together; again there was the sparkle of blades, a sprinkle of blood joining the snowflakes that drifted down around them. Tinuva jumped back, left hand going to his face to wipe away the blood from the cut across his brow which clouded his vision. The world in his eyes had gone to red: yet it was not the blood which darkened his world, but all that he had contained within himself and which had now flared back to life.

'Come on brother,' Bovai taunted. 'Finish it.'

'I will.'

Bovai mockingly extended his arms wide. 'Embrace me, brother, come on.'

Tinuva crouched.

'Our father would have been proud of you, brother. Anleah would be proud of you.'

Tinuva leapt in and Bovai crouched to receive the attack. As he advanced Tinuva shifted his dagger from right hand to his left, and then at the last instant shifted it back again. He slashed out, feigning low, then coming in high. He barely felt the icy touch of Bovai's dagger cutting into his left shoulder: poised to block his own blade and finding nothing, it had simply driven in.

The two staggered back, Bovai gasping, a bright line of blood cut across his face, his cheek slashed open from the edge of his mouth to his ear, which had been cut in half.

Crying out, Bovai clutched his face and a gasp rose from all who watched, for everyone knew how Bovai took such pride in his countenance, and now it would be twisted and scarred forever.

Instinct caused Bovai to turn, coming around even as he staggered. He dodged the blow aimed low for his mid-section, wrapping his arms around Tinuva as the two fell. Snow rose up like a gust of steam as they hit the ground and rolled.

Again and again the two slashed at each other with their daggers in their right hands, left hands fumbling to grab the blade-hand of the other. They rolled, kicking and cursing, the strength of each a match for the other. Both were covered in blood-soaked slush as they struggled and the watchers from their clan drew in closer, some now shouting for the kill and more than one crying for Tinuva.

Bovai kneed Tinuva, hitting the stump of the arrow driven into the eledhel's leg. Tinuva gasped from the wave of agony but his fury drove him on. He feigned collapse, and when Bovai rolled to gain a superior position, Tinuva suddenly pressed up, using Bovai's own momentum to roll him over yet again, and this time he drove his good knee into Bovai's stomach so that his brother gasped. At the same instant he drove his left fist into Bovai's face, tearing the cut so that Bovai screamed in agony and let go of Tinuva's right hand.

Tinuva raised his dagger.

Yet again time seemed to stand still, almost to run in reverse of the banks of the eternal river. He could see his brother as he was, as both of them had once been, hunting together, sunlight drifting through the trees, standing together in the high mountains, the wind sweeping the world.

Bovai looked up at him. 'Brother,' he whispered.

Tinuva held the blade poised, ready to drive it into Bovai's heart and in that instant he knew . . . and he remembered as well all that he had become.

Sunlight filtered down again for a brief instant, lighting the clearing, snow sparkling like diamonds.

He smiled.

The blow came as no surprise: if there was any surprise it was that there was no pain. Just a strange inner warmth as Bovai's dagger, driven to the hilt, pierced his stomach, slamming up under the ribs and into his lungs.

'You've lost,' Tinuva whispered as the breath was driven out of him.

Bovai looked into Tinuva's eyes and in that instant he felt a madness, a horror, beyond any he had known before. He reached up, pushing Tinuva back. His brother, like a great statue, seemed to hang above him, then ever so slowly pitched over.

He kicked the body away, thrashing in a near panic. Then, trembling, he stood up.

All eyes were upon him.

'It's finished,' he whispered.

He turned slowly, looking from one to the other and he could sense their contempt. He looked back at Tinuva.

So you have robbed me even of this, brother, haven't you?.

'Damn you!' Bovai screamed.

The group surrounding him was silent and at that instant Bovai knew his brother had been right: he had lost something in this moment, the pain and anger that had driven him for centuries. For a moment, he felt as if life had lost its purpose. Softly he said, 'But I won. . .'

'No!'

It was a distant scream of anguish, of a long, pent-up rage. Bovai turned, looking in disbelief at the swarm of men closing

306

in, white-and-grey capes fluttering in the wind as they ran, some wearing lacquered armour that caught the beams of sunlight and stood out like brilliant lanterns on a cold dark night.

The charge swarmed down the slope like an avalanche. Arrows snapped past. One of his cousins spun around, clutching his throat; another collapsed with a scream.

All stood transfixed, confused, startled, so sudden was the onset of the charge.

And then Bovai saw him. He had never truly laid eyes upon him before, but he knew his blood, the blood of his grandsire. It was Hartraft, storming forward, leading the charge, a short warrior wearing a lacquered breastplate by his side. Hartraft came in at the run, bow cast aside, both hands held high on his heavy sword.

Bovai spared a final glance at his brother even as he began to raise his dagger.

The sword arced in. There was a brilliant flash of light ... and then silence.

'No!'

Dennis turned even as he completed the blow, spinning around on his heel, watching as Bovai's head tumbled away, striking the snow, body collapsing. Screaming, he struck again at the body, the blow nearly cutting Bovai in half at the waist. Sobbing, he drew the blade back, ready to strike again, then saw that Asayaga had raced past, had killed one moredhel and was closing on another. Behind him another moredhel was closing in, spear lowered ... and his mind suddenly conjured the image of Jurgen trying to save Richard in similar circumstances, for Asayaga was struggling to save one of the Kingdom privates who was down on the ground, desperately trying to block a moredhel closing in with raised sword.

Dennis sprinted forward.

'Asayaga!'

The Tsurani did not hear him.

He was too far off to close in time. Still holding his blade with both hands he lofted it behind his head and threw. The sword tumbled end over end, slamming into the moredhel even as he braced himself to run his spear through Asayaga's back.

The sword struck so hard that the moredhel leapt backwards as if yanked from behind, his only sound the breath knocked from his lungs. Asayaga, killing his own opponent a second later, turned and saw Dennis standing weaponless, the moredhel between them, kicking and thrashing, Dennis's sword stuck in his side.

Men charged past, eyes wide with lust and battle-fury. The moredhel, caught so completely by surprise, had given way in panic and were running to where the goblins and human cavalry waited over the distant rise. Few made it, many falling with arrows in their backs, or were cut down as they fled. The humans and goblins on the far side of the hill came swarming up, drawn by the loud outcry at the end of the battle between Tinuva and Bovai. After hours of bored waiting many had built fires; a few were even asleep, fewer still on the crest of the hill were in armour or even had weapons.

Within seconds they, too, were breaking in panic as a squad of Kingdom and Tsurani troops, led by Tasemu, hit their flank. The watchers on the hill broke, running back down to the camp, screaming in terror that they were being attacked by hundreds.

The moredhel's advantage and the edge gained by having calvary vanished in an instant. Horsemen died before they could saddle their mounts, and in the first onslaught, so many moredhel, men, and goblins were killed that within minutes Dennis's and Asayaga's command held the edge. One more minute, and the goblins broke in panic.

More than one goblin turned on the moredhel commanders who tried to rally them, and soon men, goblins and moredhel were slaying each other in a mad frenzy as all tried to escape.

The ground was littered with the dead and dying. Tasemu marched forward, a squad of Kingdom soldiers forming a ring of archers around him. A ragged line of Tsurani crested the hill, slaying everyone in their path as they advanced, and more Kingdom soldiers fell in around their disciplined line, loosing bolt after bolt into the milling, terrified mob.

Behind Dennis, who stood in a daze, Gregory held his friend and wept.

Asayaga joined Dennis, and the two of them slowly approached the fallen elf.

Tinuva looked up at them and smiled. 'Foolish, you should have gone over the bridge,' he whispered.

'We would not leave you here,' Asayaga said.

'Bovai?'

'I killed him,' Dennis replied, voice trembling.

Tinuva sighed. 'Bury him beside me: we were brothers once.'

Dennis nodded.

Tinuva sighed. His eyes flickered and then he looked back at Dennis and Asayaga. 'Fate has made you enemies, now let honour turn that fate.'

As he started to slip away he began to chant softly. Dennis recognized the words as eledhel, but did not know their meaning.

Gregory, sobbing, spoke the words with him and at last Tinuva's voice fell silent, his spirit slipping away to the distant shore of the Blessed Isle.

Dennis reached down and gently touched Tinuva's forehead. 'Go in peace my friend,' he whispered.

Asayaga did the same, touching Tinuva's blood and anointing his forehead with it.

The two looked at each other in the grim silence, then together went to finish the fight.

SEVENTEEN

Parting

The evening was quiet.

Cresting the ridgeline, Dennis stopped and shaded his eyes from the glare of the sun. Gregory was riding up the slope, trailed by the half-dozen scouts who had been walking point.

'It's clear ahead,' Gregory said. 'Another mile we'll cross the river and be into the dwarves' territory. I dare say they already know we are approaching.'

Dennis nodded. Turning, he looked back at the column. Kingdom and Tsurani troops advanced at an easy pace – more than one had a woman from Wolfgar's fort at his side, and children were chattering, dodging back and forth. In the middle of the column was a line of a dozen horses many of them taken from the enemy dragging palanquins which bore the wounded who had been carried out from the battle. No one had been left behind this time.

Asayaga, who had been walking by Alyssa's side, broke away and came forward. As he did so, all eyes followed him and the group slowed, coming to a stop without orders. In the clearing at the top of the ridge the men gradually started to break apart from each other, Kingdom troops to one side, Tsurani to the other.

Asayaga reached the crest and nodded to Gregory.

'I take it the dwarf realm is just ahead.'

Gregory nodded.

'Then you are home safe. I doubt if they would welcome us.'

'No, Asayaga, they wouldn't.'

'Then Hartraft, our truce is at an end. We have reached the lines where our war resumes.'

Dennis nodded, his hand drifting to the hilt of his sword. Asayaga's did the same.

Tsurani and Kingdom soldiers slowly moved to take up positions behind their respective commanders. The women and children felt something coming and retreated into a small knot in front of the horses.

The two leaders stared at each other. Dennis could sense the expectant hush, and knew that everyone was waiting for what had to come. He thought of his duty, for here were thirty-one surviving Tsurani – enemies who, if he let them go today, he would undoubtedly face again come spring; enemies who might slay other Kingdom soldiers, for they had learned their skills well in the last month and would be the nucleus of a formidable unit.

'What are you thinking, Hartraft?'

'I am thinking that if I let you go now, you could do considerable damage to my side come next spring.'

'Just as much damage as you will do to us, no doubt.'

Dennis looked past Asayaga. Roxanne and Alyssa were standing nearby, watching, both silent. Behind them he could see so much more – his burning keep, Gwenynth dying, Jurgen in his cold grave, and others as well, young Richard and Osami, the look in Asayaga's eyes as he cradled his nephew and then knelt by Tinuva's side. Tinuva, buried in the woods thirty miles to the north, resting beside his brother . . . He wondered if somehow the two would find peace together in their afterworld.

Dennis smiled. His hand fell away from the hilt of his sword and he extended it to Asayaga. 'Honoured enemy,' he whispered.

Asayaga, not sure if this was the start of the challenge, or something else, grasped Dennis's hand. 'Honoured enemy,' Asayaga replied, repeating the words in his own tongue.

For a moment no one moved on either side, then Kingdom and Tsurani soldiers approached each other and repeated the gesture. Men who had bled side by side embraced and the phrase 'honoured enemy' was spoken many times.

Dennis looked over at Gregory and nodded.

Dismounting, Gregory raised his bandaged hand and pointed to the south-east. 'Asayaga. A quarter of a mile ahead there's a trail that turns to the east. Stay on it and you'll loop around the flank of the dwarf kingdoms. I will convince them that you will honour a truce. As long as you stay on the trail they shouldn't bother you. Three days' march will eventually bring you west, to where their realm borders territory you might be familiar with, ground fought over by Kingdom troops and your own.

'Once there –' he shook his head, '– well, you're on your own, but given everything you've learned, you should get through. Most of the Kingdom forces will be wintering in LaMut, Yabon and Ylith, so you'll only have to avoid occasional patrols and stay away from stockades. You should reach your own lines a few days later.'

Asayaga nodded, saying nothing. The whole time Gregory was speaking he had continued to look at Dennis as if not quite believing what was taking place.

'Asayaga,' Dennis said, drawing closer. 'I must insist that what you see as you cross through the Kingdom lines you will not reveal. You won't fight unless attacked, you'll cross through as quickly as possible and take no advantage from this truce.'

'Is that an order, Hartraft?'

Dennis hesitated, then shook his head. With a slight smile, he said, 'A suggestion, from an honourable enemy. I only ask the same as if you were an envoy travelling through enemy lines.'

Asayaga laughed softly. 'Agreed.'

'There is a problem though, Asayaga.'

'And that is?'

'What do we tell our superiors?'

Asayaga nodded and looked back at his men. After a moment, he said, 'We were cut off, we fought, we survived. Nothing more. If word leaked out on either side, all would soon know, and by the gods that would wreak havoc, wouldn't it? My master could never be made to understand.'

Dennis laughed and nodded in agreement.

The sight of the two laughing and the way Gregory pointed out the trail was indication enough of what had been decided and the mood of the men around them instantly relaxed. The two groups milled together, chattering, men searching out comrades on the other side, shaking hands, exchanging small trinkets and gifts.

Smiling, Alyssa and Roxanne approached Dennis and Asayaga,

'I'd have killed both of you if you had started to fight,' Roxanne announced. 'I'm sick to death of fighting.'

Dennis looked over at her, wanting to speak, but was unable to do so. She drew closer. She indicated to Asayaga with a nod that he should speak to her sister.

As Asayaga walked a short distance away with Alyssa, Roxanne asked, 'Do you have anything to say to me, Hartraft?'

Dennis turned away and she followed him, the circle of men around them parting to let them through. When they were a little distance from the others, he said, 'Thank you for saving my life back at the bridge.'

'We saved each other in more ways than one.'

He looked at her and nodded.

'You're going to tell me you aren't ready yet, aren't you?' She sighed.

He nodded woodenly and she looked away.

'Gwenynth still haunts me. The anger, the rage – that burned away out there –' He pointed back to the northern woods. 'Watching Tinuva die, knowing what he was sacrificing . . .' He stopped for a moment, head lowered. 'I saw it. He had his brother at his mercy, and yet he stopped, unable to strike the final blow. His love spared the one who killed him, and yet he would not have wanted it any different. At that moment it all burned away in me. From that, and from the way Asayaga held his nephew and then rose up to try and save Tinuva – I learned from all that.'

'Is that why you did not pursue Corwin?'

Dennis did not reply for a moment. As the battle-fury ended only then had he remembered that Corwin was with the band they had destroyed. But his body was not found, and he seemed to have been one of the few who escaped. Some of the men cried out to press the pursuit; even Asayaga wanted to, but he had refused. The children and women back at the bridge had been left with only four men to guard them, the men who had managed to cross the river. He had turned away from that hunt without a backward glance, which had startled many.

'He is his own poison. I'll cross paths with him some day.'

'Will you seek that path?'

Dennis smiled. 'Not everything changes in a moment. I will seek it, but I won't live for it.'

She smiled and placed a hand on his arm. Then after a moment, she drew herself close to him and kissed him, deeply.

His arms slipped around her, and he returned her kiss, then gently disentangled himself and pushed her away. 'It's true that I am not ready,' he whispered. 'I may never be ready to love again. And you should not have to wait. I'll get you and your people to safety in Yabon City, and I will visit you when I can.'

She stifled a sob and forced a smile, though tears shone in her eyes. 'I knew that is what you would say, Hartraft.'

'Dennis, can't you ever call me that?'

'Of course, Dennis.' She stood up on tiptoe and kissed him on the cheek. Then she drew back, her hand brushing his for a moment before letting go. Then she walked quickly towards the horses where the other women and the children waited.

As Dennis watched her retreating back, the striking poise of her strong, tall body erect with pride and self-assurance, he felt another crack in the hard stone that was within him. For a long moment, he felt deeply alone, and then as he saw her mount a horse and signal to her sister, a faint smile grew on his lips.

Asayaga stood on the crest of the road a hundred paces away from the others. He stiffened as Alyssa laid her hand upon his arm. 'It must be goodbye,' he said.

'Why?' she asked. 'I have no home, no family but Roxanne, and I could go with you.'

Asayaga shook his head. 'It is impossible. To my people you are a barbarian, fit only to be a slave.' He fell quiet for a moment, then added, 'To suggest we wed would bring dishonour to my house in their eyes and my lord would order me to take my own life, if he did not hang me in shame first. They would wonder why I did not keep you as a concubine.'

'Then I will be your concubine, Asayaga.'

314

He looked long at her as if weighing the offer, then said, 'It cannot be. I have come to know your people, Alyssa, but you know nothing of mine. We can be a hard people, and love is often put aside for honour and duty. Even though we shared a bed each night, during the day you would be kept apart, and . . .' he swallowed hard '. . . our children would be slaves.'

She looked at him, her eyes rimmed with tears. 'You've never told me you love me,' she whispered. 'But I see by the way you look at me.'

Softly he said, 'I have not told you because I cannot.' Then he looked into her eyes and his own grew moist. 'But you read my heart and you know how I feel.' Stepping back, he said, 'Let us end this now, for to linger only heightens the pain.'

He turned and shouted a command, and his men broke away from the Kingdom soldiers. Final handshakes were exchanged, many of the Tsurani formally saluting Dennis as he passed them. Tasemu approached, saluted, then extended his hand. 'Goodbye, friend,' he said in the common tongue.

'Goodbye.'

'I hope I not see you again in this war,' the Tsurani Strike Leader said haltingly, and then he stepped back, saluted once more and started to bark out commands.

He reminded Dennis of Jurgen in the way he moved about, showering abuse on some, and then a second later giving an affectionate cuff on the shoulder to another as they formed ranks.

'Just like Jurgen,' Gregory said, coming up to join Dennis.

'Yes, that's what I was thinking.'

'Jurgen would approve, you know.'

'Yes, he would.'

'So would your father,' Gregory added.

Asayaga walked across with a purposeful stride, once more as if on a Tsurani parade ground and Tasemu snarled the command for the men to come to attention. There was a quick inspection, Asayaga nodding with approval, and then another flurry of commands.

Six men stepped out from the column, bows in their hands, and sprinted out over the hill.

'Forward scouts,' Gregory said. 'My, how they do learn quickly.'

'I hope Tasemu is right,' Dennis said.

'About what?'

'About our not meeting again.'

Gregory said nothing.

The column started off, the horses carrying the Tsurani wounded falling in at the middle. Many of the women and children from Wolfgar's stockade openly wept at the parting.

Asayaga looked over at Dennis and nodded. Dennis left Gregory's side and fell in with the Tsurani.

'Remember, avoid contact going through the Kingdom lines: you promised that.'

'Is that an order or a request, Hartraft?'

'You know.'

Asayaga smiled and nodded. 'A request then from me, Dennis.'

'What?'

'The war between our nations might last for years yet. We serve on the same front. If a day should come when we see each other again, in the woods, or across that open field . . .' His voice trailed off.

'That we back away,' Dennis suggested.

'Yes,' Asayaga said after a hesitation. 'Yes, my honoured friend.'

Dennis nodded and extended his hand.

Asayaga grasped it firmly, then let go. Alyssa came to Dennis's side and Roxanne joined her sister, who put her arm around Dennis's waist, and he put his arm around her shoulder. He was surprised at himself for doing it, but whatever comfort he gave her was returned. He glanced back and saw Roxanne watching Asayaga and her sister with a slight smile on her lips, though tears ran openly down her cheeks as the Tsurani marched off.

Silhouetted by the evening sun, the column moved over the crest of the hill and disappeared. The world seemed strangely empty. Dennis waited, giving them time to go down the road and then turn into the woods. Then, finally, he nodded.

'Standard march,' he announced, 'Sergeant Jurgen . . .'

He fell silent, looking at his men who were gathered around. He glanced at Gregory. 'He's gone, isn't he?'

Sadly, Gregory said, 'Yes, Dennis, Jurgen is gone.'

Acting Corporal Jenkins stood at the head of the column, waiting for an order to lead the men out.

Dennis looked at him, and at the men, women and children waiting behind, all of whom depended upon him to get them to safety.

Finally, Jenkins said, 'Sir, shall I lead the trail-breakers?'

Dennis was silent for a moment, then he smiled. 'No,' he whispered, 'I'll lead. Now let's go home.'

EPILOGUE

Reunion

The day was warm.

Captain Dennis Hartraft of Highcastle, Squire of Wolfgar's Hold, shaded his eyes to look at the evening sun setting beyond the mountains which rimmed the valley.

Bow over his shoulder, he slowly walked back from the woods. He carried no game, though he had seen more than one stag. But the larder was full, the valley was rich, and he felt no desire to draw his bow on this warm spring evening. Hunting had been an excuse for some quiet time alone, to think. His conversation with Alyssa this morning over breakfast had put him in a reflective mood, making him ponder the strange twists of fate that had led him back to this valley after the war. And the children were running riot through the keep. At times he wondered why he found their noise far more stressful than the din of battle. He smiled at the thought of his eldest, Jurgen, trying to lift his father's shield, though he was only four years of age.

He paused at the crest of the small rise in the road overlooking the keep. It was a ritual which had become habit – nodding to the burial mound which held the ashes of Wolfgar, Richard, Alwin, and the others; even Sugama. He sat down for a moment. Looking at the small marker he had erected to mark their grave, he said, 'Well, Wolfgar, you old bastard, you're going to be a grandfather again. Alyssa's with child once more.' He looked down into the valley.

Where the old stockade had stood, now a sturdy keep rose. He laughed silently at the irony of life.

What had once been his land had been granted to the Tsurani with the ending of the war. Lord Kasumi, now Earl of LaMut, had been granted that office by King Lyam after the end of the war, when Earl Vandros had gain the office of Duke of Yabon, upon old Brucal's retirement. Dennis had no problem with the King taking Kasumi and the other Tsurani stranded on Midkemia into service. Better than any solider in the King's army, Dennis knew the quality of those men. For every Sugama there were a hundred Asayagas, men who would guard your back with their own lives and give everything in the name of honour and duty. No, he welcomed them as allies on the northern borders, keeping the moredhel at bay. What he objected to was them giving his family's land to a Tsurani vassal of Earl Kasumi.

The news had been a bitter blow, for he had fought loyally for ten long years and to have his ancestral home bartered away was difficult to accept. He sighed as he remembered how angry he had been at the time.

There had been, he knew, a cloud over his name. For someone had indeed talked. He could not have expected different. Soldiers were soldiers and in the days after their return to the Kingdom lines rumours had been flying about the miraculous return of what was called 'the lost patrol' and clearly someone had finally spilled the tale of what had really happened.

Then had come the night when old Duke Brucal had called him to his pavilion and pressed the charges that he had consorted with the enemy, and knowingly let an élite Tsurani unit escape.

It was ironic coming from Brucal, who was known to be one of the most pragmatic soldiers in the field. Yet, duty was duty, and if the rumours were true, Dennis could stand accused of treason.

Fortunately, none of his men would implicate him before the tribunal of Dukes Brucal and Borric, and Earl Vandros of LaMut.

Dennis was freed and returned to duty, but his reputation had been sullied. The Marauders were disbanded and he was sent to serve the last year of the war with Vandros. The Earl had been quick to realize Dennis's abilities and by the end of the war, Dennis had regained his rank and prestige, but the whispers about his mysterious journey with a Tsurani patrol never fully went away.

In a way, the new duty had been a welcome relief. The front was quiet, the patrols a boring routine, and thus he had spent the rest of the war.

And twice he had seen Asayaga. The first time was in the woods, nearly a year afterwards. The Tsurani were pressing on another front, and then launched a quick diversion into the territory patrolled by Dennis. There had been a short, shocking fight at a burning inn, both sides losing heavily. Just as he was pulling out, dragging his wounded, he caught a glimpse of Asayaga on his flank, Tasemu by his side.

He waited, not sure of what was to come next. Smoke drifted between them, and when it lifted the two were gone, and he had managed to get his command out.

The second time was on the day the Rift closed. Dennis had stood at attention with the honour company sent to attend the historic meeting between King Lyam and Emperor Inchindar, the Tsurani Light of Heaven.

Even now, five years after the war, Dennis didn't fully understand the betrayal of the elves and dwarves. One minute the two young rulers had been sitting together with a young magician in a black robe translating for them, and suddenly the woods erupted with elves and dwarves attacking the Tsurani.

The fighting had been hand-to-hand and bloody. Dennis had been battling to seize the rift machine, for he had heard Prince Arutha, the King's brother, exclaim that it had to be taken before the Tsurani could bring reinforcements through from their homeworld.

The black-robed magician and another in brown robes had finally destroyed the device, and Dennis to this day could hardly believe the fury which had resulted from the destruction of that machine – the explosion like thunder and the shaking of the ground that had accompanied it, tumbling men and horses off their feet.

The Tsurani, damn their stiff necks, would not yield, even then. Their Emperor had been safely returned to their world, but those warriors stranded on this side of the Rift continued to fight. Finally sanity reigned, and Force Commander Kasumi of the Shinzawai ordered a surrender when the bulk of the King's army arrived at the truce site.

Dennis remembered seeing Asayaga during the fight, and it had been a great relief to see him among the prisoners.

Absently, he patted Wolfgar's grave, humming a snatch of an old tune about a king, and stood up. It was nearly time for evening inspection. A patrol would go out tomorrow over the northern pass to check on the doings of the moredhel; he wanted his men in early tonight and well rested. Most of them were new recruits, a bit too eager, but then again new recruits usually were.

Reaching the open gate of the stockade he saw the men lined up. The way they were looking at him was curious: several were smiling, especially the old hands who were veterans of the Marauders. Standing in the middle of the parade ground was a short stocky soldier, wearing the tabard of the Earl of LaMut.

It was Asayaga.

The Tsurani turned, grinning, and raised his hand in a formal salute. Then he came forward and grasped Dennis's hand in his.

'Dennis, how are you?'

'Asayaga! By the gods, I thought you wouldn't get here until tomorrow.' Dennis saw the insignia above the wolf's head on the tabard. 'Squire?'

'Yes, my friend. A landed squire to my lord, Earl Kasumi.'

'Congratulations.'

'Thank you. Now I know what you meant about Baron Moyet. A fair man, but very difficult at times.'

'A stuffy prig, you mean,' answered Dennis.

Asayaga laughed. 'You said it; I didn't.'

'So, where are your estates?' asked Dennis, leading his guest to the newly-built keep.

Asayaga hesitated, then softly said, 'Valinar.'

Dennis stopped and said, 'I'll be damned.' Then he threw back his head and laughed. 'That's rich.'

Asayaga shook his head. 'The title should have been yours. I'm sorry I brought trouble upon you.'

'Don't be. We did what was right. If we had not, both of us

would be dead now, and the kingdom would be minus a good Tsurani squire.'

'And a good captain of the northern marches. At least you're answering to Baron Highcastle, and not Moyet.'

'There is that,' agreed Dennis. 'Besides, I like it here. The land is rich; it's a fine location to build a new home, to live, even to have an occasional adventure. I'll start a new Hartraft tradition here, Asayaga. I rather like the quiet now. And besides, there's something special about this place that Wolfgar found. I guess a bit of his soul lingers, for I have inherited a distinct disdain for dealings in the courts of kings.'

Asayaga nodded. 'I find that unsurprising.'

With a smile Dennis asked, 'Alyssa? She's waiting inside to greet you. Two sons now, a third on the way.'

Dennis clapped him on the shoulder. 'You're going to wear that girl out, my friend. Wolfgar would be proud.'

'Yes he would,' and Asayaga smiled, a sly sort of grin.

Just then two women appeared at the door of the keep. Alyssa hurried forward and half-flew into Asayaga's arms. 'I've missed you!' she exclaimed.

He laughed. 'And I have missed you. How has your visit been?'

'Wonderful. Better now that you're here. How long can we stay?'

Asayaga slipped his arm around her and kissed her. 'Another week, then we must both be back to court. Lord Kasumi's wife says she misses her favourite lady-in-waiting, and I must return to my duties.'

Dennis turned to Sergeant Jenkins and said, 'Inspect the men, change the watches, and then dismiss them.'

The sergeant saluted and turned to do as ordered.

Roxanne appeared at the door of the keep. She came down and kissed Asayaga on the cheek. 'It is good to see you again,' she said.

'And it is good to see you, as well.'

A shout from inside the building, followed by a wail of protest, caused both sisters to look at one another. Roxanne said, 'That's my Jurgen.' Hurrying away, she said, 'What's he up to now? He's too much like you, Dennis!'

Alyssa said to her husband, 'I'll go see if it's one of our boys, too.'

The two men stood at the entrance to Dennis's new home, surveying the valley where they had fought side by side years before, as the sun lowered in the west.

Asayaga said, 'This is a wonderful place to start a new heritage.'

'I couldn't be happier.' Dennis said. 'Roxanne is a miracle and our sons are . . . impossible.' He laughed. 'She is right. I'm sure my father is looking down from Lims-Kragma's Hall, amused at nature's revenge on his son. But, yes, life is good. Come and rest. I'll ready the bath-house if you'd care to get clean.'

Asayaga laughed. 'Yes. It's good to see some civilization has rubbed off on you, barbarian.'

Dennis frowned, 'Barbarian?'

Asayaga gave him a playful cuff on the arm. 'Let us soak and relax, and you can tell me in which part of the brook at Valinar those improbably large trout you once told me of lurk.'

'Improbably large?' said Dennis as they walked in. 'I swear on my son's head that fish was at least three feet long.'

Asayaga looked dubious, but kept his laughter in check as the two friends went into the keep to join their wives and children for supper.

To Ride Hell's Chasm

Janny Wurts

A compelling standalone tale on an epic scale, filled with intrigue, adventure and dark magic.

When Princess Anja fails to appear at her betrothal banquet, the tiny, peaceful kingdom of Sessalie is plunged into intrigue. Charged with recovering the distraught King's beloved daughter is Mykkael, the rough-hewn newcomer who has won the post of Captain of the Garrison. A scarred veteran with a deadly record of field warfare, his 'interesting' background and foreign breeding are held in contempt by court society.

As the princess's trail vanishes outside the citadel's gates, anxiety and tension escalate. Mykkael's investigations lead him to a radical explanation for the mystery, but he finds himself under suspicion from the court factions. Can he convince them in time of his dramatic theory: that the resourceful, high-spirited princess was not taken by force, but fled the palace to escape a demonic evil?

'Janny Wurts writes with an astonishing energy . . . it ought to be illegal for one person to have so much talent'
                                    STEPHEN R DONALDSON

'One to skive off work for'   *Starburst*

'An absorbing read . . . set in a delightful world'
                                    Dreamwatch

ISBN 0-00-710111-2